PRAISE FOR SUMMER OF SALT

★ "Equal parts fantasy, romance, and mystery, this book shimmers with an irresistible energy."
—*Kirkus Reviews* (starred review)

★ "Sophisticated and complex. A necessary novel that is, at the same time, so enjoyable to read that teens will have to fight the urge to crawl into the pages.
—*SLJ* (starred review)

"Combines sumptuous old-fashioned storytelling and modern feminist themes."
—*Chicago Tribune*

"A fanciful, whimsical novel. Leno mixes small-town island life and the loving bond between sisters with light magical elements as well as weightier issues that are examined with nuance and maturity."
—*VOYA*

ALSO BY KATRINA LENO

SUMMER OF SALT

KATRINA LENO

HARPER TEEN
An Imprint of HarperCollinsPublishers

HarperTeen is an imprint of HarperCollins Publishers.

Summer of Salt
Copyright © 2018 by Katrina Leno
Library of Congress Control Number: 2018933351
ISBN 978-0-06-249368-2

Typography by Alison Klapthor
20 21 22 23 24   PC/LSCH   10 9 8 7 6 5 4 3 2 1
❖
First paperback edition, 2020

to Shane
who has his own magic

Summer of Salt

I.

It was many and many a year ago,
In a kingdom by the sea.

from "Annabel Lee"
by Edgar Allan Poe

SUMMER SOLSTICE

On the island of By-the-Sea you could always smell two
things: salt and magic.

The first was obvious. It came crashing ashore in the blue
waves; it sat heavy and thick in our hair and our clothes; it
stained our bedsheets and made our pillows damp.

The second—the scent of magic—was harder to pin
down.

It floated behind my mother as she carried a woven basket out to the herb garden in the middle of the night (when
picked under moonlight, rosemary became so much more
than just something that goes well with eggs).

It gathered up in the corners of the Fernweh Inn, mixed
with the dust and the cobwebs that collected in the guest
rooms during the nine months the inn sat (mostly) empty.

And it poured off my sister on the night of the summer solstice, when she stepped up onto the ledge of my

attic bedroom window and unceremoniously pushed herself away, jumping into the night air with all the grace of a poorly trained ballerina.

Oh—don't worry.

She'll be fine.

Of all the stories about my family, the Fernweh women on the island of By-the-Sea, there are two that no one will ever forget. One is the story of how my sister, Mary, and I were born. And the other is the story of the summer we turned eighteen. This summer.

You would never know by looking at my sister that she was the type of girl who could jump from a fourth-story window and float gently to the ground on a warm and windless summer night, landing perfectly between two of my mother's enormous, prized-possession bleeding hearts, trampling not a single blade of grass beneath her bare feet. And yet here we were: A warm and windless summer night. My sister's dress floating around her like a ghost made out of cotton and lace. A fall that should have killed her. A fall that *would* have, if she weren't a Fernweh. My mother's bleeding hearts, untouched, and my sister dropping her sandals on the grass and sliding into them while looking back up at me, an obnoxiously pleased expression on her face, the scent of magic so strong and sharp (like ashes, like shadows, like dirt) that I actually sneezed.

"Bless you!" she called up merrily.

From above, leaning out of the window, I rolled my eyes.

"You're so fucking dramatic," I said.

Mary kissed the air in my general direction.

It took me a few minutes longer to make it down to the grass; we couldn't all float through the summer air. I had to crawl down the lattice that ran up the side of the house, avoiding the thorns of the roses that vined skyward and always made my bedroom smell so sickly sweet. When I finally jumped the last few feet and landed beside her, she had lain down in the grass. She was pretending to be asleep.

"Asshole," I said, and kicked her with the toe of my sandaled foot.

"Jealous," she replied.

"Joke's on you when you get a grass stain on your ass."

"Mom has grass-stain potion," Mary said, and held her hand out to me. I grabbed it hard and pulled her up. She smelled like cinnamon as she smiled at me. "Doesn't this just feel like a night of limitless possibility?" she said, suddenly serious, holding her arms open to the night like she could embrace it.

"Sure, Mary. Whatever you say."

She laughed and pushed me away, and I followed her as she turned and darted across the lawn. I paused at the edge of our property, turning only once to see how creepy the Fernweh Inn looked at night. It was all shadows and things that caught the corner of your eye. Real stuff of ghost stories. I'd always loved it.

"Keep up, Georgina," Mary called as we made our way down Bottle Hill and away from the ocean, toward the center of our island.

Oh, By-the-Sea, our home: just a handful of people with their own presumably good reasons for wanting to live on the grayest and rainiest and arguably most depressing island this side of our great mainland. (This side was east. I imagine if this side were west it would be all sunshine and palm trees and tan, muscular boys with wet suits rolled down to their waists, carrying surfboards on their shoulders as they walked barefoot down the sides of small coastal highways.)

"This is pointless. Everything is pointless," I said. I wore shorts, and my legs were already being eaten alive by mosquitoes. "Did you bring a citronella candle?"

"Oh yes, I'm keeping it in my bra," Mary said. She stopped and waited for me. "Why are you being such a grump?"

"Bonfires are pointless."

"You've already established that *everything* is pointless. I assumed bonfires fell under that umbrella."

"They do."

"What's really bothering you, my poor little grumpy sister?"

We'd reached Main Street, the longest street in

By-the-Sea. It ran north to south and cut the island in half down the middle. You could get all the way from Bottle Hill to the ferry dock on this road. I stood in the middle of it, staring down into the darkness that was punctuated every hundred feet or so by a streetlamp.

In a little over two months, Mary and I would take this road all the way to the docks. We'd board the ferry for the first time in our lives and take it to the mainland. I was going to a small college just far enough from the ocean that for the first time in my life I wouldn't be able to smell salt. Mary would get on a plane and fly south. Her school was on the very tip of the mainland, right on the water. She was tied to the water, my sister. Moods like tides, temper like a hungry shark.

"Georgie?" Mary asked, when a few moments had passed and I still hadn't moved from the middle of the road. Not like there was any *reason* to. We'd counted once; there were fewer than forty cars on By-the-Sea, and we were almost guaranteed to run into none of them at this time of night.

"Just thinking," I said.

"About . . . ?"

"College, I guess."

Mary made a noise in the back of her throat that meant something like "Really? This again?" and at the same time conveyed how unlikely it was that we had come from the same place, the same womb. At the same time, even.

Sometimes I wondered about that myself. I mean, we looked nothing alike. Mary was a blond, and I was a brunette. Mary had brown eyes, and I had green. Mary liked bonfires, and I thought they were pointless. Mary was going far away to a college on the water, and I was having heart palpitations in the middle of the road thinking about a simple little ferry ride.

"Are you still worried about that?" Mary asked. "Georgina, you're going to be fine. You're the smartest person in our class, everyone loves you, and there are bound to be more girls who like girls over there than there are here. It's a simple numbers game."

"Well, at least you have your priorities straight," I said.

"Kissing is important. You've only kissed one person in your entire life. That's weird."

"I think it's weirder that you're methodically making your way through every boy on this very small island."

"God, you *are* a grump," Mary said.

As we spoke, Mary had gradually floated higher and higher into the air. She was a solid five inches off the ground now, and I didn't think she even realized it. My sister had always been lazy about her powers—she went through week-long periods where she practiced diligently, trying to figure out how to control them, learning how to direct her body through the air, but more often than not, she couldn't be bothered.

It worried me. It was one thing trying to keep my sister's

powers a secret from a tiny island, but what would it be like for her to try and hide them from the entire mainland? From her university? From her new roommate?

"Mary," I said sternly, pointing at her feet.

She rolled her eyes and gradually sank back to earth. "There's no one around."

"That's not the point. You know you're supposed to be trying to control it."

"I can't think about it every second of every day," she said, crossing her arms over her chest.

"Let's just get this over with," I said.

I pushed past her, sure of my footing even in the darkness, because I knew the way by heart, because I knew every single way on this island, every single rock or fallen branch that might trip me up. You could walk from one end to the other in two hours, and that's if you were really taking your time.

We weren't going far. The Beach was a fifteen-minute walk from our house. That was the official, in-the-tourist-book name for where we were going, one of six beaches on By-the-Sea. (Yes, there was a tourist book for our tiny island. It was made and printed by Willard Jacoby, and I don't think he'd ever sold a single copy.) The Beach was the smallest of the six, a little cove popular with the locals and unpopular with the tourists because of a series of signs warning of frequent shark attacks. The signs, while a blatant lie designed to keep the Beach tourist-free, were incredibly effective; they featured sunblock-nosed stick figures in bathing suits missing arms or legs or huge chunks of their torsos.

The bonfire was held on the Beach every year on the summer solstice. School had been out for a month already, but this was the official start of summer and By-the-Sea's singularly minded two-month tourist season.

The island's population of young people, including the thirty-six of us who made up that year's graduating class, collected on the Beach, drank summer punch, vomited into the waves, and skinny-dipped. I had gone every year since I was thirteen, and this would be my last one. We were done now, Mary and I. Graduated. Elevated. Voilà.

I was only here because of her. She loved this sort of thing. She was born for oceanside bonfires, long gauzy dresses and uncombed hair, the scent of salt like a blanket you can't peel off your skin. She was born for the smell of water, for the way it sank into your bones, stained your skin, dyed your blood a deep, salty blue.

Me, I could never see waves again and be perfectly fine with that.

Mary linked her arm through mine and pulled me against her side, trapping me. "Just so I can adequately prepare myself, how long is your little mood going to last?"

"We've just been to so many of these. I don't really see the point in one more. Especially when we have to be up at the crack of dawn tomorrow."

"Georgie, can't you just live a little? I mean—this is the first night of the rest of your life!"

"But . . . you could say that about every night. Like, every night is the first night of the rest of your life. Because the present is always the present and the only thing in front of us is the rest of our lives."

"Here, I brought this for you because I knew you'd be like this," she said, pulling a small silver flask from her bra.

"Wait, so do you actually have a citronella candle in there?"

"It's the cinnamon stuff you like. *You're welcome.*"

She took a big swig and then handed it to me, shaking her head from side to side like a dog, with her tongue hanging out and everything.

"Georgie, just think about it," she continued. One sip of cinnamon whiskey and her eyes had already gotten all glossy. "In a couple months we'll just be *gone*, you know? This is really it. One last summer on By-the-Sea. One last summer together."

I sipped from the flask. Mary unhooked her vise grip on my arm and took my hand instead. She was swaying a little, which made me think she'd already had her fair share of cinnamon whiskey before she'd knocked on my bedroom door.

"Are you happy at all?" she asked tentatively.

"Of course I'm happy. Why wouldn't I be happy?"

"Oh, I don't know. Sometimes you just find reasons not

to be." She kissed the back of my hand. We'd reached the edge of the Beach. My sister slipped out of her sandals and held them with one finger over her shoulder.

The bonfire's flames were already dangerously high. The people around it were like little human-shaped spots of darkness against the fire. I tried not to let Mary's words into my heart: *sometimes you just find reasons not to be.* If that were true, then Mary's own vice was that she sometimes found the meanest observations and let them fall off her tongue like they were nothing.

"I *am* happy," I said, but I didn't think she heard me. She was preening: running her hands through her hair and adjusting her dress.

"Gimme," she said, holding out her hand. I gave her the flask, and she took another massive sip. "Okay. Don't go far." And she handed the flask back to me and took off running.

I was expecting that. I watched her go until I could no longer distinguish her from the other dark blobs of people.

It occurred to me that I could leave, that I could go back home and sleep for a few hours and then come out again and find her as the sun was rising, lead her home while she floated like a balloon above my head, my hand wrapped tightly around her ankle so I wouldn't lose her to the last few fading stars.

That was the extent of her powers: my sister could float.

She was, of course, hoping they evolved eventually, that

one day she'd be able to get more than a few feet off the ground, but so far, no flying, just floating.

It was a rare gift, but not unheard of among Fernweh women. We had a great-great-aunt who could fly on a God's-honest broom. We had another aunt, farther back, who never actually touched the ground; her feet were always about an inch from the soil she glided on.

And then there was Annabella.

Every year, from late June to late August, By-the-Sea played host to the rarest bird in the entire world: the Eastern Seaborn Flicker.

Although nobody actually called her that. They called her what my great-great-great-maybe-another-great-grandmother, Georgina Fernweh (my namesake, yes), the woman who'd discovered the new species, had called her: Annabella's Woodpecker.

Named after her twin sister, Annabella, who had gone missing around the same time the bird had shown up.

Her twin sister, who had started out being able to float and had, after years of practice, perfected the art of flying.

I'm sure stranger things have happened in my family than a woman possibly-maybe-probably turning into a bird.

But how else could you explain it? The same bird showing up every year, for three hundred years or so, with the same markings and the same coloring and the same mannerisms. Coming back to visit its home. Coming back, perhaps, to say hi to its living relatives (and even the dead ones, buried in the Fernweh tomb on the island's only cemetery).

Of course, the ornithologists and enthusiasts that studied her insisted that a bird with a three-hundred-year lifespan was impossible, and that the more likely explanation was that there just wasn't that much variation between individual units of the species.

They said things like that, *individual units of the species.*

They also said things like, *You should probably at least call it Annabella's Flicker,* to which my great-great-whatever-grandmother was like, *You should probably let me name this rare bird anything I damn well want because she's on my property and, if you piss me off, I'll build a very tall fence.*

And just like every summer, the Fernweh Inn would open tomorrow, and the birdheads would flock to the island in droves. Oh, By-the-Sea, island of salt and sand and rain and magic and one single solitary bird that made our tiny little chunk of rock—which would have been otherwise entirely overlooked by the rest of the world—absolutely famous (at least in certain ornithological circles).

I was rather fond of Annabella.

Not everybody had their own personal island mascot, and she was ours.

And she was a Fernweh, to boot. We Fernwehs had to stick together.

Even those of us without any powers.

Like me.

It was a well-established thing in Fernweh history: that all Fernweh women found their particular gifts by their eighteenth birthday. I had a great-great-aunt who had discovered her powers of teleportation (she could zap herself to anywhere on the island, but she couldn't zap her clothes, so it ended up being a very risqué gift) at the age of four, and she proceeded to use them gleefully, scaring her siblings and parents half to death by popping up in the strangest places. I had yet another great-great-aunt who hadn't discovered her powers of telepathy until she was seventeen and a half.

There seemed to be no rhyme or reason.

Mary and I would be turning eighteen at the end of the summer, and here I was: still resolutely unmagical while Mary had been floating since birth.

I slid my sandals off and walked down toward the water.

I found Vira ankle-deep in ocean, holding her long skirt up around her knees.

"Hi," I said, joining her.

"You smell like cinnamon."

I handed her the flask. At this rate, it would be gone before the midnight rush. (The midnight rush was all who had a mind to take off their clothes and run screaming into the water. I did not have a mind to. Mary was unpredictable; she could go either way.)

Vira took a sip of the flask and smacked her lips

exaggeratedly. She handed the flask back to me and I took the long, last sip.

Vira like Elvira. My best friend, of the non-twin variety. Shoulder-length hair the color of coal and slate-gray eyes. If you actually called her Elvira, she was known to mix crushed-up sleeping pills into your milkshake at Ice Cream Parlor, where she worked. When you woke up, you had Sharpied penises on your cheeks.

"We missed you today," Vira said.

Book club. Consisting of me, Vira, Eloise, Shelby, and Abigail. We met in the back corner of Used Books, which was owned by Eloise's mother.

"*Wuthering Heights* is a terrible book," I said.

"You got to pick the last one."

"Right, and who doesn't love a good *Bell Jar*?"

"You have to stop picking Sylvia Plath. It's making everyone cry."

"It wasn't all *Wuthering Heights*, anyway. I had to help my mom get the inn ready," I explained.

"Ah, the massive influx. All booked?"

"All booked. Check-in's at twelve tomorrow. You're welcome to come and help, Mom said the more the merrier."

"I have to be at the parlor," Vira said. "You know how those birdheads like their ice cream."

Ah, did I know a thing or two about those birdheads.

Behind us a bunch of our drunken peers fell gently into song. It was a sort of island staple, a dark and moody tune that had been around forever. Nobody knew its origins, but everybody knew it. It was what you hummed to yourself on the walk home from school, in the shower, right before you fell asleep. It was one of those songs that entered your brain and never let you forget it.

On By-the-Sea, you and me will go sailing by
On waves of green, softly singing too.
On By-the-Sea, you and me will be forever young
And live together on waves of blue.

It went on like that for many verses, dozens of voices all singing low and slow. The effect, I had to admit, was rather somber. I got goose bumps down my arms that I tried to hide from Vira. Neither of us was singing, but both of us were listening intently. The bonfire warmed the already warm night, and we took a step deeper into the freezing water to even out our body temperature.

We were joined after a minute by Eloise and Shelby, drunk and giggly, and then by Abigail, stoned and serious. The cinnamon whiskey was gone, and we all looked out at the sky, where the clouds were parting to reveal a big, heavy moon.

Abigail took a step deeper into the water, held her hands

up to the sky, and said, "I can't feel my skin anymore."

Shelby laughed and said, "Jesus, Abs, how much did you smoke?"

This side of the island faced west, and I looked out as far as I could, straining my eyes against the inky darkness, trying to see the mainland.

It was no use, of course. Even on the clearest of days, the sunniest of mornings, you could only just make out the shore. In this darkness, I could see only the dots of stars, the shadowy outline of bodies. The bonfire was bright, yes, but it also made the rest of the night somehow darker.

I felt hands around my waist and knew it was my sister by the dark smell of impossibility.

"Are you having fun?" she asked.

Nobody was paying attention; everyone was in their own little world, and that's why I didn't worry much when I felt her arms start to tug upward, sensed her feet leaving the sand behind me. I turned around to face her and placed my hands heavily on her shoulders.

"Get a grip," I whispered.

"Oh, shoot," she said, and splashed back into the water. "I didn't mean to."

"Are you ready to go home?"

"Are you kidding me? Nobody's even gotten naked yet. We have to dance naked under the solstice moon, Georgina, it's tradition."

"Well, you can get naked without me," I said.

"Just give it another half hour or so and I'll go with you. Please? Don't make me walk home by myself."

"Ugh, fine."

Vira turned around. "Hi, Mary."

"Hi, Vira."

"Are you getting naked?"

"Yeah. You?"

"I guess so. I wore my good underwear."

"I wore a bathing suit," Eloise chimed in, lifting her dress to reveal a dark-green one-piece with a skirt.

Abigail took a blanket out of an enormous straw bag she'd brought with her and spread it out. Squeezing, all six of us managed to fit.

My sister indeed got naked not long after that, and together with Vira (in her underwear), Eloise (in her bathing suit), and Shelby and Abigail (both also naked), she went charging into the great blue sea. Most of the Beach had, actually, except for me and a few other people too far away to identify.

It wasn't that I didn't *like* swimming. I just preferred the warm blanket, the bonfire blazing nearby, the inky darkness of the sky.

I guarded our blanket, my sister's clothes, and Abigail's glass pipe. ("This belonged to my great-aunt Dee, okay, so be careful with it and help yourself.")

I watched the teenagers of By-the-Sea run and jump into the freezing-cold water and thought about how many of them would be leaving for the very first time in September. After a few minutes, Colin Osmond folded his exceptionally long legs into pretzels and sat down next to me, deftly maneuvering his way around the many bras and undies and shoes that littered the blanket. We'd gotten to know each other when I'd dated his sister, Verity, last year, and we'd remained friendly after we'd broken up.

"Never understood this," Colin said. "That water is *cold*."

"Freezing," I agreed.

"Two more months, though," he said. "Can you believe it? It'll be my first time off."

Off the island. Away from By-the-Sea. Another small contingent of freshly graduated By-the-Sea teenagers stepping onto the ferry and leaving home for the first time in their entire lives.

It actually wasn't as weird as it sounded. Most kids didn't leave until college. Although small, the island had everything you might need: a four-lane bowling alley; a high school, middle school, and grade school; and one grocery store (that admittedly did sometimes run out of food, but we had learned to stock up and also cultivate little gardens).

"It doesn't seem possible," I answered finally. And it didn't. In that moment, the entire world was just By-the-Sea, just the Beach, just my sister dancing in the ice-cold water.

"I know what you mean," Colin agreed. "Like we've

been waiting our whole lives and now it's just around the corner." He knocked his knee into mine. "All right, we should at least get our feet wet."

So we waded out up to our ankles in the water, and I tried to decide what laughing, soaking-wet shape was my sister, or Vira, or anyone.

Mary found me quickly enough, running past me like a bullet to get to her dress on the blanket. She pulled it over her head and then came back to where I was standing.

"Every year," she said. "Every year I forget a towel. Hi, Colin."

"Hi, Mary," he said.

One by one our peers emerged from the water, running back to wherever they'd stashed their clothes, wrapping themselves in blankets and towels if they'd been smart enough to think ahead.

Colin wandered away, and Mary and I picked our way back to the blanket and settled around it in a lazy circle. Shelby lay down in the middle, looking up at the stars.

Abigail packed a fresh bowl and passed it around our small group. I took only one very small hit, because Abigail's stuff was homegrown and strong and I was a lightweight and didn't want to get lost on the way home. Mary skipped it altogether, probably because the last time she'd smoked weed she'd drifted lazily upward and almost decapitated herself on a ceiling fan. "This is nice," Shelby said, prone to the sentimental when she'd had a little of Abigail's stash.

"This is like the first night of the rest of our lives."

"That's exactly what I said!" Mary said.

"Every night is the first night of the rest of our lives," Vira retorted.

"That's exactly what *I* said," I said, and then I hugged Vira because she was the most perfect princess in the world.

Oh shit. See? That was the weed.

After a long stretch of quiet, I nudged Mary and asked, "Ready? You've danced *and* swum naked. Swimming wasn't even part of the deal."

"Yeah, yeah, I'm ready. Has anybody seen my shoes?"

Someone tossed them to her, and after a lot of hugging (dancing naked really endears you to people, and we were a huggy group anyway), Mary and I set off back up the Beach, back toward Bottle Hill and Fernweh Inn and our attic home and our nice warm beds.

And that was how it was: the start of every summer since Mary and I'd been old enough to figure out how to sneak out of the inn. The revelry and singing would grow louder and louder. Eventually the rest of the party (sans Mary and me, who would already be safely home) would be broken up by the sheriff or deputy, a lackluster police involvement that was more out of duty than any real passion for the laws we were breaking. (Beaches closed at dusk; underage drinking; lack of proper permits for a bonfire; indecent exposure.) We would not get enough sleep. The birdheads would arrive tomorrow, dozens of them, filling up every corner of the inn. They would bring us presents, the ones who'd known us since we were kids. They would hug us and tuck postcards and five-dollar bills into our pockets. We would get no damn rest or privacy for the next two months: the season of Annabella. Arriving like clockwork. All the fuss in the world over a silly little bird— who, I admit, I loved more than any of the birdheads, more than any of the islanders, because I felt somehow that she belonged to me, to all the Fernweh women, in a way, but especially to me.

The moon drifted in and out of existence. My sister took my hand and squeezed, and I felt that squeeze on my fingers and somehow on my heart as the singing drifted across the sand to reach us:

On By-the-Sea, you and me will be forever young . . .

Oh, By-the-Sea, island of Fernwehs and everything I had ever known and loved. How I would miss you—every part of you—but especially the smell, always the smell: of salt, of brine, of water, of spells, of potions, of feathers, and of what it would mean to leave it all in just two months.

CHECK-IN

Mary and I were born in a rainstorm that flooded the streets and overwhelmed the sewers and drowned the beaches of By-the-Sea and turned everything wet and gray for seven days.

I've heard this story many times, enough times that it feels like I actually remember it.

My mother was in the kitchen, cutting wedges of lime to squeeze into the virgin margaritas she'd been addicted to during her pregnancy. She felt off—nothing enormous, just a tiny headache, a sliver of fatigue, a faint unease in her abdomen.

She made her drink and took it onto the front porch and sat down in a wicker rocking chair and sipped and rocked and sipped and rocked.

Then one of the housekeepers saw her and said, "Mrs. Fernweh, you don't look so hot. I think you may be about to have a couple babies."

"I had just figured that out myself," my mother said, and raised her glass in a toast.

She hadn't wanted to rush her drink.

My father worked as a fisherman; my mother sent word down to the docks that the babies were coming, and then she got into her pickup truck and drove herself to the small hospital, so small it wasn't even named, so small there were only five parking spaces and four were free. She parked and went inside and filled out some forms and walked herself down to the birthing room, which was also the emergency room and the surgery room and the recovery room and, on Friday nights, the movie room.

I came first, a full five hours before my sister. I came out easily, noisily, red-faced and screaming, hardly half an hour after my mother had lain down.

I came out, and then the rains started, and then the doctor told my mother, *Hold off on pushing again, at least for a while, this second one seems to be a little stubborn.*

"Has anybody heard from my husband?" my mother asked, smiling down at me, wrapped in that generic hospital baby blanket that not even By-the-Sea's small hospital was lacking.

Outside, the skies had unzipped themselves and the rain fell so thickly that all you could see were lines of gray against gray.

But nobody had heard from my father.

"The rain is heavy; it should drive the boats in," the nurse, Emery Grace, said. "He'll be here soon, maybe even in time for number two."

My mom patted her stomach gingerly. "This one's called Mary." She touched my forehead. "This one's Georgina."

"Georgina, that's beautiful."

"It's a family name. Has somebody called the docks?"

Emery shook her head sadly. "It's the phone lines, Penny. The storm's knocked them all down."

"Can I get up? If it's going to be a while?"

"You're really not supposed to."

"I just want to sit by the window," my mother said.

So Emery raised the back of my mom's hospital bed and undid the brakes and rolled the whole thing over to the window, with me still wrapped in that blanket, trying to figure out how to nurse.

When I'd had enough milk, my mother turned me around and tucked my head under her chin, and we watched the rain come down while we waited for my sister, while we waited for my father.

But only one of them would ever show up.

Nobody ever saw my father again. His boat went down in the storm; the small crew was lost.

Now I think of him whenever it rains. And sometimes—though I know it's impossible—it rains whenever I think of him.

That was what I was dreaming about—the storm, the

flooded island, my mother with her two small babies in a rowboat—when Mary threw herself on my bed the morning after the bonfire, so early that the room was still dark. My head pounded—half from the cinnamon whiskey, half from the lack of sleep. I groaned and tried to hit her.

"You overslept, and Mom is pi-i-issed," Mary sang, catching my hand and forcing something into it. I cracked an eyelid: a banana muffin. I took a bite and chewed.

"My alarm's set," I mumbled through muffin.

"Yeah, I checked, and you actually set it for six *tonight*, which is very cute wishful thinking on your part. It's almost seven now, and I've been ironing napkins for an hour."

I grabbed Mary's arm with my free hand and pulled myself up to a sitting position. The room tilted dangerously. She held a mug of steaming coffee out to me, and I took it, gulping gratefully, not even caring about the inevitable mouth blisters I was giving myself. That little piece of skin right behind my top teeth was already shriveling up.

"Did you sleep well? I slept really well," Mary said, stretching her arms over her head luxuriantly.

"Check-in isn't till *noon*," I whined.

"Yes, well, those napkins aren't going to iron themselves, my friend." Mary hopped to her feet. "Take a shower, and I'll tell Mom you'll be down soon. I can buy you twenty minutes, maybe."

"Thirty?"

"The wishful thinking again! I wish I could be as

positive as you, Georgie, I really do. And so early in the morning!"

She left me, thankfully, alone. I propped my pillow up behind me and leaned back against the bed so I could finish eating my muffin. Five hours until check-in and I needed about forty-seven showers and twelve more muffins. And another half-dozen cups of coffee too. I finished what I had, shoved the remaining bit of muffin in my mouth, and stumbled down the hall to the bathroom.

It was just us up here: my bedroom, Mary's bedroom, our bathroom, and a room of storage stuffed so full of boxes you couldn't take more than two steps into it. The Fernweh Inn had four floors, including this one, and for ten months of the year they sat abandoned. By-the-Sea had a short tourist season, but it was also a busy one. We would make enough in two months to get by until next summer.

In the bathroom I got naked and waited for the water to heat up, jumping from foot to foot to help myself wake up. When it was hot enough, I stepped into the shower and stood directly under the stream, letting the water hit me in my face until I was sure that all the salt and sand from the night before was washed off my skin (although it would never be all washed off, not really). I felt better afterward, albeit marginally. I toweled off and then made my way back to my bedroom to get dressed.

I took my coffee cup downstairs to the kitchen for a refill. Aggie, Mom's best friend and the official cook of the Fernweh Inn, was prepping that day's dinner in the kitchen. When she saw me, she burst out laughing. Aggie's laugh was like a bus horn, loud and sharp. She was a tall woman who always wore a scarf wrapped around her long gray hair. She was like a second mother to me, especially during the summer months, when she practically lived at the inn. She laughed again now at the sight of me; Aggie was always either laughing or cooking, and often both at the same time.

"Georgina, you look like something the cat dragged in," she said. I poured more coffee and yawned.

"It was the solstice last night. I didn't want to go. Mary made me."

"Ah, it's tradition. You'll feel fine after you wake up a little. Do you want an omelet?"

"I had a muffin."

"That's a new recipe; you like 'em?"

"Really good. Thanks, Aggie."

"Well, they won't cure a hangover, but they might help a little."

"I sure hope you didn't say 'hangover' in reference to my daughter, who is, last I checked, underage," my mom said, bustling into the kitchen in her usual flurry of motion. She wore an ankle-length dress the color of midnight. *Which is not exactly my cup of tea, but adds to the aesthetic. Old inn, old island, old scary dress, you get it*, she'd once said. "Georgina, you're late," she added.

"I'm sorry. I set my alarm wrong."

"Well, I need you on silverware duty for now, okay? Wash and polish, honey, that stuff hasn't been touched since last August." She pointed to the sink, next to which was a massive pile of the good silver forks and spoons and knives. I spent five seconds of freedom staring at the pile, unmoving, and then I went and filled the sink with water.

It took ages to wash the endless pile of silverware (endless largely in part because Mom kept finding more of it and bringing it over to me with an evil, joyous smirk plastered on her face), and when I was done I set up a station in the dining room where I could polish and shine.

For not the first time in my life as a Fernweh woman, I wished magic was more like it was in the movies. On TV, people snapped their fingers and piles of silverware obligingly sprang to life and washed themselves. On By-the-Sea, not so much.

Sure, we all had our specialties (except me, who had none): My mother could make any potion she set her mind to. My great-grandmother Roberta had controlled fire; her mother before her could walk on water and breathe underneath it. My sister, with absolutely no practice or seemingly much interest at all, had mastered the act of jumping out her bedroom window, and here I was, stuck washing silver by hand.

It wasn't that I hadn't *tried* to make my powers come. I had. Especially when I was younger.

I used to put myself in the weirdest situations, just to see if anything would happen.

I'd stuck my head in the full bathtub and taken a tentative breath.

I'd placed my hand over an open flame to see if it maybe wouldn't hurt, if maybe fire was my thing.

I'd tried to talk to animals.

I'd tried a hundred things over the years, and then I'd given up, resigning myself to the fact that it would either happen or it wouldn't, and I probably had no say either way.

It was only just getting light outside when I started polishing; I was on my fourth cup of coffee (to be fair, Aggie's coffee was notoriously weak), and I had only caught glimpses of my sister as she jumped from one task to another, never in one place for very long, always with an extreme eye roll for me as Mom followed closely behind her, barking instructions. I had just managed to find a way to fall half-asleep while still mechanically polishing forks when I finished. Almost immediately, my mother was upon me with the next thing I had to do.

Hours later—*years* later—I was somehow done washing and polishing the silverware, ironing and hanging a hundred million curtains, dusting off the room keys (seriously), sweeping the front porch, beating out the cushions on the wicker furniture on said porch, and making sure Fernweh Inn's twelve grandfather clocks were all wound and set to the correct time. By then it was eleven-thirty and time for a quick lunch before the guests started arriving.

I'd checked the register earlier; of the inn's sixteen rooms (floors two and three held the guest rooms, eight apiece), I knew all but six of today's arrivals. That was to be expected: our crowd was mostly repeat birdheads, mixed in with a few random tourists who usually stayed a weekend or a week and left disappointed and confused about our priorities. The birdheads would be here until August. You'd be surprised at how easily these birdheads afforded my mother's not-shy room rates. I knew one guy—Tank Smith—who routinely sold photos of Annabella's Woodpecker to the *Geographic Times* for more money than most people make in a year. He spent the rest of the year doing God knows what, came to By-the-Sea for two months, snapped a picture, and made a cool hundred Gs.

I met Aggie, Mom, and Mary in the kitchen for lunch. Mom handed me a gray, curiously smoking drink. I looked into the glass skeptically. It smelled like a match the moment you blow out the flame. Acidic and bitter and hot.

"It will make you feel better," she said, winking. The wink meant that the stuff in my hand wasn't your run-of-the-mill smoothie.

Although people on the island didn't go around openly acknowledging the general magicness of my family, it was common knowledge that if you wanted something done, Penelope Fernweh could sometimes, with the right greasing of the wheels, do it for you. You didn't ask questions. You didn't make assumptions. You'd just slip her a little cash for her trouble and let her do her thing: bury this or that under a full moon, throw some shady ingredients into a big copper pot (you wouldn't call it a cauldron, obviously), boil a frog alive and drink the marrow from its bones (just kidding; she never hurt animals). And then you'd sit back and wait. In this case, you'd wait for it to cure your hangover.

"Wait—why wouldn't you have given this to me at *seven in the morning*?" I whined.

"I thought I should make you suffer a little. You *did* drink the rest of my good cinnamon whiskey. Do you know how long I'd been infusing that?"

I was going to argue with her, clarify that it had actually been Mary who'd stolen the whiskey, but I decided against it. She who giveth could easily taketh away, and besides, I was used to being blamed for the trouble my sister got herself into. It was just sort of the way of the world. Mary did something rash; I inevitably helped her wiggle out of trouble.

I sipped at the smoothie and instantly felt better. *Magic*, I mouthed at Mary, who rolled her eyes and held out her hand for a taste.

"Finally, the sun!" Aggie exclaimed, peering out the window. "It's been so gloomy all morning."

"You couldn't have added some strawberries to this, Ma?" Mary said, pretending to gag. "It tastes awful."

"The beggars and the choosers," Mom said.

Aggie dished out quiche to the table; I was just finishing my second piece when the door to the kitchen opened and Peter Elmhurst, bellboy/groundskeeper/jack-of-all-trades, poked his head in.

"Ms. Fernweh," he said, "the first guests are arriving."

Aggie held up a Bloody Mary I hadn't even noticed she was drinking. (If Aggie's coffee was weak, her Bloody Marys were the opposite.) "To another season," she said brightly.

"To Annabella," Mom added. "May this finally be her year."

She meant the eggs. Poor Annabella, perpetually childless. She laid eggs every summer, but they never hatched, no matter how diligently she tended to them. It was a big ornithological mystery, the will-she/won't-she back-and-forth and the letdown when, one August morning, inevitably, she would be gone, and the eggs would remain behind, useless and cold. (Every year they were carefully collected and brought back to the mainland and autopsied. Every year they could find nothing obvious pointing to why they hadn't survived incubation.)

We Fernwehs knew, of course, that Annabella wasn't strictly your average bird, and that her eggs probably weren't hatching because of that.

"To Annabella," I echoed, raising my glass.

And, fully embracing our long-held status as the biggest

weirdos this side of the mainland, we toasted to a little bird and her fertility problems: Aggie and Mom with Bloody Marys, Mary and me with a sip of legit magic potion.

It had turned out to be a beautiful day. By-the-Sea weather had always been a little unpredictable (the rainstorms of our birth come to mind), but it had only seemed to get worse lately: it would be summer and warm one minute, rainy and miserable the next, blizzard conditions the day after that. And the island paid no attention at all to conventional seasons. It had once snowed in July (the birdheads built a little lean-to around Annabella's chosen tree). It had once been a blazing 110 degrees in January (we all went to the Beach and decided not to question things). By now we were all used to it. It wasn't unusual for the birdheads to show up with both swimming trunks and skis packed into their enormous traveling trunks.

I watched the first few of them walking up the front path now, all familiar faces: Liesel Channing and Hep Shackman, Henrietta Lee behind him followed by Tank Smith, the photographer. I'd seen these people every summer since I was born, and weird as they were, they were almost like family.

Liesel reached me first. She wore pale-purple chinos with a pale-purple oxford shirt and pale-purple sneakers. And pale-purple-rimmed glasses. The only thing on her person that was not purple (luggage: purple; hair tie: purple) was her dutiful birdcat (like a birddog, but an exceptionally grumpy orange Maine coon named Horace, complete with heart-shaped birthmark on its forehead). She gasped when she finally made it up the porch steps. "It cannot be, it is *impossible*! You're a woman now! Where has my little Georgina gone to!"

"Liesel, it's so nice to see you!" I said, giving her a hug. By then the others had reached us (Hep, Henrietta, and Tank were significantly older than Liesel and had slowed down considerably over the years), and I made sure to hug and kiss every one of them. I was the front porch welcoming committee; Mary was just inside the front doors. The lucky thing was that there was only one taxi on By-the-Sea (driven by Seymore Stanners, Shelby's dad, complete with a little flatbed wagon he pulled behind it for all the luggage), and so the arrivals would be limited to groups of four. Small doses of birdheads were better.

Once this group disappeared inside I collapsed on a wicker armchair and closed my eyes, enjoying the sunshine and the warmth of the day.

I didn't have much time to myself, though. Half a minute later I heard a small cough and opened my eyes to see Peter Elmhurst standing uncomfortably close to me, smelling of firewood and smoke.

"Hi, Peter."

"Hi, Georgie," he said, then stopped.

Peter lived down the road, on a farm near the cemetery.

We'd all grown up together and used to be closer as kids, but we'd sort of drifted apart over the years. I blamed that on him—he'd been tragically in love with my sister since we were seven, and he really didn't know how to take *no thanks* for an answer.

"I brought the firewood," Peter said. "In case your mom asks. It's already out back."

"I'll tell her." He shuffled his feet but didn't make a move to leave. "Anything else?"

"I was just wondering if I could talk to you for a second?"

I already knew what was coming; if I had a dollar for every boy on this island that asked me why my sister hadn't fallen madly in love with him, I'd have enough for a ticket to the mainland. And first month's rent on a new apartment. And a brand-new car. And so on.

"Sure, Peter. What's going on?"

"I'm sorry if this is inappropriate. I know technically we work together, you know? I was actually just curious if maybe your sister had mentioned . . . Well, I wrote her a letter. And she hasn't said anything. So I'm sort of worried now that maybe I forgot a stamp? Or maybe I got the address wrong? One Bottle Hill Lane, right?"

The island was so small that you honestly didn't need addresses. If I wrote "Elvira Montgomery" on an envelope, with nothing else but a lipstick kiss for directions, it would reach her in two hours. Our postman, Albert Craws, was very good. And he was also very generous; I never used stamps. I sometimes wrote him nice things where a stamp should go—*Hope you're well, Albert! Don't work too hard, Albert!*—but I had never once actually paid to send a letter. Peter could have messed up every single step of mailing that letter to my sister and it still would have gotten here. Which meant of course she'd received it, of course she'd showed it to me, and of course she had no intention of writing him back.

"I don't think she mentioned anything about a letter," I said, hating to lie to him, hating my sister for making it necessary for me to lie to him, hating my sister for always managing to drag me into her problems. "You know my mom. She's so absentminded, she probably checked the mail and ended up burying the letter in her rose garden."

My mother was anything but absentminded, but it seemed like a good excuse; she did occasionally bury non-rose things in the rose garden.

I couldn't tell if Peter bought it. His face flushed a quick red, and he took a visible breath. Then in a small, even voice he said, "I just think if someone takes the time to write you a letter, you should respond to them."

"Maybe you should write another one and hand deliver it?"

Even my sister would have a hard time pretending she hadn't gotten a hand-delivered letter.

"Sure," Peter said, shrugging, relaxing, smiling a little.

"Yeah, I could do that. Thanks, Georgina. I guess I'll see you around."

He disappeared around the back of the house.

Mary joined me a second later, like she'd been staring out the window, waiting for him to leave.

"Why does it feel like I'm always apologizing for you?" I asked her. She sat on the arm of the chair I was in and played with my hair. We both had long hair, all the way down our backs, but that was mostly because the island's one hairdresser, Shirley Braves, was impossible to track down and also, inexplicably, hated cutting hair.

"I never asked you to lie for me. And I've never promised Peter anything," Mary countered.

"So if you don't like him, you need to cut him loose. Once and for all. Snip, snip, snip."

"You're being a real nosy Rosey, you know that?" she said, getting off the arm of the chair, wheeling around to face me. "I can hang out with whoever the fuck I want *and* I can fuck whoever I want to hang out with. . . ." She squinted, as if trying to figure out if that made sense.

"Truce. It's too hot to fight," I said.

"Yeah, what's up with that?" she asked, instantly distracted. "I thought I saw snow flurries this morning, but it's beautiful now. Oh, great. Another taxi. I'll see you later."

She went back inside.

It was like that all day, taxi after taxi bringing birdhead after birdhead to the inn.

The light was starting to change by the time my mom came out onto the front porch. "We're only waiting for a few more guests," she said. "Great turnout this year, huh? How are you feeling, Georgie?"

"I'm fine," I said. Above us, a cloud hid the sun and I shivered.

"That's probably the last of them right now," Mom said, pointing down the drive at Seymore's cab just turning into view. She put her hand on my shoulder. "You can take a nap before dinner, Georgina. Put on a happy face for now, okay?"

I smiled as big and fake as I could. She rolled her eyes and went back inside. Mary caught the door and slipped out onto the porch before it closed.

"The lobby is filled with birdheads," she whined. Then, seeing the taxi: "Oh thank God, is that the last of them?"

"Who are we missing? Nobody we know, right?"

"I looked at the register; these are newbs. A man and a woman. Two twin beds. So like, unhappily married, I'm guessing."

"Or friends."

"Right, because you take so many island vacations with your platonic male friends?"

Mary was in one of her moods, when everything you said became fair game for a fight. She was probably just as tired as I was. I looked down at her feet: the soles of her shoes were a solid half inch above the porch. I yanked her down, and she mumbled an apology but then visibly brightened. I followed her gaze down to the driveway, where our last guests were just emerging from Seymore's car.

Where our last, very young and attractive guests were just emerging from Seymore's car.

"Oh," I said.

"Oh shi-i-it," Mary whispered. "What time is it, Georgie?"

"I'm not saying."

"Georgieeeee."

"I'm not saying it."

"Georgie, what time is it?"

"Cute o'clock," I relented. "It's cute o'clock, okay, you psychopath."

I stepped off the porch, waiting on the last step as Seymore helped our very young and attractive guests with their luggage. This was no married couple. The guy looked like he was a few years older than me—twenty-three or twenty-four—and the girl seemed about my age.

Suddenly Mary's mouth was right next to my ear. *"There's one for each of us,"* she hissed, and when I turned around to smack her she leapt gracefully out of my reach. Winking, she retreated into the inn.

I walked closer to the car. The guy was paying Seymore, thanking him, laughing about something. The girl was blank-faced, unreadable, looking past me and up at the inn. She slid her red-framed sunglasses up onto her head and finally noticed me, holding my gaze for a long time, for as long as it took the guy to finish paying. When her traveling partner tapped her on the shoulder and handed her a suitcase, she took it without complaint and shifted her focus from me to him. An unkind sort of look. A look of annoyance. If they *were* married, it was definitely not a happy union.

I made the conscious shift from normal-Georgina to working-Georgina, checked that my smile was as genuine as possible, and met them on the driveway.

"Hi, there! Welcome to Fernweh Inn. Is this your first time on By-the-Sea?"

"It is!" the guy said, dropping one of his bags so he could shake my hand. "I'm Harrison Lowry. This is Prudence."

"Prue," she corrected, extending her hand and giving a weak, but not unkind, smile. Then Harrison reached over to tousle her hair, and her eyes rolled back so far in her head that I knew instantly: oh, duh. Brother and sister.

"I haven't been able to get a signal since we left the mainland," Harrison said, holding up his phone. "Is that normal?"

"Welcome to By-the-Sea," I said, sweeping my hand over the island. "That's just kind of how it is."

He smiled and shrugged a bit. "Well, I guess that can't be helped."

Harrison was cute, I had to give him that. He was tall and his hair was a messy brown and his eyes were bright and his smile was genuine. He wore long pants and actual suspenders with a short-sleeved button-up shirt. He had that nerdy-but-I'm-running-with-it thing. I wouldn't have expected him to be a birdhead, but the evidence was there: oversized leather camera bag, small binoculars already slung around his neck, dingy suitcase practically covered in antique bird patches.

Prue was more of a mystery. She wore high-waisted jean shorts that looked vintage, a blue-and-white-striped T-shirt that looked vintage and French, and faded red lipstick that just looked really, really good. Her hair was a darker brown than her brother's and hit just above her shoulders. They looked alike in a vague sort of way, just how two people who've lived together their whole lives inevitably start to blend a little around the edges.

"Where are you visiting from?" I asked.

"Just flat dab in the middle of the mainland," Harrison said, adding "kind of person who says flat dab" to my short list of things I knew about him.

"Oh, well, that's nice you're able to travel together. Are you two . . ."

"Brother and sister," Harrison finished, confirming my suspicions.

"Georgina! I'm sure our guests want to get inside and see their rooms," Mary said, bounding up next to me. I hadn't even heard the front door open. She was sneaky, my sister. She linked her arm through mine, and her smile was so bright I could feel the heat coming off her face. "I'm Mary," she continued, detaching herself from me and sticking a hand out to Harrison, then Prue.

"Harrison," he said. "My sister, Prudence."

"Perfect," Mary purred (there really isn't a more accurate word for it). "I'll get you guys all settled into your room. It's one of our nicest ones; excellent view of the sea."

Wishful thinking, maybe, but I almost swore that Prue met my eye for just the tiniest fraction of a second and smiled just the tiniest fraction of a smile.

There was a big dinner that night to celebrate the birdheads' arrival (and the, like, four inn guests who weren't birdheads but who *were* very confused and kept looking around like they had gotten off at the wrong island). Aggie went all out in the way she always did the first night of the season. We had it in the backyard and practically the entire population of By-the-Sea showed up.

Mary and I ate at a table with Vira, Abigail, Eloise, and Shelby. We were exactly two tables away from Harrison and Prue, and my sister's eyes were trained on the former in a *not-at-all-serial-killer way, thankyouverymuch, Georgina, and also mind your own damn business.*

"You *are* my business," I said. "We're twins, so people automatically lump us together. When you do asinine things, they just naturally get associated with me."

"Luckily for you I've never done an asinine thing in my

life," she said, and winked, because not even Mary could say that with a straight face. Then, more serious, settling back in her chair and using a garlic breadstick as a pointer, she said, "Do you think he's cute?"

I grabbed the breadstick from her before anybody saw the direction in which she was waggling it. "He's a *guest*," I said.

"What are you, the one-man human resource department of the Fernweh Inn?" She plucked the breadstick out of my hand and threw it across the table. "Yo, Shelbs. Hot or not?" She jerked her finger in Harrison's direction.

Shelby, picking up the breadstick from where it had ricocheted off her forehead, took a thoughtful bite and considered. "Hot," she decided after a moment. "Really hot. He's not a birdhead, is he?"

I nodded. "He's new."

"And the girl?" Abigail asked. All conversation at the table had ceased, and now seven eager pairs of eyes were staring openly at the Lowrys' table.

"Sister," Mary said.

"The girl's pretty too," Eloise said, in her usual thoughtful manner. "What's her name?"

"Prudence," Mary said.

"Prue," I corrected, perhaps a bit too quickly.

"Ohhh," Vira said, nodding.

"What oh? Oh what?" I asked.

"Nothing," she replied quickly, filling her mouth with

mashed potatoes so she wouldn't have to answer.

"Ohhh," Shelby echoed. She nodded appreciatively. "Yeah, that makes sense. She's definitely your type. She looks like she belongs on a picnic blanket under the Eiffel Tower, eating a baguette or something."

"You guys are being assholes," I said.

"*You're* being a hypocrite," Mary countered, and stole a carrot from my plate.

Eloise, angel that she was, changed the subject then to something no one could resist gossiping about for the rest of dinner: was Joel Howard, owner and proprietor of Joel's Diner, actually going to do as he'd been threatening for years and stop having free fries on Friday?

"But it's called *Free Fries Friday*," Abigail said, horrified, and they were off, a mile a minute about how Joel was on pretty thin ice with all of them, if the rumors were true.

"Thanks for changing the subject," I said to Eloise later, when the dinner was over and Aggie and Peter were setting up the dessert table.

"Honestly, they're too nosy sometimes," she replied.

"I haven't really liked anyone since Verity," I said. "I think my sister is just thrilled at the prospect. Especially if she wants to go after a guest. Strength in numbers, I guess."

"You don't have to explain yourself to me," Eloise insisted. "It's a small island. I think it's important to keep some sort of privacy."

I waited until the guests had had the first pickings of the

dessert table and then grabbed a plate for myself. Aggie's cinnamon cheesecake was unreal and aside from that she'd made four different kinds of brownies, twelve types of cookies, an assortment of mini pies, and a cake made as the exact replica of the inn. I took a little bit of everything.

It was cooler out now, but Peter had gotten the fire pit going, and the fire caught on the wind and blew warm air all over the yard. I brought my plate over to one of the benches that dotted the lawn, looking out over the southern tip of the island and the dark ocean beyond. I'd been avoiding Mary and the others pretty deftly so was both annoyed and discouraged when I heard footsteps behind me—and then immediately terrified and thrilled when Prue asked if she could sit with me.

"Yes! I mean, sure. I mean, if you want to," I said, sliding over, hating myself for how hard words could be.

"If you don't mind," she said. She sat down and showed me some fluorescent-colored liquid in a paper cup. "Do you know what this is? It was in that enormous, car-sized bowl," she said.

"Ah, that's Albert's Postal Punch. Be careful with it; it's sort of disgusting and also unrealistically strong."

"Unrealistically strong, I like that," she said, smiling. The moon was out and high in the sky, and that, coupled with the lights from the lanterns that were scattered around the lawn, made Prue look ethereal, almost too pretty to focus on. Then she took a sip of punch and immediately spit it out in an impressive arc onto the grass, and I couldn't help it, I burst out laughing, just barely managing not to snort.

"God, what *is* that?" she said, coughing.

"I warned you."

"I've learned my lesson; I'll listen to you from now on." She spit again, then poured the rest of the punch onto the grass. I offered her my dessert plate.

"To get the taste out of your mouth."

"This is a liberal spread you have here," she said.

"I haven't had Aggie's cooking since last August, so I'm just remembering how good it is."

Prue picked a peanut butter brownie off the plate and took a big bite. "Oh wow," she said through a mouthful of chocolate. "Oh geez."

"I know, right?" I set the plate on the bench between us. "Be my guest."

"Technically, I *am* your guest," she said, swallowing. "You live here, right? At the inn?"

"Since we were born."

"Oh, yeah. Mary . . . she's your twin, right?"

"In everything but looks and personality."

"Yeah, you don't look alike. Is it cool, living here? It's kind of . . ."

"Creepy?"

"No, I like the inn. I mean the island. Does it ever seem . . . small?"

Did it ever seem small, this island I had spent every minute of my waking life on, this island I knew like I knew my own body, this island where every tree was named and everyone knew each other and every person played some intimate, vital role in making sure it functioned smoothly, day after day after day until the day I left, until the day we all would leave, to seek our fortunes elsewhere.

"Do you know how the Amish leave home and spend a year just sort of doing whatever they've always wanted to do?" I asked.

"Rumspringa," she responded.

"And you know how almost all of them return home after that and never leave again? That's kind of like this island."

"Heavy."

"Yeah. But that's how it is everywhere, right? It's hard to leave the place you grew up."

"I wouldn't really know; we've always traveled around a lot. My father's an archaeologist and my mother's a linguistic anthropologist. Harrison and I were homeschooled, dragged all over the place. Our parents have settled down now, retired, but I still feel kind of . . . untethered."

"How did you end up here?"

"My brother. He's in graduate school for ornithology; this is part of his research. It was either tagging along with him, official sister-cum-lab-assistant, or stay with my parents until college. They're great, don't get me wrong, but

I'm used to traveling. So I picked the lesser of two familial evils, and here I am." She paused, took a bite of cookie. "It's kind of charming, this island. I hope that didn't come across like I didn't like it."

"Oh, no. It *is* small. I think I'm just used to it."

Behind us the birdheads were loud and rambunctious, stretching their legs after a full year of doing whatever they did when they weren't looking for Annabella.

As if she could read my mind, Prue asked, "So what's the deal with the bird? My brother wouldn't stop talking about it for the entire trip over here, but honestly, I get a little sick on boats, so I think I missed most of it. She only shows up during the summer, right? Where does she go for the rest of the year?"

Where did Annabella go? Somewhere far, far away, if she knew what was good for her. Somewhere where the rumspringa never ended. Somewhere where she didn't have to deal with birdheads documenting her every turn, photographing every tiny movement of her head, singing songs to her at night before they left her to get some sleep. Somewhere where she didn't have to worry about eggs that didn't hatch and summers that kept feeling shorter and shorter. Somewhere where you couldn't smell the ocean, somewhere where the ocean was the faintest memory. A rumor heard from a friend of a friend of a friend. Somewhere where the color blue did not exist.

"Georgina?" Prue asked.

"Sorry. What was the question?"

"Forget the question," she said with a wave of her hand. She forked a bite of Fernweh Inn–shaped cake and handed it to me. "Questions later. Cake now."

I took the fork obediently.

The sound of crashing waves—never really absent on By-the-Sea but only sometimes, for a few minutes, faded enough into the background that you didn't really notice them—swelled up and momentarily overwhelmed the night. I ate the cake. Prue took another cookie.

Mary could fly. I wished I could stop time.

"I saw you talking to that girl," Mary said later in the bathroom we shared, a long piece of floss woven through her fingers. It was past midnight, and it felt like I'd been up for a hundred years. I sat on the edge of the claw-foot bathtub and waited my turn at the sink.

"Prue. She seems nice."

"You *li-i-i-ike* her," Mary said. She lifted herself onto the vanity and sat facing me, not flossing with the floss, just playing with it.

"I only just met her."

"You can like people you just met. You can even like people you haven't even met yet. You can even like people—"

"Did you talk to her brother?"

"What, am I allowed? You told me he was a guest.

Which, by the way, I thought was pretty rich since you flirted with Prue all night."

"It was twenty minutes, it wasn't all night, and I've come to accept the inevitability of you sleeping with Harrison this summer. Despite the fact that he's a birdhead, which sort of goes against all laws of logic."

"I dunno, his birdheadedness just somehow adds to his charm," she said, winking. "Is Prue nice?"

"She seems nice."

"How come she's here? She's not a birdhead too, is she? She doesn't seem like a birdhead."

"She's just tagging along with her brother."

"Poor girl. She probably has no friends."

"You're an asshole."

"No judgment! Who needs friends?" She hopped off the vanity, threw the floss in the trash, and spread a line of toothpaste on her brush.

"You have friends, Mary."

"I have you, Georgie. I don't need anybody else."

"Well, you won't have me at college, so you'll have to make some new friends."

"Ugh. That sounds exhausting. They should assign you friends like they assign you a roommate. By the way, have you gotten yours yet? I'm with someone named Mildred Miller. That's a truly unfortunate name. I hope she's, like, unreal hot. For her sake, you know."

"I wouldn't lead with that in your introductions."

"God, you think I'm such a jerk," she said, rolling her eyes and brushing her teeth.

"I don't think you're a jerk."

Mary spit, rinsed, and turned to look at me again. "Are you nervous?" she asked, suddenly serious.

I knew exactly what she was talking about, of course, and it wasn't college. But I had no desire to get into it at the current moment. I gave a noncommittal shrug and pushed her out of the way so I could wash my face.

"I mean, I'd be nervous. If I were you. I'd be just a little nervous," she continued, moving to the toilet, sitting down on the closed lid, and crossing her legs. "I'm not saying *you* should be nervous, but *I* would be nervous."

"Can you shut up?"

"Do you not want to talk about it?"

"The queen of deduction."

"Our birthday is two months away."

"Thank you, Mary, I remembered."

"And you still haven't shown any signs of—"

"Grandma Berry was seventeen years and three hundred and sixty-four days old before she showed any signs of—"

"Lower your voice! Do you want to wake a birdhead?"

"Grandma Berry," I repeated, hissing, "did not show any signs of magic until the day before her eighteenth birthday."

"And I bet *she* was nervous," Mary said thoughtfully. I

wanted to grab the nearest hairbrush and beat her over the head with it, but I settled for brushing my teeth so hard my gums turned bright red.

When I finished, Mary was staring intently at me, her forehead knitted up in lines.

"But what about the twin thing?" she asked quietly.

"What twin thing?" I asked, although I knew exactly what she was talking about, of course I did.

"The first Georgina. She never got powers, but her sister Annabella did. Her twin. There haven't been twins in our family since."

"Our great-great-aunt's daughter never got powers either, and she was an only child. It's not like I'll *die*, Mary, I'll just go on living like every other person in the history of the world who isn't in our family. Being able to float three inches off the ground isn't the fucking miracle you make it out to be."

Mary's shoulders lowered a fraction of an inch, the only sign to indicate that I'd struck a nerve.

"I'm sorry," she said. "I shouldn't have brought it up again."

"Look, it's okay. Of course I keep thinking about it. Of course I'm nervous, or . . . not nervous, really, but just . . . curious. But I do mean that; it's not the end of the world if I'm not a . . ."

We didn't say the word out loud—that little word assigned to the women in our family—there was rarely a need. Mary reached her hand out and squeezed my fingers, squeezed every knuckle.

"I'm tired," she said.

"A long day of annoying me, I don't blame you," I said, but softly, so she'd know I was joking. She got up and hugged me quickly, then slipped out of the bathroom. I shut the door and took her place on the toilet, next to the open window. And fuck, although I didn't want to, although I really didn't want to, I started crying.

Outside, a massive crack of thunder and the unmistakable patter of rain.

Like a sign from the heavens. We feel you, girl. We got your back. We'll like you no matter if you get your powers or not. We could really care less.

Me too, Sky. I could care less too.

DAYS LATE

Annabella didn't show up the next day or the day after that. I was busy at the inn, my mother constantly had me shuffling between housekeeping duties, cooking duties, concierge duties (those were the best, our four non-birdhead guests asked easy questions and had seemed to accept that their weeklong summer vacation was being shared with a bunch of weirdo bird enthusiasts).

Wherever Annabella was, she was making the birdheads antsy, even though her absence wasn't that unheard of. Yeah, she *usually* showed up promptly on the day after the summer solstice, but she was also just a bird. You couldn't count on birds.

"The record lateness is one week," Lucille Arden said at breakfast, three days since the solstice. Lucille was the youngest birdhead—besides Harrison now—and celebrating her tenth summer on the island. She accepted a muffin from Aggie, who was walking around with a tray of them. "So three days isn't anything to panic about. You can't give a bird a datebook."

I thought *You Can't Give a Bird a Datebook* would be a good name for a really boring romantic comedy. I liked Lucille—she was about as normal as a birdhead could be, and talking to her helped alleviate some of my own anxieties about where Annabella was. I remembered the year she was a week late; Mary and I had been thirteen and the entire island had dissolved into near-hysteria levels of panic. I had never thought *that* much about Annabella before, and so I surprised even myself when her lateness affected me to such a degree: I had insomnia, nightmares when I *did* manage to sleep, and I felt anxious all the time.

My mother had crept into my bedroom in the middle of the fifth or sixth night of waiting and sat down on my bed with her jasmine-and-lavender sleeping draft.

"I could practically hear you tossing and turning from the first floor," she'd said, sitting on the edge of my bed and handing me the mug.

"Why do I care so much that Annabella is late?" I'd asked, pulling myself up to a sitting position and sipping the drink.

"She's a part of our history, whether we like it or not," my mother had said. "The Fernweh women are all related. What happens to one of us happens to all of us."

"You don't mean . . ." We had never directly acknowledged it, that this bird might *actually* be my great-great-great-namesake's sister. It was hinted at heavily, sure, but never confirmed nor denied.

"My second cousin could turn into a black cat," my mother had said, as if that answered everything. She'd bent over to kiss my forehead and then slipped the mug out of my hands; I was already falling asleep, so strong was her magic.

"Anyway," Lucille was saying now, "I don't love that she's late either, but I'm not quite ready to panic. We'll all be laughing about this at the festival, just you wait."

Held three weeks exactly from the solstice, the festival started at six in the evening and ran well into the night. In theory it was a celebration of our island's founding, but in actuality, it was called the Fowl Fair, and I think we can agree on what we were really celebrating.

Yes, Annabella had her own festival.

"I look forward to it every year," Lucille continued, taking a bite of her muffin. "I just hope the little darling shows up in time."

"You should play a little hard to get. Maybe that'll piss her off and she'll come looking for *you*," Mary said—I hadn't noticed her come into the dining room. She stood in the doorway, looking pissed off herself, but I doubted that it had anything to do with the birdheads' concerns.

"Ha! You're funny, Mary," Lucille said, and she took her muffin and wandered off. She had a habit of doing that, wandering in and out of rooms and conversations like she'd never quite grasped the concept of saying *hello* and *good-bye*.

"What's your problem?" I asked when Mary had joined me at the table.

"It's been three days, and I haven't made out with Harrison Birdface yet," she said, scowling.

"I believe his last name is Lowry. And also, he's a bird-head. He doesn't care about kissing girls; he cares about Annabella."

"He could care about both."

"There's no precedent."

"There's no precedent because there's never been an attractive birdhead before," Mary argued. She had a point. "What about his sister? Any luck there?"

Actually, Prue had been about as absent as Annabella. I hadn't seen so much as the back of her head since the inn's opening night party.

I shrugged. Mary sighed loudly.

"We're both losers," she said.

"I don't think not having makeout partners makes us losers," I said.

"First of all, it does. Second of all, I have plenty of makeout partners."

"What's it like being so popular? Like just the most popular little flower in the whole world?"

"It's really nice," she said seriously.

And then, like Lucille, she wandered away.

Having exhausted all hope of further conversation, I decided to ride my bike to the town square and visit Vira at Ice Cream Parlor.

The town square of By-the-Sea was actually more like a rectangle, and it was the only place on the island where, looking east, west, north, or south, you couldn't see any water. There was a gazebo and a small playground on the northern end and a farmers' market at the southern end on Sundays. All around the green were the shops and eateries and businesses of the island: the post office, Used Books, Joel's Diner, Ice Cream Parlor, the coffee shop (named Coffee Shop, because apparently we're really boring), etc. The high school and lower-grade schools were at the northern tip of the square, and the town hall was at the southern tip. It was a five-minute bike ride to reach Ice Cream Parlor, the ice cream and candy parlor owned by Vira's mom, Julia Montgomery.

It was Vira's dream, once her mother retired, to take over the business and rename it Skull & Cone. Already she experimented with making her own flavors, slipping them next to the normal stock so customers had a choice between Dutch Chocolate, Vanilla, Strawberry, Pistachio, and Broken Hearts of Lovers (one of her recent creations, which was basically just raspberry and cream and an unexpected dash of cardamom).

I arrived at Ice Cream Parlor at eleven, right when they were opening. Vira wore her unreasonably cute candy-striper outfit (plus white apron and matching hat!) and was busy setting out the ice cream labels next to their corresponding buckets of ice cream.

"Hi, Vi," I said.

"Oh, I'm sorry, are we still friends? Are we talking now? Do we know each other? Did we have a class together once or something?" Vira said. "First you ditch book club and then you haven't come to see me in three whole days."

"Vira, you know how busy the first days of the season are," I said. "I thought of you every minute."

She shrugged, too elbow-deep in ice cream to argue much. "What do you want while I'm in here?"

"Could I have a Bloody Sundae please?"

That was another Vira original, consisting of whatever her flavor of the day was (today: Lies of Our Elders) with plenty of strawberry syrup and whipped cream on top. She made two and joined me at one of the parlor's little tables.

I could tell even before Vira opened her mouth what she was about to ask me, so I beat her to it. "I haven't seen her since the party. Also good to keep in mind: we don't even know if she likes girls."

Vira took a thoughtful bite of her gray-and-white-swirled ice cream. "Well, let me just say that Colin Osmond was *also* sitting on a bench overlooking the very romantic ocean and moonlight thing that was going on, and she chose to sit with you and not him. And everybody says Colin is the cutest boy on the island. I guess. Right?"

Vira didn't pay much attention to gossip like that, especially when it came to romantic stuff (she was, as she'd once put it, "as aroace as they come"), so it was kind of charming that Colin was still on her radar, at least as far as his island sex symbol status was concerned.

I thought about this for a moment. Given the choice between Colin and me, Prue had picked me. "And he was really sitting alone on a bench?"

"Alone, yes."

"And she picked my bench instead?"

"She made a beeline right toward you. We can't be sure yet whether or not she wants to kiss your face, but your chances are looking up."

"I knew there was a reason I liked you," I said.

"My sage, sage wisdom. And also my ice cream," Vira said.

"And also your ice cream, yes."

I took a circuitous route back to the inn, because it was a beautiful day and the sooner I got back, the sooner my mother would find something for me to do. Mary and I didn't have shifts so much as we had two months of being at our mother's beck and call. But it was worth it, as she often reminded us, because in return we got food and shelter and the occasional magic potion.

I ran into a small herd of birdheads just south of the town square, milling about in the parking lot of the town hall

(Annabella had once nested on top of a streetlamp there).

"Anything yet?"

Tank Smith, busy setting up a complicated-looking tripod and camera, looked over and scowled. "Nothing at all. Not so much as a feather."

"Oh, she's here all right," Henrietta Lee chimed in, adjusting her thick glasses on her face. She had a set of binoculars hanging around her neck that were bigger than my head. "I can feel her. Can't you feel her, Liesel?"

Liesel held a series of instruments I couldn't even begin to guess the use of. They were small, metallic, and had a trio of glass balls attached to them, each filled with a different color liquid. She harrumphed at being addressed, but didn't offer anything in the way of an opinion. By Liesl's feet, her birdcat, Horace, regarded me with a look of distrust. I gave him a little wave.

"Well, let me know if you find anything," I said.

"You will be the first to know, Georgina," Tank said. He raised his enormous camera and snapped a photo of me before I could protest. Then, looking at the little screen, which no doubt showed my unready camera face, he added, "Ah. Strange to imagine where all the years have gone. I remember when you were just a babe."

The birdheads—especially the older ones like Tank and Henrietta—were prone to random bouts of reminiscing; I took that as my cue to leave. I waved to Tank and the rest of them and went on my way.

Without really meaning to, I ended up at the graveyard. The one graveyard on By-the-Sea was small and old and quiet—a few of my favorite things. I got off my bike, left it leaning against a tree, and walked deeper into the crooked rows of graves.

In the graveyard, it always seemed to be late autumn.

The perfect season for graveyards.

The dead trees had spilled their dry leaves all over the grass, and they'd billowed against the tombstones in big piles.

I found her sitting on a bench outside one of the mausoleums. Prue. Of course. She held a red cardboard box of fries from Joel's Diner.

In the few days since I'd seen her, I'd kind of forgotten how pretty she was, and now it hit me all over again. She wore a dark-green sundress, and her hair was tied with a silk scarf. She had red sunglasses on, even though it wasn't that bright out.

I walked up the steps to the mausoleum, clearing my throat to announce my presence, because I didn't know a *ton* about flirting, but I knew terrifying someone in the middle of a graveyard probably wasn't the best approach.

She looked up and maybe smiled a little, maybe happy to see me? Or else just really happy with the fries, which was possible, because Joel made some really good fries.

"Hi," I said.

"Hi, Georgina," she replied. She patted her hand on the

bench beside her. I guess benches were now my favorite pieces of furniture, taking the place of beds and rocking chairs. I sat.

"I haven't seen you around much. There aren't many places to hide on By-the-Sea; you're talented," I said.

Oh wait.

Was that creepy or cute? I couldn't immediately tell.

Prue laughed a little and put the fries on the bench between us. "I've been spending a lot of time in the library," she said.

"The library? In summer? Why?"

"I like books," Prue said. "And we had to pack light, so I couldn't bring any. And the library dude is really strict; he won't let me check anything out because I'm 'not a By-the-Seathian, and therefore ineligible to acquire a library card.'" She paused, considered. "Do you guys really call yourselves that? By-the-Seathians?"

"Oh, absolutely not. Stevie is the only one. And he's a stickler for those book rules." Stevie Carmichael, the librarian, acted like he wasn't guarding books, but lives.

"Good. I mean, it's actually a little cute. This whole island is a little cute, you know?" she said.

"How do you mean?"

"Like . . . the one inn, the one diner, the one ice cream parlor, the whole town-green situation. An actual gazebo. A beach called the Beach. A mysterious ladybird whose absence so far has made my brother very anxious."

"When you put it that way . . ."

"It's like a different world here. A very quaint, sort of creepy world."

"Creepy?"

"No offense," she said quickly. "I'll shut up now."

"No, please, don't shut up." Never shut up, never leave my sight, let's move into the graveyard together, some of the mausoleums could actually be pretty homey with the right amount of sprucing. It was just so easy to talk to Prue, like she was a complete open book. And she was funny, and interesting, and her smile was like a small revelation. Like she had invented smiling.

"I didn't mean creepy in a bad way," Prue insisted. "I just meant . . . it's like a storybook. Sort of dark, sort of cute, a little too perfect. Take this graveyard, for instance."

"What about it?" I asked.

"Well, I mean . . . it's *fall*," Prue said. "It is literally fall in this graveyard. Brisk air and fallen leaves, and that *smell*. Does that make any sense?"

"I'm sure it's just a geographical anomaly," I said. "You know, how like some cities are always gray and rainy? I'm sure it's just in some weird position on the island. And so it makes it seem . . ." I paused. I didn't know if eternally autumn graveyards were strange or normal or not. "I've never been anywhere else," I admitted, in way of an answer: I don't know any better.

"Really? You've never been off the island?"

"Nope," I said. "I mean—I'll be leaving in two months, for college. So that will be my first time."

"Wow," Prue said, taking a bite of fry and chewing it thoughtfully.

"I know. It's weird, right?"

"I don't want to say it's *weird*," Prue said carefully. She looked at me out of the corner of her eye and laughed nervously. "All right, it's a little weird, yes. But I've done weird things too! I traveled across the ocean to help my brother chase after a bird. So we've both done weird things."

I thought of the weird things I'd done over the course of my life.

When I was eight I'd had to untangle my sister's hair from the branches of the tree she'd floated into.

When I was ten I'd helped my mother mix a tincture that would make the roses that vined up the side of the inn bloom overnight.

When I was twelve, the year my grandmother died, I sat by her deathbed as she spun hay into gold and told me to put it toward my college fund.

When I was seventeen, I met a girl who'd traveled the world and had the kind of hair you wanted to just touch, just see what it felt like, and who when she talked to you stared so intently into your face that you felt just the tiniest bit like you were going to catch on fire.

"Oh, I don't know," I said. "I've had a pretty normal life until now."

Prue ate the last fry and moved the empty container to her other side. I could smell her hair; it mixed with the salt and the magic on the air and made something new, something unique.

"I don't think anything about your life is normal," Prue said quietly, a little distractedly, like her mind was on something else entirely. After a minute she looked at me and asked, "Do you want to do something tonight? I've been hanging out with Harrison a little too much. I love my brother, but he's currently only able to talk about one thing."

"One bird thing?" I asked, trying to ignore the irritating hammer of my heart and the imminent spike of my expectations, trying to remind myself that more likely than not, Prue was straight and just wanted to be friends.

"One bird thing," she confirmed. "I'll find you around the inn later? If you're free?"

"Sure," I said quickly. "Sure, I'm free."

"Great."

She smiled, picked up her trash, and left me alone in the graveyard to dissolve into a puddle of actual sunshine.

With Verity gone, I was one of only four out lesbians on our very small island. Two of them—Bridgett and Alana Lannigan—were in their sixties and had been happily married for thirty-five years. Wisteria Jones was a year younger than I, and while a perfectly nice girl, there had never been a spark between us. Same with Sally Vane, a bisexual girl in Wisteria's class, and Polly Horvath, who was two years younger and had dated both Sally Vane and Sally's second cousin, Marcus.

But here was the problem with all of that—because I knew everyone on the island so intimately, had grown up with all of them, Prue was basically the first girl I had met who was a mystery. Did she like boys? Girls? Both? Neither? I could only guess, which was proving to be hugely irritating.

Was this what it was going to be like off the island? In two months, when I left for college, was my entire dating life going to be a constant cycle of guessing and getting let down? And although I felt accepted here, I couldn't help but wonder about life elsewhere. Would the people at my college be as accepting as the people on By-the-Sea? Would I know how to do this better? To navigate the weird is-this-a-date-or-isn't-it?

Because even now, even as I reminded myself over and over again that what was happening tonight was probably not a date, I could *feel* the sloppy smile plastered across my face, the highest of hopes building in my chest.

Mary noticed it the second I walked into her bedroom (she was reading comics in her underwear in the middle of the day, hiding from our mother). She made a long, drawn-out noise in the back of her throat that sounded a little bit like she was choking.

"Gross, you have a date with her, don't you? It's not fair that you have a date and I don't. I'm prettier."

She probably was prettier, although as far as womb-sharers go, we really couldn't look less alike.

"It's not a date. Have you tried being forward?" I asked, though even as I said it I remembered who my sister was and, duh, of course she'd tried being forward.

"I all but took my clothes off in the dining room and climbed up on his table to perform a jig," Mary said. Then, raising a hand to her chin: "Do you think that would work?"

"I think that would accomplish many things, yes, including Mom banishing you from the island and burning your name off our family tree."

"But at least I'd have a date," Mary said, like she wasn't ruling it out.

"I don't even know why you like him so much. Is it just because he's fresh blood?"

Mary wrinkled her nose. "That's a decidedly gross way to put it, Georgie."

"But you're not saying no . . ."

"I'm not saying no," she agreed. "There are only so many people on this island, as you are well aware. It's nice to have a couple new faces around here."

"So . . . just go up to him and ask him if he wants to get a coffee or an ice cream or take a stroll on the beach or something. What's the worst that can happen?" I sat on the edge of Mary's bed and started flicking absently through a comic.

"Every time I see him he has his nose buried in a book about birds. These fucking people, I tell you. Up to their eyeballs in feathers. What do they *do* for the rest of the year? Sit around and pine for Annabella?"

"Absolutely they do, no doubt in my mind. You just have to shift his priorities a tiny bit."

"Oh, what, now that you have a date you think you're the dating expert? Are you going to open up a matchmaker's business on the island? You're so weird."

"Look—Annabella isn't even here yet; he can't spend *all* of his time out looking for her."

"He can," Mary said mournfully. "Trust me, he can."

"Well, then, maybe you need to shift *your* priorities."

"Meaning?"

"Meaning maybe it's time for you to get a little more interested in Annabella."

"Ah," Mary said, doing the chin-stroking thing again. "Intriguing idea."

"You know practically everything about her: where she likes to nest, what her favorite color is—"

"It's lilac, duh, that's why Liesel only wears purple."

"See how much you have to offer Harrison? Now you just have to show him that."

I could tell she was thinking about it.

"Are you *actually* a dating expert?" she asked after a few

seconds. "Oh, maybe that's your thing, Georgie! Maybe your"—she looked around and lowered her voice for dramatic effect—"*magical power* is being a dating expert!"

"Being a dating expert is not my thing," I said, rolling my eyes.

"Maybe rolling your eyes is your thing."

"I thought we agreed that we weren't going to talk about this anymore."

"If you don't get yours, I'm going to renounce mine. I've already decided," Mary said, suddenly serious, ditching her comic and pulling herself up to a sitting position.

"Don't be silly."

"I've already looked up the spell; it's in Mom's book. It's not hard, I can do it."

"Mom would kill you. And that's not even what I want."

"It's not fair. I can't do that to you. Mine is useless anyway; I've never even gotten more than ten feet off the ground."

"It will grow over time, and you're *not* renouncing it. Absolutely not."

"The night of our birthday. If you don't have yours by then, that's it for me. No more. Renounced. A return to normalcy. You can't stop me."

"You can't *return* to normalcy if you've never *been* normal."

When Mary was finally born, five hours after I was, the doctor had a hard time holding on to her. She kept floating out of his grasp, slippery and wet. Luckily the doctor was already eighty-four at that point and chalked the whole thing up to his budding case of dementia. My mom, overjoyed at Mary's immediate displays of power, became increasingly underjoyed when she realized I was just sitting there like a lump of baby fat. But whatever, she eventually decided that one floating baby was enough. She was already dragging stepladders around the house to pry Mary off ceiling fans and light fixtures; it was nice that I generally stayed where she plopped me.

"You can't renounce yours," I said firmly. "And there are still two months left. Anything can happen."

Mary shrugged. She didn't like being told what to do, and I didn't like the determination I saw in her eyes. It was a little scary.

I didn't have time to dwell on it, though—we both heard our mother's footsteps on the attic stairs at the same time. Our attempt to dive under the bed didn't work; there wasn't room for both of us.

"Mary, put some pants on. Georgina, stop encouraging her. I need you both downstairs," Mom snapped.

"Figure out how to turn invisible," Mary said as soon as Mom had gone. "That would actually be something useful."

Prue found me around eight, as I was dusting and winding countless grandfather clocks in the foyer of the inn.

"Cute apron," she said before I saw her, and I whirled

around so quickly I lost my balance and fell sideways into a Howard Miller. It chimed loudly in defiance, and I picked myself up again, red-faced and unbelievably happy.

"Prue!"

"Fancy meeting you here," she said.

"Is it nice outside?" I asked.

She had a pair of tiny binoculars looped around her neck, and she wore a wide, stiff sunhat.

"It's beautiful out," she said. "I thought we could go down by the water?"

Eighteen years minus two months of living on an island and I had never wanted more to go and look at the waves.

"That sounds perfect," I said. I ditched the feather duster and the apron behind the concierge desk, and we walked out into the evening, which yes, was beautiful: warm and quiet and filled with the scent of the roses I usually hated, but right now adored beyond measure.

I led the way, not to the Beach but to Grey's Beach, which was just north of the inn, where the cliffs dwindled off. Long ago someone had carved steps into the rock face leading down to the sand; it felt a little like descending into a fairy tale. Where tourists avoided the Beach because of the shark attack warnings, they simply didn't know how to get to Grey's, so it was usually equally deserted.

The steps were long and winding and a little claustrophobic. I glanced back at Prue, and she flashed me a smile so wide I swear the moon got a little brighter.

"Are you all right?" I asked.

"Never better," she said.

I felt rusty and out of practice. Verity Osmond and I had dated for almost five months, but that was a year ago. She'd been the only girl I'd ever dated. I suddenly wished I had paid better attention, taken notes, done *something* to prepare myself for whatever this night was.

Prue and I reached the bottom of the staircase and emerged abruptly onto Grey's Beach, moonlit and loud with waves crashing against the cliffs. She took a deep breath and said, "I think I could get used to living by the water."

We were on the east side of the island; there was no land to see off the coast here, just an endless expanse of ocean.

"It's nice," I agreed, but it would have been more accurate to say, *I don't know anything else.*

When I thought of other places, other cities, they were shadowy and blurred. There were two places you could be in this world: on By-the-Sea or off of it. Like every almost-eighteen-year-old who'd grown up here, I was leaving to go to college. Would I be among those who promptly returned from my rumspringa, or would I be among the far lesser number who created a new life, learned how to live outside of this tiny place?

Prue sat down in the sand, her dress pooling around her, and I lowered myself beside her. "Do you regret traveling so much?" I asked. "I mean—do you wish you had somewhere you could say was *home*?"

"I've always had my brother," Prue said thoughtfully. "I think a person can be a home, sometimes, just as much as a place or a house can. Even though he's a few years older than I am, we've always been close. He looks out for me, you know?" She paused, picked up a handful of sand, let it sift between her fingers. "Do you feel that way about your sister?"

"Yes," I said automatically. I felt that way about her even though she was a bit of a vapid, self-absorbed princess. I felt that way about her even though she could fly (okay, hover) and I could not. I felt that way about her even though she put herself first in every situation and I was so often left behind to pick up the pieces of whatever terrible decision she'd made.

It was the way of the Fernweh women; Mary was certainly not the first Fernweh to be born a little bit nasty. My mother had been an only child, but her mother had been one of three sisters. My grandma Berry hadn't gotten her powers until the day before her eighteenth birthday, and my mother told me that her sisters, Samantha and Matilda, brutalized her for it.

"Why would they be so mean?" I'd almost asked, but then I'd remembered Mary, and how you never really knew what you were going to get: the nice, thoughtful, kind Mary, or the raging evil bitch.

"She's trying very hard to sleep with my brother," she said.

"To be fair, she tries very hard to sleep with a lot of people."

"Good for her," Prue said. "She should do what she wants."

"She does *exactly* what she wants."

"And you? What do you want?"

What did I want? So many things, an impossible number of things. I wanted this beach and this moment to last forever, to never fade away into memory. I wanted to peek inside Prue's brain to find out the answers to questions I didn't know how to put into words. I wanted to kiss a pretty girl on a beach and not have to worry about whether eighteen would come and go and I'd be the first Fernweh woman since my great-great-great-great-great-great-namesake to remain as normal as I currently was. I wanted a hundred million things, but I knew how to ask for zero of them.

I pointed east, across the water, my arm indicting the entire world, the entire known planet.

"What more could I want?" I said.

But I think we both knew the answer to that question was:

Lots lots lots lots lots.

WEEKS LATE

A week passed, and then another, and Annabella still didn't show up. The entire island descended into an acute kind of panic. The birdheads organized groups to diligently comb every inch of By-the-Sea, searching well outside Annabella's usual nesting areas, tearing frantically through places she had never once been spotted in. They went door-to-door asking to check people's attics, people's cellars, people's spare bedrooms and linen closets. I saw little of Prue, as Harrison had employed her as his personal bird-hunting assistant, and the two of them were gone from early morning until late at night, when I sometimes spotted them in the dining hall, raiding whatever leftovers they could find. I was too embarrassed to approach her; part of me worried that she was spending so much time with her brother because she didn't want to spend that time with me.

"That's just silly," Mary said when I told her, late one afternoon as we sat on the porch drinking lemonade mules (Aggie's answer to virgin Moscow mules and what to do with my mother's out-of-control ginger plants). The last non-birdhead guests had departed that morning; we had a party of two due to check in soon.

"You don't know. I don't know. Maybe she didn't have a good time. Maybe she figured out I'm gay and she's staying as far away as she can." I shivered; the weather had turned colder recently and that morning had dawned rather gray and misty and had only gotten more miserable as the day wore on.

"She clearly digs you. Obviously her brother is a serial killer psychopathic meanie face who won't let her have any fun."

Harrison still hadn't shown the least bit of interest in making out with her, despite her best attempts. (Her best attempts: stealing a pair of binoculars from Liesel and prancing around the inn wondering loudly if anyone wanted to go Annabella hunting with her. Harrison had been the only one in the dining room at the time. He hadn't looked up from his cup of tea.)

"She probably doesn't want to lead me on. Ugh, it sucks even more that she's a decent person," I said.

"Look, Georgina, if Annabella had actually shown up when she was supposed to, we wouldn't even be having this conversation, because you wouldn't be able to talk, because you would currently have another mouth on top of your mouth."

"When you put it that way it sounds really gross."

"Kissing *is* gross," Mary said. "Think of all the germs."

Two things I didn't really want to think about: mouth germs and the fact that Annabella still wasn't here. The island felt incomplete without her. My mind thought of all the terrible things that could have happened to her on her journey. Maybe she had hit her head and damaged the part of her brain that contained the instinctual knowledge of migration? Maybe she was flying around aimlessly, looking for land, eventually succumbing to exhaustion and drowning in the waters below?

"Are you fucking thinking about Annabella again?" Mary asked.

"You're telling me that you're not the *least* bit concerned about where she is?"

"She's a *bird*, Georgie. I am not concerned about where a bird is, no. She'll show up or she won't."

"She's not just a bird, Mary, Jesus, even you can't be that cruel."

"You don't really believe that, do you?"

"Of course I believe it. It's the only rational explanation."

"Rational? That one of our weird old relatives turned into a *bird*? Honestly, sometimes I think hanging out with a birdhead's sister has rubbed off on you in terrifying, unprecedented ways. You're one step away from changing your major to birdologist."

"Ornithologist," I corrected her.

"Eww, see?" she said. She had finished her drink; she took mine and sipped deeply.

"She's probably dead. She's never been this late. You wouldn't care if she were dead?" I asked.

"Don't be an asshole, Georgina, of course I'd care if she was dead."

"Every year. Since we were *born*, Mary. Every single year."

"Fuck. Is it raining? That's just great. Everything is great."

Mary went inside, leaving me alone on the porch with two empty glasses. The rational part of me knew that I didn't need to be so bothered about Annabella's absence; she was bound to show up sooner or later, she always did. And the birdheads would calm down, and Prue would have more time to spend with me, and Harrison would relax a little bit, and Mary would finally talk him into making out with her, and maybe everything would go back to normal.

But it was hard to let that rational part of me get too much airtime. Everything felt on edge now, buzzing and sharp to the touch. It couldn't even stay hot on this weird island for more than a week; the weather was as inconsistent as my own moods. Ups and downs, sun and rain.

I stayed on the porch until the new guests arrived, a

young married couple on what they charmingly referred to as a "babymoon." She looked almost ready to give birth, and I was tempted to tell her that babies born on By-the-Sea tended to always smell like salt, always crave the ocean on their skin, always look for the full moon or North Star to guide them home. But instead I said nothing, led them into the lobby, got them their room key, and brought them upstairs while they trailed behind me, arms interlocked, kissing and whispering things to each other that were just past the range of my hearing. I knew already that we would not see them for the entirety of their stay, that they would come down for breakfast, maybe, and sneak enough food back up to their room to last them until evening. I was happy for them, a brief moment of happiness that only increased as soon as I shut their door and turned around to find Prue, like a beautiful deer in headlights, standing outside her room, staring at me.

"Hey," she said, smiling. She looked tired. "New guests?"

"They're on a babymoon."

"Really? That's sort of cute."

"I know." I pointed to Prue's binoculars. "Any sign of her?"

"Nope, nothing." She yawned loudly, covering her mouth with both hands. "Gosh, sorry; I think I've slept for about five hours this week. My brother has based his entire scholarly career on this trip. If he doesn't see Annabella, he's going to have a heart attack."

"She'll show up," I said, trying to sound convincing. "She always does."

"I hope so," she said. "Hey—what are you doing now? Maybe we could take a walk."

The six most beautiful words that had ever been uttered in the English language. Maybe! We could! Take a walk!!!

"I could do that, sure," I said, trying desperately to find some appropriate balance between *unmatched excitement* and *casual, cool indifference.*

"That's great. Let me change quickly? I'll meet you out front."

"Yeah, sure, of course," I said. She slipped into her room, and I tried not to actually skip for joy as I walked back through the inn and took up a post on the porch.

She joined me a few minutes later, wearing a dress with a full sailor's collar complete with a little bow just below the hollow of her neck. It would have looked absurd on anyone else, but on Prue it looked off-handed and sweet. She had one of those old cameras with her, a clunky box that you had to look down into to focus.

"Has it stopped raining?" she asked, holding her hand flat to the sky. "That's nice."

That's because you brought the sun with you to By-the-Sea; it follows you like a doting celestial body, I wanted to say, but miracle of miracles, I managed to keep my mouth firmly shut, choosing instead to only nod and smile, the far, far, far wiser choice.

"Where should we go?" Prue asked.

"I know someplace," I said, and we stepped off the porch together.

The sun was low in the sky, just an inch or two off the horizon. We weren't going far. The big oak tree was a short walk, sitting directly on the southern tip of the island, so close to the edge of the cliffs that some of its roots actually lurched out over the air, and the bravest of souls could climb carefully, carefully out, holding their breath while their friends snapped a picture. I thought it was hilarious, because what I knew that they didn't know was that the cliffs held no danger for them. My mother's grandmother had placed a protection spell on them after a birdhead with his nose in an ornithology magazine had walked straight over the edge to his death. "There are enough ways to die on this Earth," my great-grandmother had famously declared, "let 'distracted reading' be one less thing to worry about."

For the less daredevilishly inclined, there was a tire swing attached to one of the tree's largest branches. At full swinging power, your feet came almost to the edge without going over—if you looked straight ahead and angled your chin toward the sky, it was exactly like you were flying into nothingness, into air, into blue, into clouds. When I was younger I used to think that's what Mary must have felt when her feet left the ground: the soaring, stomach-dropping punch of potential.

When Prue saw the tree, she gasped a little, and then when she saw the tire swing, she gasped again, and she ran the rest of the way to it with her camera bouncing painfully on her hip.

"Georgina! Did you know this was *here*?" She shrieked, and then she laughed and said, "Wait, duh, of course you knew this was here. This is unreal."

The tree was pretty impressive, even to me, and I'd grown up with it. I had seen it and climbed it and hugged it and carved my initials into it and hid behind it. It looked like a tree straight out of a Southern gothic romance; all it was missing was the Spanish moss.

Prue unslung the camera from her shoulder and set it gently on the ground, and then she threaded her legs through the center of the tire swing. I wondered if she would ask me to push her, but she didn't, just backed up slowly on tiptoes and kicked her feet up in front of her, flying forward and back, pumping her legs, gaining speed quickly.

To our right, the sun was just dipping into the ocean. Everything was bathed in orange, peach fuzz, candy apple-y colors that made By-the-Sea seem like something out of a storybook.

"Georgina, come on!" Prue said. She'd dragged her toes into the grass to stop herself, and she was currently waiting impatiently for me to join her. There was not enough room for us both to sit, and so I climbed carefully to the top of the swing, standing straight up on the tire with my hands wrapped around the rope for balance.

And the sun blinked its final glow, and Prue reached a hand up and touched my left ankle briefly, and this, too, must be what flying felt like: stomach-dropping, indeed.

FOWL FAIR

The day of the Fowl Fair dawned to a low buzz of disappointment. There was nothing to celebrate. Annabella still hadn't turned up. She had never been this late before. The island was in disarray, and the inn was the epicenter of its specific breed of chaos. Everywhere you turned there were birdheads in various states of mental unraveling. The energy was cluttered, confused, frantic. It seemed absolutely absurd that the Fowl Fair would continue despite Annabella's absence, but everything had been planned, and we were an island of routine and tradition. It was impossible that we would forgo something as steadfast as the festival.

Willard Jacoby came to the inn to see my mother. He was the mayor of By-the-Sea, the first selectman of By-the-Sea, the town chairman of By-the-Sea, and basically the elected official of everything you could be an elected official of.

I knew what he would ask even before he reached the front door.

He wanted to see if Penelope Fernweh knew how to fix this. If she could throw some things together in a big black pot and magically pull Annabella out of it. "Truth be told," he said, standing nervously on the front porch, "I was hoping maybe your mother . . . well, maybe there's something she could do?"

I had to think that if my mother could have done something to find Annabella, she'd have done it by now, but nevertheless I led Willard into the house and brought him into the kitchen, where my mom was polishing silver (was my mom obsessed with polishing silver? I would have to look into this later). She looked up when we walked in, and I knew she'd figured out what Willard was going to say before he even opened his mouth, just like I had. She made a shooing motion with her hands, an indication that she wanted me to leave, but I hung back toward the door and watched. It was always fascinating to me, seeing the people of By-the-Sea trip over their words in an attempt to ask Penelope Fernweh for a favor. It was almost better than a movie.

"Penny, dear," Willard began. "You know I wouldn't come to you unless it was an emergency."

I actually knew for a fact that Willard had come to my

mother last year when he'd noticed his hair was starting to thin, which could hardly be considered an emergency, and the faintest smirk on my mother's face told me she did too.

"What's on your mind, Willard?" she asked, because she wasn't the sort of woman who just handed things to people. She liked to make them work for it.

"Penny, the people are panicking. Annabella is so late, and . . . well, you know. I thought there might be something you could . . . do."

"You don't think I would have done it already, if there were?"

"I don't know how all this works," Willard said quickly, holding his hands up in front of his chest, like he hadn't meant to offend her. "Maybe I can help?"

"You want to help?" she asked. "Hmm. Well, that's a different story." She replaced the fork she was currently polishing back into its case and wiped her hands free of some invisible dust. She walked over to the coffeepot and poured a mug of coffee. With her back turned, so neither Willard nor I could see what she was doing to it, she fumbled around in a cabinet. She took out small, colored bottles of different things, moved them to the counter, placed them back. When she turned around, she was holding the mug in her hands. Her face had settled into an expression of compassion.

"There's nothing I can do to help find Annabella. She has always been above my abilities," she said sadly. "But there's something you can do. Taste this, and it will reveal the right answer of whether or not the Fowl Fair should continue."

Willard adjusted himself to his fullest height, standing straight and looking important as he took the mug from my mother. He looked into its depths, took a tentative swallow—then a deeper one—and then nodded once.

"Well?" my mother said, holding her hands in front of her like she was eager to hear what he'd learned. "What do we do?"

"The show must go on," Willard announced confidently. He set the mug on the counter. "Penny, I thank you for your help, but there is much work to do!"

He turned and practically ran me over on his way out of the kitchen.

I walked over to the mug, picked it up, sniffed it, and took a cautious taste.

"Cinnamon and vanilla?" I guessed.

"And a bit of myrrh. People love myrrh," Mom said.

"How did you know what he was going to say? What if he canceled the fair?"

"It's Willard. He's not going to pass up the chance for an islandwide shindig. This way, he feels important, I didn't have to cook anything up, everybody's happy. Besides, I see no reason to cancel the fair. I think it might be nice. People need a little distraction. Tensions are high."

Tensions are high qualified for the understatement of the

year; just that morning, Liesel Channing had started crying so hard that her contacts washed right out of her eyes.

My mother sighed loudly and dumped the rest of the unmagical coffee down the drain.

"Are you all right?" I asked her.

"There's a lot on my mind, Georgie," she admitted.

"Like what?"

"Like how long these birdheads are willing to wait before they ask for their money back and get the hell off this birdless island."

"Do you think that might actually happen?"

"I couldn't begin to guess," she said. "It's not easy reading minds. Complicated recipe. Takes too much energy. And besides that, people don't always think the truth."

"But would we be okay? If they did that, would we have enough . . ." It was hard to say the word *money* aloud at the end of a sentence like that.

"Let's just say it was your grandmother who could spin hay into gold, not me. And her gift had its limits too. We have a bit saved up, but not enough to last forever." She paused, put her arm around my shoulders. "Tell me, you haven't been feeling any tingling in your fingertips lately when you see hay?"

"Sorry, Mom," I said.

"I thought not. Ah well. We better pray for a bird-shaped miracle, my love."

***

Mary and I rode our bikes to the town green a little before six. The sight of the town square transformed—food tents, a small area of carnival rides, a little midway with games impossible to win—made me strangely calm. See, we could still function as an island, as a town, sans Annabella. We did not need some magical bird to make us interesting. We were unique all on our own! Look, a festival! An actual, proper, midsummer celebration of life! How very quaint and lovely of us!

Mary and I were on ride duty; our kingdom consisted of a thirty-foot-tall Ferris wheel, a bouncy castle mid-inflation, a little merry-go-round made up of a mermaid, a brightly colored fish, and a blue whale.

"Is this how we die?" Mary mused. "Of boredom?"

"I don't think we're that lucky," I whispered back to her.

Vira showed up soon after with her ice cream cart. She gave us both cups and spoons, and we dug out the flavors we wanted ourselves, praising her good name.

As expected, just about every living soul on By-the-Sea showed up to the festival, anxious and hopeful that something, *anything,* might happen—that Annabella might swoop down from the sky and alight on the gazebo, maybe.

The time passed quickly.

The same few kids rode the rides and bounced in the bouncy castle for hours. Then Jimmy Frankfurter stuffed himself with cotton candy and jumped immediately on the

Ferris wheel and puked at the very top, an impressive spray of sick that landed on the two unfortunate souls in the cars underneath him.

"Holy mother of shit," Mary said when she noticed a few minutes later (having been occupied with a small technical glitch over at the carousel). I was trying to clean up vomit with some paper towels stuck to the end of a broom, because if I got too close to the mess I felt like I was going to puke myself.

"Jimmy Frankfurter," I mumbled. At the last islandwide Halloween party he'd bobbed for and ate so many apples that he puked a brilliant pile of red. I hated that kid.

"Why did you let him on here?"

"I wasn't paying attention," I said.

In truth, I'd been diligently scanning the crowd for Prue; I was ready at the drop of a hat to very casually ditch my post and bump into her.

"Well, I can do the rest of this if you want," Mary offered, which was uncharacteristically generous of her.

"That is uncharacteristically generous of you," I said.

"I could change my mind at *any* moment," she said, and I thrust the broom into her hand without another word.

I wandered over to the bouncy castle and found it filled with more drunk adults than bouncy kids, which is how I knew it must be after nine, the unofficial time when the festival dissolved from a place of good, clean family fun (at least in theory) to one of debauchery.

"If Willard sees you guys, you're gonna get kicked out," I said to the unidentifiable jumble of limbs and feet in the castle. At least they'd taken their shoes off.

I figured now was as good a time as any to turn off the rides for the night (there was something very satisfying about the idea of the bouncy castle deflating around the group of drunk adults now residing within it), and I did so quickly, turning the last few kid stragglers away with the musings of a seventy-year-old woman ("Shouldn't you be in bed? Where are your parents?"). I found Willard by the cotton candy cart and gave him the keys for the Ferris wheel and carousel.

"Another successful turnout!" he said, beaming, clutching the keys in his hands as if they were the keys not only to the kiddie rides, but to *the entire world*.

I decided not to tell him about the vomit.

As the night grew darker, more lanterns were lit, including fairy lights that strung back and forth overhead. This was By-the-Sea in a nutshell: a weird little island with a festival dedicated to a bird who was late to her own party.

When I got back to the rides, the castle was fully deflated, the people within seemed not to have noticed, the vomit was mostly cleaned up, and my sister was gone.

I found Vira with her shoes off, sitting on the grass with her back against the ice cream cart and her legs spread out in front of her.

"We're all out, girl scout," she said, patting the cart.

I sat down beside her. "I don't want your ice cream; I want your company."

Vira put her hand on her chest. "Be still my heart."

"How are you?"

"Tired. Stained with Frozen Blood." An ice cream flavor; she held out her arms to demonstrate.

"Why don't you go home?"

"To be honest, I was just saving up my energy for the trip. I am *tired*."

"I'm tired too. Have you seen my sister?"

"Not for a while," Vira said, shrugging. "I think she was talking to Peter earlier." She put her head on my shoulder and actually started snoring. I resigned myself to being her pillow for at least a few minutes.

And then, there in front of us—not there one moment, there and beautiful the next, was—

"Prue," I said. This single name was meant to convey a lot of things: *Prue, I am so happy to see you* and *Prue, you look so beautiful tonight* and *Prue, if you keep looking at me like that I will have to kiss your entire face, societal etiquette be damned!*

"Hi, Georgina," she said, and I couldn't even begin to translate that into anything more than exactly what it was. A simple greeting? A declaration of love? A hello, a good-bye? The secret of the universe and our purpose here on Earth?

Vira lifted her head and blinked sleepily. "I'm Vira," she said, sticking her hand out. Prue shook it, still smiling, ever smiling.

"Prue. Nice to meet you. That's an interesting name."

"It's short for Elvira. My mom went through a pretty intense vampire phase."

"I was named after a song," Prue said. "Not as fun a story."

"Well, it could have been worse for both of us," Vira said cheerfully. She held her hand up to me, and I pulled her to her feet. She stretched and hugged me. "I better get this thing home." She patted the ice cream cart. "Nice to meet you, Dear Prudence." She winked and was on her way.

"I like her," Prue decided.

"My best friend, of the non-sister variety," I said. "I'm officially done with ride duty—should we go for a walk?"

"That sounds great," Prue said, and we started off across the town green as the Fowl Fair slowly packed up around us. "I wish I could have gotten here earlier, but my brother had me out all day again." She sighed and looked at me. "Still no sign of her. Do you think something bad happened?"

"I don't know. It feels . . ."

Like it.

But I didn't want to say that.

Because saying things out loud imbued them with a

certain kind of power, and I did not want to give power to the idea that something might have happened to Annabella.

"The birdheads are all losing their minds," Prue said. We reached the edge of the green and started walking south. In the moonlight Prue practically glowed. A trick of either the light or my heart, I couldn't be sure.

"She'll show up," I said. I was so used to reassuring people—the birdheads, various islanders who thought I might have some pull in the matter, *myself*—that my words ended up sounding hollow. Even though I wanted to believe them. I *needed* to believe them. What would it mean for the future Fernwehs if Annabella never arrived? What would it mean for the inn, for our livelihood? For the real human woman who had turned into a bird?

"Either way, I'm glad I came here. Bird or no bird," Prue said.

"Oh?"

A translation of the word *oh*:

WHY TELL ME WHY TELL ME WHY TELL ME WHY TELL ME—

"Because I met you," she continued.

"Oh."

A further analysis of the word *oh*:

OHGODOHGODOHGODOHGOD.

"Yeah," Prue said, and she reached over and took my hand and held it, and every star in the night sky blinked brighter and brighter until the world was as lit up and bright as a midday in summer, a blazing wonder of incorrect light levels.

"Is this okay?" she asked.

"Yes!" I said. I shouted? I was talking too loud. I made a conscious effort to lower my voice. "Yes. It's okay."

We kept walking.

We kept walking WHILE HOLDING HANDS.

It felt like a very specific sort of miracle, this hand holding. It felt good and necessary and gentle and real. Neither of us spoke, we just kept walking and holding hands and then we'd reached the inn and we were still holding hands and then we walked around the back of the inn and we were still holding hands, holding hands, holding hands.

We sat on the bench we'd sat on the night of the inn party; the first time we'd really spoken.

And Prue

still

held

my

hand

and the ocean had never looked so beautiful

and the smell of salt had never seemed so warm and good

and I thought:

possibly this is the best night of my life.

"It's really beautiful here," Prue said.

"It is," I said, but what I meant was *you're* so beautiful here.

"If she doesn't show up soon, he's going to want to leave," she said.

"Your brother?"

"He's already searching for the next place to go, the next rare bird he can study," she said in way of an answer.

That stock, empty, fake response again, because I didn't know what else to say. "She'll turn up."

"And if she doesn't?"

She has to.

Prue lifted her feet onto the bench, pivoted, and leaned against me, her back against my chest.

And we sat like that for a long time, long enough for my heart to slow down. And then Prue finally got up and walked closer to the cliffs, the magic cliffs you could not fall off, not even if you wanted to. I got up too, and went and stood a few feet away from her.

And then she said:

"I've been trying to get up the courage to do this for a few weeks now."

And then I said:

"Do what?"

Prue took one step toward me, another step toward me. The grass stretched on for a million miles; it would be years before she reached me. She covered her face in both her hands and took another step. I wanted to move, but I thought if I did that, I would explode. My whole entire body would erupt into stardust. Maybe we aren't meant to be so happy, so warm, so absolutely, batshit joyful. Prue was right in front of me, I could smell her clothes, the lavender laundry detergent the inn provided to its guests.

I raised my hands and closed them around her wrists, gently prying her fingers from her face. Her eyelids were squeezed tight. She needed sleep. I could feel the exhaustion coming off her in waves.

And because she had crossed all of that distance, because she had come so close, I thought I could at least be the one to do the rest of the work, and so I kissed her. Lightly. Like how I imagined a bird would kiss another bird.

And she kissed me back. Like how a bird might ask for more.

When we pulled away, I was light-headed from holding my breath and Prue was smiling.

And I think—I *think*—she would have kissed me again, had Harrison Lowry not chosen that moment to come jogging across the back lawn of the inn, binoculars bumping against his chest and a complicated camera in one hand.

"I've been looking for you everywhere!" he said. "Are you coming or not? Hi, Georgina."

"Hi, Harrison."

"Oh no—Harrison, I completely forgot," Prue said, her

smile disappearing. "Georgina, I'm so sorry, I promised Harrison I'd go out with him again after the festival."

"Looking for Annabella," Harrison explained a little impatiently. "I thought all the lights and sounds might attract her. Plus the fried dough. Hep Shackman told me she *loves* fried dough, but he also talks to his binoculars, so I was taking that with a grain of salt."

"I'm sorry," Prue told me. "I promised."

"It's totally fine," I assured her. "Honestly. I should get some sleep, anyway. Long day."

"I'll see you tomorrow?" she asked, as Harrison sort of hopped up and down on the balls of his feet, looking like he was contemplating whether it would be okay to take her hand and pull her away.

"Definitely. See you tomorrow," I said.

I waited until they had walked back up to the house and veered off down the side of Bottle Hill before I went inside. The inn was empty and so was my sister's room, her bed made sloppily and her pajamas thrown in a pile on top. I collapsed in my own bed, feeling the edges of sleep already pulling me down, the gentle yelling like some sort of lullaby.

The gentle yelling?

I opened my eyes to pale sunlight filtering in through the roses vining past my windows.

It was morning already? I must have fallen asleep more quickly than I thought.

And it was quiet now so the yelling must have come from my dreams—

Except, no, there it was again. Someone in the inn was yelling. Multiple someones, a clash of voices that reached all the way up to my attic bedroom.

I got myself out of bed and pulled on jeans and a T-shirt and, rubbing sleep from my eyes, I walked down the short hallway and pushed Mary's door open.

Her bed hadn't been slept in. It was exactly as I'd left it last night.

I felt a thrill of fear as my brain struggled to put the two things together: the many rising voices downstairs and my sister's empty bed. Had something happened to Mary?

I ran down three flights of stairs and found myself in a lobby filled with people—birdheads, Aggie, my mom, and—

Relief flooded through me as my sister appeared out of nowhere, grabbed my hand firmly, and pulled me around the corner and into the library.

"What's going on in there?" I asked, but she just kept pulling me, into the dining room and around the back of the house to the back porch, down the stairs and onto the grass. She was wearing the same outfit she'd worn to the Fowl Fair. There was a small tear in her shirt. She hadn't slept, and her eyes were big and wide. Her hair was escaping her braids and falling down around her face. "Mary, what is it?"

"I was here last night. Got it? I had too much to drink, and I fell asleep like this," she whispered hurriedly.

"What? What are all those people—"

"Georgie, got it? Do you understand?"

"Fine, yes, obviously I'll cover for you, can you just tell me—"

"She's dead," Mary said.

"What—who?" I asked, and all of these faces cycled through my head, all of the girls and women of the island, starting with Vira and Eloise and Shelby and Abigail and Prue and—

"Annabella," Mary said. "They found her, and she's dead."

"No," I said. "That's not true, Mary, she's not even here yet, she's not even here. Why would you say that?"

But she couldn't reply. I saw her words catch in her throat and I saw her swallow them back down and I saw the tears begin to fall down her face.

I pulled her toward me and felt her heart beat against my chest, a broken beat, something shattered and taped back together.

And as we stood there—

Just like on the day of our births—

The skies opened up.

And it began to pour.

II.

I *was a child and* she *was a child,*
In *this kingdom by the sea.*

also from "Annabel Lee"
by Edgar Allan Poe

DAYS AFTER

If Annabella's absence had brought with it a building sense of panic, her death brought with it a terrifying crash, a cacophony of noise that descended over the island and made our ears ring. I dragged Mary home, leading her up the back stairway and into her bedroom.

"You need to lie down," I told her, helping her into the bed, pulling her shoes off her feet, and letting them fall to the floor.

"I was here all night, okay?" she whispered.

"Fine, Mary, fine. Just don't worry about it, okay?"

I pulled the blankets over her and went downstairs again. The crowd of birdheads had dispersed; I intercepted my mother as she pulled on high, black boots in the kitchen.

"Is it true?" I asked her.

"I know as much as you know," she said.

"But Annabella's dead?"

"I know as much as you," she repeated. She looked up at me then, finally finished with her boots, and I saw that she looked sad, and worried, and maybe a little scared. "They said she's dead, yes. I'm going now."

"Who said she's dead?" I asked.

"Frank and Nancy Elmhurst," she replied. "They found her in their barn."

Peter's parents. They lived near the cemetery.

"I'm coming with you," I said.

"Hurry up and get your shoes on."

We were soaked by the time we reached the Elmhursts' farm. The birdheads had beat us to it; some of them held umbrellas, some of them had rain jackets, but most of them just stood in the open and let the water rush over them.

I should have anticipated what a shitshow it would be. Birdheads were dramatic under the most benign of circumstances; now that they had something to actually be upset about, every single one of them had forgotten how to conduct themselves as adults. There was open, messy weeping, long hugs with no end in sight, low keening moans that started and ended as if from everywhere and nowhere at once, and more yelling—Liesel, her purple dress soaked to the bone, was arguing loudly with Henrietta as the latter fought a losing battle of keeping her thick eyeglasses dry. Horace paced nervously by their feet, ducking in between their ankles and over Liesl's purple rainboots.

"What happened?" I asked Tank, who was sitting

outside the barn, under the overhang of the roof. He had his camera in his lap and his hands wrapped around it like it was the heaviest thing he'd ever had to carry.

"Georgina?" he said, looking up at me slowly. "Please don't go in there. It's terrible in there. I couldn't bear it if you saw."

Hep Shackman, who was just a few feet away from Tank, mumbled something then, and I almost went to him before I realized he was just talking softly to his binoculars, holding them in his lap like he'd gotten confused and thought they were Annabella. When he looked up and saw me, he acted like I'd startled him, like for just a moment he was afraid of me. But then he returned his attention to his binoculars.

"Should somebody call the police?" I asked to no one in particular, because wasn't that what you did when someone died? I tried to remember the practicalities involved in death, and that was the only thing I came up with: somebody should call the police.

"Harrison did," Prue said, suddenly beside me, looking even more exhausted than she had last night and soaking wet. I suddenly remembered the bird-lightness of her lips on mine and felt a pang of anger that that memory was being interrupted by something so sad. "It's really terrible," she continued, lowering her voice, taking me by the hand and pulling me away from Tank. "We were one of the first ones here."

"I have to see," I said.

"Are you sure you want to?" Prue protested.

"I have to."

I walked slowly into the barn, letting my eyes adjust to the dimness. There were three overhead lights, large industrial-looking things that gave out just the faintest whisper of a glow, humming with the effort. There was only one person in here, standing directly in the center of the space, eyes trained on the floor.

My mother.

She took one step to the side and held her hand out to me.

It was worse than I could have imagined.

Annabella was lying next to a thick wooden support beam, broken and small in death. Her wings were spread limply open, as if she had died in an eternal flight. There were clumps of straw and feathers and twigs around her, and it took a moment for my brain to understand what it was—her nest. Her nest was lying in pieces all around her, as if someone had taken it in their hands and ripped it apart.

"Mom," I said. "Did somebody . . . ?"

"I don't know," she said. "It certainly looks that way."

"Her nest . . ."

"I know."

"Harrison called for the police."

"I know."

She knelt down on the dirt floor of the barn and held

her hand over the broken body of the bird, as if she could feel something I couldn't. She plucked a thin straw of hay from the dirt and held it, considering.

"It was an accident," I insisted. "It had to have been an accident. Birds fly into windows all the time, right?"

"I think we both know Annabella was no ordinary bird," she replied softly. She let the hay drop to the floor, and then she stood up and took my hand. "Somebody did this to her."

But I didn't want to believe it. The thought that somebody could have hurt Annabella was so sharp and toxic it made my stomach curl.

I felt something brush against my side, and Charlene Brooks stepped around to the other side of Annabella. She was By-the-Sea's sheriff, a woman about my mother's age with dark-brown skin and short curly hair mostly covered by a baseball hat.

"I didn't want to believe it," she said.

By-the-Sea's one deputy, Whitey, had followed her into the barn. He put his hand over his heart. The four of us stood there looking at Annabella.

"What do you make of it?" Whitey finally said. He was talking more to my mom than to Charlene.

"I don't think this was an accident," my mom answered softly.

Charlene nodded. "The ripped nest. That break there, in her wing." She crouched down and pointed to Annabella's left wing, twisted and stretched at an unnatural angle. "She couldn't have done this much damage herself."

We were silent again.

There was no crime to speak of on By-the-Sea. We were all quiet here; we all liked minding our own businesses and doing our jobs. There was no theft, no assault, no abuse. Until that day, the most Charlene and Whitey had had to do was write out parking ticket after parking ticket, which nobody ever bothered to pay and they likewise never bothered to follow up on. The one jail cell was used by Whitey to take his midafternoon naps. They were utterly out of their element now, moving uncertainly around the corpse, taking notes, taking photographs, and they both looked a little sick. The barn was stuffy, and I imagined that Annabella was starting to smell, the sharp tang of decomposition, even though it was too early for that.

Finally it became too much for Whitey—he clicked the lens cap onto his camera, bowed his head to us and to Annabella, and left the barn.

Charlene took a shallow inhale and turned to us, shrugging. "I have no idea what to do."

"Let me think about it," my mom said quietly. "I may be able to come up with something."

"I don't know about all that," Charlene said, "but I'll take all the help I can get."

Don't ask questions. Don't pry too hard. It was the By-the-Sea way.

Charlene left us alone. My mother inclined her head slightly toward me. "Are you okay, Georgina?"

"I don't know. I don't know what I am," I said.

She took my hand again. My mother's hands had always been firm and cool, but there was something different about them now.

Now, they were shaking.

I hope it doesn't seem strange, the bird funeral that took place the next night, the way the entire island met once again in the backyard of the inn to bury Annabella near the cliff. So she would be close to the water, people said, as if the entire island wasn't close enough to the water. But I knew it was really so she'd be close to *us*, to her once-home of the Fernweh Inn, to her living relatives, to the girl who shared her dead sister's name.

I hope we don't seem silly, the people of By-the-Sea and the birdheads (even though I have made fun of them plenty of times, but I'm allowed), everyone arriving with bowed heads and somber expressions.

I hope I have accurately described the island and all its eccentricities. I hope I have accurately detailed what Annabella meant to all of us: our tiny claim to fame, but even more so than that—she had been one of us.

My sister had avoided me since yesterday morning, emerging from her room only to pee and brush her teeth and find something to eat. She ignored me when I knocked on her door and even though our bedrooms didn't have locks, I left her alone. It's not good to disturb a Fernweh when she doesn't want to be disturbed. Like vampires, you should wait until you're invited in.

Now she stood on the outskirts of the little group that had formed in the backyard of the inn. She wore a tattered, oversized black sweatshirt, and she pulled her hands into the sleeves and hugged her arms around herself.

The funeral was not a huge production. It rained the entire time. The grass was spongy and soft. Everyone held umbrellas over themselves but came away wet anyway. Peter dug the small grave for Annabella. My mother had put the bird's body into a wooden cigar box, and she placed it inside the hole with a tiny sprig of rosemary on top. Then Peter covered the box up with dirt and people just wandered away, unsure of what to do or where to go, unsure of how much grief was allowed when the person you were grieving wasn't a person at all, at least not anymore, but just a little flicker of a bird.

Pretty soon there was a small handful of us left, sitting in the grass in the twilight: Vira, Prue, Abigail, Eloise, and me. Shelby hadn't stayed after the ceremony; she hated things like this, big showings of sadness. My sister had disappeared somewhere after the first fistful of dirt was dropped onto the grave.

Abigail smoked a long skinny joint and passed it around

our lopsided circle. Eloise cried silent tears, wiping at her cheeks every few seconds. Vira put her arm around Eloise's shoulders and squeezed.

Prue sat beside me, as close as she could manage. I didn't know the last time she had slept; her head kept nodding forward. Finally I leaned close to her and said, "I think you need to get some sleep."

"I can't sleep," she said. "I don't feel tired at all."

I stood up and helped her to her feet, and we walked together into the house. I found my mother in the kitchen while Prue waited in the dining room.

"Can I have a cup of tea? For Prue?"

"Tea tea or *tea* tea?" my mother asked.

"The latter."

"Poor girl." My mother poured a mug from a kettle already warmed on the stove. She handed it to me and said, "Make sure she drinks it all."

Harrison had joined Prue in the dining room; they were sitting at one of the tables together and looked more like twins in that moment than Mary and I ever had. Equal in sadness, equal in exhaustion.

I set the mug in front of Prue and then pushed it closer to her when she didn't immediately pick it up.

"It's good for you," I said. "It will help you sleep." *It will knock you literally unconscious* was closer to the truth.

She took a tentative sip, and then another, and then

finished the rest of the mug in one giant gulp.

"Oh," she said when she was done.

"Are you okay?"

"I have to lie down. No. I'm fine. Sleeping. Fine. Immediately."

"Do you need help upstairs?" I asked, but she stumbled out of the room without answering.

Harrison watched her go, bemused.

"I don't think she's gotten much sleep lately," I said.

"Nor have I," he admitted. I realized this was the first time I had been alone with Harrison. He looked completely devastated and suddenly a lot younger than I knew he was. He put his face into his hands and sighed heavily, his shoulders rising and falling. Then he looked at me and rubbed his eyes. "What do you think happened to the eggs?" he asked quietly.

"The eggs?" I thought back to the Elmhursts' barn, to Annabella lying in the dirt with pieces of her nest strewn about her. "There weren't any eggs."

"I know. But I also know that Annabella only builds her nest when she's ready to lay. She's never been found before she's laid her eggs. Not once."

"So what are you saying? That somebody took them?"

"Or broke them, I don't know. I don't know what I'm saying. I just think it's weird they weren't there."

"I don't know who could have done this."

"It couldn't have been a birdhead," Harrison said.

"They all love her too much."

"Hey, you're a birdhead too," I pointed out.

Harrison smiled weakly. "Fine—*we* all love her too much."

"But it couldn't have been an islander. We love her just as much."

"What about that really pregnant woman I've seen darting around here?"

"I don't think the babymooners snuck out of the inn in the middle of the night to murder a bird," I said.

The truth was, I had no idea why someone would want to kill Annabella. She was responsible for the fiscal success of our tourist season, a source of pride, our sole claim to fame. I couldn't imagine anyone on By-the-Sea would have wanted her dead.

"We're the only newcomers here," Harrison said thoughtfully, a little quieter. "It would stand to reason . . ."

"I don't think you had anything to do with this."

"I'm only saying, it would be an obvious conclusion. New birdhead comes to the island; Annabella ends up dead."

"Nobody is going to think that."

"Well, *somebody* killed her," Harrison said. Then he looked at me quickly, a little worried. "I think I'm panicking a little. I don't know. Perhaps I'd better get some sleep too. Is there any more of that tea?"

"Go see my mom," I said, pointing toward the kitchen.

"She'll take care of you."

I went out to the backyard. Abigail and Eloise had gone, but Vira was still there, sitting alone, a dark smudge in the middle of the rapidly darkening night.

She held a bright-yellow umbrella, a tiny refuge against the downpour of rain.

I sat down beside her, and she put her arm around my shoulder.

"Fuck, Georgina," she said.

I couldn't answer her. I had begun to cry, and I thought in that moment I would never, ever be able to stop.

It rained throughout the night. When I woke up, it was still raining and the driveway was under a half inch of water. The door to Mary's bedroom was slightly ajar, so I went in. She was asleep on top of the covers, still dressed in that black sweatshirt from yesterday. I woke her up and brought her into the bathroom, then handed her a towel and ran the bath. She didn't protest, just waited patiently while the water filled and I sprinkled bath salts on the surface, something of my mother's invention that smelled of lavender and camphor and made the room hazy and warm.

I shut my eyes as she undressed and got herself into the tub, and when I opened them she was submerged to her neck, her head tipped back and her hair spilling over the edge of the tub, already damp and frizzy from the moisture in the air. I sat on the toilet so I could make sure she didn't fall asleep and drown. She washed herself methodically with a bar of peppermint soap, raising her arms one by one over her head, lifting her feet gingerly out of the water. Her movements were slow and heavy, like she was in pain. The water was milky enough that I couldn't see into it, but once, when she lifted her neck to wash her face, I saw what I thought was the dark edges of a purple bruise blossoming on her back. When I looked again, it was gone. An effect of my mother's bath salts or a trick of the eye, I couldn't be sure.

When she was done, I handed her a towel and she stepped out of the tub and onto the tile floor. She looked smaller, like she'd lost weight and inches overnight. My poor sister, who loved Annabella as much as I had, who had to imagine, as I had imagined, a murderer flinging the bird against a pole, breaking the fragile, hollow bones that held her together, twisting her wings, ruining her flight forever. I knew that great terrors could shrink a woman, and I knew that my sister would never be the same. That maybe none of us would.

I moved from the toilet so she could sit down, and then I towel dried her hair and combed it with my fingers, braiding it into a long plait that I twisted into a bun on the top of her head. She smelled like lavender, like fear.

"I never knew how much I cared about a little bird," she said when I'd finished with her hair.

"It's all going to be okay."

"She's never nested in the Elmhursts' barn before," Mary

said. "I don't even think anyone looked there. She was in the rafters, high up. They found pieces of her nest up there. Do you think she was hiding because of the weather? It's been raining so much lately."

"I don't know. It's possible."

I imagined someone placing a ladder against the loft in the Elmhursts' barn, taking their time climbing up to Annabella. She was trusting; she was used to people getting too close, taking her picture, measuring her eggs with delicate tape measurers. She would let you put a finger on her head and rub. When she'd had enough, she would nip you ever so gently, like a cat who doesn't want to hurt you but just wants you to leave it alone.

"I keep dreaming about it," Mary whispered. She squeezed her eyelids shut and shook her head back and forth.

I put blush on her cheeks, because I didn't know what else to do, because she looked so pale.

"I think you need some more sleep now," I said.

I brought her back into her room and handed her pajamas, waited while she got dressed and then helped her crawl into bed.

"Is it even bedtime?" she asked, her eyes already closing, her hair quickly soaking the pillow.

"It's bedtime. Look, it's dark outside."

Mary looked to the window, where it was, indeed, dark and gray and wet.

"It feels like I'm still there," she said quietly.

"Where?"

But she didn't say anything, so I covered her and tucked her in, then sat on the edge of the bed while she struggled to stay awake. I didn't know what else to do for her, how to help her. She looked lost, too small, a shrunken shadow underneath the blankets.

"You don't think it's weird, to be so upset?" she asked again, eyelids heavier, face relaxing.

"Of course I don't."

"Because everybody is upset about Annabella, right?"

"They are. You just need a little rest. When you wake up, Mom will make you something to drink."

"You'll get yours, Georgie. You'll get yours or I'll renounce mine," she said, and her eyelids shut with an almost audible, minute crash.

I waited a few minutes just to make sure she wasn't going to get up again, and then I pulled all the curtains shut and turned the lights off and closed the door behind me when I left.

I got dressed and went downstairs. The inn was packed with people but eerily silent; the birdheads didn't know what to do with themselves, so they were eating a very long and slow breakfast, and Aggie was quickly running out of food.

I made myself a plate of pancakes and went into the kitchen, where my mother was sipping a cup of coffee and picking at a muffin.

"Is your sister still asleep?" she asked when she saw me.

I nodded and poured myself a cup of coffee. I looked down at the brown liquid as I raised the mug to my lips and paused. "What about if you put something in everyone's drinks? And if they're a murderer, their hair would turn blue?"

My mom smiled and touched my own hair. "It doesn't work quite like that. Any kind of big thing like this . . . It takes a bit of planning. A lot of time, energy."

"But you're working on something?"

"I'm working on something, yes, Georgina."

"And how long do you think it will take?"

"A few weeks, at least."

"Weeks?"

"The moon needs to be good again. These are difficult things to do; they take time."

"And until then?"

"Until then, I don't know. Maybe Charlene will come up with something."

"And the birdheads? What if they leave? What if the *murderer* leaves?"

"If anyone attempts to leave the island, they will find the ferry to be quite nonoperational," she said quietly.

So my mother had broken the ferry and trapped us all on the island with a bird murderer. Probably not the route I would have taken, but I didn't exactly have anything to contribute, at least not in the way of magic. I had no choice but to wait until the moon was good again, to see what else my mother had up her sleeve, to hope it would be enough to figure out who had killed Annabella—and *why*.

That was the most frustrating part; I couldn't begin to imagine what sort of motive they might have. And what if it *was* an islander who had done it? Did that make things better or worse? Worse, undoubtedly, because that meant that someone I'd known my whole life had an evil in them that I had never even noticed. My brain cycled through islanders' faces. I wasn't even hungry anymore; I left the pancakes on the counter and took my coffee out to the front porch. Everything on the porch should have been soaking wet with the downpour, but the cushions were warm and dry. My mother's doing, no doubt. And I had a feeling she'd done something to the coffee, as well, because the warmth it provided spread quickly through my body and left me with a feeling just shy of utter relaxation. I bet she'd slipped in a little valerian root, a sprinkle of chamomile, a few muttered, quiet words; just enough to calm down the birdheads who would otherwise surely be beside themselves right now.

If I'd had any bit of real magic of my own, I'd summon up whoever'd killed Annabella and . . .

But I didn't.

So it was pointless to consider.

I was almost finished with the coffee when Peter showed up. I hadn't seen him since the funeral, and there was something about him now, some straightness to his back, a somber way he walked. Annabella's death was affecting all of us differently, I knew. It was like we were all strangers now.

"Hi, Peter," I said.

"Hi, Georgie," he said.

"She's asleep."

"Good. She needs her rest." He swung a wicker end table over with one hand and sat down.

"Are you doing okay?" I asked.

"I don't know how I'm doing," Peter said honestly. "The whole thing . . ." He shook his head, wrung his hands together. "I just wish I could do something to help."

"We'll find whoever did this," I assured him. "The truth will out."

"Tell her I stopped by? I was supposed to do some work in the gardens today, but . . ." He motioned at the rain. "I just want her to know I'm around. If she needs me."

"Of course." Though I couldn't imagine my sister ever needing Peter.

Peter left, replaced quickly by Henrietta Lee, her thick glasses askew on her face, who moved so soundlessly that I didn't notice her until she had sat herself in the chair next to me.

"Geez, Henrietta!"

"I'm sorry, Georgina. I thought I'd get some air."

Henrietta was a tall, thin woman, a reed of a woman.

She'd celebrated her seventieth birthday last year, and Aggie had made her a cake in the shape of an airplane, for her late husband, who'd been a pilot. She was quiet, gray-haired, aloof. She generally stayed to herself, and I don't think she needed much sleep anymore; I'd caught her in the living room at three in the morning, reading books about ornithological case studies in the near dark. Whenever I tried to turn on a light for her, she'd said there was no need: she knew the books by heart.

"Then why hold them at all?" I'd ask.

"They're a comfort. Plus, it'd be a little weird sitting alone in the dark without a book."

I tried to imagine Henrietta killing Annabella, but the image felt immediately wrong to me. I had seen Henrietta scoop spiders into the palm of her hand and walk them outside to the grass to live another day. I had seen Henrietta cry buckets of silent tears at the end of every summer when Annabella's eggs refused, yet again, to hatch. There was no way on this green earth that Henrietta had anything to do with Annabella's death. It just wasn't possible.

"Strange weather we're having," she said, looking out over Bottle Hill. "It's like the island itself is in mourning. Feels a little . . ." She trailed off and looked at me out of the corner of her eye.

I could fill in the blank.

Feels a little spooky.

Feels a little magicky.

Feels a little unnatural.

"Nobody checked the barn," she said after a pause. "She's never nested there before. She could have been there for days. She could have been there all this time, just nestled up high in the rafters, waiting for her eggs to hatch, with nobody the wiser."

"It's not your fault."

"Oh, I know that. It's not anybody's fault." She paused, laughed—but a sad laugh. The saddest laugh I'd ever heard. "Well. It's someone's fault."

I didn't like the way she said it. But I couldn't quite pinpoint why.

She rose from her seat without another word and walked back into the house. I swear, none of the birdheads knew basic conversational etiquette, like *hello* and, God forbid, *good-bye*.

I took my empty coffee mug back inside. My mother was in the kitchen still, sitting by the window, finishing the pancakes I'd left behind.

"You shouldn't drug people," I said.

"I've hardly drugged anyone," she said without looking up. "You can buy those herbs anywhere. And you seemed fine with it the other night, bringing tea to Prudence and her brother."

"That was different." I stole back a forkful of pancake. "Mom . . . Harrison said something last night, and I thought it was a little weird. But you know how Annabella only builds her nest when she's ready to lay her eggs? Well . . . where *were* they? They looked all over the barn, right?"

"I've been wondering that myself," she said quietly. "Yes, they looked all over the barn. They didn't find anything."

"So what does that mean? Why would somebody want a couple of useless eggs? They never even hatch."

"Why would somebody kill a beautiful thing like Annabella?" she asked. "Why do these people do anything they do?"

When my mother said things like that—*these people*— I think she meant everyone in the world who wasn't a Fernweh.

FLOOD

My mother's coffee had made me sleepy, but not in a tired way, in a sad way, a mournful way. I wanted to lie down, to close my eyes, to try and forget about Annabella for a while, only my room seemed too empty and lonely, so I went to check on Mary. I found her floating at least a foot off her bed, which proved my theory about why her mattress was so much more comfortable than mine (less use) and *also* seemed a bit dangerous to me; surely her freshman roommate wouldn't be as understanding about a floating girl?

But now that I was up here I realized I wasn't tired anyway, I just didn't want to be alone. I tugged on Mary's arm until she woke up and fell back on the bed.

"Is it tomorrow yet?" she said, sitting up.

I unbraided her hair, still damp and now falling curly down her back. "It's the morning," I said.

Mary stretched her arms out and said, "I had a dream I was flying."

"That's not a bad dream to have," I said, still unbraiding. "Peter came by to see you."

She sat up straighter in bed. "Is there coffee made?"

"Yeah, but I'd make your own pot."

"Tainted?"

"Definitely tainted."

Mary swung her legs over the side of the bed but didn't make any immediate move to stand. Instead, she looked at her feet and the floor beneath them, a good six inches away.

"Mary?"

She shook her head, smiled, looked at me, and gingerly put her feet on the ground. I saw an unmistakable wince on her face, the slightest giveaway of discomfort.

"I'm just a little sore," she said. She used my shoulder to lift herself up and then swayed gently, as if caught in a breeze.

She really did look smaller, and like her features had resized themselves appropriately.

"You're still floating," I said.

She looked down at her feet and laughed gently, a laugh not unlike the trill of birdsong.

"What would I do without you?" she said.

"Be burned at the stake."

"Or crushed to death with rocks."

I tried to smile, but really I was thinking about Mary's college roommate again, and about how my sister was no closer to being able to control her powers than she was when she was a kid, getting stuck on the ceiling in the living room or tangled up in the branches of a tree.

Then she winked, and she was Mary again, no longer something more fragile and lost than the sister I'd grown up with. She left me alone in her room, and I sat on the bed, feeling the coolness of the blankets that hadn't been slept in. I lay down, folding my arms behind my head, shutting my eyes, and taking a deep breath of rose-filled air.

The roses were out of control this year. Peter trimmed them, cut them back, but they just kept persisting. They were thriving in this rain; if we weren't careful, they'd take over the entire house. You wouldn't be able to see anything of the Fernweh Inn except bloodred blooms and dark-green vines and sharp little thorns. Like Sleeping Beauty stuck in a tower surrounded by things that could prick. Except there weren't any princes on By-the-Sea. We didn't need princes; we saved ourselves.

"Georgie?" came Vira's soft whisper from the doorway.

I heard her walk over to the bed and felt the mattress dip as she sat down next to me. I scooched so she could lie down, then I opened my eyes and looked at her. Vira's signature cat eyes were smudged, like she'd been rubbing her eyes. Her hair was knotted into a bun on the top of her head. She wore black lace gloves, and she smelled like rain.

It was still coming down; the attic was filled with the patter of water hitting the roof and running down the windows.

"The streets are starting to flood," Vira said, nudging her chin toward the outside, toward the enormous double windows that faced the front yard.

"Really?"

"Just an inch or two. I saved a kitten on my way over here. It's in the kitchen now; Aggie is trying to feed it cucumbers. I think I'll name it Rain."

"Poetic."

"What are you doing in Mary's room?"

"I didn't want to be alone."

"But you *were* alone."

"Now I'm not," I said, and snuggled against her side. "I sent out a siren call to you, and then you appeared."

"The ferry's broken," Vira said.

"That was my mom."

"I sort of guessed." She turned so she was on her side, propping her head up with her hand. "Is she . . ."

"She's doing something; I'm not sure what. She said she had to wait until the moon was good again."

"Mysterious."

I rolled onto my side too, so we were facing each other. "I think something is going on with Mary," I said. "She seems . . . this is going to sound weird."

"I've known your family my entire life; it sort of takes a lot to faze me now."

"When I look at her I just get this feeling, like . . . I don't know. She seems smaller. She wasn't here the night Annabella was . . . the night she died. She told me not to tell anyone. I don't know where she was."

Vira fell onto her back again. She considered what I'd told her with a serious expression on her face, her forehead a mess of wrinkled lines.

"You don't think she . . ."

"Of course not," I said quickly.

We let the sound of the rain drown out the silence that filled the room.

Of course I didn't think that.

I just didn't know what I thought.

According to Fernweh legend, seven days after Mary and I were born, the rain finally stopped. The entire island was covered in water, five- and six-feet deep in parts. Aggie picked us up from the hospital in a small rowboat. My father and the rest of his crew were still missing; they'd searched the waters off the eastern coast of By-the-Sea every day for seven days and come up with not even a scrap of clothing.

Emery Grace put my mother into a wheelchair and wheeled her to the front door of the hospital, where Aggie waited in her little boat, one hand holding on to the wall of the hospital to keep the boat in place. My mother handed her babies to Aggie one at a time, and Aggie tucked my sister and me into a wicker basket stuffed with blankets. She rowed us all home with powerful, deep strokes.

Back then, our nursery was on the first floor, next to my parents' bedroom. Aggie and my mother tucked us in our cribs and then went onto the porch.

"I'm so sorry, Penny," Aggie said.

My mother's face was stoic, unreadable.

I knew all this because Aggie had told me, because my mother had told me, because I'd dreamed it. Fernweh history belongs to every Fernweh woman. I knew what my great-grandmother ate for breakfast fifty years ago on a random Tuesday in March. I felt the tightness in my mother's chest as she stood on the porch of the inn and looked out at an island drowned and soggy and colorless.

"I'll have to build a widow's walk," she said, and then she looked at Aggie and smiled so Aggie knew that she could smile, too, that the rest of their lives wouldn't be all sadness and loss.

And she did build a widow's walk.

And she never once used it.

Until now.

My mother, sick of birdheads clogging up every room of the inn, procured a sizeable collection of umbrellas from who knew where and kept them in a row at the front and back doors. The birdheads made use of them at once; it was unnerving to stand at my bedroom window and look down at them over the lawn of the inn—dozens of little black umbrella spots of mourning. The entire place was quiet, eerie, still.

I went around and opened every single window in the inn, trying to let out the stench of grief.

But grief was stronger than rainwater, so I didn't think it did much good after all.

I found my mother at the very top of the house, at that very widow's walk she'd built almost eighteen years ago and never used.

The stairs were pulled down from the attic ceiling hall-way. That's how I knew where she was. I climbed up to meet her, emerging into the gray, wet morning. She was holding a large umbrella and drinking a cup of coffee. It was steaming hot, and she gave me a sip without asking. It warmed every inch of my skin. I pressed myself against her side and handed the mug back to her.

"I wouldn't have thought I'd feel so sad," she said. "With Annabella gone. But she was one of us, I suppose, even though we only knew her in a peculiar way." She meant as a bird, and not as a woman who had learned how to grow feathers. "I've heard so many stories about her. From my great-grandmother," she continued. "She lived to be one hundred and six, my great-grandmother. I was named after her."

The original Penelope Fernweh, whose portrait hung

in the library with every other Fernweh woman who had lived on the island and on Bottle Hill and in this house. That Penelope Fernweh had been a storyteller, and she'd left behind journals filled with the history of the Fernwehs— thick, heavy tomes that served as a reminder of the past.

"What was she like?" I asked. "Annabella?"

"She was just an ordinary girl," my mother said, as if that meant anything at all. In a family full of girls, you realize quickly that no girls are ordinary. Whether or not they turn into birds, girls could fly and make magic all their own. But I knew what she was trying to say—that Annabella Fernweh, before she was *the* Annabella, *our* Annabella—was just a girl who, like my sister, sometimes floated an inch or two off the ground.

"Tell me about her," I prompted. Unlike Penelope Fernweh the First, my own mother took a little prompting to open up. She sighed now, took a long sip of coffee, and began.

"Well, you know she was a twin. Annabella and Georgina. I had never planned on naming you after any of us, but I just loved that name so much. I thought there was something poetic about naming you Georgina, about being a better mother to you than Clarice was to her girls."

All I knew about Clarice Fernweh, the mother of the twins, was that she was a dark smudge on the history of the Fernweh name. She kept her girls on leashes so short they were rarely allowed to leave Bottle Hill. They were homeschooled, locked in their bedrooms at night, and not allowed to have any friends.

No wonder Annabella turned into a bird.

"When I was pregnant with you, I used to read Penelope's journals over and over again," my mother continued. "There's a story, about the three of them—Clarice was like me, you know, she could make things, except she wasn't very good at it. She got her concoctions wrong all the time, it got to the point where, if you knew better, you wouldn't even accept a cup of coffee from her. One night, she forgot to lock her daughters in their room, and they took their chance and escaped for the night. They were just teenage girls; they wanted to go explore their island and have some fun and see the ocean at night."

She paused. Her eyes burned with anger at this woman who'd lived so long before her. "Clarice was waiting for them when they got back. She had two cups in her hand, filled with some terrible, smoking liquid. It's a very tricky mixture, to get people to tell the truth. Even I have trouble with it. But for someone like Clarice, it was a disaster waiting to happen."

My stomach felt tight; I had never heard this story before. "She made them *drink* it?"

She nodded, her mouth tight. "Every drop."

"And what happened?"

"Annabella's drink had come out all right. She told her mother exactly where they had gone that night, exactly who they had seen. But Georgina . . . something in her drink turned against her. She grew gravely ill. She was only sixteen, and people say it almost killed her. People say . . . that maybe if it hadn't been for that night, she would have found her powers."

My heart felt like it had shrunk to half its size. I couldn't believe I hadn't heard this story before. Clarice had been a *monster*.

"That's terrible," I said.

"Magic is never guaranteed in this world, not even for a Fernweh," she replied. "I think Clarice wanted to protect her children so much that she ended up ruining them. One of them flew away, and the other . . . Well, if you a stifle a child, you stifle every part of them. Who knows what Georgina could have been if she'd been given the chance to shine. Who knows. She could have been as amazing as you are."

She put her hand on my cheek, and even as she smiled at me, a little voice in the back of my head reminded me that I hadn't found my powers either. I was no better than the original Georgina.

Well—at least I didn't have Clarice for a mother. Magic wasn't everything, not even for a Fernweh.

"I'm so happy you're normal," I told her.

She laughed. "I think that's the first time in history a teenager has ever called her mother normal. I'll take it."

"What about this?" I asked, gesturing out at the rain,

my head still reeling from everything she'd told me. "What do you think is causing this?"

She thought for a moment, letting her coffee cool, staring out over Bottle Hill. "The first Penelope could control time. Nothing too severe. She could pause things for a few minutes, maybe speed up a day if she felt like it. But my mother told me that whenever she did it, things got a little wonky on the island. Using magic always has consequences. It rained frogs once. All the roses bloomed in winter. That reminds me a little of this."

"Are you saying all this rain is a consequence of using magic?"

"A consequence, a result . . . I'm not sure yet. But it smells like magic, doesn't it?"

She turned to face the backyard of the inn, which had been transformed into a memorial for Annabella. Her grave was marked with a little flat piece of wood sanded smooth by Peter, and although the islanders of By-the-Sea were not, as a rule, religious, there were still offerings left: old coins and pots full of seawater and small mounds of beach sand.

My mother had tolerated these gifts until they became too cumbersome, until half the backyard was taken up by trinkets and tchotchkes, and then she went out and collected the items in a cardboard box, which she left on the front porch. When people complained, she said, "I don't dance naked in your backyard," which made them a little confused and a little uncomfortable but also a little less likely to leave their old junk at the inn.

Still, it did not escape me: how strange it was to sit by the grave of a bird who had been so much a part of your identity as a Fernweh woman, and as an islander, that her sudden absence felt like a loss so sharp and profound that it took the place of even your father, of even your grandmother, of even every Fernweh woman who'd come before you and every Fernweh woman who might come after.

Except Clarice.

I don't think I could count Clarice in my mental list of ancestors anymore.

"I'll find who did this," I said.

My voice sounded more confident than I felt. My mother handed me her umbrella and kissed me on the side of my head. She left me alone on the widow's walk; I looked down at the backyard and the smattering of people taking turns crying by Annabella's grave.

Peter had carved into the wood of the grave marker: A.W.

Annabella's Woodpecker.

Secretly I thought he probably should have made it A.F.

Annabella Fernweh.

Once a Fernweh, always a Fernweh, no matter how far you flew.

SUSPICIONS

I started to notice something unexpected.

It began as a whisper in the inn, a low murmur that followed me through the halls and crept around corners and slunk in between the sheets of my bed, waiting for me. It began with Shelby leaving Annabella's funeral and casting distrusting looks at my sister. Then Hep Shackman, sitting outside the barn, looking scared when he saw me. I would enter a room and it would fall silent. I would sneeze and everyone nearby would jump. I would cough into the crook of my elbow, and if someone was sitting at the table next to me, they would get up and move.

I thought I was being paranoid at first.

But then I saw Lucille sitting alone in the library of the inn, reading a book about the stages of grief, and when I sat next to her and said hi, she smiled politely, placed the book on an end table without marking her place, and left the room.

My sister wandered in shortly after. She took Lucille's place, crossing her legs under her body, looking like a small child in the overstuffed chair.

It was twilight and there were heavy bags underneath her eyes. I realized I hadn't seen her in days; she had been walking around the house from shadow to shadow, like something that didn't want to be caught.

"Why do you look like you just saw a ghost?" she asked. Then, looking around, "There *are* ghosts here, you know. Vira told me once."

"She was just trying to scare you."

"I don't know. I trust Vira when it comes to creepy things."

"Hey, have you noticed . . . ," I said, but stopped, because I couldn't figure out how to phrase what it was I wanted to say.

Have you noticed people are avoiding us?

Have you noticed nobody will talk to us?

"I passed Lucille in the hallway," Mary said. "She practically climbed the wall to get away from me. So yeah. I've noticed."

"What do you think it is?"

"You know what it is, Georgina, you just don't want to admit it to yourself, because it sucks too much," she said.

She pulled two cookies out of the pocket of her dress and handed me one.

"They think we've got magic," I whispered.

"They've always thought that," Mary corrected. "But now they think I've killed Annabella."

This small crumb of knowledge had been sitting low in my stomach, wiggling around in my gut, trying to get my attention. To hear Mary say it out loud made it real. They thought—the birdheads, the islanders—that my sister killed Annabella.

"It's not fair," I said.

"You can ask me," Mary offered. "I won't be offended."

"I never for one second—"

"Right, but it's fine if you did. I can see how it makes sense. I'm a bitch. People love blaming bitches for things. And plus—you don't know where I was that night."

"You're a bitch, Mary, but you're not a murdering bitch."

"*Murdering Bitch* will absolutely be the title of my memoir," Mary said. She popped the last bit of her cookie into her mouth and chewed slowly.

"Well, where *were* you that night?" I asked.

"At the Fowl Fair. With you."

"And afterward?"

"Here and there," she said, and her expression clouded over. "Do you want to go out tonight? Colin Osmond is having a party."

Even under the black stain of death, the island loved its parties.

I shrugged. "If you want to go, I'll go with you."

"I want to go," she said. "Can you believe it's almost our birthday?"

"Why won't you tell me where you were?"

"I didn't kill Annabella."

"Mary, I would never think that."

"I'll meet you in an hour, okay?"

And she got up. And she floated across the room. And I knew I should go and yank her back to the ground, but instead, I just watched her leave.

Mary knocked on my door an hour later, and didn't wait for me to respond before she let herself inside. She was holding an umbrella, and she'd changed into black, ripped jeans and a boxy T-shirt, heavy black boots that I thought she must have stolen from our mother's closet. Her blond hair was braided into two long plaits that lay over each of her shoulders and she wore a dark plum lipstick that matched the circles underneath her eyes.

My sister always wore long, flowy dresses and not a stitch of makeup. I wasn't sure who this was, but she looked more like Vira or my mother, twenty years ago.

"Is that what you're wearing?" I asked.

"Is that what *you're* wearing?" she shot back. I had on jean shorts, a flannel shirt. My hair was pulled into a bun, and I wore plain white sneakers, dirty now from years of use.

It had taken me the full hour to decide what to wear. What if Prue was there? I doubted the news of a party at Colin Osmond's house would have reached her, but if it *had*, I didn't want to look like I'd gotten dressed up for her, but I didn't want to look like a jerk either. Half my wardrobe was spread out across my bed, and I saw Mary sneak a glance at it.

I hadn't told her about Prue and me kissing in the backyard, but in my defense, I hadn't seen more of her lately than the back of her head disappearing around corners. And I would have told her then, but there was something so disconcerting about the way she was dressed, about the plum lipstick that colored her pout into something unrecognizable. Something a little creepy.

"Are you ready?" she asked, crossing to my window and lifting it open.

I thought of Clarice Fernweh barricading her children in their bedrooms. I thought of the original Georgina so sick with accidental poison that she almost died. I thought of Annabella, seizing her one opportunity to get away forever.

I didn't blame her. Given the chance, I think we all would want wings.

"Georgie?" Mary said. She already had one leg out the window, and she was ducking her head to get outside. I thought I would always remember my sister like this: poised to jump.

And she did.

And she waited for me to climb down the latticing, and then we set off together across the island, huddling under one umbrella, just like we had the night of the summer solstice—minus the rain, minus the umbrella, minus my sister's dark lipstick. That night felt like a lifetime ago; everything had changed since then. The island was a different place, my sister was a different girl. Even I was unrecognizable.

My sister pulled a little silver flask from her bra, just like the night of the solstice, but unlike the night of the solstice, she drank with a singular purpose: long, deep pulls without asking me if I wanted any. When she was finished, she handed it over as an afterthought. There was hardly a sip left.

"What's going on with you?" I asked her.

"What do you mean?"

"This outfit? The amount of alcohol you just drank?"

"I'm getting ready to party. Can't you tell?" she said, and then she slipped away from me, out from the protection of the umbrella, and she was running down the middle of Main Street, following the road to Colin Osmond's house, which was just north of the Beach. I lost sight of her in between the streetlights, and I slipped the empty flask into my back pocket and tried to keep up.

By the time I reached Colin's house, she was gone—already inside or else disappeared into the night. Colin's parents were always traveling; they owned the only general store on the island and they left often, on buying trips. They'd been gone before Annabella had been murdered, before my mother had disabled the ferry. I wondered how they would even make it back.

Colin was standing on his front porch, and when he saw me he waved me up. I had been to this house with Verity so many times that it felt weird to be here now, without her, but I was glad that Colin was here, one friendly face against the darkness of the night.

"Hey, Georgina," he said. His usual upbeat energy was more subdued, and I was reminded for the second time that night that everything was different now. "How are you holding up?"

"It's been hard," I admitted.

"I saw you at the funeral, but I didn't know what to say. Things like that . . . they just mess with my head. You know?"

"It's fine. I get it."

"I should have reached out to you, though. I'm sorry." He took the umbrella from me now that I was safely under the roof of the porch, and he shook the water out over the railing. There was a bucket full of umbrellas outside the front door; he added mine to the bunch. "There are all kinds of things to drink inside. Help yourself, okay?"

he said, but I didn't get a chance to respond, because Billy
Kent erupted from the house in a mess of alcohol fumes
and noise. He seemed to pause midstride when he saw me,
a burst of laughter dying on his lips as he pulled the front
door shut behind him and froze.

"Oh," he said. "Georgina. I didn't realize you would
be here."

"Georgina is my friend," Colin said, putting his arm
around my shoulders in a protective way that set me immediately on edge. "Why wouldn't she be here?"

Billy rolled his eyes, but then he seemed to catch himself. He took a slow breath. "I don't know. I guess I just
thought she might have other things to do."

"Other things to do?" I asked. It took me a minute to
catch on, but then I had a flash of Lucille falling all over
herself to get away from me, of Shelby leaving the funeral
early, and something clicked together. "Are you kidding
me?" I hissed. "Billy, you've known me my entire life."

"Have I?" he said. He was drunk; I could tell by the way
he swayed almost imperceptibly back and forth, by the way
his eyes didn't quite seem to focus. "Because right now it
feels like I've never really known you at all."

"Oh, give me a break—" I said, shrugging out from
under Colin's arms. "Don't worry, I'm not staying. Let me
just get my sister and we'll both go."

"Your sister? Mary isn't here," Colin said.

Billy recoiled further at the mention of my sister, and a

big part of me wanted to whisper some singsongy mumbo jumbo in his general direction and see how quickly he sobered up, afraid I was turning him into a cat or a frog. But then Colin's words caught up to me, and I looked at him.

"What do you mean she isn't here? She was just ahead of me."

Billy opened his mouth to speak, but Colin stepped in front of him, pushing him bodily away from me.

"Enough, dude," Colin said, disgusted. "Yeah, I don't know, Georgina, but I've been out here for a few minutes. She's not here."

"Fine. What about Vira? Is Vira here?" I asked.

Colin shook his head. "She's not either, sorry."

"Great," I said. I reached behind him and plucked my umbrella out of the stack.

"Georgina, wait—"

"It's fine, Colin," I snapped. "Everything is fine. Enjoy your party."

I opened the umbrella and stepped out into the rain, ignoring Billy's jeers and Colin's attempts to both call me back and shut him up. My body felt hot with anger—at Billy Kent and every person who shared his opinion, and at my sister, for inviting me to this party in the first place and then vanishing without a trace.

I didn't even realize where I was going until I was half-way to the town green, to Ice Cream Parlor and the small two-story apartment above, where Vira lived with her mother, Julia.

I didn't meet a single soul the entire way, and the water came up to my shins and soaked my sneakers and splashed up my legs until I was soaked to my waist. I had a single word stuck in my head and it played over and over to the tune of every nursery rhyme my mother had ever sung me.

It was the word they had called all the Fernweh women before me. The word they would call all the Fernweh women after me. The word that could seem like either a blessing or a swear, depending on how you said it.

When I got to Ice Cream Parlor, it was closed. There was a funny sign on the door, handwritten by Vira:

closed due to inclement weather;
also, stop being assholes

I felt my heart swell with love for my best friend because I knew that second part was directed at all the people like Billy Kent and Lucille Arden, all the people who were suddenly convinced we must have had something to do with Annabella's death.

I walked around the building to the metal stairs that snaked up the back, leading to the second floor and the door to the Montgomerys' apartment. I knocked a little melody on the glass windowpane and Vira appeared a second later. She scowled when she saw me but she flung the door open, reached a hand out, clamped down on my wrist, and pulled me inside.

"I've called you a thousand times in the last three days. Did anyone see you come up here? Geez, you're soaked."

"Nobody saw," I said. "There isn't anybody out there *to* see."

"Good."

"What do you mean, *good*?"

"Sorry. But I think I'm the only person on the entire fucking island who hasn't lost their mind. Aside from you, probably. Unless you *have* lost your mind since I saw you last. I wouldn't really blame you."

"People are avoiding you because they know you're my friend," I guessed.

Vira rolled her eyes, which was always an impressive sight, because she could get them so far in the back of her head that only white was left. "I'm so sorry, Georgie. On top of everything."

"Your mom?"

"I've been working on her. But it's me against the whole world, you know? Thankfully she's not here right now."

"I think I'm uninvited to book club," I said.

"Eloise is sympathetic to your cause," Vira countered. "Shelby and Abigail can go fuck themselves."

She steered me farther into the apartment, finally pressing my shoulders down until I was sitting in one of the yellow plastic chairs around the kitchen table. The Montgomerys' home was a strange, strange place. The entire decor was 1950s and very bright and cheery, but Julia, a taxidermist in her spare time, had filled the apartment with every animal that had died on By-the-Sea during the last twenty or so years. The centerpiece on the table was a family of squirrels, perpetually frozen in a snugly, sleeping bundle of bones.

Vira got me a towel and then poured me a cup of tea from a teapot that had been warming on the stove. She sat across from me and watched as I half-heartedly toweled off and then tried a sip of the tea.

Vira in this kitchen would never get old to me. Her black dress, her black hair, the tiny silver stud in her nose— all of that set against the backdrop of bright yellows and blues and oranges was at once both alarming and deeply satisfying. The one place I felt more at home than home was sitting with Vira in her kitchen.

The tea was citrusy and light. Vira made her own tea of herbs she grew in a small garden on the metal landing outside her bedroom window. The rains had probably ruined it now.

"First things first," Vira said. "Did she?"

"No."

"You're sure?"

"Yes."

"I don't *like* asking. But I have to ask."

"I know."

Vira sipped her tea thoughtfully.

"I promised my mom I would find out who killed her," I said. "But I don't know where to begin."

"'Begin at the beginning,'" Vira recited, "'and go on till you come to the end: then stop.'"

"*Alice in Wonderland?* I don't know what that means."

"Sure you do. You're here, aren't you?"

"I don't know where I am," I said, brushing away a tear that was making its way down my cheek.

Oh.

I hadn't meant to cry.

"Georgina," Vira said, producing a tissue from a quaint ceramic tissue box, "you always cry when it rains. Come on; let's get you out of those wet clothes."

We moved into Vira's bedroom. This was the only room of the apartment not decorated in chirpy fifties decor. Vira's bedroom walls were black, and her twin bed had a canopy of black lace and her windows were fitted with black lacy curtains. Everything was black and lace, basically, which gave the room a strange Victorian, haunted-dollhouse-type feel.

The one place I felt more at home than home and Vira's kitchen was Vira's bedroom.

Vira rummaged around in her closet, and I stripped while her back was turned. She tossed a fluffy black robe over her shoulder. It smelled like rosewater and lemons as I slipped it on.

I moved to sit on the bed but was greeted by a furious yowl from something moving underneath the blankets.

"Careful!" Vira shouted, diving over to the bed to pull a little bundle of fur out from under my butt.

"What *is* that? And what was it doing under your sheets?"

"My cat! Rain. Don't you remember? She likes to sleep under the blankets." She presented the kitten to me proudly. Rain was scrawny and twisty and very, very cute. "When she dies—in, like, eighteen years—I think I'll have Mom turn her into a lamp."

I scratched Rain between the ears. "May you live a long and happy life."

Vira put the kitten down, and Rain burrowed herself underneath the covers of the bed again. Vira pushed her to one side, lit some tall white pillar candles in her defunct fireplace, and then we sat across from each other on the bed.

"I'm so sorry all this is happening to you," she said.

"Ain't no thing," I said, but we both knew that it *was* a thing, and that it was a thing that really sucked.

"I know why you came here," Vira said.

"Because I love you and I missed you and I wanted to spend time with someone who doesn't think I did something to Annabella?"

"Nope. Because you want to solve a murder and you know the best way to start—"

"Oh no."

"—is by contacting the spirit world and giving them a quick *hello, how do you do?*"

I groaned. Vira slid off the bed and crossed the room to her closet, standing on tiptoes to pull something down from the top shelf.

Vira's Ouija board was made of wood the color of stained tea, and it said *Talking Board* across the top in curved letters. The word *yes* was written in the top left corner, the word *no* was written in the top right. At the bottom: *Good-bye*. The middle of the board held the alphabet and the numbers, zero through ten. The planchette was cool when Vira placed it into my hands. She set the board on the bed and arranged it just so between us. Then she sat down again and looked at me expectantly.

"You know how I feel about this," I said.

How I felt about it: very creepy.

I wasn't entirely convinced that the spirit world was so easily accessible that an old wooden board would suffice to serve as mediator between this plane of existence and theirs, but if that *were* the case, I also wasn't entirely convinced that was a good thing to play around with. And I didn't know what sort of spirits would be so eager to talk to two teenaged girls sitting on a flooded island in the middle of a rainstorm, anyway, but I couldn't imagine it would be the good ones.

"What do you intend to accomplish here?" she asked,

even though technically this wasn't even my idea. But I knew intentions were important. Especially when it came to creepy things like Ouija boards. Intentions were everything.

"I want to ask about Annabella's killer," I said. "Who killed Annabella? And where was my sister the night it happened?"

She took my hand and maneuvered it and the planchette onto the board.

I suddenly didn't feel well; my belly ached with some vague discomfort and my palms felt a little sweaty.

"Vira?"

"I'm concentrating."

The room felt suddenly warmer, like the candles were throwing off more heat than their tiny flames would suggest.

"Vira, is something happening?"

"Who killed Annabella?" Vira said, but she wasn't talking to me, she was directing her words toward the board between us. We both had the tips of our fingers on the planchette and the absolute scariest part of how it jumped into motion is that I knew Vira would never, ever push it. She took this shit way too seriously.

"That's not me, that's not me," I said.

"I know, shush," Vira said. She looked positively radiant, alive with excitement.

The planchette moved to point at the letter *E*.

The planchette moved to point at the letter *V.*

I wished desperately that it would spell out something non–sinister and light, like how about: *E-V-entually the rain will stop and Annabella's death was just a joke, she's actually fine and well and also you guys are totally safe and everything is great!!!!!!*

The planchette moved to point at the letter *I.*

The planchette moved to point at the letter *L.*

Evil.

Of course the planchette spelled out the word *evil,* because life could never be calm and easy, life always had to be scary and dangerous and mean. The planchette kept moving.

The planchette moved to point at the letter *M.*

The planchette moved to point at the letter *A.*

The planchette moved to point at the letter *N.*

The planchette stopped moving.

"Evil man," Vira said, mostly to herself, but also, I thought, because she considered the phrase *evil man* to be too good and creepy not to say out loud. "Do you know his name?"

The planchette moved to point at the word *no.*

"Hmm," Vira said.

"I'm going to pee myself," I whispered.

"At least we've ruled out some genders," Vira said, choosing to ignore me. "Of course it's a fucking *man.* Men are always killing things. Okay. Where was Mary Fernweh the night Annabella was murdered?"

The planchette moved to point at the letter *W*.

The planchette moved to point at the letter *I*.

The planchette moved to point at the letter *T*.

The planchette moved to point at the letter *H*.

The planchette moved to point at the letter *H*.

The planchette moved to point at the letter *E*.

The planchette moved to point at the letter *R*.

And then, as if it wanted to be very clear that it would share no more knowledge with us, the planchette moved to point at the word *good-bye*.

Vira didn't look up from the board. She let her fingers fall away, but she just stared at the planchette like it was going to do something. For its part, the planchette sat motionless on the board, like a completely innocent thing. I thought the silence in the room was going to kill me but as soon as I opened my mouth to speak, Vira held a finger up. *Shush*.

Then she said, "With her. The planchette spelled—"

"I know—"

"With her." She finally looked up at me. She looked more confused than anything, like she was trying to wrap her brain around what we'd just learned. "Do you remember what I said? Maybe I wasn't specific enough? We don't know who the *her* is."

"Vira, I think if we can be confident about anything in this world, it's that you know how to be specific with your Ouija questions."

Vira put her hand to her mouth and bit one nail, almost methodically. She shook her head a little. "And Mary told you—"

"That she didn't do it. Yeah."

"So if she didn't do it—"

"Then why is this thing saying she did?" I finished.

Vira shook her head again. "Well, it's not saying she *did* do it. It's just saying . . . she was there, maybe? Or maybe she saw Annabella before? Honestly it would be really nice of the spirit realm if we could get another question or two," she said, and poked the planchette for emphasis. Nothing happened.

"Well, I guess we've figured one thing out," I said after a minute.

"What?" Vira asked, her voice barely a whisper.

"There's a whole lot my sister isn't telling me."

So maybe Billy Kent had a reason to be wary of us, after all.

Maybe everybody did.

I cut through the graveyard on the way home. Autumnal, eternal, welcoming. The rain here was not as fierce; it died down to a steady, light trickle. The ground was soggy with wet leaves. Although it must have been after midnight by that point, the moon was bright in the sky and lit everything with a soft, yellow glow.

Vira had given me dry clothes to wear (black jeans,

black turtleneck, black lacy bra) but those, too, were already damp. I propped the umbrella up against a grave and sat down on a stone bench. Because I couldn't go home, because I couldn't think of *where* to go, so I figured I might as well stay there and make myself comfortable.

Vira had given me a spoon and a pint of Broken Hearts ice cream for the road, which seemed appropriate. I pulled the top off the carton and started eating. It was that perfect temperature: soft and creamy, not too melty. I was halfway through the pint when I heard the whistling, and somehow, though I didn't think I'd heard him whistle before, I knew who it was.

Harrison Lowry.

He hadn't seen me yet, and so I was gifted the rare pleasure of watching the movements of someone who thinks he's completely alone. Harrison whistled a somber, depressing tune that sounded a little bit like the By-the-Sea shanty. He walked with his hands in the pockets of his trench coat, which was just a little too big for him, in an adorable sort of way, in a way that made him seem a little younger than he was. His hair was wet and messy, and he didn't have an umbrella with him. And he looked sad, distant—like he was in another world entirely. That was probably why he hadn't noticed me yet, although he'd come to rest not ten feet away from me.

Not knowing what else to do, I cleared my throat.

Harrison jumped a mile, and then he saw me and smiled

and put a hand over his heart. "Geez Louise," he said, adding "geez Louise" to the list of things that made Harrison Lowry strangely appealing. "Georgina! What a strange place to meet."

I felt an overwhelming happiness—that he didn't run away the moment he saw me, that he didn't seem that bothered at all to be so close to me, and that he even seemed, maybe, pleased to have run into me. I held the ice cream out to him, and he came and sat next to me on the bench and took it.

"Tell me," he said, taking a bite of Broken Hearts, "what brings you to the graveyard in the middle of this rainy night?"

"I didn't have anywhere else to go," I said. "You?"

"A little bit of insomnia, I'm afraid. I spent so many nights looking for Annabella that now I can't seem to sleep. I didn't want to wake my sister, what with all my tossing and turning."

Ah, Prue.

Her name still sent a little rush of warmth down my arms, even though I hadn't seen her since the funeral. It was nice to know that she was well, even in the chaos of everything.

Harrison chuckled, took another bite of ice cream. "I bet it gets old, dealing with all these bird lovers, doesn't it?" he said after a minute. "I think we're all prone to the sentimental. Even those of us who didn't know her well."

"It doesn't get old," I said softly. "It's nice. What made you want to find her in the first place?"

"Just the idea, I think, of seeing something that so few people before me have seen . . . It became a bit of an obsession. My sister would say it's a *big* obsession, I'm sure."

"It's nice that you have each other," I said.

"It's nice to have sisters, isn't it? You would know," he said, and looked at me out of the very corner of his eye, like he was trying to hide how eager he was to hear my response. Like he had heard something.

"I do have one of those, yeah."

"It's nice," he repeated. He looked so suddenly sad, sitting there, and more like a little kid than ever, his shoulders hunched and his arms hugged around his knees and every inch of him completely dripping wet.

"I'm glad you don't hate me," I blurted out. I wished I could pluck the words out of the air and force them back in my mouth, back down my throat. But you can't unsay things once they're out in the world. Not even Fernweh women can manage that.

Harrison swallowed. He put the pint on the bench between us, resting the spoon carefully across its top. "How do I put this," he wondered aloud. "All right. Georgina, I don't believe for a second that your sister—or anyone in your family, for that matter—had anything to do with Annabella's death."

"How come?" I asked.

I really needed to learn how to keep my mouth shut unless it was to say *thank you for not thinking we're murderers*.

"You're all smart women," Harrison said. "And it would be decidedly *un*smart to sabotage your only means of livelihood."

"We wouldn't kill the bird because without the bird there won't be any birdheads, and without the birdheads there would be nobody to stay at the inn," I translated.

"Exactly."

"How come you're the only one intelligent enough to figure that out?" I asked, even though I was thinking something more along the lines of *you don't know my sister; her motivations are a little harder to pinpoint*.

"I've been thinking about that," Harrison said, picking the ice cream up again, taking a thoughtful bite. "And I think it's because we're the newbies."

The word *newbies* coming out of Harrison Lowry's mouth made me laugh out loud. He smirked in response.

"I just mean," he continued, "that of all the birdheads here, I'm the most removed. I've never been to By-the-Sea, I've never met you or your sister before this summer. I don't have a real attachment to you yet. No offense."

"None taken." The ice cream was exchanged from Harrison's hand to mine. A symbiotic ice cream relationship in a graveyard. One could do worse.

"There's a lot of emotion running around. The birdheads just want to blame somebody and get it over with.

And with all the rumors floating around about your family already, I think it makes sense they've chosen Mary as their scapegoat."

"Not rumors," I said. I suddenly didn't care much about the Fernweh family secrecy. It hadn't gotten us anywhere but suspicious looks and whispered accusations.

"Not rumors," Harrison repeated.

"If you're referring to the general spookiness of the Fernweh women then no, not rumors," I clarified.

"Spookiness."

"You know. Boil and bubble and all that."

"Ah. Well, I guess that changes things a little."

"Oh?"

"Back to the drawing board. No telling what you may or may not have done."

But he was smiling. And there was also an earnestness there, like he was taking my magicky revelation at face value. That was sort of nice.

"Have you ever heard that poem?" he asked, suddenly distant, looking past me.

"What poem?"

The ice cream was almost gone.

"'In her tomb by the sounding sea,'" Harrison said.

"Ah. Of course I've heard that poem. Poe was quite taken with the theme of death."

"Of women in particular. Sort of morbid, no?"

"What about it?"

"Hmm? Well, it's been in my head since I stepped off the ferry. I never considered myself much of a poetry person."

"Well. Islands. The sea. Rain. Graveyards. Dead things. It's hard not to feel poetic here."

"I think you have a point."

"Harrison—will you take a walk with me?" I asked.

That declaration on the widow's walk buzzed around in my head, loud and angry, *I will find who did this.* Even if that person might be my sister.

"Where?" Harrison asked.

"To somewhere unpleasant."

"Ah," he said. "I am at your disposal."

And we began to walk.

The entrance to the Elmhursts' barn was roped off by bright-yellow police tape. It was raining in earnest over here, just a short walk from the graveyard. We huddled underneath my one umbrella as Harrison fiddled with the lock on the door, wiggling a paper clip around inside it until it popped open with a soft *click.* He let it fall into his hand and then, looking around to make sure no one had seen us, we ducked into the dark mouth of the barn.

Harrison pulled a flashlight out of the pocket of his trench coat (where he'd also pulled the paper clip from, which begged the question: what *else* did he have in there?) and clicked it on. I put the umbrella near the door to dry out.

"What exactly are we doing here?" he asked.

"Didn't you know? We're solving a murder," I said. I grabbed the flashlight from him and put it under my chin.

"And what do you expect to find here?" he asked.

I handed the flashlight back to him. "Something the police missed."

"When you say *the police* like that, it implies more than just a sheriff and a deputy," Harrison said. "It's sort of false advertising."

"Fair."

He scanned his flashlight around the interior of the barn. "There's an overhead light in here somewhere, isn't there?"

I found the light switch on the wall and turned it on. The barn was washed in pale, dusty light. I half expected there to be a bird-shaped white chalk outline in the dirt marking where Annabella was found, but the ground was clear. The nest was gone. It looked like nothing out of the ordinary had ever happened here.

"I don't even know what I'm looking for," I admitted.

Harrison tossed the flashlight from hand to hand. He looked around the barn. "So far we don't seem to be showing much promise as sleuths."

"I know." I took a deep breath. "All right. You take the loft. I'll look around down here. Shout if you see anything."

So Harrison climbed carefully up the wooden ladder that led to the lofted area, and I explored the ground floor, the wood underneath my feet creaking as I walked around. I had "Annabel Lee" stuck in my head now, and I kept seeing shadows moving out of the corner of my eye because the half-light made everything spookier than it was.

Then Harrison started whistling again, and *that* made everything spookier than it was, too, and so finally, my nerves shot to hell and my skin crawling with goose bumps, I climbed up the ladder to meet Harrison in the loft. Because I didn't want to be alone. Because the phrase *higher ground* was suddenly ringing in my ears. Because outside the rain beat a torrential staccato against the roof, and I thought my heartbeat might be trying to match it.

It was brighter up here (closer to the overhead lamps), and I felt instantly more relaxed. I forced myself to breathe, breathe, breathing through the panic I could feel welling up in my chest. A sort of buzzing around my rib cage. The ever-familiar feeling of fear.

"Harrison?"

He turned around to face me, and as he did, the beam of his flashlight caught on something by his foot. A flash of gold. I bent down to pick it up and held it in my cupped hands. I felt that icy trickle of horror when you are home alone and hear a sound too loud to be just the house settling, or when you are walking at night and suddenly hear footsteps following too closely behind you.

It was my sister's necklace.

I would know it anywhere. It was a delicate heart-shaped locket, identical to the one given to me on our sixteenth birthday. Matching lockets. Mary wore hers often; mine was tucked safely inside the top drawer of my bureau. I'd never been one for jewelry.

The Ouija board had said: *with her.*

And now I had proof of it: Mary was here, in the barn, the night Annabella was murdered.

I knew if I opened this locket I would find a picture of the two of us on one side—Mary and me—and a picture of my mother and father on the other.

The clasp of the necklace was broken.

I held it up to Harrison, so he could see it. "It's my sister's."

"What would your sister's locket be doing in this barn?" Harrison asked, his voice careful and measured, like he was trying to keep something out of it.

"I know she didn't kill Annabella," I said, but even as the words left my mouth I wondered—did I really know that? It was my sister's word against the Ouija board, against this locket. It was my sister's word against everything piling up against it.

"But if she was here, she must know something," Harrison said. "Have you asked her?"

I shook my head. "I don't know what she knows. She's being . . . strange."

"Strange," Harrison repeated.

"Oh, please don't change your mind about us," I said quickly.

"Not changing my mind. Just . . . processing."

"Did you find anything else up here?"

"Feathers," Harrison said.

I took a step closer to him. "What?"

"Feathers," he repeated. "But not Annabella's."

"Not Annabella's."

"Look."

He took one step to the side, revealing a small, neat pile of feathers. They were white and long and clean. Not Annabella's.

"What kind of bird did these come from?" I asked.

I felt sick to my stomach.

"It's hard to say," Harrison said. "They don't look familiar to me."

"I think I need some air," I said.

"Mmm," Harrison said. He picked up a feather and carefully put it into a pocket of his trench coat.

I wondered again what else he might have in those pockets. The reason why it was raining so much? The location of my missing magic powers? That which my sister refused to tell me? The identity of the evil man who'd killed Annabella? What part my sister must have played in her death?

My head was spinning.

I descended the ladder quickly and raced across the barn to the door, which was standing ajar just an inch or so. I pushed out into the cold, wet evening. The moon was fat and almost full in the sky above me. I leaned against the outside wall of the barn and breathed and breathed and breathed.

Until I heard the barn door creak open and closed, and I felt a hand on my shoulder.

I opened my eyes.

Harrison, holding my umbrella.

"Are you all right?" he asked.

"Just needed a little air."

He offered me his arm. "Let's go home, shall we?"

I took it, gratefully.

And we set off into the dark.

That night, late, Mary crawled into my bed. I moved over to make room for her.

"I can't sleep," she said.

"Where did you go?"

"When?"

"At the party, Mary. Where did you go?"

"Oh. I just got there and I saw the lights and I heard all the people laughing, and I couldn't do it."

"You're cold."

"Can I stay in here?"

Usually it was cramped with the two of us in one bed,

but tonight Mary felt smaller, like she took up less space.

"Of course."

"Did you have fun? At the party?" she asked.

"I didn't stay either. Why are you so cold?"

"I don't know," Mary said.

I reached down to the foot of the bed and found the extra quilt that was folded there. I draped it over her, tucking it under her chin.

I knew I should have told her about the Ouija board, about finding her necklace in the barn, but I couldn't. She was shaking she was so cold, and I couldn't make myself ask her why she had lied to me. I couldn't make myself ask her what had really happened.

The bed felt so much colder with my sister's shivering body next to mine. I moved an inch away from her.

"Stop that," she said. "You're my *sister*."

When she said that word it felt more like a curse than a familial relation.

I took her hand in mine, and my fingers froze to ice.

"Mary?"

"Not now," she said.

When I woke up, she was gone.

In her place: plain white feathers.

FEATHERS

The next morning I picked white feathers off my white sheets and stuck them into a white pillowcase I'd taken off one of my pillows. My mother came in when it was halfway full.

"What's all this about?" she asked.

"I think something's going on with Mary."

My mother picked up a feather and held it between her thumb and her middle finger. She looked at it. She smelled it. She licked it (gross).

"What are they?" I asked.

She sat down on the bed, causing a small swarm of feathers to rise up and float around her. She collected them in her lap, examining each one, twirling them around.

"I'm not sure," she said.

"Are they coming . . ."

"From your sister?" She exhaled slowly, thinking. She

looked very unmagicky today. I think, given everything, that was a deliberate choice. She wore faded baggy jeans and a white sleeveless collared shirt tucked into them. She had rainboots on and her hair was tied into a ponytail at her neck. I felt a sudden rush of emotion for her, this woman picking feathers from my bed and piling them into a careful mountain on top of her thighs.

"Your sister has had an emotional upset," she said finally. "We all have." That seemed to be putting it lightly. She opened her mouth to say more but paused, decided against it, dumped the feathers from her lap into the pillowcase. Then she sniffed. Once. Twice. "Georgina," she scolded. "You smell like cheap tricks."

"Oh, it was nothing—"

"The spirit world is not *nothing*!"

"I don't even believe in that stuff, really. It was all Vira's idea."

"Cheap tricks and hay," she amended. "What exactly are you up to?"

"Okay, well, we *did* use the Ouija board. But just a little," I admitted, sitting next to her on the bed.

"Did you learn anything?"

"The person who killed Annabella is a man," I said.

"It's always a man," she said grimly. "Anything else?"

If I wasn't ready to tell Mary that I knew she was in the barn the night Annabella was murdered, I certainly wasn't ready to tell my mom. I was suddenly thankful she had never fed us a truth serum (that I knew of) and did my best to make my face as neutral as possible.

"That's all. The spirits were pretty unforthcoming."

"And the hay?"

"What?"

"Why do you smell like hay, Georgina?"

"Oh."

"You went back to the barn."

"Just for a minute."

"And you found?"

"Nothing at all," I said. The locket burned in my bureau, announcing my lie, and I was afraid it would set the whole thing on fire. But my mother just nodded to herself.

"Throw those over the cliffs," she said, getting up, pointing to the bag of feathers. "Or bury them, or burn them, I don't care."

"But if they came from Mary, isn't that a little harsh?"

"If they came from Mary, I'm sure she'll just go ahead and make more," she said. She looked tired, strange, worn thin around the edges.

"You don't think this is like . . ." I paused. I held up a feather in the hopes that it could convey what I meant without me having to actually say it. That Mary wasn't the first Fernweh woman to leave feathers on her pillow when she woke up in the morning. That was how it started with Annabella too.

My mother sighed. "If it is," she began, "then it's your

sister's business. And I suppose, for now, we'll just have to wait and see."

"Mom, that's not helpful at all," I said.

She kissed the side of my head and let herself out of the room.

"That's not helpful at all!" I called after her.

She did not come back.

Among the small number of people not avoiding Fernwehs like the plague was Peter, who gladly obliged my request to get rid of the feathers. It felt like something much more illicit than it was, handing him the overstuffed pillowcase and relaying my mother's instructions to make it disappear.

I'd found him in the backyard, trying his best to sweep rainwater off the porch, and he wrinkled his nose as he peeked inside the case. "Feathers?" he asked.

"It's sort of a long story."

"All right," he said. "I'll take care of it now."

"Only not the pillowcase," I said. "I'd like that back."

"Sure thing, Georgina."

I watched him take the pillowcase around to the front of the house, and I was about to go inside when I heard a sharp whistle from the back door of the house. It was Harrison, but he shook his head when I went to meet him, and instead vanished and reappeared a few moments later at an open window. He made me sit in a wicker chair on the porch, and he hid himself behind the curtain.

"It's better like this," he said. "More undercover. If they think I hate you, they're more likely to talk to me. Let something slip."

"That sleuthing yesterday really went to your head, huh?"

"Look what I found," he hissed.

He held up a feather to the window screen. I stared at it for a long time and then he scolded me for being too obvious, so I looked back across the yard.

A feather.

But not a white feather.

He'd found one of Annabella's feathers.

"Where did you . . ."

"Don't be mad," he said.

"Where did you find it?"

"In your sister's room."

"What were you doing in my sister's room?" I hissed.

"I said don't be mad! I was just looking around. For clues." He paused. "Maybe that sleuthing *did* go to my head. Just a bit."

"And where exactly did you find it?"

He paused again. It was a heavy sort of pause. The kind that made my stomach twist in anticipation. "In her nightstand," he finally said.

My stomach twisted again. "Her nightstand?"

"Look, Georgina, I still don't think your sister did it, but obviously she knows something. And she's an easy target;

public opinion weighs heavily here, and as far as they're all concerned, she's as good as tried. Which, if true, makes it very lucky that I went snooping and found this before somebody else did, so you should go ahead and forgive me for that."

"I'll take it into consideration."

"Also . . . ," he said, rather uncomfortably, with a little less bravado in his voice than just a moment ago.

"What?"

"Have you considered . . . You know. The *actual* legal implications here?"

"What legal implications?"

"Animal cruelty. Does By-the-Sea have a judge?"

"Of course By-the-Sea has a judge."

Eleanora Avery.

I was unsure whether she'd actually ever tried a case or not.

"You don't think they'll take her to court, do you?" I asked.

"This is your island," Harrison replied. "You tell me."

This was my island, all right.

Where nothing ever happened.

Where people loved a good drama.

"Give me that feather," I said.

I took the feather up to the widow's walk, where I knew I'd be alone, where I knew no other guest would find me.

I carried an umbrella and a large jar candle up to the roof and was surprised to find my sister already there, almost like she was waiting for me. She wore a long white dress that blew wildly in the breeze.

"The island's flooding," Mary said, not turning around. "Have you noticed?"

She was right. Bottle Hill rose gently above the shallow pond that surrounded it. An island on a bigger island. The rain fell in a loud roar. It sounded like static turned up high on a broken television set.

My sister had feathers in her hair.

Every so often one would dislodge and float away on the manic breeze, sailing rockily on the wind until it succumbed to the rain and drowned.

"Mary, where the fuck are these coming from?" I asked, my voice frantic. I picked one off her shoulder.

"Hmm? Oh. I'm not sure," she said. She plucked the feather from my fingers and considered it. She smelled it, exactly like my mother had. That must be some instinct lost to me, the non-magical Fernweh. I had no desire to smell the feathers falling from my sister's hair. I already knew they'd smell like the whole island. The salt. The magic. And now: the rain.

"Harrison found this in your room," I said, and held out the single feather that was unmistakable in its origin.

"What was he doing in there?" she said sharply.

It was hard to describe how my sister looked. Smaller.

Scared. But more than that—like something was missing. Like something had been taken from her. But I had no idea what that could be. Comfort? Safety? All of the above?

"I was going to burn it." I showed her the candle, to demonstrate. "Mary, where did it *come* from? If somebody else had found this . . ."

"They already think I did it. It's not like having proof would change anything."

"So this is proof?"

"I didn't do it," she snapped, and for a moment, there she was: my sister, the bitch in all her glory, long hair whipping about her face, her feet leaving the floor of the widow's walk to hover an inch above it. I could have hugged her. And I would have, if at that moment a strong gust of wind hadn't ripped the feather from my fingers, sending it floating in a vicious cyclone down to the backyard . . .

In front of the waiting eyes of two of the birdheads— Hep and Lucille—who were sharing the same umbrella as they took a stroll around the yard.

"Mary, get *down!*" I yelled, and yanked her to her feet so hard that she fell to her knees.

So when Hep and Lucille turned as one to look up at the house to see where the feather—Annabella's feather—had come from—

All they saw was me.

At that point, it seemed like there was only one thing to do.

I was used to cleaning up my sister's messes. I was used to taking the blame.

So I raised my hand—

and waved.

Blame shifted from my sister to me as easily as a feather caught on a strong breeze.

It didn't bother me at all.

I considered a lifetime of living with Mary, of cleaning up after all of her messes, big and small, to be practice for this. I held my head high and looked every birdhead I passed in the eye. I walked with my shoulders back and a jaunt in my step that I hope conveyed the message: *Don't bother fucking with me. You won't get very far.*

I tried to pretend that I thought my sister was innocent.

I tried to pretend that I didn't think about Clarice Fernweh and her two locked-away children almost every minute of every day.

I tried to keep my promise to Annabella: *I will find who did this.*

That promise seeped into my dreams.

I was in the barn again, only this time it was filled with water, and this time my sister was drowning. I woke up choking, terrified, and I went to see Harrison that evening—to inform him of my renewed sense of purpose, my rekindled desire to clear not only my sister's name but now mine as well.

And I was genuinely surprised when Prue answered.

With everything going on, Prudence Lowry had been mostly removed from the forefront of my mind. But now, standing before me in a simple striped cotton dress, her mouth opened in surprise, her hands holding what smelled like a cup of peppermint tea, I felt a rush of affection, a rush of hope, and a rush of . . .

Something else. Because Prue wasn't looking like she was that happy to see me. In fact—it was kind of the exact opposite.

I felt my heart sink to somewhere around my stomach as it occurred to me that Prue might be of the same mind-set as most of the island: that the Fernweh women had something to do with Annabella's death.

"I was just looking for your brother," I said quickly, feeling my face grow hot as Prue continued to stare at me in a way I could not begin to discern. "If he's not here, I can go."

"What? No, you don't have to—he's not here, no, but you should come in," Prue said, shaking her head, moving aside for me.

"I can just come back later," I said, turning around. I felt her hand close softly around my upper arm, and I hated myself for noting how warm it was.

"Is something wrong?" she asked.

I turned around again. "Do you think my sister killed Annabella?"

Prue looked confused. She removed her hand (*put it back, put it back*) and took a step away from the door. "Can you come in for a second?"

"I don't know," I said. But I didn't move.

"There's something I've been wanting to talk to you about," Prue said quietly. She gestured into the room. Two twin beds, one made neatly and one made messily, with clothes scattered across the quilt and a straw hat on the pillow.

I stepped inside and closed the door behind me.

Prue sat on her bed (the messy one, which made my heart soar with I didn't even know what) and gestured to the other. Harrison's, perfectly made with not an inch of fabric mussed. Figured.

We sat across from each other. Prue still held that mug in her hands, so tightly that her knuckles were turning white.

Then she laughed. "Okay, I definitely don't think your sister had anything to do with this," she said. "Sorry, that actually . . . I wasn't expecting that."

"Oh. Really?"

"Really. Promise. The thought never crossed my mind."

I felt a welcome rush of relief and relaxed a little on the bed. "Okay. That's good. That's great." But Prue still looked a little . . . strange. "Is there something else?"

"There isn't really an easy way to say this," she said.

"Prue? Whatever it is . . ."

She stifled a yawn, and I noticed how tired she looked. Her mascara was smudged a little underneath her eyes; her hair hadn't been washed in a few days. Her dress was wrinkled. She looked like she hadn't slept either. I remembered the time, a few summers ago, when Hep Shackman had stayed up for forty-eight hours taking notes on Annabella's nesting habits. He'd become convinced that he, too, was a bird, and Annabella's eggs weren't hatching because he was the one who was supposed to sit on them. My mother had given him a cup of tainted tea and he hadn't come out of his room for a day and a night. When he finally did, he had to admit that he was not, in fact, a bird, and that sitting on eggs would do nothing more than crush them. There was something about Prue now that reminded me of that—maybe the way her eyes seemed to take a few extra seconds to focus, the way she kept gripping that mug in her hands.

Finally she took a deep breath, set her mug on the nightstand, and said, "I think I've been avoiding you. Just a little bit. But not because of Annabella, it's nothing like that. It's just . . . you're the first girl I've ever kissed. And I didn't know how to tell you that."

"Oh," I said. "Wow."

"I mean, I know I'm . . . I know I like girls. And guys. The girl thing is sort of newer. Harrison is the only one who knows."

"Oh," I said again. And for good measure: "Wow."

"I know kissing you shouldn't have thrown me as much

as it did, and that's not even the right word for it, really, it just sort of . . . it sort of made everything real. Like a confirmation of everything I thought I was feeling." She was pulling on her fingers, bending them back. "And then with everything that happened . . . I just haven't been getting that much sleep."

"You're not alone."

"So I was avoiding you, yes. Not because I thought your sister killed Annabella, God. No, I was avoiding you because it was easier than having to process what it means to have kissed a girl. And I'm sorry, I just couldn't . . . I didn't know what to do. After that night . . . I mean, we kissed, it was this huge moment for me, and then my brother totally interrupted it, and then the next morning . . ."

"Kind of killed the vibe," I said.

"I'm sorry. It's just been . . . a lot."

"Well, we don't have to . . . I mean, that could be it. We could just forget it ever happened."

"I don't want to do that either," Prue said, so quietly that her words were almost blown away. I had to catch them in my hands, bring them to my ears, strain to decipher what exactly it was that she meant.

"Me neither," I said.

"I like you. Like, I *really* like you. I'm sorry this is so hard for me."

"Whatever you need," I said. "However slow or fast or whatever. Anything is fine with me."

And I meant it.

It had been easy for me; I'd been born into a long family of women who didn't give a single hoot about who you chose to love. I'd known I was gay since I was six years old, when I'd fallen in complete and all-encompassing love with my kindergarten teacher, Miss Farid. I was twelve when I told my mother I was gay, and it had been like asking her to pass the coffeepot. She'd only been so happy to lend her blessing. Mary had been equally easy; she'd rolled her eyes, said "Duh," and remarked that it was a relief she didn't have to compete with me for guys, even though, she was quick to point out, I wouldn't have been much competition.

Vira was the easiest of all. I told her I liked girls. She told me she didn't like anyone, at least not in a sexual way. We breathed huge sighs of relief and that was that.

So I had absolutely no idea what it might be like to contemplate your sexuality under anything less than ideal conditions. I had no idea what things were like for Prue at home, what the rest of her family and friends were like. Did her friends know? What was it like to be Prue at that moment, quiet and thoughtful, her fingers tapping out some foreign rhythm on the bed. I wanted to hold her hand, to quiet the impulses that made it impossible for her to sit still, but I didn't want to disrespect whatever music she heard.

I couldn't remember whose turn it was to speak, so I

finally said, "How long have you known?"

"That I like girls too? About a year."

"What happened?" I asked.

Prue blushed a little. "I was at a coffee shop with my friend. There was this piano player, a woman . . ." She paused. "There have been a few others since then. And you, of course. You sort of confirmed things."

I was very close to getting up the nerve to close the space between us and possibly kiss her again when the door to the room flew open and Harrison raced inside. He was soaking wet, and he started talking to me like it didn't surprise him in the least that I was there, that he'd maybe even been expecting me.

"You have to come with me. Right away. No time to waste. Put some shoes on. Quick as you can."

"What's going on?" I asked.

"Your sister has climbed a very big tree, and she's threatening to jump."

I was torn.

On the one hand, Mary wasn't in any real danger. She'd jumped and/or fallen out of plenty of trees before (the ability to float didn't necessarily go hand in hand with the ability to keep one's balance) and she just drifted lazily down to the ground, landing on the grass with a gentle bump that didn't so much as bruise her skin.

On the other hand, Harrison and Prue didn't know

about Mary's gift. I guess I *had* told Harrison, more or less, that we had magic, but he didn't know what kind, and as far as I knew, Prue was still out of the loop. And while my mother had never sat me down to explicitly forbid me from spilling the beans, it was also sort of just known.

People knew we had magic.

It wasn't spoken of.

But this felt like a new By-the-Sea—one untethered from the rules of time and space, one floating higgledy-piggledy on an ocean that kept tossing it this way and that—and I couldn't for the life of me figure out my best course of action. And I hadn't even yet taken into account *why* my sister might have climbed the tallest tree on the island and was now threatening to jump off it. That was a mystery all on its own.

"And you're absolutely sure no one else saw her?" I asked Harrison, for the eighth or ninth or twentieth time.

"She's pretty hidden. You know. By leaves. Rain," he said. He was out of breath due to running full speed back to the inn and now, running back. "I'd just stopped under the tree for a bit of shelter. And then she called down to me, 'Hi, Harrison! Just wanted to warn you that I'm going to be jumping soon. Didn't want to startle you.'"

"That's all she said?"

"That's all she said."

"Does your sister have a history of jumping out of trees?" Prue asked.

"Well . . . ," I said.

"Well?" Prue repeated.

"Okay." I stopped running. Harrison and Prue stopped too, and we all huddled underneath an umbrella that wasn't even a rain umbrella at all, but a beach umbrella that somehow belonged to Prue, because of course Prue owned an enormous yellow-and-white-striped beach umbrella and had casually packed it for summer vacation. It felt a little bit like we were inside a tent. "I have something to tell you."

Prue and Harrison were rapt listeners. They both seemed to have guessed that I was about to drop something important on them.

"Right. So. All the rumors. The boil and bubble stuff," I said, repeating the phrase I'd used in the graveyard with Harrison. "All that's true, okay?"

I tried to gauge Prue's reaction without being too obvious about it. She was nodding her head, and when I looked at her she said, "Harrison told me."

"I hope that's okay," Harrison said quickly. "We don't have many secrets."

"I know what it's like having a sibling. I'm glad you told her," I replied. "So, going along with that whole thing . . . Mary can float."

"Fly?" Harrison exclaimed.

"She might use the word *fly*; the word *float* is a tad more accurate," I clarified.

"Wow," Prue said. "So she *does* have a history of jumping out of trees."

"No. I mean, not really. This is new. She knows . . . we don't use our powers . . . I mean, she doesn't use her powers in front of other people. It's not how it works."

"What can *you* do?" Prue asked.

"I'm a dud," I said quickly, in the vein of pulling a sticky bandage off a wound in one unthinking breath. It felt like I was admitting something not only to them, but to myself. We were almost eighteen, and it was time I came to terms with it: I wasn't getting any powers.

"What do you mean?" Harrison asked.

"I'm just normal. I'm just a sidekick."

I started running again, forgoing the relative dryness of Prue's umbrella for the chance to move faster. As a result, I reached the tree before either of them. And I also reached the tree soaking wet.

The impressive canopy *did* provide fairly adequate cover from the storm. I found Mary immediately, looking strange and languid, sitting far up in the tree with her back against the trunk and her legs spread out on a branch and crossed at the ankles.

"Mary?" I called up to her.

She didn't look like herself. Her dress was too big, her hair was too messy. When she looked down at me, I could have sworn her eyes flashed black.

"Hi, Georgie," she said.

"Can you come down?"

"I kind of like it up here."

"You told Harrison you were going to jump."

"I don't think I'm ready to jump quite yet."

"You know I don't love heights."

"You don't have to do anything you don't want to do."

But alas, the rules of sisterhood: if your sister took residence in the boughs of a tree, you were obligated to go and visit.

I rubbed my palms against my clothes, drying them.

"I'm not great at climbing trees," I said to Prue, who'd appeared beside me.

"And just to be clear, if you fall, you won't float?" she asked.

"Sink like a stone," I confirmed.

"Be careful," she said.

I started to climb. A few feet up I realized I'd blown a perfectly good opportunity for a tearful farewell kiss, but it was too late to go back and rectify that. I concentrated on the task at hand.

Mary watched me with some interest, but she didn't offer any tree-climbing tips. It was just as well. I didn't think I could listen to tips while at the same time not plummeting to my death.

Luckily, the tree was fairly easy to climb, offering many sturdy branches at very manageable intervals. I was on level with Mary after only a few minutes. I immediately made the mistake of looking down.

She put a hand on my arm to steady me.

Her fingers felt like feathers, but when I looked at them, they were just fingers.

"What the fuck are you doing up here?" I asked.

"I woke up this morning and I thought to myself, I suppose I'll go climb a tree," Mary said, shrugging, like it was perhaps the most normal thing in the world for young women to spend their free time in the branches of big trees.

"'I suppose I'll go climb a tree'? Nobody talks like that, Mary."

"My legs hurt. From walking."

"So you thought you'd give them a rest *in a tree*?"

"It's not as weird as you're making it sound."

"It feels pretty weird. Harrison and Prue think it's pretty weird."

Suddenly nervous, Mary asked, "They didn't tell anyone else where I was, right?"

"I don't think so. I mean, no—Harrison came to get me."

"Okay. You're sure?"

"Who else would he tell?"

"I just don't want anybody to know where I am." She frowned and rubbed her fingers against her temples, like she had a headache. Her eyes, her mouth, her jaw, her shoulders . . . everything looked smaller. Was something wrong with my eyes?

"Are you hiding from someone?" I asked.

"Evil man," she said, and I tried to remember if I'd told my sister what the Ouija board had said.

And then something clicked.

"You were in the barn with him," I said. "You didn't kill Annabella, but you know you did."

"It's not fair to read minds," Mary said, squinting. "Is that your thing?"

"No, it's not my thing, I—I found your necklace. In the loft."

Mary's face clouded over and for just a moment I saw something dark and broken there.

"Mary, what were you doing in the barn?"

"Gathering eggs," she said after a long minute. Then she smiled. "Do you want to know where they are? I'll tell you, but you have to promise not to tell anyone else where I am, okay? I'm safe here."

"Eggs? You have her eggs?"

She nodded and ran a hand through her hair, sending a small cascade of feathers down over the bough of the tree, down to where Harrison and Prue waited patiently below.

"I took them," she said. "To keep them safe."

"To keep them safe? From what?"

"If a man is angry enough to break a bird into a million pieces, what do you think he could do with her eggs?"

"Where are they?"

"In my bedroom. Under that floorboard in my closet."

She wiped at her cheeks as if she were crying, but her eyes were dry. "Eggs are so fragile, Georgina."

Around us the tree swayed gently in the breeze and a few drops of rain were blown into Mary's safe haven. She put her hand in her hair and pulled out one feather. It wasn't white anymore. They were getting darker.

"Who killed her?" I asked.

She made a motion, and I held my hands out flat as she placed a feather in my palm.

But just like the other feather on the widow's walk, this one only rested for a moment before it caught on a sudden gust—

And blew away.

And Mary leaned forward and whispered in my ear—

In a voice that sounded exactly like a birdsong—

In a voice that made it unavoidable, that thing I'd known for so long already—

My sister was turning into a bird.

And just like my namesake—the Georgina who came before me—there would be no magic I could use to save her.

III.

But our love it was stronger by far than the love
Of those who were older than we—
Of many far wiser than we—

once more from "Annabel Lee"
by Edgar Allan Poe

EVIL MAN

I realized halfway down the tree that our birthday was tomorrow.

In that post-Annabella world, it was hard to keep track of time. Days seemed to melt together. It could have been weeks that Mary and I were stuck up in that tree, weeks more before I reached the bottom and started walking back to the inn with Harrison and Prue.

The waters were so high that we were forced to overturn Prue's beach umbrella and use it as a makeshift boat. We paddled with our hands, ineffective scoops of water that propelled us forward at a snail's pace. The island was covered in water. The cliffs to our right had become a waterfall to the ocean. We steered clear of them; I didn't know if the magic would hold now or if we would plummet to our deaths below.

I told them about Mary.

"This is a strange island," Harrison said, dipping his hand into the new freshwater sea, as if to illustrate that not *only* was my sister turning into a bird, but we also had this flood to deal with.

"It's never been quite this strange," I said. "You missed many, many years of no floods and boring birdwatching and movie nights on the town green and uneventful summer solstices where hardly anyone even got naked."

"Yeah, but . . . there was still magic and stuff, right?" Prue pointed out.

"Super-boring magic. Honestly. We don't even own wands. Or pointy hats. It's nothing like it is in the movies. It's way more . . . normal."

"Normalcy is underrated," Harrison said.

When we got back to the inn, it smelled like vanilla and cinnamon; Aggie's island-famous birthday cake. The three of us—under better circumstances I might have called us something cute, like the three musketeers or the three amigos or the three stooges, but under these circumstances I couldn't bring myself to do so—stood in the kitchen and peered into the oven and watched an overlarge yellow circle rising to perfect golden perfection inside it.

"What's this for?" Prue asked.

"Tomorrow's our birthday," I said.

"Really?"

"Yup."

"Well, happy early birthday," Harrison said weakly.

We decided to break for a few minutes to change into dry clothes. It seemed like a losing battle; as soon as we stepped outside again we'd be waist-deep in water and any cute thoughts of being warm and not soaking would be far behind us. But still, for now, it felt nice to peel off my underwear and bra and pull on warmer clothes: jeans and a turtleneck I hadn't worn in five years at least, a heavy sweatshirt I used to wear to help my mother harvest herbs in the moonlight. I found thick wool socks and put them on under my rainboots. I piled my hair up into a bun on the top of my head. I wrapped a scarf around my neck and then I met the Lowrys outside Mary's room. We wanted to see the eggs, to make sure they were safe. Safe from what, I couldn't say.

Prue had pulled her hair into a wet ponytail; the back of her clean shirt was already damp where the end hit it.

The inn was strangely quiet. We hadn't run into a single birdhead on our way to the attic.

The door to Mary's bedroom was closed.

I wanted to know why my sister didn't feel safe and who she was hiding from up in that tree. When I'd asked her, when she'd leaned in to whisper to me, all she had said, all she'd repeated, was *evil man*.

"Well," Harrison said. "Should you do the honors?"

I reached out and gripped the doorknob with a hand that hopefully looked a lot sturdier than I felt, and then I twisted and pushed the door open.

It creaked a little, an appropriately creepy creak that made Prue cross her arms over her chest and made Harrison take a tiny, imperceptible step back. I took a big, steadying breath that didn't actually do anything to steady myself, and I stepped into the room and flicked the light switch on.

And of course nothing happened.

And of course then the hall lights winked out, and we were plunged into sudden, blinding darkness.

Prue grabbed my arm. Harrison shrieked. I reached back into Harrison's trench coat pocket (him wearing that trench coat indoors seemed very Harrison-appropriate) and pulled out the flashlight I knew would be there. I flicked it on just as a low rumble of thunder echoed through the house.

"It's the storm," I said. "It must have knocked out the power lines."

"It chose a most inconvenient moment to do so," Harrison pointed out.

My sister had candles scattered throughout her room. I found a book of matches in her nightstand drawer and went around lighting them. A massive bolt of lightning pierced the sky and lit up our faces in severe yellow. The roof was alive with the sound of rain. Harrison shut the door and locked it, then, after a moment's consideration, he pushed Mary's bureau in front of it.

"Can't really be too careful, can we?" he asked.

The candlelight caused a hundred different shadows to

come alive and dance across the walls of my sister's bedroom. I placed the flashlight on the bed and pointed it toward the closet. The door was shut.

I thought of the floorboard that lay within it, the one Mary had pried loose years ago; in its long history, it had hidden other such treasures as jewelry stolen from me, cookies stolen from Aggie, cinnamon whiskey stolen from our mother.

I thought back, but I didn't think it had ever held anything quite so precious as the last eggs Annabella would ever lay.

I opened the door.

Harrison and Prue stood sentry on either side of me as I knelt down and felt along the floor.

The loose board jiggled when my fingers ran across it. I forced my fingertips into the cracks between the boards and pulled upward. It popped up with ease.

And there, bundled in many of my sister's clean wool socks, were the eggs.

They were perfectly white, not a blemish on any of them.

I felt a rush of sadness for these eggs. They had no chance of hatching. A poor track record for their siblings combined with a lack of their mother's brooding left them no chance at all. They were cool to the touch and most likely already dead. I wanted to gather the pair of them in my hands and bring them over to a candle, warm them up and sing them to them and whisper to them and tell them stories of their mother and the legacy she had left behind. I wanted to wrap them in my sister's socks and tuck them into my pocket and walk around so, so carefully, as not to upset or disturb them in any way. I wanted to cuddle them and hide them and find out who'd killed their mom and do something terrible to him. Something to match the terribleness of what he'd done to Annabella.

"Georgina?" Prue said.

"They're here," I said.

And I left them alone, undisturbed, and stepped back so Prue and Harrison could have a look. Harrison had come all this way to see Annabella, so it felt right that at least he was able to see these eggs, perfect and eternal, although, for all intents and purposes, useless.

"They're beautiful," he said, and they honestly were. An entire lifeform self-contained in one smooth white sphere.

Prue left her brother and went to look out the window. "The waters are rising," she said.

We had dragged our boat-umbrella onto the porch, but now the porch was under a foot of water and the boat-umbrella was drifting languidly away, passengerless, a spot of bright against the dark blue of the rainwater.

"My sister was hiding from someone," I said, watching Harrison put the loose board back in its place and move a pair of Mary's shoes on top of it. If you didn't know exactly where to look, you'd have no idea two of Annabella's eggs were hidden there. "I think whoever killed Annabella might have done something to Mary."

"Done something?" Prue said. "Like what?"

"I don't know."

And when I didn't know something—like what sort of thing could happen to a girl to make her shrink and shrink and then ultimately, potentially, turn into a bird—there was one person who might.

Penelope Fernweh the Second.

The ladder to the widow's walk was folded into the ceiling, so I knew my mother wouldn't be up there. I went down to the kitchen, where Aggie was carefully icing the birthday cake. She quickly moved her body in front of it when she heard me at the door.

"I already saw," I said, smiling.

"Oh, the surprise is ruined," she said, and she went back to icing.

Aggie was a good cook, but she was an unreal cake maker. The yellow cake was completely covered by a smooth, creamy layer of buttery white frosting. She was working on the icing flowers now; there were at least twenty pastry bags spread around the counter, each holding a different shade of buttercream. There were delicate roses, vines that wound around the circumference of the cake, bright peonies, and yellow sunflowers.

"Aggie, it's beautiful," I said.

She set the icing bag on the counter and gathered me up in a hug. I realized it had been so long since I'd heard Aggie laugh. The kitchen felt empty without it.

"Your birthday snuck up on me this year," she whispered into my ear, then held me at arm's length to look at me. "It's been such a strange summer."

What would Aggie do now that Annabella was dead? If there were no birdheads to stay at the inn, if there were no birdheads to cook for . . .

I hugged her again, trying to imagine a summer where Aggie was not here, in this kitchen, every waking moment of the day. It felt impossible. When I finally pulled away from her, I could feel the tears in my eyes. She dabbed at my cheeks with her apron.

"I know," she said. "But everything is going to turn out all right."

I wanted to ask her how she knew that, how she could say that with even an ounce of conviction in her voice, but instead I shook my head, composing myself, and asked, "You haven't seen my mother anywhere, have you?"

"She's out back. In the rowboat. Have you seen the moon? I don't think I've ever seen the moon as full as it is tonight."

The back porch was under a foot of water, but my mother was waiting next to it in her rowboat, standing up, holding the railing for balance, like she had been waiting for me. Her hair was billowing all around her face in the breeze: long and brown and messy. I waded across the porch and stepped carefully into the rowboat. She sat down across from me and said, "This reminds me of the night you and your sister were born."

I had heard the story a million times, but I let her tell it to me again, and I listened like it was the very first time, because I loved to hear my mother speak.

She told me about the birth. About how I'd been her only child for five hours. About how I'd waited patiently with her to meet my sister. About how the rains had started the first time I'd cried.

"What are you doing out here?" I asked when she had finished talking.

She rowed the boat out into the backyard, navigating the floods with a deft hand. Somewhere near where the flower beds used to be, she stopped rowing. She raised the paddle above her head and then plunged it into the water like a spear, so it stuck into the wet earth below.

"Hold this, will you?" she said.

I took hold of the oar. I could feel the current underneath the water and the boat struggling against it. I held on tighter.

"What are you doing?" I asked again.

"The moon is good again. See?"

My mother lifted something from underneath her shirt: a tiny bottle she wore on a chain around her neck. I watched as she uncorked the bottle, smelled it, held it over the water and carefully poured it in.

The liquid inside was the color of sunshine. It smelled like leaves.

"What is that?" I asked.

"Your sister is hiding something," my mother said.

"You know?"

She nodded. "I found that loose floorboard when you were both eight. She hid a slice of cake inside it. I followed a trail of ants."

"The eggs are already cool," I said. "They must be dead."

My mother stood up and found her balance in the rocking boat. "*Nearly* dead," she said, and dove into the water in an elegant little arc. Her body made just the tiniest ripple as it disappeared beneath the surface.

She was gone for long enough that I got nervous. I was just preparing myself for a rescue mission when she broke the surface again. She held something out to me, treading water with her free arm.

I took the thing from her.

It was a nest.

Impossibly dry, impossibly beautiful. I put it in my lap. It was made of intricately woven twigs and pieces of cloth and hay and white feathers. My mother held the boat tightly and then lifted herself up and over the side.

"I made that," she said proudly.

"Mom—do you know what happened to Mary? Do

you know why she's turning into . . ."

It was hard to say it out loud: *a bird*.

My mother's face darkened. She shook her head.

"Is there any way to stop it?" I asked. "I sort of like her human."

"It's something she will have to learn how to control. Right now, she's not in control at all. Right now, we're lucky she doesn't just float away."

"But *why*?" I asked. "What could have happened to her?"

"I don't know," she said, her face darkening. "Something bad." She pulled the oar out of the ground and laid it across the boat. "You don't know who she was with that night?"

"We were together at the Fowl Fair," I said, thinking back. "And then she just kind of disappeared. Vira said—"

But I stopped, because I remembered what Vira had said that night, when I asked if she'd seen my sister: *I think she was talking to Peter earlier.* There wasn't anything unusual about that; Peter had a tendency of always being underfoot, especially when Mary was involved. But why hadn't I thought to ask him earlier, if he knew anything about where she had gone that night?

"What is it?" Mom asked.

"Maybe nothing," I said.

She began paddling toward the house. Harrison and Prue were waiting on the porch, watching us. Harrison helped Mom out of the boat. I stepped onto the porch;

Prue took my hand and touched the nest.

"Is that for the eggs?"

I nodded. "Will you take it to them?"

She took the nest from me and ran into the house.

"Excellent diving, Penelope," Harrison told my mother.

"Thank you, Harrison. And thank you for helping my daughter."

"Mom—can we borrow the rowboat?"

"Be my guest." She put her hands on either side of my head and kissed my forehead. "It comes from here," she said, and pointed to my belly. I felt a strange flutter where her fingers had touched but I had absolutely no idea what she was talking about. I smiled and nodded, which was always the safest response.

She swayed a little. Harrison reached a hand out and steadied her.

The effects of the magic she'd done. Strong magic; she was completely sapped.

"I'll just go lie down for a while," she said with a weak smile. She went into the house, and Harrison climbed into the boat.

"She found a nest in the water?" he asked.

"It's a long story."

"Magicky?"

"Very magicky."

We waited for Prue.

"All tucked in," she said when she finally came back.

"Do you guys want to go on a little trip?" I asked, gesturing toward the rowboat.

"Where to?" Harrison asked.

"Well, first, I want to make sure Vira's okay. Who knows how high the waters are down there. And after that . . . I think I need to go talk to Peter Elmhurst."

"I'm in," Prue said. She stepped gingerly into the boat. Harrison and I followed suit.

We started paddling for the town green.

The island was an unrecognizable, treacherous beast.

We passed a few people in boats (both actual boats and those of the makeshift variety: plastic storage containers, garbage cans, bathtubs, wooden wine barrels), but once they got close enough to see who we were (or who *I* was, more specifically) they paddled hurriedly in the other direction.

The entire first floor of the Montgomerys' building, including the Ice Cream Parlor facade, was underwater.

We steered the rowboat around to the back of the building, and I pulled myself onto the metal staircase. I promised Harrison and Prue I wouldn't take long, and then I knocked on Vira's front door.

She appeared a moment later, threw the door open, and squeezed me into a hug.

"I've been worried sick," she said. "It's getting bad out there."

"We found the eggs. And my sister is turning into a bird. We're going to talk to Peter. I think he might have been the last person to see her before whatever happened to her in the barn."

Vira took this news in stride.

She looked past me to where Prue and Harrison waited in the rowboat. "Is that your ride?" she asked.

"Yeah. It's a little slow, but it's all we have."

Vira put her hand over her eyes to shield them from the pouring water. She scanned the island, left to right, and then smiled.

"She's almost back. Just give me a second."

She went into the house and emerged a moment later in a bright-yellow raincoat covered in cheery cartoon ducks. She fit a matching hat on her head.

"Wow. I've never loved you this much," I said.

"And you're about to love me even more." She pointed over my shoulder. "Behold, our new ride."

I turned around to see Julia Montgomery pulling up to the second-floor railing of the building behind the wheel of a squat little red tugboat. Julia threw the lines to her daughter, and Vira tied the boat up. Julia stepped onto the landing.

"Georgina, it's so nice to see you," Julia said, and although her voice was a little strained, I thought she mostly meant it.

"Can we take the tug out? Errands," Vira said.

"Do I want to know what kind of errands?" Julia asked.

"We're going to clear my name," I offered. "And Mary's, while we're at it."

Julia considered for just a moment, and then she dropped the keys to the tugboat into Vira's waiting hands.

"Why does your mother own a tugboat?" I asked Vira as the four of us ditched the rowboat for our upgraded ride.

"Tugboats are really useful," Vira said, as if it were obvious, and then she pointed her chin at Prue and winked at me approximately eight hundred times.

"Okay, okay, you've made your point," I said.

She took her place as the captain of the tugboat, and it was like the universe shifted just a little bit back into place, as if to say, *Yes, of course this is where Elvira Montgomery belongs: behind the wheel of a tugboat wearing a matching raincoat and rainhat.*

Then she called, "I recommend life jackets! It's been a while since I've actually driven this thing," and that feeling shattered just a tiny bit. Harrison, Prue, and I dutifully slid into our bright-orange life vests (I helped Vira put hers on) and with a slightly worrying lurch, we were off.

We made our way to the Elmhursts' farm through water that was growing more and more unruly. The tugboat had been a lifesaver; there was no way we could have rowed ourselves through waves this high and choppy. Prue turned green and gripped the railing, keeping her head over the side of the boat, staring into the dark water like she might, at any given moment, hurl.

The rain had become a thing alive and dangerous, pouring down around us in buckets. It was impossible to see more than five or ten feet in front of the boat. Vira took it slow, and I stood at the bow with an actual lantern, feeling very 1800s-whale-hunting-expedition, yelling back to her if we came too close to buildings or trees sticking up out of the water. We found the Elmhursts' barn almost by accident, after weaving back and forth with no real idea of where we were.

The barn doors were open—the yellow police tape gone—and the water poured in and out of the entrance freely. Together with Harrison I guided the boat carefully through the doors. The lights were off—I wondered if the power outage had affected the whole island—but I held the lantern up and Harrison took his flashlight out again and pointed it around. The beam landed on Peter, sitting on the loft with his legs dangling over the side. The water was so high that the bottom of his sneakers skimmed the surface every time they kicked back and forth.

He had a strange expression on his face. I felt like I had stumbled upon him in a too-intimate moment.

Vira killed the engine of the tugboat.

Prue finally vomited.

Harrison rubbed her back.

The three of them presently occupied, I turned to Peter.

"Hi," I said.

"Hey, Georgie," he replied.

"What are you doing in here?"

"I went for a little swim, but the water's too choppy now. I was waiting to see if it would go down."

"You went for a swim in your clothes?" I asked, because Peter was wearing jeans and a dark T-shirt and even a pair of sneakers, all sopping wet now.

"I figured—I was already soaked," he said lightly. "Why not?"

It actually made sense; what little time I'd spent in the storm since I'd changed my clothes had left me as dripping wet as Peter.

"And your parents? Are they okay? The water's getting high."

"They're fine," he replied, gesturing vaguely. "They found higher ground." Then he looked at me like he was seeing me for the first time. "What brings you over here, Georgie?"

"Peter, I wanted to ask you about the night of the Fowl Fair. Did you talk to my sister? Do you know where she went?"

"Has she said something?" he asked.

"Not really. She's . . . waiting out the storm," I said, because there was some edge to his voice, something that told me to choose my words carefully.

"I miss her," he admitted, and his face softened a little, and whatever strangeness I'd sensed in him just a moment ago vanished. He was Peter again. Peter the jack-of-all-trades. Peter the shy and quiet and in-love-with-my-sister boy.

"Do you know anything about that night?" I asked.

"Of course I do. But I love your sister, Georgina. I was trying to protect her."

"Protect her? From what?" My heart felt like someone held it in their hand, like someone was squeezing it tighter and tighter.

"Georgina," he said slowly. "Isn't it obvious?" He paused to rub at his eyes with wet hands. Then he looked at me again. "Mary killed Annabella."

And (oh timing, oh you silly, silly timing) the roof of the barn gave in under the weight of the rain.

Prue screamed as a piece of roofbeam, soggy and bloated with rain, came crashing down on the boat. The loft collapsed underneath Peter and he went plunging into the black water. I heard Vira shouting for a life preserver and before I could react, Harrison found one and threw it over the edge to Peter, who was struggling to stay afloat in water now riddled with debris. A massive piece of roof came plummeting down from the ceiling; I felt something crash into me, and the next thing I knew, Vira was on top of me, her face inches from mine.

"Did you just save my life?" I asked shakily.

"Thank me later," she said, scrambling to her feet and hoisting me up.

Peter was too far away to reach the life preserver; Harrison was struggling to pull it back into the boat so he could throw it farther. I grabbed the end of the rope and we pulled together, heaving as the boat pitched back and forth and sent us stumbling, more than once, to our knees.

Vira got behind the wheel again and the boat stuttered forward, dangerously close now to Peter, who flailed in the water and kept disappearing for longer and longer periods of time, getting weaker and weaker.

Harrison and I finally managed to haul the life preserver onto the boat, and he yelled back at Vira—"Hold her steady!"—before he grabbed it and dove headfirst into the water.

"Harrison!" Prue screamed from the back of the boat. She picked her way across bits of roof and beam that had landed on the boat, finally reaching me and half flinging herself over the railing. "Harrison!"

I grabbed on to the back of her lifejacket so she wouldn't pitch over the side, and we both searched the water for Harrison, who was paddling toward where Peter was struggling to stay afloat. When he reached him, Harrison slipped the life preserver over Peter's body and then used the rope to start pulling them back to the ship.

"In the stern!" Vira shouted over the rain. "There's a ladder in the stern!"

"Go around, Harrison!" Prue said, pointing frantically. She ran toward the back of the boat and made sure the ladder was extended. Harrison and Peter reached it after a moment and then they were on the deck, breathing heavily, Peter leaning over the side and retching water.

After a few more harrowing moments of navigating backward out of the barn, we were safe.

Well. *Safe* was relative.

I gave Peter a life jacket—he seemed shaken, but mostly unharmed—and Harrison found a compass in (of course) the pocket of his trench coat. We made our way slowly south, through squall-like winds and rain that came in sideways, soaking every part of my body, soaking even the *inside* of my body.

I wanted to grab Peter, shake him, ask him what he meant when he said that Mary killed Annabella, but I made myself take a deep breath and give him a minute to recover. Besides—my sister told me she hadn't done it. The Ouija board itself had said it was an *evil man*. I had to trust my sister.

But I couldn't deny, either, the newly formed smudge of doubt that had been born within me. A worm of evil that questioned my sister's story and her motives and her innocence. A worm that slithered its way through my body, slowly eating me from the inside out. That was what happened when you stopped trusting your sister, your twin: you were eaten alive in a gale, shivering and soaking and miserable.

And Mary had been acting so *weird*.

I had to get back to her.

Whatever she was doing in that tree, I had to make her tell me the truth.

And since it didn't seem likely that I'd be able to get to her *alone*, I'd take the compromise of me plus four others.

As it turned out, Prue wasn't quite done being sick.

She sat on the floor of the boat, her back pressed up against the aft side, her knees bent and a bucket between them. She was a pale green, the color of new grass. I left Harrison to navigate at the bow of the boat, and I went to sit next to her.

"I'm so sorry," I said.

"It's the back and forth," she said, illustrating with her hand. "It's the rocky-rocky. It's the—"

She paused to vomit.

When she was done, I helpfully tossed the contents overboard and handed the bucket back to her.

"Thanks," she said. She gripped it like a security blanket. "You must be really attracted to me right now."

"Surprisingly enough, I am."

"You don't believe him, do you?"

I paused just a moment too long, just a half a second, but it was enough time for Prue to see the worm inside me.

"The eggs," I whispered. "The feathers."

"Georgina, she's your *sister*," Prue said.

"But the whole island . . . Everybody's so sure . . ."

"Well, *I'm* not so sure. I'm not so sure at all," Prue

replied, and to punctuate this point, she vomited again.

The fierce loyalty of Prue made the worm shut up for a few seconds. I emptied the bucket again and then hugged her, kissing her wet hair and the side of her face.

"Georgina!" Vira called then, and I gave Prue back her bucket and joined the captain at her post. "Tree ho!" she said, and pointed. Then she turned back and saw how confused I looked. "It's like 'land ho,' but it's a tree. Tree ho. Get it? Because there's no more land; it's all water. Anyway, we're here."

My sister's tree. The water now reached halfway up its trunk; the tire swing was floating useless on the waves. Peter looked nervous; he stood up and did his best to pace with what limited deck space he had.

I climbed the tree again.

My sister was still a girl, sitting right where I'd left her. She was making a tiny nest in her lap with strips she'd torn from her dress and feathers she'd pulled from her hair and twigs she'd pilfered from the tree.

"Did you find them?" she asked.

The eggs.

"Yes, Mary."

"Are they safe?"

"They're safe. Mom made them a nest."

"Why did you bring him here?"

"Peter?"

"I told you I was hiding, and you brought him right to

me. I can't say I understand your approach," Mary said, and she sounded so much like herself that I wanted to cry.

But then I heard what she said, as if on a delay.

"Peter?" I asked. "You were hiding from *Peter*?"

"Why do you look like that?" She shook her head and laughed. "Wait—let me guess. Did he tell you I killed Annabella? That I used my magic powers to cut off his dick?" She rolled her eyes and in that moment I swear she grew taller. "I should have. I *wish* I had dick-chopping magic powers."

"Mary?"

She shrank again.

She closed her eyes, squeezed her eyelids together.

When she opened them again, I saw real fear there.

"Why did you bring him here?" she whispered.

And on the bough of this tree, in the middle of a gale, with my sister so small and fragile in front of me, I could suddenly see—with such sharp clarity it made me squint— how dense I'd been.

My sister hadn't killed Annabella.

Of course my sister hadn't killed Annabella.

But I knew who did.

Evil man.

"What did he do to you?" I asked.

But I already knew.

And I was already climbing back down the tree.

And I was already back on the boat.

And I was already throwing myself at Peter, who looked suddenly terrified, caught, *guilty*.

I felt Harrison grab my arm and pull me back.

"Georgina?" he said. "What's going on?"

I stopped fighting.

The four of us—Prue, Harrison, Vira, me—were at the bow of the boat.

Peter backed up and up until he was at the very back.

Harrison let go of my arm.

"Tell me what you did to my sister," I whispered.

And the minute the words left my mouth—

The minute they touched the air—

The rain stopped.

BIRTHDAY

Everything suddenly felt very, very clear.

"Tell me what you did to my sister," I repeated, and Peter put his hands up in front of him like I was threatening to shoot.

"What did she tell you?" Prue asked, moving to my side, slipping her hand in mine. "What did he do?"

"He has to say it. I want to hear him say it."

Peter looked terrified.

I remembered Peter as a child, playing tag with Mary and me in the backyard of the inn. I remembered Peter red-faced and mumbling at the beginning of the season, asking me if Mary had gotten the letter he'd written to her, the sharp flicker of anger on his face that he'd quickly gotten under control. I remembered Peter stacking wood for countless summer fires in the backyard of the inn. There was no appropriate place in my mind for the version of

Peter that was currently forming there.

Above us, a bolt of lightning streaked across the sky. Prue jumped and let go of my hand.

"Tell me, Peter," I said.

"You better talk, asshole," Vira chimed in. "It's four against one."

"I have no idea what you're talking about," Peter said. "Look, we went to the barn after the Fowl Fair. We fell asleep. When I woke up—she was standing over the bird, okay? She killed the bird; I saw her throw it against the beam. I'm the innocent one here. You should be interrogating *her*."

I took one tiny step toward Peter.

Above us, a low rumble of thunder.

"I don't believe you," I said.

"I'm telling you the truth," Peter insisted. "And there's more. I saw her *fly*. Everything they say about your family is true, and I'm going to tell everyone. Who do you think they'll believe? Me? Or a *Fernweh*."

He said the word like it was a swear, like something dark and twisted. He said the word like it was a stone that fell out of his mouth and shattered into bloodred crystals on the floor. He said the word exactly like he was saying another word entirely. He said the word like he was actually saying the word—

Slut.

All of the pieces of that night were shifting and clicking

into place inside my brain. My sister's torn shirt. The bruise in the bathtub. My sister's broken necklace. My sister's nightmares. My sister's terror.

Peter saw it.

Peter saw everything that I knew about him, and he was suddenly scared of it.

Good.

Let him be scared.

"Georgina," he whispered. "You *know* me."

"I know my sister," I countered.

"I would never do anything to . . ."

But the lie was too big for him to even say.

Because he *had* hurt my sister.

I took another step toward him.

He held his hands up in front of him. Like he could stop me.

His face changed.

A shadow passed over his features, and I saw him how my sister must have seen him that night in the barn, that night when she said *no* and he said *yes*.

"Do you have any idea," he began, his words dipped in acid, "what it's felt like, all these years, watching your sister go out and . . ."

He put his hands over his face. His shoulders bounced in some silent, hate-filled laugh.

"I *loved* her," he said. "I wrote her letters and brought her presents and walked her home in the dark and made her tea and left flowers on her bed. I did *everything* for her, and do you know how it's felt to watch her pick every single guy on this island except *me*?"

His eyes were flashing now.

The sky had turned a deep, dark purple. The lightning split the clouds in half and set the whole world on fire. Someone put a hand on my arm, and when I tried to brush it off, whoever it was just held on tighter.

I turned around.

Mary.

Out of the tree and (thank God, thank God, thank God) still a girl.

"Let's just go home," she said. "It isn't worth it."

"Go *home*?"

"He's right, Georgina. This is why I didn't tell you. Nobody's going to believe me. Everybody knows I'm a . . ."

Fernweh.

Bitch.

Slut.

"That's bullshit," I spat. Another crack of lightning, a flash so bright we all paused and looked upward.

When I looked back at Mary, her mouth was open just a little. She was staring at me.

"Oh my God," she said.

"What?"

"This whole time," she said.

"Mary, *what*?"

She grabbed my hand. She pointed up at the sky.

It had started to rain again. Tiny drops of ice-cold water.

Mary stopped pointing at the sky and pointed, instead, at my face.

"Georgina, you're crying," she said.

It felt like time was moving only for my sister and me. Everyone else on the boat stood silent and still, frozen, suspended.

"So?" I said, and wiped at my cheeks. "What's your point? I always cry when it rains; you always say that."

Mary smiled. "It's the other way around," she said. "It always rains when you cry."

"That's the same thing."

"It's not the same thing at all. Don't you see?" she said. "It's your *thing*, Georgina. This is your thing. It's *always* been your thing; it was just too big for any of us to see!"

Mary had both my hands in both her hands, and she was smiling for the first time in days, in weeks, in who could tell how long in this timeless, broken summer. I looked down at the floor; her feet were hovering an inch or two above the wooden planks of the tugboat. "Happy birthday," she said.

And then Prue screamed.

And the world around Mary and me came unpaused and leapt into motion.

I turned around.

And Peter had a gun, an old and tarnished pistol that he

held like a thing he did not know how to hold, gripped in two hands so tightly that his arms shook with the effort, the almost-imperceptible quivers that radiated up to his elbows, his shoulders, his chest. His lips had turned white. He looked almost as scared of the gun as we were.

"Peter, what are you doing?" I asked.

He tightened his grip. I imagined Peter sneaking into his parents' room, taking this gun from his father's nightstand, trying to figure out if it was loaded.

I wondered why Peter thought he might need a gun.

I wondered if he guessed I would find out eventually.

Behind me I heard Vira whisper, "Evil man."

"Just put it down, Peter. Don't be like this," I said.

"No way. I don't know what you two are capable of," he said, almost frantically, gesturing between Mary and me like we were bombs instead of girls.

"Surely no more than what *you* were capable of," I said.

"If you just let me go, if you just . . . I'll go home, and I won't even tell anyone what she did. I won't even tell anybody," Peter said.

"What *I* did?" Mary repeated. "I didn't do anything, Peter. All I did was say *no*."

"You make yourself sound so innocent," he snapped. "Did you tell them how *you* were the one who wanted to go to the barn in the first place? How *you* were the one to start it all?"

"And how you threw Annabella against the beam when

I wouldn't go further? And about how I started screaming, and how you put your hands over my mouth so I'd shut up, and about how you climbed on top of me? How you told me what you would do to me if I told anyone . . ."

Mary covered her face with her hands.

I imagined my sister, broken and violated, slipping Annabella's eggs into her pocket so Peter wouldn't hurt them. I imagined my sister saying the word *no.* I imagined my sister shrinking, shrinking . . .

Peter held the gun in his sweating, shaking hands.

Could guns fire after they'd been soaked in floodwater?

"Peter, just put the gun down," I said.

"No. No way," Peter said, and he tightened his grip.

For the first time in my life I felt the power of the Fernweh women, ready and waiting at my fingertips.

Exactly like my mother had said: a burning, tight feeling in my gut.

Next to me, my sister shrank. And shrank.

Prue and Vira and Harrison were completely silent and motionless behind me.

I had never really given much thought about what my eighteenth birthday might look like. There'd be cake, sure. There'd be a colorful banner strung across the dining room: *Happy Birthday!* There'd be Mary and my mother and a quiet dinner. A bonfire in the backyard maybe, a small pile of presents wrapped in brown paper and twine.

I'd never considered the possibility of that summer

leading me here: standing on a boat, a gun aimed at my chest and my sister sprouting feathers next to me, long shiny feathers that erupted out of her skin at an alarming rate.

I made myself not look at her.

It seemed private, somehow, this moment of transformation. It seemed like my sister's business.

I focused my attention on Peter.

I knew that he would use that gun, because that is what small, scared men did: they used things more powerful than themselves to make up the difference. They hid behind weapons of mass destruction: big guns and bigger bombs.

They were small, small, small—

Peter was small, but I could see him becoming bigger in his own mind as his finger inched toward the trigger.

"I'm giving you one last chance," I said.

He laughed. "*You're* giving *me* a last chance? I'm the one with the gun!"

And I watched as his finger wrapped around the trigger.

And I lifted my hand into the sky.

And I didn't know quite how I did it, only that the tightness in my belly was moving upward. A tightness that demanded to be released.

And I raised my hand higher—

And the skies opened up—

And the skies poured down—

And I heard a loud *crack*—the loudest of cracks—the
crack of an old evil gun held by a young evil man—
   And the flash lit up the entire world—
   And everything went white.

AFTER

I woke up in my bed.

The world was dark.

There was a bandage wrapped around my head, covering my eyes.

I started to unwind it, but I felt my mother lay her hand on my wrist.

Call it a Fernweh thing or a daughter thing; I knew my mother's hand even with bandages wrapped so thickly around my eyes that the light couldn't even peek around the edges.

"Easy," she said. "Close your eyes."

I closed my eyes underneath the bandage. My mother's hands started to unravel it for me. My mother's hands were steady, cool things, and I could feel them trembling through the thin fabric.

When she slipped the bandage off, she put one palm over my eyes.

"Give it time," she said.

Without the bandage, even with my eyes closed and my mother's fingers blocking the sun, the world seemed so, so bright. My eyes ached with it.

"What happened?" I asked.

"Don't you remember?"

"Is Mary okay?"

"Are *you* okay?"

"Are you going to answer every question with a question?" I said, and gently pulled her hand away.

The insides of my eyelids were a bright, painful red.

"Has the sun exploded?" I asked.

"I imagine if the sun had exploded, we wouldn't be around to comment on it."

"There was a bright flash."

"Yes . . . ," my mother answered, prodding for more.

"I thought that might have been what it was. The sun exploding."

"Not quite."

I still had my eyes squeezed shut. I tried opening them the tiniest crack. My bedroom was a blurry, bright mess through the crosshatched black lines of my eyelashes. I shut them again. My head throbbed.

"I don't feel so great."

"You've exerted a fair amount of energy. On your very first try. You've been asleep for a long time. It doesn't surprise me that you don't feel well."

"I remember . . ."

"Yes?"

"He had a gun," I said. Suddenly that was the only thing I could see: Peter holding a gun. What was Peter doing with a gun?

Peter saying the word *Fernweh.*

Peter meaning the word *slut.*

Prue screaming.

Vira, the captain of a tugboat.

Harrison pulling flashlight after flashlight from a trench coat with impossibly deep pockets.

It came back to me in fits and starts, flashes and snapshots.

I opened my eyes again. Slowly. The light felt like an invasive, heavy thing. My mother was blurry.

I had raised my hand up toward the sky and called a bolt of lightning down from the heavens.

"Just like fucking Zeus," I whispered.

"Ah, so you're remembering," Mom said.

"Holy shit. Did I kill him?"

Peter had forced himself on my sister in a gross, dusty barn, and Peter had thrown a three-hundred-year-old bird against a wooden beam and snapped her wings and neck, and Peter had aimed a gun at my face, but—despite all that—I didn't think I was prepared to add *murderer* to the list of attributes I used to describe myself.

"Not quite," my mother said. Her face came slowly into focus, and I saw how sad she looked, how tired.

"I think I was trying to."

"Oh, you were certainly trying to. But luckily you have three very eager witnesses who've all given testimony in your favor. Plus, the gun was found. Albeit a little worn for the wear."

"Worn for the wear?"

"Your aim was very precise. Your . . . how did you put it? Your Zeus bolt hit the gun."

"So he's alive."

"I said *a little* worn for the wear; I think I should amend that to *a lot* worn for the wear," my mother said thoughtfully. "He was blown into next Tuesday. Really. I had to go and drag him back to the present. He smokes when he opens his mouth and he's covered in burns, but he'll live."

"He fired the gun," I said.

"Yes."

"He tried to kill me."

"You were very lucky."

"You knew," I said. "You must have. You knew I was making it rain."

"I had a feeling it was you, yes."

"When did you figure it out? Have you known all along?"

The storm when I was born. The snow in summer. The blazing heat in the dead of winter. The weather of By-the-Sea had always been laughably temperamental.

But no—not always.

Just for the last eighteen years. Because of me.

"Not all along," my mother admitted. "Not for a while. No Fernweh woman has ever had this particular gift before. I didn't know what to look for."

"And then? When you realized it? How come you didn't tell me?"

But I already knew what she was going to say.

I had to come to it when I was ready.

As if she could read my mind (and who knows, stranger things had happened), she kissed me on the forehead and said, "Exactly."

"What will happen to Peter?"

"You don't have to worry about Peter. He'll be going to jail for a long time."

"There will be a trial?"

"Of course."

"But who's going to believe him over us? Who's going to believe him over Mary?"

"Like I said, Georgina, you have witnesses. And that young Harrison Lowry has proved to be quite the advocate on your and Mary's behalf. We'll make sure Peter's punishment matches his crimes."

My mother's eyes darkened.

We hadn't said the word yet.
Words had power.
Just like the words—
Slut.
Magic.
Fernweh.
They had power.
So did the word—
Rape.

BIRD

In the bright flash of a bolt of lightning called down from the sky by magic I never knew I possessed—

My sister had disappeared.

I remembered now.

The smell of burning flesh.

The light so bright it had washed the entire world away.

The tiny flutter on my shoulder.

Like the smallest, most delicate little body had landed there for just a moment—

Before flying away.

As if to say—

Thank you.

LEAVING

The island drained of water as I lay recovering in my bed.
It ran off over the cliffs in dramatic waterfalls.

It drained into the sea.

The ground was soggy underfoot.

But we knew it would dry eventually.

Peter enjoyed a swift trial with a jury of his peers, who convicted his raping, bird-murdering, illegal-possession-of-a-firearm, attempted-murdering-of-a-human ass to fourteen years in prison. He also had to register as a sex offender. He was shipped to the mainland on the next ferry out.

His defense—*she deserved it because she had already had sex with so many people*—made the judge, the Honorable Eleanora Avery, laugh the fuck out loud.

As if out of a fairy tale, nobody asked:

What was my sister wearing the night she was raped?

How much had my sister had to drink the night she was raped?

How many guys had my sister previously had sex with?

Because—again, out of a fairy tale—they realized that none of those things mattered.

Because there was nothing in a girl's history that might negate her right to choose what happens to her body.

The last days of summer settled into a quiet rhythm.

The island was hot and humid and somber.

I spent the days washing the sheets and pillowcases and towels of the inn, preparing for the end of the season, getting ready for fall. I spent my evenings with Prue—pushing ourselves out into nothingness on a tire swing or running full speed into the ocean or lying on the cool grass of dusk, flicking mosquitoes from our skin and letting our hair tangle up together.

I woke up every morning and went into the kitchen and poured myself a cup of coffee.

Aggie laughed again. The inn became a place I recognized.

I let the birdheads apologize, one by one, a steady stream of humiliated people I had known my entire life.

I forgave everyone who asked me to.

I said to good-bye to them, one by one, these people who had dedicated their lives to a thing that had been so violently taken from them.

I watched them lay their hands on the top of Annabella's grave.

I watched them pull the grave marker out of the

earth—the one Peter had made—and fling it into the sea.

The rule of the cliffs did not apply to grave markers carved by rapists.

Our good-byes were short and perfunctory (Hep Shackman) or long and drawn out (Lucille Arden) depending on who was leaving.

Liesel Channing gave me a sweater she had knit out of truly hideous purple yarn. On the front was a rather sloppily rendered crest of the university I was slated to attend so soon that it took my breath away when I thought too much about it. She hugged me for a very long time and whispered in my ear, "I'll be back next year. Annabella or no Annabella, this is my home too."

Every morning I went into my sister's empty, quiet room and checked on the eggs.

The nest, magically rendered and pulled from the flooded ground under a full moon, kept them warm and safe under the floorboards.

We took turns watching over them: Harrison, Prue, Vira, me. We stacked books and magazines on Mary's bed and read stories and watched Annabella's babies.

I thought it was too late for them.

Vira told me that they had a magic nest to help them along, and I should have a little hope.

When I missed my sister, I held her necklace in the palm of my hand. The broken clasp told an entirely different story now.

I wondered if I should have seen it earlier.

I listed all the reasons a girl might have to keep something like that a secret, even from her own sister.

I went through the motions of leaving.

I packed my things into three steamer trunks.

I got a letter in the mail with my future roommate's name and address.

Hattie M. Hipperson.

I sent her a letter.

> *Excited to meet you.*
> *Excited for school.*
> *Excited.*

(The word *excited* falls flatter and flatter the more times you write it.)

And then—through some trick of time, a slow bleeding of hours—it was the day before I was supposed to leave.

I woke up and poured myself a cup of coffee and brought it up to Mary's room.

Vira was already there.

Vira, too, was getting ready to leave By-the-Sea for her own rumspringa. She was going to a big city on the opposite coast, the western coast, a city full of sun and palm trees and surfer boys and long-haired girls she could care two shits about. When I pictured Vira in a midnight-black bikini standing with her feet in sand almost too hot to bear, I wanted to cry tears of absolute joy. Like Vira in a candy-striped apron scooping ice cream the color of rusted nails, like Vira at the wheel of a tugboat in a yellow raincoat, like Vira, my best friend, whose house was covered in roadkill taxidermy—it just made so much sense.

I suspected that Vira, of the vampire name and the no-fucks-given attitude, had it all figured out in a way I could only one day hope to.

I sat on my sister's bed and threw my arms around Vira's shoulders. She put her hands on my forearms and said, "I'm going to miss you so much. But you can be from my school to your school in five hours. Flying through the air! What will they think of next?"

We stayed like that for a while, me hugging her, her patting my arms, the eggs out of their cubby hole, resting on the floor of Mary's closet.

After a few minutes I realized that Vira was humming. And then her humming turned into words: a familiar eerie tune that filled the room with its simple, somber melody.

On By-the-Sea, you and me will go sailing by
On waves of green, softly singing too.
On By-the-Sea, you and me will be forever young
And live together on waves of blue.

I thought I saw the eggs twitch, but when I looked closer, they were still.

"We're leaving tomorrow too," Prue told me that evening.

There was one ferry off the island per day (ever since it had miraculously recovered from its mysterious ailment) and the very idea of getting onto it with Prue by my side made things seem suddenly a million times more bearable.

But still.

When I tried to actually picture myself leaving By-the-Sea, I couldn't.

All the signs pointed to me leaving.

The packed steamer trunks.

The envelope of money my mother had tucked into my hands that morning, for me to open my very own bank account once I reached the mainland. (*"The By-the-Sea Bank doesn't count for much off these shores,"* she'd said.)

The week's worth of food Aggie had packed carefully into a wicker picnic basket. (*"For the journey,"* she'd said, although there was more than enough food for one ferry ride and one train ride.)

My ferry ticket.

My train ticket.

The response from my roommate, Hattie M. Hipperson, who somehow managed to seem much more sincere every time she wrote the word *excited* in her letter back to me. (Which was seventeen times in four neatly printed pages.)

The thick black knitted hat Julia Montgomery had made for me and delivered that afternoon, with matching gloves and scarf for good measure. (*"The winters get so cold in that city, Georgina,"* she'd said, and hugged me for so long that it began to feel less like a hug and more like an extended apology.)

The feather I found on my pillow that night, the beautiful pale-brown feather placed perfectly where I would later lay my head.

The magical nest in my sister's room that somehow, between watches of its diligent guardians, had gone empty. Not a piece of egg nor fluff of feather left to be found.

I put the nest in Mary's nightstand drawer.

I didn't worry about the eggs; I knew they were in good hands.

I woke up that night to my sister hovering over me.

She clamped her hand down over my mouth before I could scream and then she fell, laughing, to the bed.

"You should have seen your face," she squealed.

"Am I dreaming?"

"Don't be a doofus. Did you really think I turned into a *bird*?"

"Sort of, yeah," I admitted.

"Well, yeah, I sort of did," she admitted back.

"You took the eggs?"

"Yeah. Don't worry. They're safe." She snuggled under

the blankets with me. "I heard about Peter."

"He got what he deserved."

"You should have killed him," she said. Then, worried she'd hurt my feelings, she added, "Just kidding, of course. He wouldn't have been worth the extra energy."

"Mary, why didn't you tell me?" I asked.

Her face darkened, and she wiggled herself deeper under the blankets, pulling them over our heads so we were totally covered.

"I was afraid nobody would believe me," she whispered, her voice soft and muffled by wool.

"*I* would have believed you. I will always believe you."

"This island, Georgie . . . ," she began. "This island is so small. People talk. I hear what they say about me. The whispers. I've heard them call me things. They would have said I was asking for it."

In the darkness, I reached out for her and put my index finger on the tip of her nose.

"I'm sorry this happened to you. And I'm sorry I didn't figure it out before," I said.

"You don't have to be sorry for anything. You saved my life, remember? You pulled a lightning bolt down from the sky like fucking *Zeus*."

"I think that was mostly an accident."

"You blew Peter to kingdom come! Honestly, who cares if it was an accident or not."

"I should have known. Mary, I'm so sorry I didn't know."

"I thought about telling you," she said, her voice a whisper again. "Maybe I should have. I just felt so lost, so confused. I felt like I didn't know which way was up anymore, which way was *right*. Whether I *had* done something. To deserve it."

"I love you. I'm sorry. I hope you know now that you didn't do anything."

"I know," she said quickly. "You have to stop apologizing to me; it's not your fault. And you need to snap out of this mood, because the island's been gray as shit the past couple of days, and I know it's because you've been moping around."

"I'm leaving tomorrow."

"I know that too. I know everything. I can fit into really small places now. I can just listen."

"So you *are* a bird?"

"Details are unimportant." She paused, lifted the blankets a little so we could breathe, so a sliver of light found its way into the bed. She looked sad and small with the covers pulled up over her head and our faces inches apart. Her breath smelled like tea and rain. "I heard something," she said. "A secret."

"What kind of secret?"

"Did you know," she said, fiddling with the collar of

my pajama shirt, "that no Fernweh woman has ever left the island before?"

"What? Where did you hear that?"

"I was hiding in the eaves. I was *literally* eavesdropping."

"And?"

"It's true. Mom and Aggie were talking. I knew Mom had never left the island, and Grandma, but I didn't realize *none* of us . . ."

"Well, I guess that's going to change. Because I'm leaving the island tomorrow. And you."

Again, in the darkness, Mary was quiet.

"Poor Mildred Miller," she whispered. "Robbed of the distinct pleasure of sharing a very small cinder block dorm room with me."

"You're not going? Because of what Mom and Aggie said?"

"It feels like I was never going," Mary whispered. "And it doesn't have anything to do with . . . Peter or what happened or . . . There are just some things I need to do now. Here."

"Like what?"

"Like, I dunno. Could you actually picture me at college? Could you picture me away from this weird little island? Plus, it looks like I'm going to have to raise some babies."

"You aren't talking about the eggs, are you?"

"Of course I am. Although if those little fuckers think

I'm going to chew worms and then vomit them back up, they're sadly misinformed about how far I'll take my maternal hen duties."

"Disgusting."

"Yeah, well. Somebody's gotta do it."

She stretched herself out on the bed, taking up all the room. I kissed the side of her face, and she pretended to barf.

"I'm going to miss you so much," I said.

"Don't worry. I can *fly*. I'll come and visit."

Mary was gone in the morning.

I thought I might actually scream if I found one more feather in my bed, but . . .

Nothing.

I got dressed and left the house early. The ferry left at noon, but I had one little thing left to do.

The island was quiet and warm in the soft morning light. I filled a thermos with coffee and set out down Bottle Hill wearing my rainboots, even though the ground was dry and hard by now. The island was back to its usual self, heavy with the thick heat of another summer's end, a mugginess that could be picked up in your palms and saved for a later day. I filled my pockets with it and kept walking.

Oh, By-the-Sea—how the place you grew up could feel at once so safe and so much like a trap. I had never wanted to leave it, but here I was, my bags packed and my good-byes all ready and waiting in the back of my throat.

"I'm not abandoning you," I whispered to the island, my island, but of course it didn't respond. Islands were like that. Always listening. Never replying.

The graveyard was orange and crisp and autumn as usual. I slipped a fleece button-down on and wandered through the graves. It was the place I'd miss most, I knew. The always-autumn graveyard.

And although I knew now that I must have been the one controlling the weather, I had no idea how I might reverse the effects.

Not that I wanted to.

It had always been perfect, this graveyard. It had always been empty and autumn and mine.

And now I was leaving it.

Who knew how long this rumspringa might last? I guess that was the point, sort of. A jump into the unknown with your hands pressed over your eyes.

I settled myself down in between the graves, crossing my legs and cupping my hands around the thermos to warm them. I thought of rain, of wind, of sunshine, of rainbows. All these things that suddenly felt like they might actually be a part of me in a way that felt huge, unfathomable.

I had brought a flood to By-the-Sea—

But had it been the first time?

The Fernweh mausoleum was the largest in the grave-yard. The outside was carved in Annabellas, a tribute to Annabella Fernweh and her sister, Georgina, my great-great-great-great-whatever-grandmother who had been among the first people to inhabit By-the-Sea. I bent down and found the loose stone near the door and removed the little key we kept hidden there.

When Mary and I were younger, we'd play in here. A morbid setting for our dolls to have teatime, but we had liked the stone floors and the way the light turned into rainbows from the stained-glass windows.

I found my father's empty tomb. There was nothing inside this stone container, no earthly remains of Locke Caravelle. His name wasn't even etched into the door. My mother wouldn't allow it. But this is where my father would go, should anyone ever find his body. This is where all the Fernweh women and the men who loved them were buried.

I put my palm against the cool stone.

I had heard the story a hundred times. The story of our birth. Of the final push that delivered me into the world, the push that coincided with the skies opening up. An island flooding around my mother and me as we waited for my sister to show up.

The great storm of our births—the one that had sunk my father's ship.

It had started the moment I was born.

And now I knew that my father's ship had gone down because of me.

My father's tomb was empty because of me.

I would never know my father because I was born with a power I didn't even want, one I didn't even know about for eighteen years.

And now I had it, and there was no sending it back. There was only going forward, and living with the knowledge that the newborn tears of baby Georgina had done so much more damage than anyone had realized at the time.

I wouldn't forget that. This power had blood on its hands.

"I'm so sorry," I whispered to his empty tomb.

"I'm so sorry," I whispered to all the women who had come before me.

And then I left them alone and promised I'd return one day.

The dead loved promises; the living loved promising.

I returned home and stood in my bedroom and turned in a slow circle, looking.

The day had turned bright and sunny.

I guess that meant I was in a good mood.

I had almost no clue how my powers worked. That

little knot of warmth in my gut—when I'd Zeused-out on Peter—that was gone.

If I stood at my window—

And looked up at the sky—

And concentrated very, very hard . . .

I could almost make a cloud appear.

"You'll figure it out," my mom said at the door to my bedroom. She was dressed less conspicuously now that all the birdheads were gone. Jeans and sneakers, a Smashing Pumpkins T-shirt. Her hair was in a long, straight ponytail and she held a cup of coffee, which she offered to me.

"Just coffee?" I asked, taking it.

"You're leaving me for nine months. You think I'm not going to make you a little protection spell?" she responded. We sat on my bed, facing each other.

"Mary came to see me last night."

"Me too," she said.

"She was a human."

My mom nodded. "She's not leaving."

"She told me."

"But I'm glad you are," Mom continued. "If it was going to be anyone . . ."

"Am I really the first? Out of all the Fernweh women?"

Mom nodded again.

Then: "You'll be great, Georgina. You've always been great. Since the minute you were born, sending floods after your enemies." She stared off into space, as if savoring the memory: her and Aggie and my sister and me in a wooden rowboat, making our way safely home.

Without my dad.

I couldn't imagine leaving her.

I couldn't imagine leaving this place.

And yet.

I went to say good-bye to Annabella.

My mother had made her a new grave marker. A flat little rock worn smooth from the ocean. Magically engraved words read: *We loved with a love that was more than love.*

And I thought—

In a million years, if some archaeologists unearthed the remains of By-the-Sea from the bottom of the seafloor (an Atlantis for a distant generation!), and found this rock with these words guarding these tiny, fragile bird bones, they would have no fucking idea what to make of us.

And that was fine with me.

With Aggie and Harrison's help, I loaded my three steamer trunks and one picnic basket into the bed of my mother's pickup. Harrison and Prue added their luggage, and I remembered, so vividly, the moment they'd gotten out of Seymore Stanners's taxi in the driveway of the inn, two months and an entire lifetime ago.

There's one for both of us, my sister had said.

But I'd promised myself I wouldn't cry (mostly because I really didn't want it to rain on all my stuff), and so I pushed that memory down somewhere to save until later.

"Are you okay?" Prue asked me.

"I'm okay," I said, and kissed her.

We lay down in the truck's bed as my mother drove us to the docks, watching the whitest, puffiest clouds crash against each other in the sky over what had been my entire world, what *would* be my entire world, at least for the next thirty minutes.

I closed my eyes and let the roar of the wind rush over me, drowning out as much as I could.

Everything would be okay.

The birdheads would come back.

The inn would stay open.

My sister was alive, and Peter was in jail.

The sun was shining.

And Prue was holding my hand.

You couldn't ask for much more than that.

I'd seen the ferry before, of course, many times, but somehow, today, it looked smaller.

"Are you sure this thing is seaworthy?" I whispered to my mother.

"I vomited twenty-seven times on the way over," Prue

said, overhearing me, dragging her suitcase out of the back of the truck. "But I survived."

"You're going on a great adventure," my mother said.

"Oh no. Are you going to cry?"

"Fernwehs don't cry," she said quickly, wiping at her cheeks.

Without warning, she threw her arms around me and hugged me so tightly I couldn't breathe.

When she let go, she was not crying, but her eyes were wet and red.

"I'll write to you every day," she said. "I'll even use a telephone. You know how much I hate the phone."

"And email?"

"And smoke signals, and carrier pigeons," she added. She kissed the tips of her fingers and then pressed them against my cheek.

"I love you."

"I love you too."

She got back in the truck but didn't drive away. I saw her shoulders shaking, her hands covering her face.

"Georgina? Are you ready?" Harrison asked.

I hadn't thanked him for everything he'd done, for showing up at Peter's trial and speaking out for my sister and for believing me without so much as a moment's hesitation.

"Harrison," I began.

He held his hand up. "It doesn't need to be said."

"But you did so much."

"Not any more than any decent birdhead should have done."

"Then I guess you're the only decent birdhead."

"Nah, cut 'em some slack. They're old. And mass hysteria is a dangerous drug. Let's not forget Salem." Then, darkening, "That probably wasn't the best parallel I could have made."

"An apt one, though. A literal you-know-what hunt."

"I'll never let them burn you at the stake," he said, and bowed to me, and I added *person who bows to other people* to my growing list of things I knew about Harrison Lowry.

Harrison and Prue started up the gangway from the dock to the boat. I followed afterward, but only made it halfway up before I heard my name being shrieked at a deafening pitch from behind me.

I turned.

Vira, of course, leaping off a bright-yellow bicycle and running toward me with her arms out and wide. She flung herself into me so hard we fell backward on the gangway.

"Did you think I wouldn't come and see you off, you *ass*?" she shrieked, hugging me tighter and tighter. "I'm going to miss you so much. You're like my favorite person in the entire world. Okay? Okay, Georgina?"

"Okay, okay! I love you too, Vira."

Vira climbed backward off me and kneeled there, her eyes so wide and her face so beautiful that I wanted to put her on pause, pull out a canvas and easel, and paint her picture right there in bright and beautiful oil paint, the last memory I'd have of her on By-the-Sea for who knew how long.

"You *can't* love Hattie M. Hipperson more than me," she whispered.

"Elvira, don't be ridiculous," I said.

"Call me as soon as you get there."

"Of course I will."

"I'll be sitting by the phone."

"Even before my mother."

"Okay," she said, breathing deep, trying not to cry. "Don't shoot anybody else with lightning bolts unless they *really* deserve it."

"I promise."

"Oh! I brought this for you," she said. She fished around in the folds of her coat and withdrew a small black journal, pressing it into my hands urgently. "Don't forget me. Don't forget anything. Write it all down."

"Do you really think I'm going to forget you, Vira?"

She didn't answer, but she squeezed my hands so hard they turned white. And then she kissed my cheek and helped me up and she ran down the gangway and I knew she wouldn't look back, I knew she'd jump on her bike and peddle away as fast as she could.

And she did.

Prue was waiting for me at the top of the gangway. She

was smiling so wide and—honestly, was *everybody* on the verge of tears?

"I wish I had a friend like that," she said.

"You have me."

"You're lucky, Georgina. This whole world is yours." And she pointed out across the island just as the gangway was lowered back onto the pier and the boat sounded two enormous horns and we pulled away from the dock.

My mother waved violently from the window of the pickup.

I waved back—

Until I couldn't see her anymore.

And then I saw them.

Three little birds, flying recklessly over the strong ocean wind, flying right toward the boat.

Three Annabellas.

One a little bigger.

Two little babies, just testing out their wings.

Learning how to fly.

And I waved to my sister too—

Until I couldn't see her either.

And then I sat down at a table inside the ferry's open cabin. And while Prue and Harrison ordered lunch from a little old lady who worked the concession stand, I opened the journal Vira had given me.

I found a pen in my bag.

And before I could forget—because it was even now

fading from my senses, it was even now too far away to properly identify—I wrote:

> On the island of By-the-Sea
> you could always smell
> two things:
> salt and magic.

ACKNOWLEDGMENTS

Every ninety-eight seconds, an American is sexually assaulted.

One in six women has been the victim of a rape or an attempted rape.

One in thirty-three men has been the victim of a rape or an attempted rape.

Transgender, genderqueer, and nonconforming individuals are at a much greater risk of sexual assault.*

---

*Statistics were provided by www.rainn.org. To reach the free, confidential, and 24-7 National Sexual Assault Hotline, call 1-800-656-HOPE.

This book is first and foremost for every single person who has been the victim of sexual violence.

To the people who had a direct hand in the making and shaping of this book, I could not possibly thank you enough, not even if I were to buy you a pint of every flavor of ice cream offered in Skull & Cone.

For sound advice, solid wisdom, and a great partnership that gives me confidence every single day, thank you to my agent, Wendy Schmalz.

To my family for their persistent support of everything I do and for having faith in me even when I fail to find that same faith in myself. And especially to Elliot, Alma, and Harper, who continue to be just the best-ever spots of light in my life.

To the real-life Georgina and the real-life Mary, thank you for lending your names to this book, but more importantly, thank you for always being two of the first readers of anything I write, and for always being honest and forthcoming in your feedback. And thanks for being two of the dearest friends I have—I am lucky to know you.

For the brilliant lending of many puns for this book (Skull & Cone, Fowl Fair, some others that got cut from the book but not from my heart) and for willing to stress text with me whenever I feel certain I'm going to abandon writing and become a long-distance trucker, I owe heaps of debt to Aaron Karo.

To my team at HarperTeen for standing behind me for

FOUR books (!!), and especially to my editor, Jocelyn Davies, for fielding all my questions and ideas and comments and concerns with only grace and care.

To the readers who have been with me since the very first book and put endless energy into promoting, sharing, blogging, tweeting, photographing, Instagramming, smoke signaling, yodeling, etc., etc. just to get the word out about my writing. Especially to Molly, Crini, Sana, Catherine, and Alice, who have been among the loudest and loveliest.

To Sandra Bullock's and Nicole Kidman's hair in *Practical Magic*. This book would frankly not have been written without it.

And to Shane, for everything and for always.

DON'T MISS

Keep reading for a preview!

ONE.

There are long stretches where I don't remember anything.

I wake up in my car.

I'm driving, but I don't know where I'm driving to and
I don't know where I'm driving from.

But it's my car. And my things are in it.

I just don't know how I got here.

It's only been a couple hours. I remember what I put on
this morning and I'm wearing the same clothes. A pair of
black tights. Jean shorts, a tucked-in flowered shirt. A gray
sweater, worn and pilled. My favorite sweater.

The clock in my car doesn't work and I can't find my

cell phone, so I don't know what time it is. But it's still light out and it's October now, a warm October, and it must be around two or three. The sun goes down so early. Did I miss school again? Sometimes I miss school. What's the last thing I can remember? Ten o'clock? Eleven? History—I can remember history. We're studying the Second World War. I'm in precalculus. I can't remember calculus. I've been out since ten thirty, eleven.

I check my body for bruises, for cuts, pressing fingers into my stomach and arms, checking to make sure I'm okay. Sometimes I'm cut up all over and sometimes there are twigs and leaves in my hair and once I was halfway to New York, driving too fast, and I had to pull over to the side of the road and catch my breath and figure out where I could turn around.

I live in Massachusetts, by the shore. A town called Manchester-by-the-Sea. That's the whole name of the town. The people here, they get angry when the tourists abbreviate it. But we can call it Manchester.

It took me four hours to drive back. Two tanks of gas. I broke curfew by three hours and I was grounded the entire weekend. Grounded for something I can't even remember doing.

It started a year ago and I haven't told anyone about it, even though it's only gotten worse. I can't tell anyone about it because . . .

There are a lot of reasons.

I'm scared they'll think I'm crazy.

I'm scared they won't believe me.

I'm scared there's something really wrong with me.

And so far, I'm handling it. I'm dealing with it.

Usually it's no more than an hour or two and sometimes it's only ten minutes. Sometimes I'll be watching a TV show, and then I wake up standing in my backyard and the same TV show is still on. So I can catch the ending, which I guess is good. Although I have no idea what's happened up until then.

And apparently I don't do anything too obvious. Because I've been around people before and nobody ever seems to notice. Nobody except Hazel, really. But Hazel notices everything.

Hazel is my sister. She's thirteen. It's her and me and Clancy, our brother. He's fifteen, a sophomore. I'm Molly. I'm a senior. I'll be eighteen soon.

Clancy never notices anything.

But Hazel.

She's asked me about it.

I act like she's crazy, which is the easiest thing to do.

Once I asked her if I ever seemed different.

She said yes.

But it was in a way nobody else would ever notice.

I said, What do you mean?

She said if I was going to keep secrets from her, she was going to keep secrets from me.

It happens once a week, maybe. Every other week. Sometimes more.

I don't know what it means.

I've thought about it and . . .

It scares me.

It leaves me feeling sort of hopeless and unable to control my own body. We're supposed to be able to do at least that, right? To tell our feet to move and suddenly we're walking. To tell our arms to lift and our tongue to talk.

To tell our brains to remember.

To commit something to memory.

I think there's something wrong with me.

I mean . . .

I guess I know there's something wrong with me. There has to be.

I get these headaches. Migraines. Sometimes they're really bad; sometimes I have to stay home from school and I have to lie still in bed and keep the blinds closed and sometimes I throw up into the yellow mixing bowl my mom puts on the floor next to me.

My therapist says they're related to my "emotional difficulties."

Those are his words, not mine.

He also calls it depression.

I don't like calling it that.

My mother calls it my melancholy. But I don't like calling it that, either.

But it's something, sure.

It's just . . .

I have to see a therapist once a week and I have to talk about my life and about my problems, but I won't take the pills anymore. I took them for a while, but I don't like them and so I stopped taking them. They take away the lows but they take away the highs, too, and so you're left floating in a strange in-between of colorless, tasteless moments.

And it's not like . . .

I don't want to kill myself.

It's just that sometimes I can't understand anything, and sometimes it feels like the whole weight of the universe settles itself on my shoulders and I can't see the reason for anything. I don't want to die, really, but I don't particularly want to live.

Sometimes I wish I could slip away while I sleep. Wake up someplace better. Someplace quieter.

But I don't believe in heaven, so I'm not sure where that place would be.

I made the mistake of telling people this. So I was sent to a psychiatrist.

And it's gotten better since then.

I don't know.

Sometimes it's fine. Sometimes I'm fine.

Other days.

It's hard for me to have a conversation. It's hard for me to get up, brush my teeth, comb my hair.

It's hard for me to face my friends at school. It's hard for me to write a research paper. It's hard for me to take a breath. Air, sometimes, seems too thick. Tastes like smoke.

I don't know why I feel that way. I have a great life. It's perfect, really. My parents are fine. My brother is fine. My sister is fine. My friends are fine. Things are fine.

This is what I keep telling my therapist, but he keeps making me go back and back and back.

He says, Do you sometimes get the feeling you'll never be happy?

I say, Don't we all?

He writes something down on a little pad of paper.

I say, I was just . . . That was a joke. I was joking.

He says, Do you always joke like that?

I say, Oh god, Alex.

He lets me call him Alex.

I haven't told him about my missing time.

Like I said, I haven't told anyone.

I kind of want to . . .

Just figure it out. See if I can figure it out by myself.

I just hate thinking there's a part of myself I don't understand. That I can't control, that I can't tame, that I can't stop. That I can't change. It makes me crazy. It makes me angry. It makes me scared. It's scary.

One minute you're in history class and it's ten thirty in the morning, and the next minute you're driving your car and you can't find your cell phone and you don't know what time it is and how many hours you've lost and where you've been and what you did and whether you haven't just lost your entire fucking mind.

That's what it feels like. Like I've lost my entire fucking mind. Like I've gone crazy and like I'll never be normal and like I should just pack my things the second I turn eighteen, move to Alaska or Scotland or Romania. Get as far away as I can from everyone I love and just lead my life in a quiet town, knitting sweaters and selling them on street corners to pay my rent and buy food.

I can't knit. I would learn.

I look at myself in the rearview window. I look the same as I looked this morning. I have my hair in a bun and I look tired. I'm on Water Street, I'm driving through the touristy section of town; there are small shops on either side of me. My parents own a shop here. Was I coming to see them? There it is, on the right. By-the-Sea Books. I work there after school some days. They only pay me minimum wage. I know for a fact the other cashiers get more. My parents say yes, but the other cashiers do not get dinner and a place to live and clothes to wear and a car to drive.

Fair enough.

I put my signal on and take a left onto Prince Street.

Should I go back to school? Make up some excuse about where I've been? Sick grandmother? I use that excuse a lot. My grandmother is dead. All my grandparents are dead. No one knows that. You say sick grandmother and people don't usually ask questions.

Right on Allen Street.

I'll go back home, take a shower, take a nap. Be back at the bookstore by five and hope they don't call my mom before then. Tell her I skipped out again. Maybe they'll call my dad. He's a lot easier to deal with. He gets flustered and takes any excuse I give him with a hint of gratefulness. He just wants to believe I'm not crazy.

I don't want to go back to school. It's hard to get back into the sway of everything after you've been outside yourself for a few hours. Or inside yourself. Or next to yourself. Somewhere else. Who knows?

Left on Prescott.

That's when I see him.

There's more traffic on Prescott. It leads into the center of town and it spans the length of Manchester. Quickest way through.

I see him from far off in my rearview mirror. I don't know what makes me see him. The motorcyclist. He's dressed in black. Black jacket, black helmet. He's going too fast. He's weaving in and out of traffic and I know something awful is going to happen before it happens. I feel like I've seen him before, the boy on the motorcycle, and I feel like I know it's inevitable, what's about to happen. He's speeding through cars, he's riding the yellow line, he's gaining on me, and I know it's me he's coming for. It's me, I'm the reason he's speeding. He's trying to catch up to me.

But that's crazy.

I look up as the light turns yellow, but I'm already

halfway through the intersection so I keep going.

The boy on the bike, he's not slowing down. The cars around him are stopping for the red light, but he's speeding up and he's trying to beat the traffic that's already crossing Prescott on Jacobson.

For a second I think he's going to make it.

But then he doesn't.

The truck hits his back tire and he's in the air and I'm screaming without realizing it, braking without meaning to, and I lose him somewhere over the roof of my car. The squealing of tires and the crash as a second car hits the truck that hit his bike and suddenly the boy has landed on the road in front of me. He's flown off his bike and clear through the air over my car, and I don't know how I've gotten out of my car but I'm out and I'm still screaming and I'm running over to him like, I don't know. Like I can save him. But there's blood on the pavement and there's blood leaking out of his helmet and his leg, one of his legs—it's broken, it's bent all wrong. And I know he's going to die. I don't know how I know but I know, and I fall to the pavement in front of him and I pull his helmet off. Because why? Because I don't know. It's all I can do.

His eyes are open. He's gasping for breath. His eyes are green, his hair is black, his lips are red with blood that's choking up out of his mouth.

Fuck, fuck, fuck, fuck, I say and I pick his head off the pavement and cradle it in the crook of my elbow and there's blood all over my sweater. My favorite sweater and there's blood all over it.

Fuck, I say. Please don't die. I can't watch you die.

He catches his breath a little. I wipe the blood away from his mouth with my spare sleeve and I'm crying suddenly; I didn't realize I was crying. This stranger is going to die and I don't want him to die. Please don't die. Please don't die.

His eyes focus on my face. His eyes meet mine and run over my mouth, my neck, my ears, my hair. Back to my face, my eyes.

"Mabel," he says.

Mabel?

"I'm not . . . Look, it's okay, you're not going to die."

"Molly," he says.

He said Molly?

He said my name?

How do you? How do you . . . How do you? How do you?

"How do you know my name?" I whisper.

"I fucked up," he says.

"How do you know my name?"

"It's me," he says. "It's Lyle."

"I don't . . ."

I don't know you.

"Please don't leave me."

"I'm not going to leave you."

"I fucked up again. I always fuck it up. I just. I wanted to see you again. I couldn't . . . I had to try."

"I don't know who you are."

"You can't leave me," he says. "You have to stay with me until I die."

"You're not . . . Don't say that. You're not going to die."

You can't die in front of me.

"I'm going to die," he says, "of course I'm going to die. I feel like I'm going to die."

"You're . . . you're not making any sense."

"You were starting to . . . Molly, please. Don't leave me."

"How do you know my name?"

He's choking again; fresh blood is bubbling out of his mouth and all I can see is the red of it spreading out in one big puddle on the pavement. His eyes are rolling backward in his head, and suddenly I'm aware there are people standing around us. People screaming, a woman crying. He's going to die.

"Lyle!" I yell. I shake him. "Lyle! Wake up!"

His eyes flutter open again; I wipe the blood from his mouth.

"Don't die, please," I beg.

"Get in the ambulance," he says and then I can hear it, the ambulance, the sirens. "Ride in the ambulance with me. Tell them you know me. My name is Lyle Avery. My cell phone is in my pocket. Call my brother. Tell him . . .

tell him where to meet us."

"I don't know how you know me," I say. I choke. "I don't know who you are."

"I know," he says, "but I had to try."

The sirens are getting closer. The ring of people around us is growing, but nobody tries to help. "Please don't die," I whisper.

"You have to call my brother. In my phone. His name is Sayer."

Sayer Avery.

"I don't know who you are," I say weakly.

"At least pretend," he says. "I need you to pretend."

The woman sobs louder. Lyle coughs again, and blood sprays from his lips and gets all over me.

He's going to die. He's going to die and there's nothing I can do.

In the times I'd like to black out, I am forced to live. To be aware. To witness.

In the times I'd like to wake up hours away from where I am, miles away from where I am, I am here. Here watching this boy I do not know take ragged, choking breaths. His teeth stained red. His eyes all white. His cheeks draining of color.

"Lyle," I say, and he focuses on my face again. "Lyle. You're going to be okay."

I love you and you're not going to die.

PRACTICAL
SOCIAL WORK
Series Editor: Jo Campling

(BASW)

Social work is at an important stage in its development. All professions must be responsive to changing social and economic conditions if they are to meet the needs of those they serve. This series focuses on sound practice and the specific contribution which social workers can make to the well-being of our society in the 1990s.

The British Association of Social Workers has always been conscious of its role in setting guidelines for practice and in seeking to raise professional standards. The conception of the Practical Social Work series arose from a survey of BASW members to discover where they, the practitioners in social work, felt there was the most need for new literature. The response was overwhelming and enthusiastic, and the result is a carefully planned, coherent series of books. The emphasis is firmly on practice, set in a theoretical framework. The books will inform, stimulate and promote discussion, thus adding to the further development of skills and high professional standards. All the authors are practitioners and teachers of social work, representing a wide variety of experience.

JO CAMPLING

PRACTICAL SOCIAL WORK

Series Editor: Jo Campling

BASW

PUBLISHED

David Anderson
Social Work and Mental Handicap

Robert Brown, Stanley Bute and Peter Ford
Social Workers at Risk

Alan Butler and Colin Pritchard
Social Work and Mental Illness

Roger Clough
Residential Work

David M. Cooper and David Ball
Social Work and Child Abuse

Veronica Coulshed
Social Work Practice: An Introduction

Paul Daniel and John Wheeler
Social Work and Local Politics

Peter R. Day
Sociology in Social Work Practice

Lena Dominelli
*Anti-Racist Social Work:
A Challenge for White Practitioners and Educators*

Geoff Fimister
Welfare Rights Work in Social Services

Kathy Ford and Alan Jones
Student Supervision

Alison Froggatt
Family Work with Elderly People

Danya Glaser and Stephen Frosh
Child Sexual Abuse

Bryan Glastonbury
Computers in Social Work

Gill Gorell Barnes
Working with Families

Jalna Hanmer and Daphne Statham
*Women and Social Work:
Towards a Woman–Centred Practice*

Tony Jeffs and Mark Smith (eds)
Youth Work

Michael Kerfoot and Alan Butler
Problems of Childhood and Adolescence

Mary Marshall
Social Work with Old People

Paula Nicolson and Rowan Bayne
Applied Psychology for Social Workers

Kieran O'Hagan
Crisis Intervention in Social Services

Michael Oliver
Social Work with Disabled People

Lisa Parkinson
Separation, Divorce and Families

Malcolm Payne
Social Care in the Community

Malcolm Payne
Working in Teams

John Pitts
Working with Young Offenders

Michael Preston-Shoot
Effective Groupwork

Carole R. Smith
*Adoption and Fostering:
Why and How*

Carole R. Smith
*Social Work with the Dying
and Bereaved*

Carole R. Smith, Mary T. Lane and
Terry Walshe
Child Care and the Courts

Alan Twelvetrees
Community Work

Hilary Walker and Bill Beaumont (eds)
Working with Offenders

FORTHCOMING

Gill Stewart with John Stewart
Social Work and Housing

Working with Families

Gill Gorell Barnes

MACMILLAN

First published 1984
Reprinted 1986, 1987, 1988, 1990

Published by
MACMILLAN EDUCATION LTD
Houndmills, Basingstoke, Hampshire RG21 2XS
and London
Companies and representatives
throughout the world

Printed in Hong Kong

British Library Cataloguing in Publication Data
Barnes, Gill Gorell
Working with families.
1. Family social work—Great Britain
I. Title
362.8'2'0941   HV700.G7
ISBN 0–333–35221–1
ISBN 0–333–35223–8 Pbk

*For my children, Lucy and Christopher; and in memory of Henry,
my husband, to whom social work and family therapy were
familiar for eighteen years; with my love*

Contents

4   Initial Work with the Family   **35**

The professional family: convening the network   36
The home interview   36
The agency interview   38
   Who makes up the family and how do you involve them?   38
   Who comes to the interview?   40
   Opening the session: practical issues   41
   Middle stages   43

5   Divorce and the Single-parent Family System   **46**

The divorce process   46
Mother on her own   50
Father on his own   51
One-parent families   52
Who becomes the 'other parent'?   53
Becoming the 'other parent'   54
Grandmothers   54

6   Step-families and Foster Families   **56**

Structural features of step-families   57
What makes reorganisation difficult   60
From one to two   60
   The Rose family   62
   The Knowles family   65
Foster families   67

7   Young Children and Violence in Families   **69**

Babies and their impact on parents   69
   'He's doing it to get at me' – non-accidental injury 72
   Immaturity   73
How can family work with abusing parents be done?   73
Where the family is not viable: authority issues   76

8   Adolescence   **78**

Early adolescence: the suicide attempt   79
Young people who have got too big for their parents   81
The use of supervision and care orders   85
The crisis of leaving home: a foster family   87

Foreword

The publication of a new British book on family therapy is a welcome event. Whilst the deluge of American contributions to this increasingly complex subject-area continues, European participation is still minor by comparison. Much family therapy theory is generic, but its contextual premise makes it necessary that a range of books should be available that focus on the particular culture from which families and therapists are drawn.

This book is especially important because it is less dependent on American sources than were the first British books published in the mid-1970s. Family therapy has developed rapidly in Britain during the last ten years and it is appropriate that a book published in the mid-1980s should reflect the particular flavour of British practice and British research.

Few practitioners are better qualified to produce a book that is so relevant and informative as Gill Gorell Barnes. Her experience includes working in and consulting for both statutory and non-statutory agencies. Her previous writings and research have included work with immigrant families, children at risk, violent families and the seriously disadvantaged. She has made major contributions to teaching family therapy to multi-disciplinary groups through her work for the Family Therapy Programme at the Tavistock Clinic and she has been consistently attentive to the learning needs of social workers in statutory agencies. She is certainly one of the most competent people I know at conceptualising highly complex ideas and yet she possesses that rare skill of being able to convey their meaning through commonplace and homely examples, reducing (enlarging!) a discussion of systems theory to a matter of cornflakes and wellington boots!

The book describes a broad range of family problems and a variety of approaches to treatment. One of its many strengths is its transcendence of methodological sub-divisions and its ability to integrate ideas from psychoanalytic theory with strategic and structural approaches and to see them all as contributing to a broad systemic view of family treatment.

Social workers will welcome the life-cycle format of the book and the attention paid to several family forms, including single-parent families, stepfamilies and foster families. The changing forms of commitment in intimate relationships makes 'family' as central as ever in most people's experience, holding out the possibility of intimacy and continuity but also the twin threats of fusion or disintegration. But for most people the family is a different kind of social group from the so-called 'ideal' or 'norm' and requires of the worker a deep understanding and knowledge, and new and relevant approaches to helping when the family encounters difficulties. As the author rightly points out, social workers are required, more often than other professionals, to help families who are in varying stages of fragmentation and transition and who are experimenting with new and atypical structures. Sources of knowledge for such work are derived primarily from clinical experience and the clinical literature but they also come from a close familiarity with family studies and particularly from recent British work directed towards understanding the context of the family at risk. Unlike the work of some writers in the field, who seem to work in a sort of therapeutic vacuum, Gill Gorell Barnes is clear that the work of sociologists and family theorists 'helps to develop the professional eye as to which families are most vulnerable'. This in turn enables the worker to understand the needs of the particular family more sensitively and accurately, and to introduce appropriate and perhaps novel tools for helping the family to evolve an unusual but satisfying pattern of group life during treatment.

Family therapy has proved to be a creative method of work for social workers. Despite the criticisms made by some social work theorists regarding its elitism and clinical bias, no such criticism is justified in relation to the present work. Indeed, the book represents just that blend of practical application, innovation and sound theoretical underpinning which makes the family therapy paradigm, at its best, of particular relevance to the social worker.

SUE WALROND-SKINNER

Acknowledgements

A book written by a working mother is necessarily a cooperative effort and I would like to acknowledge the many different kinds of practical support that enabled the words to reach the page. Firstly, to my husband and children for putting up with absence and preoccupation at weekends; and to the other working mothers who form part of my extended family network, especially Diana Butt and Ros Gray. Secondly, to my colleagues in the Tavistock Clinic Family Therapy programme and Mrs Elsie Osbourne, then Chairman of the Department of Children and Parents. Thirdly, in different teams Elsa Jones and John de Cartaret; David Campbell and Sebastion Kraemer at the Tavistock Clinic and Alan Cooklin at the Institute of Family Therapy (London) for joint exploration and development of ideas over the last four years.

I would like to thank the following members of training teams at both the Tavistock Clinic and at the Institute of Family Therapy (London) for the use of family examples, and extracts from their work – Lorraine Christie, Bjorg Eimstadt, Irene Gee, Elsa Jones, Jonathan Hill, Jessica Saddington, Jenny Treble and Mike Wilkins. I would like to add that wherever a piece of work appears in a critical light the work cited is my own.

I would like to thank Nicola Madge for allowing me to read her invaluable research review 'Families at Risk' prior to publication, and for permission to quote therefrom.

I would particularly like to thank Elsa Jones, Sue McCaskie and Sue Walrond-Skinner for their help in reading and commenting on the first draft of this book. I would also like to give special thanks to Margaret Walker, Sally Launder and Melissa Ford whose support from the library at the Tavistock Clinic is invaluable. Finally my thanks to Nina Spellen for her patience in the typing of this manuscript and Janice Uphill for her meticulous attention to the references.

GILL GORELL BARNES

1

Introduction

In this small book I have attempted to address some of the dilemmas as well as some of the pleasures that social workers thinking about direct work with families will encounter. The next chapter outlines some ideas about families, family pattern, and the differences between families whom social workers may encounter, and families who may never be seen by social workers except in a resource capacity; the second chapter considers some of the particular issues for social workers in undertaking family therapy both in terms of agency context and the family structures of the client populations, which will include both deprivation and fragmentation. This chapter looks in particular at some of the cycle of deprivation research, and indicates famly factors related to the development of resilience in children and their mothers. These two chapters also consider why a family approach makes sense, drawing from systemic thinking and research in related fields.

Throughout the book I have drawn considerably on research findings which I hope will be of interest and stimulus to all social workers, whether or not they wish to develop work with whole families. The use of research from other related fields links to my own interest in giving a family and social systems approach to work with people under stress a scientific frame wherever it is possible, to complement that aspect of therapeutic intervention which must always be an exploratory human encounter.

I have always enjoyed learning theory by illustration and I have therefore included clips from the transcripts of work with families where space allows. Where possible I have selected examples of families from social service, probation and mental hospital settings, except where the peculiar clarity of the family's expression of a common aspect of family pattern warranted taking it from a client group that is more likely to come direct to clinic settings. A main purpose behind all the work transcribing involves is not to show the excellence of professional work, but to give social workers in pressurised contexts the direct experience that families brought together *do* talk, expand their own ranges of problem-solving possibilities and skills and with a bit of professional warmth, pushing and clarification, may even arrive at conclusions that satisfy them and in addition expand their problem-solving repertoire for the next crisis that will confront them. This is not a characteristic of families who go to child guidance clinics, but a characteristic of families *in principle*, when given encouragement by professionals to do so, plus some professional know how to help them get going in a safe way.

I have now been working with families for over fifteen years. Teaching and supervising the direct family work of others over the last ten years, as well as working face to face; and simultaneously experiencing the dilemmas of becoming a parent and recognising the circular and systemic aspects of family life in which children become a force for continuous and radical change in adult perception, emotional experience and adaptive management, has given me both an intensively subjective experience of the complex demands created by intergenerational tensions, as well as a more objective appreciation of the many skilled and strategic ways in which other families manage them. I am particularly aware of the interdependence of different families with one another for aspects of their successful survival, an aspect of family life, especially with young children, which I still believe needs more recognition both by social workers and policy makers. In addition the management of family and marital tension by legal separation, and the *choice* of single parenthood, as well as the complexity of multiple parenting arrangements in step families has become an increasing part of both personal and professional experience. This book is not therefore primarily about working with a mythical 'norm' that still haunts the field – the two-parent, two- to three-children nuclear family – but discusses and gives examples from a variety of work with different family forms.

There are certain deliberate omissions. I have chosen not to write in detail about the specific contexts in which family work takes place, because others have covered this (Bentovim, Gorell Barnes and Cooklin, 1982) or are currently addressing themselves to this (Treacher and Carpenter, 1984).

I have focused rather on the universal dilemmas that families bring to different agencies, related to different aspects of the life cycle of families; birth, growth, illness and the fear of death, and the transitional stress that accompanies these inevitable but normal changes, presented in the form of inability to achieve a sufficiently adaptive form of family organisation.

Because I do not have enough direct experience of work with families with homosexual parenting relationships, and have only consulted to unhappy situations arising from this family form, I have not written about this group of families whose particular structures for dealing with the universal dilemmas of child rearing and parental ageing will develop its own survival patterns to handle risk factors more adaptively. I am also aware of the absence of case examples from different cultural family forms, such as Chinese or Asian families. Throughout I am interested in promoting creative thinking about the different structures families have developed for managing the requirements of children, in tension with the requirements of society. Such adaptiveness is sometimes related to culture, sometimes to poverty or deprivation and sometimes to the attempt to break old boundaries of pattern and create new forms, which are not yet realised.

My experience in family social work has always maintained a balance between practice and teaching, since I have never wanted to lose touch with the basic anxieties that face-to-face work with families arouses. Working with families can be exhilarating, but it also involves disappointment and cost. While the resources of the family may be greater than those of the single person, they may not be adequate to deal with all the dilemmas posed by life and society. The social worker wants to tap those resources, but also has to face how to help the family find outside resources if their combined efforts fail. When the social worker has to do this he or she is simultaneously managing personal disappointment at needing to bring alternative care and control measures in, as well as the famly disappointment and anger. A framework for doing this that is seen by the family itself as a resource or extension of family concern, rather than a deprivation of their parental rights, is a better framework for subsequent family life and ongoing relationships betwen its members, and can be achieved where prior deprivation is not too great and current experience not too harmful.

Families often assess themselves correctly and tell social workers that they cannot manage a particular situation at a particular point in time; that their capabilities, emotional or intellectual, or their life experience and skills are inadequate to deal with particular developmental crises or aspects of life stress. One of the most difficult social work tasks is to judge whether parents are right or whether there are untapped areas of competence that can be fostered by a new look at the pattern created by the interplay between the family and its surroundings. If parents are feeling 'incompetent', how long will this last? Might the family, given other crucial connections such as the development of more intimate bonds between adults or adults and children, or a particular social resource which created the preconditions for such a development like a home, or the space of a less intrusive environment, cope well enough? Other parents are correct in their self assessment of not coping, and may need to be helped to continue parenting in a limited but possibly essential capacity. Others still will need active help in giving up and mourning a missed opportunity in recognising their incapacity to parent.

Underlying the focus on the family in this book is a belief that the meaning of 'family' continues for individuals despite the radical changes of shape and structure that they may undergo in a lifetime. Part of the work that social workers do, more than other professionals, is to work with family fragmentation. It becomes particularly important, then, that they have some concepts themselves that help them think about this dimension of the individuals they see, internalised aspects of family patterns of relationship, in the many different contexts they are required to meet them. Divorcing families, single-parent families, step families, foster families, the assessment of future families in fostering and adoptive work, and the recollection of families for children in homes, hospitals and containing institutions, or for adults in mental hospitals and for old people living alone, all require some (systemic) concepts of family relationship. Each lonely individual holds some notion of family form and shape inside, and may need help in thinking this out more clearly. Arriving at a better understanding of this internal map of family relationship, as well as looking practically at the external arrangement of the family, will help the social worker plan with the client the thinking about their requirements for closeness to and distance from other people in the future.

2
Understanding Families

What is family pattern and family system?

The idea of a family system is based on the notion of the organisation of pattern over time. The patterning of daily life in any family is built up over the lifetime of the current family, and incorporates what has been learnt from the patterns of previous generations. Much of this patterning in every family operates at the level of habit, and is therefore no longer within the conscious awareness of family members. Where ideas or strongly held beliefs or ways of doing or seeing things come from in the family may no longer be remembered, in spite of the power these ideas hold in current reality. Social workers, by helping families look at the repeated occurrence of certain events that do not lead to satisfactory outcome and the non-occurrence of other possible events which might help the family if they did occur, can make their own map of the systematised elements of family pattern alongside the family (Watzlawick, Beavin and Jackson, 1967). In understanding where and how the pattern repeatedly gets stuck and fails to generate new thinking and behaviour or appropriate feeling, the social worker can begin to plan the kind of information or additional resources the family need.

The development of family patterns
Family pattern is made up of interpersonal relationships involving people with individually specific constitutions and past histories, living in a particular social network in a particular culture. Many different variables will have affected the course of their development. The interactions between any potential couple will develop certain features, some of which are specific to a particular piece of interaction, and others which are longer term properties in the relationship over time. For example, a wife may hate her husband over the interactions around why he never does the washing up and the husband may hate a wife over why she never takes trouble with the maintenance of the family car. These will be emotional aspects of short-term behavioural interactions which may or may not affect other interactions in their lives. They may hate specific aspects of their children's behaviour at

meals or in shops, and again this fierce emotion may be confined to those specific interactions in a particular context, or may reflect other interactions in the family. Each of these family sequences will have a rhythm, a time span, and a closure form of their own (Cooklin, 1982). Put together, these create the unique features of particular family patterns, which, when problems are thrown up, will influence the need for short or for longer-term intervention.

The emotional properties developing from the patterning of interaction can be thought of as the relationship's dynamic aspects. Subtle aspects of a relationship may become observable only as the professional joins the system, and gets to know the family, but other aspects of relationship and dynamic will be immediately observable in behaviour.

When a mother, Mrs Berg, tells a seventeen-year-old girl in a family interview to take off her coat because it is warm in the room, the social worker may infer from the interaction that one of the dynamic aspects of the relationship as a whole is over-protectiveness or overcloseness which is inappropriate to the age and developmental capabilities of a seventeen-year-old. Similarly where a mother Mrs Sharpe, complains of a thirteen-month-old toddler 'He's always been set against me right from the start', it may be inferred that mother is attributing negative attitudes to the baby that are developmentally at odds with an adult recognition of infants and their usual range of demands on a mother.

Over time in a relationship, interactions, and the thoughts and feelings about interactions, affect further interactions and patterns begin to develop. Mrs Berg may expect her daughter to keep her closely in touch will all her thoughts and feelings so that they can be monitored within the context of her own ideas about what is right and proper. This may make it difficult for her daughter to develop thoughts or feelings of her own which differentiate her from her mother. Mrs Sharpe may anticipate every demand from her infant as an attack that needs correction, and perpetuate a relationship based on antagonism, and physical intimacy maintained through chastisement. Mrs Berg's husband will affect the interaction between herself and her daughter, just as Mrs Sharpe's mother will do. In order to understand *how* they affect it, we may need to understand something about the relationship that each of these parents had with their own parents when they were younger, and the kind of attitudes and behavioural patterns that they observed and learnt over time. The more that a group of people in a family interact on a regular basis in relation to certain repeated daily events, the more it can be predicted that the patterning itself affects the properties of their relationships, that is, that each relationship within that group will have systemic properties related to a larger pattern of mutual influence.

Thinking about family patterns

For family therapists the connections between interactions, relationships, the pattern of the relationships overall and the symptoms 'shown' by any one member, is the focus of attention. However, thinking about how to work with families, about how to intervene in the organisation of pattern over time that we call the family system, is divided. The debate, as in other aspects of social work, is related to the level at which intervention takes place. Should the professional aim at intervening in the behavioural and emotional interactions as they occur in the room, or should he or she be aiming to understand their meaning in the context of each person's previous life experience? In a family group this would mean understanding the behaviour of an individual at the wider level of its systemic meaning for the family *as a whole*. This might be limited to the family in the present generation or it might necessarily include the dimension of the previous generation, or of more than one generation. Is intervention more effective when it is offered at the level of *observable behaviour* in the immediate present? Under what conditions is it more effective when it is focused on less overtly definable aspects of relationship which can only be inferred on the basis of observation and enquiry? This question has not been answered, and is likely to depend as much on how the professional works most effectively as any other variable. Here the question will be framed in terms of the need for the professional to define for each family the information or the ideas that will make a difference to the balance or rigidity in systematised aspects of pattern, which does not currently allow them to find new solutions.

Ideas about the systemisation of pattern and habit form the basis of family therapy theory and practice. Bateson has referred to habit as a major economy of conscious thought, 'a sinking of knowledge down to less conscious and archaic levels' (1973, p. 155). This sinking process involves simplification. In the process of coding and classifying knowledge about the world, much of the original information is lost (Foss, 1973). Ideas and information about events as originally received, may be deleted, distorted or condensed in such a way that only one or two attributed meanings for the remaining 'habit' may be available. For example, out of a complex sequence in which Jim spilt something, Mum shouted at him to clear it up, Dad told Mum not to shout at the boy, Susan pinched him for causing an upset and Jim bashed Susan for pinching him, it may only be remembered by the family that Jim bashed Susan, if Jim already has a family label as an aggressive or naughty child. The family will pre-select from sequences such as this, involving the *whole* family, aspects which fit their prior set towards *Jim*, and ignore those other aspects of sequences involving themselves which may have contributed to the behaviour. In this sense pattern 'organises' the freedom of perception in families, and can prevent the intake of 'new' information or ideas. Such pattern is preserved by the continuous repetition of daily acts, by lack of variety in family interactions, and by the ease with which people can lapse into old quarrels and repetitive rows that are never really resolved.

All these aspects of habit may preclude the intake of new information which in turn makes for increased inflexibility in problem solving. Further empirical evidence for the validity of these ideas as a basis for intervening in family pattern can be found in Gorell Barnes (1982, 1984).

Nadia 26, discharged from a long spell in mental hospital following a breakdown at work and a long 'phobic' spell in the home without working, provides an example of a young adult patient playing a part in family patterns. Her critical analysis of her family in terms of the disorganisation of the household as a whole, was seen by the hospital staff (who never met the family) as related to her paranoid state and was written into her profile as part of her 'paranoid, persecuting delusions'. On her discharge, by chance connection, she was referred to a social worker working with a small group interested in developing their work with families, who invited the family as a whole to come along to discuss the rehabilitation of Nadia, and see what plans could be made. Nadia had two brothers living at home and a younger sister who had moved away, the only one of the four children over twenty who had successfully moved away from home. The family were open in their criticism of Nadia and her controlling ritualistic behaviour. She forcefully replied in terms of their contribution to a chaotic home which she maintained 'drove' her into obsessional rituals as a means of self-preservation. Just as they spent a lot of time avoiding her rituals she had spent a lot of time avoiding their chaos. Following a pattern of mother and father working different shift hours, there was no pattern of night and day for the family. Members went to bed at any hour from 7 p.m. to 7 a.m., while others correspondingly began their day as the other's day was ending. Meals were eaten as and when individuals pleased; territory within the house was unclear since rooms, or bits of rooms belonged to different people at different times of day, but might be fought over if members by chance used the same room at the same time of day. The family expressed a wish for a warm household which was better planned and was always open to everybody. They felt they needed a 'housekeeper'. Nadia's paranoid outbursts were placed within a context of family reorganisation of time and space; an issue on which each member felt strongly although they had not got together to plan or change any of the things they revealed themselves disliking. Over eighteen months, working on a basis of fortnightly and then monthly interviews, Nadia's creation of a limited personal structure in which she could function better as an individual took place, within an overall re-balancing for other family members and the creation of a clearer structure of daily living within the household.

The question then for each family is how they can be helped to move from habits which preclude them from finding solutions to the problems that are currently confronting them, to new experience which enables them to think, feel or act differently.

In Nadia's case, two things made a difference in the first interview. The first was that some of the protective aspects of her behaviour in staying at home were pointed out to the family in the light of what they had said about 'needing a housekeeper' – the second was that they were able to reframe some of her 'rituals' as an attempt to make order out of chaos, and link that to a wish for more order that each had expressed in different ways. This understanding was linked to tasks that helped them to work out new patterns of living together. For Nadia, as well as for her family, a more workable reality was created which eventually enabled her to move out from the family, with each of them more convinced that the other would be able to manage without them.

Family systems and intervention

The Social Worker perhaps more than most professionals other than psychiatrists working with adults, comes up against interactions that seem to be intractable and fixity that is impossible to change; either in the social situation in which the client finds him or herself or in the client's internal capacity to experience hope and think about a different possibility. Such situations may call for professional action on more than one front; indeed for the kind of understanding, and social work planning which other psychotherapists have criticised family therapy for including as part of its brief.

One of the peculiar talents of social workers however, has always been to translate insight into action modes, both in individual, group work and community work. Social workers are thus well equipped from their prior experience to help families to think about what may make a difference to their perception of the problem, that may then enable them to act upon it in a new way.

Defining a family

Traditionally the family is the primary social group into which individuals are born and upon which they initially depend for nurture and for the physical and psychological protection offered by intimate relationships. Again by traditional definition it is a unit of more than one generation. Normally a proportion of the members of a family live in one household. It would however be a mistake to attempt any such simple definition of the many family forms that social workers work with. Social workers work not only to 'preserve' old forms but to create new forms. They are often working with 'families' that are in the process of mourning and re-constitution at the same time, and tackling 'systems' with life spans of only weeks or months. Similarly they often have only one generation, a sibling subgroup for example, to work with.

A notion of what is 'family' that provides a coherent theme for social work, centres round the construct of attachment (Bowlby, 1982) and the necessary provision of protective intimate bonds for successful human development and adequate mental health (Rutter, 1979). Social workers spend much of their time not only trying to preserve these constructs on behalf of vulnerable individuals, but in actively creating and recreating them in different family forms such as adoptive and foster families and in small group situations in homes, hostels and other institutional settings. Robinson (1982a) has categorised the variety of reconstituted family forms with which social workers may be engaged. These include adoptive families, foster families where the child's relationships with the original family are maintained and foster families where such contacts are not required, as well as different forms of step families. Social workers have to be concerned not only with the current structure and pattern in which these notions of family are housed but with previous family patterns which may be interfering with the successful development of these. This may be happening actively, as when a blood relative cannot decide about future care for a child, or when parents actively and destructively undermine the success of a foster placement, or it may happen through the internalisation of learnt pattern that the individual carries into the new situation and which is always available to be triggered into action replay. In family situations where the present structure will very often be discontinuous from the past structures, it will not be adequate to look only at the current situation. The social worker will necessarily have to include in a personal assessment of how to work with the disturbance in the current structure, that part of the map which relates to the previous family structures the individual has experienced in his or her lifetime, and see how those impinge on the situation here and now. This will be essential information in the social worker's own *thinking* however he or she chooses to use it in *practice*.

In natural families, forms will also be varied. The traditional system to be worked with is a man, a woman and some children. Many families however will have only one parent, although an essential part of the family system will be the person or group to whom mother or father turns for support and confirmation of their own adult capabilities, as well as for sexual needs. These partners may be either male or female. The importance of adults' protective relationships with one another should not be underestimated. Recent research (Brown and Harris, 1978; Rutter *et al.*, 1983) has shown the difference that a confiding relationship with a man makes to the mental health of mothers. As yet we are relatively unknowledgeable about the family structures, strengths and dilemmas of homosexual couples. A developmental focus may help in thinking about how to help any family organise more successfully around some of the essential requirements of child rearing, and the complexities related to the nurturing of attachment and protective intimate ties in ways that are age appropriate. For example, in a family where the nominal parents are a white lesbian couple, the children are all Black British boys, and there are problematic issues of cross-'generational' attraction, it seems particularly important to be linking professional thinking to the developmental needs of the children. Focussing on those things that any parent, or those who stand for parents, regardless of their sex, has to be able to do on behalf of a child of a particular age and stage may help the 'family' discover what they can do as a healthy parent-and-child unit and what can't be managed.

Structure and hierarchy

Members of a family are connected by a series of interactions over time which create relationships. These connections influence and constrain individuals, both externally and internally. Individual freedom is of necessity constrained by any system in which degrees of mental interdependence will be a key feature. Families are organised to carry out a number of tasks relating to nurture and socialisation for which the parent or parents are normally responsible. One of the most common problems that families deal with in practice is the question of *who* is in charge, and while authority is constantly handed around at both conscious and covert levels, the right of those designated parents to have the decision-making power over children who are still dependent is a crucial boundary marker, defining who is 'in charge' both within the family and between the family and the outside world as it is embodied in various laws. Parents are still the primary executive sub-system in the eyes of the world. Social workers are often the professionals who have to take responsibility for changing this boundary marker, and for divesting parents formally of their parental authority, often taking aspects of this same parental authority upon themselves.

The family life cycle
The adaptation of principles of work with families for social workers has to take into account the variety of family structures a social worker will meet with, as well as the discontinuous nature of much of the family pattern that will be present in any current system that is being worked with.

A life cycle framework for thinking about how a family is functioning is always constrained by cultural and social norms. What is and is not accepted and acceptable behaviour within a nuclear family and the family's social network at any point in their lives is inevitably affected by difference in cultural expectations. Biological development offers a frame around which to build thinking about how parent figures and children are relating and provides additional focus for family assessment and for many aspects of thinking about family functioning, as an alternative axis to the socio-cultural dimensions. A systemic view of why the dilemma the family brings is as it is, which includes the cultural and socially determined perspectives, can be placed alongside a series of questions that may help in answering urgent problems about whether the family is a viable developmental unit from the stance of its more vulnerable members; and indicates more clearly where reorganisation needs to take place and whether the professional resources available will enable this or not.

Minuchin (1974) conceptualised the natural family as developing through a number of stages that require it to restructure within its own organisation, while at the same time maintaining a continuity on behalf of its members. He defined family structures as 'the invisible set of functional demands that organises the ways in which family members interact' (p. 51). Families and their behaviour are governed by two broad systems of constraint. The first of these can be described as universal constraints since all families have to wrestle with them; nurture, complementarity, the organisation of authority and power, interdependence versus autonomy. The second set of constraints relates to the ways in which these universals are housed within any particular family; the structure, organisation and daily behaviour within which they are negotiated.

Minuchin's particular contribution to the development of life-cycle ideas as a way of thinking about family stress has been the emphasis on the normality of stress, and the inevitability of transitional crises for *all* families. A change such as a marriage, a new baby, a second child, a death in the family, the housing with the family of an old person, are changes forced upon the 'pattern as it was' from which a new pattern has to evolve. A new balance has to be established within the range the family can manage. Since many families are not able to transform themselves to provide necessary and age-appropriate continuity, the concept of the 'under-organised' as an alternative to the 'disorganised' family was developed.

Particular difficulties for each family in terms of their current life experience will need clear understanding. This may include attention to a 'higher organising principle', the weight of expectation, attitudes and taboos from the past. Equally powerful may be a lack of adequate experience from the past which is affecting the current situation; for example, girls who, having spent all their lives in care, are as young mothers struggling to find a family form that they themselves never experienced (Rutter *et al.*, 1983).

Carter and McGoldrick (1981) have defined these two axes of stress usefully as the horizontal and the vertical stressors. The horizontal stressors includes the predictable developmental stresses and the unpredictable events, the hazards that life deals families, handicap, long-term illness, untimely death as well as environmental stressors outside the family over which the family have no control. The vertical stressors include the experience of previous generations as the parents in the family have incorporated and transmitted them. Obviously the family will be most vulnerable at a point where a current crisis regenerates some previously transmitted anxiety which has left the parents unprepared to cope in relation to that area of life.

An intact family progressing through the life cycle would go through transitional stages which can be outlined theoretically and oversimply in Table 2.1.

Families in crisis

Many families whom social workers see are unlikely to have had rhythm and continuity in their histories and will have either poor family experience or an absence of family experience to bring to bear on their current dilemmas. They are also likely to be suffering from a number of current life stresses which threaten their own mental state, so that they present in a state of crisis.

14

TABLE 2.1

Family life cycle stage	Transitional issues	Changes required in the family system as a whole
A Leaving home and living alone	Separation Independence	(i) Allowing young person to be separate from family; (ii) Not calling them back each time there's a crisis.
B Forming a couple marriage	Emotional involvement in the new system	(i) Acceptance of spouse as part of family; (ii) Rebalancing of relationships to acknowledge privacy.
Family with young children	Changing from a two-person to a three- or four-person unit	(i) Making space for children; (ii) Being available in a new way; (iii) Reconciliation with grandparent role.
C Family with adolescents	Increasing flexibility further to include independence of views and behaviour, including sexual behaviour, from younger members plus maintenance of authority	(i) Recognition of value of change initiated by younger members; (ii) Recognition of the value of fights, arguments and negotiation; (iii) Recognition of importance in maintaining own difference.
D Launching children 'empty nest' phase	Accepting fluctuation in coming and going; drawing new boundaries round the couple after children have gone	(i) Negotiating relationship with children as adults (as in *A*); (ii) Re-thinking opportunities in the world outside the family: time, space, finance.
E Later life	Accepting more dependence on the children	(i) Maintaining couple or individual functioning in the face of old age; (ii) Accepting dependence of elderly without overprotecting or managing them; (iii) Facing loss or death including one's own.

NOTE   For alternative pathways see Dare, C., Life Cycle Table, *Journal of Family Therapy*, vol. 1 (1979) no. 2, pp. 142–3; Carter, E. A. and McGoldrick, M., *The Family Life Cycle* (1981).

When the normal parameters of family pattern are exceeded by a series of events or a particular constellation of events, people's usual coping mechanisms and the family's way of keeping its balance are thrown out of action. The family may either make a creative leap directly into some totally new way of approaching the problem; as many of the self-help groups that have grown up around crisis areas of family life such as child abuse, or other forms of family violence have moved parents to do; or people may enter a state in which they are temporarily at sea before new solutions are sought. This may include the dissolution of previous family structures. Crisis implies the breakdown of old patterns and the possibility of new patterns developing. It also raises the probability that the family itself will never settle down in the same way again. The outcome of crisis is not necessarily positive.

Crisis intervention theory has focused on the reduction of anxiety in the client alongside the mobilisation of hope and the restoration of a sense of autonomy and control over the situation. Step by step planning is of great value in this process. Sainsbury (1975) highlighted how many disorganised families will value talking through aspects of the problem situation in the smallest detail in order to obtain greater mastery over the event.

Social workers are more likely than other professionals to be faced with the possibility that the original family system has burst its boundaries, or exploded in ways that have led to expulsion, exclusion or disappearance of some of the members, so that what is being mastered is the creation of new systems which may be acceptable or totally unacceptable. An essential feature of contact between family and professional at such a time will be the way in which the family feels the worker can hold the crisis and help them. Family systems can be placed at three potential points in a notional spectrum from flexibility through rigidity to chaos:

1. Families with enough flexibility of interaction and freedom of expression for the development of individual autonomy including disagreement and the development of new patterns.

2. Families where the maintenance of outward conformity is of paramount importance at the expense of any individual disagreement.

3. Families with chaotic interactions based on perpetual disagreement and resulting 'crisis' (from which no learning takes place).

Families of the *first* type are more likely to be met as clients in normal life hazard situations such as accident, severe illness, handicap, premature death or enforced disasters such as temporary homelessness. They will also be met in resource capacities, as adoptive and foster parents, as community aides, as sustained volunteer helpers. They will be more able to make use of professional ideas to enable them to rethink and reorder that temporary sense of chaos.

Families of the *second* type are met in situations where there may be acute mental illness in one or more members (psychotic illness in particular) both in teenagers and adults; in many cases where violence is covert and denied such as persistent child abuse; and unfortunately in some cases where resource families such as foster families or family group home parents, or house parents, cannot bear to face the violence and distress in aspects of their job; and respond by more and more sustained surface smoothness which denies any possibility of disagreement with the way things are being handled.

Families of the *third* group, chaotic families, may be similar to though not necessarily the same as, the under-organised family as originally described by Minuchin *et al.* (1967) in *Families of the Slums*. These are families for whom crisis, violence or wide swings from what most people regard as 'normality' provide a sense of being alive. The danger for more vulnerable members lies in a failure of protective ties and inadequate boundaries between the generations. A family for example where the dogs are used as sexual partners in the children's evening games arranged by mother and her boyfriend for amusement, shows formidable cross-generation confusion and the children, more vulnerable family members by virtue of their developmental position, may need long-term protection.

Family balance and resistance to change

The concept of 'homeostatic mechanisms' operating in families to keep the balance of emotions and behaviour within particular limits now has some clinical and experimental support. Its conceptual value in assessment is that it offers social workers a way of thinking about key characteristics of the family which are interrelated with the present problem, their centrality to the family in terms of its own definition of itself and its 'coherence', and the amenability of these characteristics to change. Criminality for example may be a key aspect of the way a particular family defines its cohesiveness. It may also help the social worker consider what the likely effect of 'improvement' in one member of the family may be on other members; since a change in the referred person if he or she remains in the family will require a change in the others. This may either be resisted or resolved by the appearance of a problem in a different family member (which allows the overall family balance to remain unchanged) or in the exclusion of the person posing the problem.

A number of studies relate good mental health to families that can tolerate much wider differences of opinion and behaviour, and greater freedom to act independently without weakening the balance of the family as a whole. Such families showed greater receptivity and responsiveness to new ideas from outsiders (including professionals) which enabled them to develop solutions to problems.

Severely dysfunctional families, in contrast, are seen as having a narrower range of responses with little attention paid to individual perception and feeling or to difference of views that do not fit the family's agreed group norms. Both very rigid families and highly chaotic families would share this common characteristic of wishing to preserve the family as it was and of being unable to process new ideas and therefore be amenable to change (Lewis *et al.*, 1976).

The question of how information is received or how a family system changes, however, relates not only to its own characteristics, but to the way in which the outside agent, the social worker, conceives of his or her own input in relation to the process set up with the family, the map made of the process and the assessment of how the 'system' can receive 'information' and move towards a more adaptive organisation. Such moves are more likely to require changes in *both* attitude and behaviour but either may follow upon a change in the other. A fuller analysis of systems ideas and terminology in family work can be found in Gorell Barnes (1982, 1984).

Family assessment

A number of different groups have now developed interesting and thorough ways of making assessments of family strengths and problem areas. In Great Britain any form of assessment based on a single dimension of family functioning such as communication, *or* affective functioning *or* behavioural functioning is not in favour. Rutter (1975) detailed eight areas of family functioning as correlated with psychiatric stress in children, which in an earlier publication (1978b) I listed in an overall assessment procedure that includes the physical assessment of the child and parents. Family functioning needs assessing in those areas that relate to the successful physical emotional and psychological growth of children:

1. absence or gross distortion of affectional bonds;
2. gross disturbance in the feeling of the family as a secure base from which children can safely explore;
3. absence or gross distortion of parental models which child imitates (consciously or unconsciously) and on which identification is formed;
4. presence of dysfunctional styles of coping with stress (for example, disproportionate aggression; perpetual recourse to illness);
5. absence of interaction or gross distortion in the interaction between parents;
6. absence of necessary and developmentally appropriate life experience (food, warmth, play, conversation and interaction leading to the development of social skills);
7. absent or exaggerated disciplinary techniques;
8. absent or distorted communications network (inside the family and between the family and the outside world).

A number of authors who have studied families over time have looked at the different ways in which families cope with stress, either by coming closer together or by moving further apart. Minuchin distinguished the movement towards either cohesiveness or greater distance from one another as enmeshment and disengagement, Jordan (1974) as integrated versus centrifugal families and Byng Hall (1981) has looked in detail at ideas in which children may regulate closeness and distance between parents in order to keep the right kind of balance for that family going.

Although ideas are couched in different descriptive terms they all hold the notion of a central 'balance' in the family which is being maintained in relation to the crisis. Reiss (1981) in a series of experiments with over a thousand families has shown how families manage self regulation within certain parameters and take on different aspects of one another's functioning in order to protect the 'balance' of the family as a whole.

Core characteristics of 'balance' may include persistent acting out or the expulsion of a member from time to time in many of the families whom social workers see. How this form of dealing with a problem was arrived at may well require explanation along the historical axis of a previous generation, to be understood fully as a systemic family feature rather than a piece of individual pathology. To have children received into care for example or to enter mental hospital from time to time may be a solution learned from earlier life experience or from a previous generation.

The social worker seeing an individual who is a parent, a spouse or a child will understand that here is someone who carries aspects of the family pattern and organisation in the way he or she thinks, sees and feels even while the social worker is in the room; and take this into account in helping the individual to think about the dilemma presented.

3
Families and Social Workers

Social work and family therapy

The Barclay Report (1982) suggests that social workers require knowledge of two kinds: practical knowledge, the structure of the daily world of neighbourhood, area, and agency and how these can be made available to people, and knowledge that gives meaning to behaviour and illuminates different human processes. One of the particular talents of social workers has been the capacity to combine these two aspects in working forms that relate to the specific requirements of different client groups – insight in action rather than in words alone. The value placed on casework as one form of social work activity was always counterbalanced in practice by other forms of group work in communities, settlements and psychiatric hospitals. How do those many forms of work with families that have taken place over time and continue to burgeon in everyday social work differ from the thinking and practice of people who think of themselves as doing family therapy, and do such differences have important implications for practice or not?

Much social work time is spent with families who are temporarily changing shape through the loss of a member by illness, death, or flight from home, separation, abandonment or expulsion. Social workers thus have to be concerned with helping families reorganise in a different way, with helping them monitor what is lost, and with creating new family structures. In these areas of disrupted family life they have a great deal to teach other professionals who are more familiar with intact families and have focussed on systems that have become fixed over time. Social workers' special skills in family work may therefore be seen as linked to the active reorganisation of family structure. Some of the innovative work in supporting families by the use of intensive volunteer neighbourhood schemes (for example Harrison, 1982), in maintaining aspects of family system by keeping brothers and sisters together in fostering placements (Cox, O'Hara and Bruin, 1981) or by creating new family rather than institutional forms for children of all ages in care, as the work of the Kent Fostering Scheme has done, shows the commitment to the central importance of attachment and growth within a pattern of protective bonds as a fundamental human right, on which one of the best impulses of social work practice is based.

Similarly the determination to clarify confused aspects of family and professional pattern by structuring more clearly the position of children in care in relation to their sense of 'belonging' to a family, has been forcibly taken on by the British Association of Adoption and Fostering (Rowe, 1982; Adcock and White 1980, 1982). This painstaking work on carving out boundaries and structure where previously confusion existed, also requires work on the relinquishing of inappropriate ties with non-functioning aspects of family pattern, the parents who no longer parent.

Family therapists are concerned with both the relationship between the functioning of the family as a whole, its overall organisation and capacity to deal with the demands and stresses of a complex society, and with the disturbance shown by any one member as a message about this functioning at a particular point in time. The professional move would therefore be towards understanding why the resources of the family unit were not able to handle the disturbance at issue, and why this was different now in comparison with some previous occasion which had been manageable. Any problem or disturbance brought by a child or young person still living with their parents would therefore be viewed within the context of the family, and any changes taking place; and the views, opinions and ideas of the family canvassed for solutions. The difference from a social work perspective that was not taking any kind of systemic view of the presenting problem might be in the weight accorded to the *current context* in which the child was living, the success of organisation of that context in terms of the developmental needs of the individuals living within it and an awareness of the interrelationship of *previous contexts* in which an individual had lived with the present situation. This would apply for example in step families where the impact of previous marriages and ex-spouses living outside the current constitution of the family would be considered, both in terms of the expectations each current spouse brought to the family and the expectations children and parents had of each other based on previous patterns. It would also be considered in terms of the *current* interaction ex-spouses had with the present family – both parents and children – and how that boundary was managed. Similarly in a foster home the same considerations would apply. What are the expectations the children bring to the family from previous families and what expectations do the foster parents have of them? In addition how does the *current* management of the boundary between the natural family and the foster family affect the presenting problem? For some children a series of foster families or patterns of previous attachment (constellations of relationship that the child carries as a picture inside) might be relevant to consider. An attempt should always be made therefore, to view the problem within the largest manageable or relevant system so that the interrelating pattern of factors could be considered which might well show the problem in a very different light from that originally presented.

Parsloe, in a DHSS survey of social service teams (1978), points out that social workers were not sufficiently helped in their training to understand the *context* within which they had to work with clients, and that much social work methods teaching was still overinfluenced by the casework formerly taught to medical and psychiatric social work students, where the focus was almost entirely upon the relationship between client and worker. On other courses, she suggested that casework may have been replaced by sociological theories at a very high level of generality. 'Our studies would suggest that there is still a great deal to be done in helping students to understand how to use their interactional skills in relation to particular practice theories.' Family work was very little used, although a look at different studies of social work intake suggests that direct family work might be appropriate in about one third of presenting problems (Davies, 1980).

Training in work with families has changed in the five years since the DHSS study although this may be predominantly at post-qualifying level, with a move on all training courses towards looking at the interactional behaviour between social worker and client family as well as the worker's views of what he is doing. Much of the training offered takes place in agency settings, using role-play skills and rehearsal or re-enactment of aspects of the case where the worker has felt 'stuck' in the family pattern. Thus the move has been towards both skills development and recognition of context. Although the first area has moved faster than the second, the current preoccupation and development in family therapy teaching is towards the application of concepts and methods in different settings.

My own study during the same period (Gorell Barnes, 1980) of social workers already attempting family therapy methods (selected by virtue of their membership of the Association of Family Therapy and therefore not a random sample) showed a variety of methods slowly infiltrating practice. Respondents were practising in a variety of settings including social service departments, psychiatric hospitals, the Family Service Unit, the probation service and departments of child and family psychiatry. Reasons for valuing a family therapy approach were ranked in the following order:

1. Offers an open model of communication and sharing which is enjoyed by the family.
2. The method was enjoyed by the social worker.
3. It moves the focus of concern from the individual to the family with positive results.
4. It offers a realistic way of working.
5. It is effective in problem solving compared to other methods.
6. It improves the quality of family life outside problem solving.

The preferred method of working with families was short term, problem focussed and goal oriented. The study revealed the highly complex variety of theoretical approaches covered in training courses which, while clearly offering stimulus, had little coherence with one another. Respondents were struggling primarily to put together two different but essential elements of their practice bases, the understanding of the individual represented by psychodynamic theory, and the recognition of the influence and effect of context represented by sociological theory.

A small number of people had extended their range of work into the community network including relatives, neighbours and professionals central to the family support system, as part of the definition of 'family' that they made.

How can previous writers help us?
A great deal has been written about work with families using other series of frameworks both sociological and psychoanalytic. I am referring briefly to only a few texts which have informed social workers over the last ten years. Younghusband (1967) provided a starting point for thinking about work with families as a group, in a collection of papers that combined sociological and psychodynamic points of view. Other texts that will have influenced most social workers will have been Mayer and Timms (1970), Jordan (1972) and Sainsbury (1975) since they were written with particular reference to the social work task with families. Walrond-Skinner (1976) provided the first comprehensive account of a systemic approach to family work and techniques for working with the family.

Jordan (1972) in 'The Social Worker in Family Situations' presented a communications view of systems thinking in relation to families; and in looking at the dangers of an approach in which the family rather than the individual was seen as patient, focussed on the need to recognise the protective aspect for the family as a whole of keeping the problem in one member. The social worker is required to ensure the 'safety' of the family in removing the problem. Jordan drew attention to the 'balance' of the family:

> Patterns of family life, not rigidly defined by a set of rules but gradually evolved as a result of the delicate emotional balance between the needs of the members of the family. Such norms represent the sum total of all the years of conflict, compromise and concern for one another through which the family have built up all they have in the way of happiness, security and mutual support; and protected themselves against the potential miseries and uncertainties of life together.

He recognised that to have a social worker looking at the pattern of the family, with the possibility of its 'overthrow' as he terms it, may be a threat of greater consequence to the family than the loss of one of its members, particularly where the family has a history of reliance upon the institutionalisation of one of its members as a means of preserving the stability of the others.

It is the recognition of the power of these 'protective mechanisms' in the family balance which has recently returned to family therapy thinking, particularly in the work of the Milan group (Palazzoli, Boscolo, Cecchin, Prata, 1978). This will be described later (Chapter 10). Research discussed in the previous chapter (Reiss, 1981) also looks in detail at the mechanisms by which this protectiveness is displayed. However, what Jordan did not include in his analysis of the family 'resistance' to change, and what offers more hope to the social worker than he himself was able to experience as he describes the process of his own work, is the protective part played by the 'problem' person in 'agreeing' to be thus labelled to maintain the status quo. It is this aspect of protectiveness which is a powerful ally to possible change in how the family perceive themselves and their interrelation with the problem person. Suggesting to a family that the problem behaviour is serving a protective or loving function on behalf of other members, is a powerful message which also testifies to the intrinsic strengths in a family who have developed such loyalty in one of their members, strengths which may have been temporarily lost sight of during the crisis. Obviously it would be foolish to suggest that all behaviour can be reframed positively in a way that leads to family harmony but to hold on to an awareness of mutual protectiveness, and the problem behaviour having a positive function for the family balance as a whole, and to be able to put back a different quality of perception to the family, can often lead to a better outcome (see

Chapter 7 and Chapter 10 for examples of learning to reframe 'deviant' behaviour).

Social Work with Families (Sainsbury, 1975) develops many of the themes discussed by Mayer and Timms (1970) in describing clients' perceptions of social work in action. Sainsbury's particular concern was to identify what clients regard as good practice and appropriate personal qualities among social workers. His chosen client group, families helped by the FSU, are a group who have been of particular research concern in the last ten years. In 1972, the DHSS funded a number of projects to look at intergenerational patterns of social disadvantage and this research is discussed briefly on pages 30–4 as it relates to the likely characteristics of families who will be requiring social work help.

The emphasis of Sainsbury's research findings about the kind of social work help this group of clients valued, is towards the intimacy of family and worker, towards working with the details of family life and the practical problems that arise from it, and recognising the 'daily reality' of the clients' framework. It is away from the development of a 'dependence' model in which the clients or families see the worker as the main resource. It incorporates clear thinking and the use of authority that is given where the worker has established a basis of intimacy with the family.

Systemic thinking and social work

Systems ideas which link the relationship of one person or event to another, have been offered to social workers by many authors. Vickery (Specht and Vickery, 1977) points out the difference in thinkers and teachers between those who try to think according to a single organising principle (an organised conceptual framework) and those who think and know many things that are different, unrelated and even contradictory. Family theory and the ideas underlying family therapy in social work thinking have suffered the same problem of whether to unify a number of different conceptual frames which offer different ways of looking at how families 'organise' themselves, each of which may have logically different developments for the methodology of social workers. Unifying concepts that link social work theory and family theory are held in most compact form in Specht and Vickery (1977) with the chapters by Vickery, Goldstein and Pincus and Minahan being of particular relevance. They discuss a number of shared constructs including that of seeing the problem as the unifier – believing that a wide range of conceptual frames should be taught to social workers around the nature of shared human dilemmas, with the purpose of the work to be done kept in the foreground. 'Although the needs of the clients system enable the agency to define its goals, the points and methods of intervention cannot be selected properly without an awareness and substantial knowledge of the social system within which the problem is rooted.'

Goldstein discusses the personal move from a psychodynamic individual-oriented approach, to a more systems-oriented approach and the way in which this allowed him to use problem-solving concepts from systems theory, and communication theory. This move allows not only the development of different ways of *thinking* about clients' problems, but different ways of developing problem solving skills such as better communication with others. These authors remind social workers that individuals can be known both as unique beings in their own right and simultaneously as integral elements of some larger social structure. Conversely these larger systems – families, groups, neighbourhoods and communities need to be seen both as complex entities and as composites of individual beings, each with his own needs, hopes and ambitions (Specht and Vickery, p. 67). This key point is the one that unifies all social work approaches. Families and communities are part of individuals, just as individuals form families and communities. The difference between professionals is about methodology; where do you go in and how do you proceed?

Within the family therapy field the ways social workers are offered organising principles to help them to think about their work can become divisive. For example, long-term arguments about whether working with the behaviour of the family is a more effective way of problem solving than working with the family affect – their feelings – is irrelevant unless placed in context. A systemic approach, by recognising interconnection, would ask the question only in the context of the family–worker system: 'Which will work best here?'; not within the context of methodological argument. 'Who is doing the work; what is the area of concern; what is the worker's setting; what methods of operation has he or she been taught?' These are all essential contextual questions.

Similarly within family therapy, theory has become divisive and the 'organising principle' often gets lost in endless skirmishing about which 'method' of working with families is the 'truth'. Family work in this country is moving beyond that phase. There is now a greater concern with the principles of systems theory as they apply to making conceptual maps to think about families, their behaviour, emotions and the meaning they give to these in different contexts, rather than to whether psychodynamic, structural, systemic or strategic work offers the truth (Walrond-Skinner, 1981; Gorell Barnes, 1982; Bentovim, Gorell Barnes and Cooklin, 1982; Whiffen and Byng Hall, 1982; Treacher and Carpenter, 1984).

Why social workers should not do family therapy
Before we continue however it is important to approach the question rather differently, and ask why social workers should *not* do family therapy. In an earlier survey of social workers using family therapy methods (Gorell Barnes, 1980) the hazards of taking a systemic view on board were noted. Two main areas of concern were raised. The first was around the question of where and how the boundary of professional intervention could be defined once the individual as the primary focus for attention was abandoned. One despairing respondent commented on the flexibility and confusion engendered as part of the process of taking systemic thinking on board and felt that what was involved was a wish to do 'world therapy'. World therapy or an overall ecological viewpoint seems essential if the world is to survive, but as Haley succinctly put it 'whatever radical position he takes as a citizen, his job as a [therapist] is to advise the social unit that he can change to solve the presenting problem of the client' (1976, p. 5).

The second major dilemma stated by social workers, was to do with the change in the nature of boundaries that they experienced in relation to their own professional system, since the arbitrary nature of hierarchy, and aspects of boundary in decision taking, become far more apparent when family therapy is tried out. Where older systems of theory, treatment approach or administrative structure, originally developed in response to a different way of thinking about change and professional–family interrelationship are challenged, new questions about who should be in charge arise. Haley (1975) developed this problem strategically in an article called 'Why Mental Health Settings should Avoid Family Therapy'. British social workers in the last five years have added their particular contextual experience to the debate, bringing it 'home' for people in different settings (Adams and Hill, 1983; Dimmock and Dungworth, 1983; Treacher and Carpenter, 1984). Readers are referred to these authors for detailed accounts of survival strategies and particular skill development. Adams and Hill in particular draw attention to the impotence the social worker experiences within his own agency about the possibility of achieving a change in work method, and the difficulty this impotence creates in creating a context for a *family* in which they feel they have the power to create change in themselves. For the family the difficulty is additionally linked to having to label themselves as 'in need' or 'inadequate' in order to obtain a resource they know is available under particular categories which they may experience 'family work' as trying to do them out of. The authors point out that once the social worker has perceived how he or she becomes part of the 'problem' by maintaining categorisation, solutions may be forced to develop that may not be within the accepted field of operation of the agency of which he is a part. These dilemmas have been further discussed by De'Ath (1983), who points out that while most families suffer set-backs at some stage, related to health, unemployment or because of some permanent feature of their environment, support services are *not* geared to the healthy aspect of the family which would boost their view of themselves as capable of doing something about it through a community-based activity. Instead services are geared to intervention, requiring the clients to identify themselves through a problem and therefore casting the family in an inadequate or helpless role.

Why social workers might enjoy working with families

How can the social worker learn to help the family discover their own resources? We need first of all to accept that we are just ignorant outsiders, who do not understand how the family works, or why it works the way it does. Nonetheless by asking the unaskable questions that only outsiders can ask, we may promote a different cycle of thinking and possibly of expertise in the family. It may mean abandoning much of the *formal* professional front by working directly while being able to move back and use the professional and agency resources the family may need at any time.

This chameleon way of working from a stated position of relative ignorance means recognising that families often find their own 'problem free' answers which do not suit society as the social worker has to represent it. Social workers, of all professionals, have to represent the reality of a variety of systemic perspectives that are different from those the family hold. These are to do with human values as well as how our society has acculturised these. Social workers have to work as negotiators on the boundaries of very different philosophies born of each family's historical and contextual experience. In some cases to accept the family's solution will be incompatible with the agency's requirement of the social worker (to accept stealing from others as a solution, for example). The worker may not become deviant and stay in the job, although perhaps understanding the requirement on someone else to do so.

Examples include the youngest boy in a family of stealing boys who steals just enough to keep his mother well provided with a focus of concern and the attention of the courts and a probation officer, at a time when she is otherwise seriously depressed and has been making overdose attempts, following her other sons growing up and leaving home; or the boys who are loyal to their mother's pattern of keeping a close circle of protective friends by receiving stolen goods, by stealing the kinds of things that she is used to handling. These are *overt* not inferred solutions to problems; recognised and voiced by the offenders involved. The solution from the social worker's viewpoint cannot include condoning the offence, and has to incorporate authority, clear seeing, the spelling out of the consequences of alternative paths of action as well as commending the protective position from which the choice of the anti-social action was determined.

In order to do their job, social workers are aware of their need to use their authority as well as their understanding (Sainsbury, 1975). We can only be effective if we help the client or family within the realities of the relevant social contexts. If the social worker sees the job as changing those realities he or she will work with communities, institutions and in politics. If however the choice of work is with individuals or families, he or she will focus on how to help them discover possibilities of change in their social realities as the primary task. Both may be done alongside one another, as in some of the most powerful work with community groups. The worker must not however confuse his or her own contexts by imposing personal anger at some of the contexts confronting the family upon *them*, if this depresses and immobilises them further. Such a technique may only be used professionally if one can be sure that it has an empathic or mobilising effect. Such confusions are common because social workers have to bear the same realities, frustrations and constraints as their clients, with the same upsurges of anger that accompany such an experience. That is why they need colleagues, action groups and effective political channels in addition to their daily work. The focus of a social worker's professional energy is to enable the family to confront these alternatives themselves as options, with some element of their own volition and choice built in. Families can be moved from experiencing themselves as passive victims of social forces (a view with which social workers themselves often concur) to having some choice of action. Such movement often involves techniques more familiar in radical politics or community work than in the therapeutic field, such as confrontation, argument and the linking of family and outside resources. These are tactics that many social workers use in relation to their own agencies but are less comfortable using in relation to families. If we think of families, like institutions, as having similar features of inflexibility of patterning in relation to certain problems, it is easier to accept that similar tactics of confrontation or persistence in holding an alternative view are part of what is sometimes required to achieve a shift.

Thinking different and thinking small

The greatest dilemma for social workers however, as we have seen, is how to link what they have learnt as professional behaviour, to some form of intervention that makes sense to the family itself. This may mean giving up something of what has been learnt both at the level of theory and of behaviour in the conduct of an interview. It can feel difficult and 'disloyal' to give up something which has been won by hard work, and approved by a qualifying body for sets of alternative behaviours (which may even require social workers to be less 'professional' – learning to be rude with clients, how to interrupt, how to play with children, how to fight with adolescents, how to share jokes). These skills often come more readily to residential workers who are used to working close to their residents. The question each person must ask for themselves is related to what makes more sense to the family. Much professional time has been spent trying to negotiate families into an ethos which is culturally alien to them. Social workers have always been taught that they should start where their client is, but they have often *not* been taught frames for freedom of exchange between where their client is and where they themselves are, and may not feel the trivia of daily life is actually the medium of where work should be.

In fact, I believe the freedom not to act with a professional front can be a mark of high professionalism where it is linked to an exact understanding of the meaning of what is taking place. Having a mother talking seriously with an eight year old about farting on top of a bus; recognising the meaning behind the sexual acting-out of adolescent boys in expressed rudeness 'Fucking child mental health people keep your bollocks small'; refusing to allow a family to move off the issue of who makes the son's school sandwiches until a different solution which does not end in a punch-up between mother and son is reached; taking seriously a step-mother's rage with her step-children when they arrive for each weekend with a bag full of dirty clothes, is the stuff of family life. The relationship between these 'bits' and the family whole will become clearer more quickly as the experience of working with families grows.

Families at risk and the implications for direct family work

The 'cycle of deprivation' thesis

A number of studies arising from the DHSS/SSRC programme of research initiated in 1972 have now investigated in detail many aspects of deprivation and the process of transmission of deprivation through the generations. Many of the empirical studies, together with literature reviews, have now been published. Madge (1983) has summarised features of this research into families at risk, and developed some guidelines for predicting the families in which children are most likely to suffer. These are important for social workers in that research shows that in spite of the odds being stacked against certain children and families, there is very mixed support for the cycle of deprivation thesis; and more interest in the concept of resilience in children and the difference that enables many families to cope, and to do much better than the pattern of the previous generation suggest.

Coffield (1983) looking at the most severely disorganised families in the study, pointed out that there was no inevitability that parents and children would have particular difficulties in common, and some of the children from very adverse backgrounds were doing well at school. Similarly Tonge *et al.* (1983) found very favourable outcomes in *some* of the families of children of problem parents, and marked discrepancies between the adult circumstances of mothers and sisters brought up in the same household. McLaughlin and Empson (1983) in a study of sisters and their young children found that mothers (the grandmothers of the study) had a negligible influence on styles of child rearing in their own daughters, who were more likely to take advice from Health Visitors of the Infant Welfare Clinic.

Madge (1983) has neatly summarised the research for intergenerational continuity on identified families at risk in the following way:

> Not all studies have defined family risk in the same way and not all have adopted similar methodologies. Nevertheless the findings combine to confirm and illustrate these general conclusions on cycles of deprivation . . . Our research has verified that under certain conditions, some family members display consistent patterns. This indicates that like can beget like. At the same time however it has provided convincing evidence of widespread discontinuities which suggests that rags to riches and other family contrasts are also found (p. 198).

She has identified an 'at risk ABC', which if used in detail helps to develop the professional eye as to which families are most vulnerable. While social workers are likely to know about the risks or poverty highlighted by research they are less likely to be aware of the difference that it seems good family relationships can make as can intimate peer relationships outside the family. Also there are pointers from many of the studies quoted that very specific work done with parents and children to *improve the quality of talking and interaction between them in a focused way* makes a great difference to the subsequent development and overall emotional and educational progress of the children.

There is now some concensus on the important dimensions of parenting (Rutter, 1975; Rutter, Quinton and Liddell, 1983). There are parenting skills which reflect sensitivity to children's cues and a responsiveness to different needs at different stages of development; social problem-solving and coping skills; interaction skills, knowing how to talk to and play with children; discipline skills, effective in the double sense of bringing about the desired behaviour in the child, doing so in a way that results in harmony and increasing the child's self control. As a specific type of social relationship, parenting also has broader social and interactional qualities that leave enduring impact on children.

Mothers in care as parents
An interesting question for all those involved in maintaining families as social matrices in which to nurture children, as opposed to other forms of social group setting like children's homes, is whether children who go into care and are not placed with families suffer additional difficulties when they themselves become parents. Recent research (Rutter, Quinton and Liddell, 1983) suggests that they do. From a contrasting group of women matched for age and social class the findings were eloquent, although the reasons for the difficulty are complex.

Mothers who had been in care were twice as likely to have *parenting problems* themselves. For example nearly half found it hard to express warmth to their children, nearly two thirds appeared insensitive to their children's distress and a third did not play with their child. More of them found it harder to discipline their children than mothers who had not been in care.

In comparing current family circumstances the 'in-care' mothers were more likely to lack supportive relationships in the home or with their families, less likely to be in a stable marriage or cohabitation (43 per cent *v.* 93 per cent) and where they were cohabiting three times as likely as the comparison groups to have a severely discordant relationship. Perhaps unsurprisingly, 71 per cent of the in-care group versus 15 per cent of the comparison group wished they had someone to turn to for help on practical matters. They were more likely to have large families and for the children to have different fathers (43 per cent *v.* 93 per cent).

The mothers had a much higher rate of *psychiatric disorder* than the control group, 44 per cent as against 2 per cent in the comparison group having spent time in mental hospital, and 78 per cent were assessed as having some currently handicapping psychiatric problem at time of interview. Their cohabitees were more likely to have probation or prison records (over half, compared with 13 per cent in the comparison group) and twice as many had a psychiatric disorder.

On the other hand, one third (51 per cent) showed good parenting. What accounted for the difference? Early admission (under two years old) to the institution made one difference, since this group had the most severe parenting problems.

However the factor making *most* difference to parenting were good qualities in a husband. Although the group as a whole were four times more likely to marry men with problems than the comparison group and were therefore less likely to find supportive relationships, where they did this exerted a powerful protective influence.

The conclusion of this study seem to me worth summarising since a high proportion of the work social workers are faced with is in the families where a member has been in care, and the implications for developing protective mechanisms both during the in-care experience and after leaving care have not been thought through, in terms of how support might continue to be available. Minimal indications for support might include:

1. Support of an intensive and long-lasting kind to *mothers*: (a) through the use of groups for themselves; (b) to discuss parenting problems and increase the range of parenting skills – either in individual family work or in work with groups of families; (c) through very specific focus in family work on improving the amount and quality of talking, and increasing positive rewarding interactions between mothers and children and decreasing negative sequences leading to violence.

2. Helping *parents* negotiate marital rows in ways that are more likely to lead to successful outcome and less likely to involve the children.

3. Recognising that a request for alternative care for a child may be part of a mother's inbuilt survival kit. In families where the social services have literally been the extended family from time to time such a request may have a positive function on behalf of the future life of the family and need special recognition in that light.

The effect of unemployment on families
Children in large families with an unemployed head are particularly likely to be living in overcrowded conditions, be poorly clothed, have

inadequate bedding and a poor diet. The evidence of the effect of unemployment on family roles and relationships is unclear because it is out of date. The effect in the 1930s (and 1940s) should not necessarily be seen as similar today. However Komatovsky (1940) found that families who had got on well before unemployment got closer, and those with existing earlier difficulties grew more distant. There is no hard evidence that desertion or marital breakdown correlates more strongly with unemployment.

Poverty however has other effects on children, such as more hospital admissions through higher illness (Brennan and Stolen, 1976). Fagin (1981) notes more sleeping and eating disturbances and more accidents. Portsmouth Social Services Research and Intelligence Unit found that 43 per cent of the fathers of children in care were unemployed in 1976 and over half of those requesting financial support to enable their children to remain at home had in the recent past been in receipt of unemployment benefit. In 1979, Birmingham Social Service Department found that over half of the families of children received into care were dependent on state benefits and over two thirds of the households received no male wage due to unemployment or single parent status.

Most important in distinguishing between families in ostensibly similar circumstances who survive resiliently and those who don't is the quality of family relationships. Family cohesion and support are protective against stress. There is an accumulating body of evidence which indicates the value of close relationships for health and well being (Brown and Harris, 1978; Madge, 1983).

4
Initial Work with the Family

Most people working with families regularly now agree that certain sorts of beginning are more productive than others. Within the creation of a temporary security made by the social worker sitting down with a family, there are processes that help the family to work on their own anxiety, that enable them to begin to define in more conscious ways why they think they have come or have sought outside intervention (or face the reality of why it has been imposed upon them by law), and that are more likely to help them begin to do some work on this between them. Families themselves are as likely to see no point in their coming as to be well motivated, and may very well be violently opposed to being involved. The social worker therefore needs to have some conviction about what is being done, and needs a good 'selling line' to convey the integrity of his or her purpose, either by letter or word of mouth, to the group he or she is hoping to see. In this country, a greater proportion of social workers see families for first interviews than continue to work with them as a group (Gorell Barnes, 1980) since nearly all family work takes place in agencies that believe in offering a variety of professional interventions to the families they see.

The setting in which the family are seen will itself affect the process of the initial interview and the expectations of the family before the interview begins. Pollitzer (1980) has discussed some of the contextual elements of the agency work and the way in which the building itself creates expectations for families.

The majority of families still come to social workers because someone other than the family itself is experiencing stress as the result of the behaviour of one or more of the family members, although it has been found that the more localised the office the higher the rate of self referral. As a result of the services available to all families, such as the Infant and Child Welfare Clinics and the Education Service there is also a choice open to families about where they make their problem known. Historical attachment to certain aspects of Welfare State provision may make referral to a hospital department for help with a 'disguised' problem more acceptable to some families than open discussion with someone based in a social service department with its inevitable ticket of 'not coping'. For other families however, previous experience of help with particular focal problems such as the short-term care of children during a hospitalisation may make social services a part of the extended family (Jordan, 1972; Madge, 1983). A high proportion of mothers seeking care for their children will have had in-care experience themselves, and therefore will have very mixed feelings about looking for help with their own children.

Others may come out of habit rather than choice; in principle it is likely that social service departments will have to deal with the highest proportion of families in crisis and in need (see Chapter 2).

The professional family: convening the network

The extended-family aspect of the way in which some families use and depend on more than one agency for different aspects of their own support, means that it may be vital to consider the professional network of the family as a part of the thinking about what is going on, who is involved and what is to be done. Social workers will need to use their own experience to make intuitive hunches about who else in the network or a family may hold an essential piece of information that helps put the problem before them in perspective. Auerswald (1968) has written a classic paper demonstrating parallels between agency and family fragmentation. Roberts (1982) has given many examples of multiple agency allegiancies in which families are being fragmented between difering services, and explores this in terms of problems within and between agencies related to trust. Balancing short-term time available against long-term time is always problematic but gathering crucial information may save time in the long run and lead to more relevant intervention.

The home interview

A very high proportion of first-interview family work takes place within the family's own home. Bloch (1973) discussed the clinical home visit in a detailed way that reads strangely to social workers used to conducting much of their work in the home. He highlighted many potential aspects of making a visit to the home that can be adapted for different purposes. These include a tour of the house, including rooms not organised for show, and consideration of the contrast between public and private areas, the assessment of emotional exchange through the serving of food and a considered view of the style and management of family space. While social workers always resist the policing role that is implicit in such an idea, Davies (1981) points out that a failure to take such overall assessment on behalf of society seriously, may lead to some other less humanist group of professionals being given such a role; especially in cases of suspected or known child neglect or abuse. Going to the 'right part of the house' when assessing the deprived or depriving aspects of family organisation can be of great value in planning future work with the family, especially if social workers talk their way round getting mother and children to tell them about the use of different spaces and what they mean to each of them. Cade and Southgate (1979) have shown how the use of house space can be a highly effective feature of family work and marking family change. This can be especially valuable if the assessment of standards of child care is one of the purposes of the visit, since the contrast between 'front' rooms (a term which has after all a double meaning) and the barren cheerlessness of rooms to which children are relegated, can be startling information on the quality and stresses of family life. Lindsey (1979) has emphasised the importance of establishing a setting which makes clear to all the members of the family that the purpose of the home visit is for therapeutic work to be done. She points out how a 'setting' can easily be avoided by the worker assuming the habit of 'dropping in', thus being forced to see whoever is there rather than those whom he or she believes to be important. A boundary can be made by the social worker acknowledging the difference between time spent in the family which is necessarily 'arranged' time, and time when he or she is absent, which is family time.

Lindsey also highlights some key aspects of maintaining authority while the interview takes place: sit where you can see everyone and have eye control; leave social exchange which takes up time like cups of tea to the end of the interview; don't begin until everyone you want to be there is there. (The cup of tea however can be an important 'marker' that the family are now ready to talk seriously, so I think in this as in all things, the context will help the worker decide whether it is merely a distraction. Sainsbury (1975) has some nice comments on how the worker's capacity to wait for the tea to be 'mashed' is taken as an indication of their patience and interest.) I have also found it useful to mark out the physical space in the interview in terms of everyone being able to see and hear what is going on. It may be that if someone retreats to the corridor in rage they can still hear what is going on and are therefore part of the session. If they go to the lavatory and lock themselves in however, that is clearly 'leaving the session' and the family will have to take a decision about how to deal with it. Byng Hall (1982) has also written about the inclusion of key neighbours and relatives who may, by their being 'around' at the time of the visit, be indicating their necessary involvement in the work. Clarke (1980) has given some imaginative examples of how to make use of meal-time issues in helping deeper family problems.

The agency interview

An interview will start better if the therapist feels he or she is providing a reasonably comfortable environment for the family to be in. Pollitzer (1980) and Adams and Hill (1983) have described the difficulties of achieving this in social work departments. While it is unsatisfactory for family work to be attempted in rooms that are too small for the right number of chairs to be included, families are very adaptable. A small table with some toys or drawing material, for children who will get restless without things other than 'words' to relate to, is an asset. Most agencies are able to provide at least one room which can be seen as a family or group room, in which adequate furniture is available for both purposes. It helps to have a large cardboard box labelled with the family name into which any drawings, or other offerings can be put, along with small toys or plasticine. Children of all ages, as well as adults seem to enjoy plasticine. Felt tip pens and sheets of paper are useful but not for very small children.

While it would be ridiculous to aim for too much 'planning' in many departments, it is possible to create a working environment for a family fairly quickly if the social worker has a small personal space to keep things in. This can be a desk drawer, a shoe box on a shelf, or a coat pocket. It indicates preparation to the family, and awareness of their different ages and capacity to participate in different ways. It will also save the social worker time and energy for the interview itself if the children feel contained.

Who makes up the family and how do you involve them?

It is apparent from studies I have referred to (SSRC, 1978; Gorell Barnes, 1980) and from my experience of teaching introductory work with families over twelve years, that social workers in hospitals and clinics still feel more comfortable about inviting whole families in, than do social workers who do not feel that the agency *itself* is seen as having a caring function in the eyes of the community. If the profession's own anticipation is that inviting a father or boyfriend in to the session means inviting an angry man who will not want to be there, it is not surprising that there is reluctance to do so. Dealing with angry parents comes high on the list of things given in response to the question 'What do you find difficult handling in family interviews?' which I ask in training sessions. It is therefore vital that the social worker experiences a purpose in having the family there. Using your own wording; and wording that will suit the family; variations on the following truths can be developed to fit the family and its cultural expectations, in a letter to both parents in the home and to the other children.

1. We like to see all members of the family because you all know each other much better than I do, and you can all pool your ideas on what's wrong and what can be done to put it right. My job will be there to see where I can add anything to that. *Or where culturally appropriate:*
2. Fathers, as head of the family, are very important when matters like this have to be discussed (decisions like this have to be taken) and we can't act without you. If you are not able to take time off work because it threatens your job I can arrange to see the family with you at the beginning or end of the day. If you would like me to contact your place of employment please let me know.
3. In families everybody has a point of view and these are not always the same. In our experience it is very important to hear what everybody has to say, so I would like to visit you on 10 Jan. Please can everybody be there even if it's only for a short time.
4. We often find other people in the family have ideas about how to deal with the trouble that's going on and that a chance to talk about it altogether produces a much better plan than mum and I could make on our own.

In families of different cultures different people will be seen as vital to problem solving. This could be mother's mother or mother's brother in a West Indian household; father's mother or mother's brother in an Indian household or indeed numbers of brothers on both sides of the family to balance up the 'fairness of assessment' in a domestic row. This knowledge of who is necessary in assessing family resources requires a working awareness of the different structures in households of different cultures. Part of this can only develop with experience but part of it can also be studied in the work of others (Ballard, 1982; Gorell Barnes, 1975; Barrow, 1982; Oakley, 1982).

As I hope is apparent from the tone of these letters the emphasis is on seeing the family as a resource group, rather than as an aspect of the pathology which the social worker wishes to study. Sainsbury (1975) shares comments from families which show how they experience difference between workers who are 'with' them and who are 'studying' them or too official. Initial approaches often failed, either because of a tone that was too remote, or because it was too official or threatening. Where it is thought that all members of a family may not speak English, translation into the appropriate language or dialect shows seriousness of purpose.

Who comes to the interview?

When the first interview takes place my personal approach is to see whoever turns up or whoever is at home, rather than insisting on 'whole family', since if the preparatory work has been properly done, this is itself information about the way this family operate in relation to the outside world and the current problem. The meaning of the absences and the absent members of the system always needs to be borne in mind during the interview, since it is a communication that may be important. Who comes instead may also be a surprise. In the following extract, the social worker is mistakenly trying to focus on the meaning of the father's absence and is floundering in the face of the united solidarity of the three-generational system of the women in the family. The precipitating crisis involved the theft of large sums of money in the home and the possible reception into care of the thief, Brenda.

Mother (Loretta), Maternal grandmother (MGM); Brenda (14, identified troublemaker) Paul (3).

MGM: Well he's been bullying her and ignoring her because she's not conforming.
S.W.:   Tell me about Bill, why isn't he here.
Mother: Well, his job is important.
S.W.:   You obviously don't think that's why he's not here.
MGM: (*Shakes head sadly*) He's not mature enough love, look I'll tell you what, he's got thousands in the bank and he won't buy himself new clothes. They have their food and he makes sure they have their £40 every month, but we buy in between – I do. Loretta hasn't had new clothes – she's had that coat three years – You couldn't go to Bill for help, he needs help himself in my opinion. (*Three-year-old son of Bill and Loretta bashes radiator loudly during this.*)
S.W.:   Is that why you think he isn't here.
MGM: He's not here because you can't tell him and you can't tell him lots of things.

Mother: (*simultaneously*) Because he's at work.
S.W.: I know he's at work but I wrote to both of you offering to make a time when he could come. Did he read the letter?
Mother: No, well to tell you the truth I didn't show it to him.
MGM: No, nor would I. Not Bill.
Mother: He would have gone mad.
MGM: Well, we don't know if he would have gone mad.
S.W.: Why didn't you show him the letter? Does he act for Brenda as her father – I'm not clear what happened to her own father.
MGM: Oh well, Loretta divorced him, he was no good for her, she'd known him as a child and she said, 'I'm going to marry him', and I said I'd never interfere with my kids and I didn't. And what he wanted was a mother – he loved *me* – he needed *my* help.
S.W.: You're telling me now your daughter has married two men who need help – (*looks to Brenda who is now giggling*) is that right – you've a strong Nan there Brenda (*patting MGM – all laugh – youngest son stops bashing radiator and joins group*).

This extract shows some of the problems of beginning. It is only when the social worker 'joins' the system by acknowledging the strength of the grandmother that she begins to make headway. In this family it became clear that the two independently powerful systems, that of maternal grandmother, daughter and granddaughter, and that of husband – wife – children could not meet in the same room. In order to begin work with that part of the family that took primary responsibility for the children, it was first necessary to work with and make a boundary between that family and the family to whom the children ran away when things got too hot: their 'dear hardworking-nan' and her cohabitee. Work with this family therefore took place in three settings, to fit the different family sub-systems; at home with mum, Bill, Paul, and Brenda; at her nan's house with her cohabitee, Jim; and in the office with Brenda's elder brother, Brenda and mum to do some work on their first family, especially including the children's own father who was in prison.

Opening the session: practical issues
Whatever style of addressing the family the social worker chooses, there are certain areas of family behaviour and family functioning he or she will want to attend to. It is a good idea to dispel the anxiety to do with the setting itself in order to concentrate on the purpose for which the family have come. Preliminary courtesies are part of all therapeutic work. There should be enquiry as to whether everyone knows why they are here today, personal contact with each family

member to find out about their anticipations in coming to a family interview, discussion of neutral topics such as schools and work and clarification of family names and ages, and forms of address.

In the course of this process the social worker has the chance to begin to learn about the relationships between family members, as well as demonstrating respect for the family by his manner. He begins to assess their mood and pace. Is it appropriate to the occasion?: too angry, sad or hilarious? How do the parents treat the children, and how do the children respond to the requests of the parents? Do the family present a united front. . . if not, who looks at whom before speaking and who disagrees? Who sits next to whom is used as information by all social workers, and commented on by some. In all this noting of the process, the social worker has to maintain an open mind about the meaning of the information.

Although each of us as professionals begins to clock up detail from the beginning of an interview we are not in a position to use that detail valuably on behalf of the family until we have a greater overall view. One may or may not wish to use observations to change the rules of behaviour *in* the session: 'I notice that you always let your mother speak for you . . .' while we are together I want you to speak for your-self.' This decision to change family patterns by intervening during the session, and how it is done, depend on the style and theoretical frame of the social worker. In general, in the first half of the session, it is of greater value to observe what is going on accurately and try to understand it, rather than to be intent on creating new patterns for the family. In some families, however, the problem is stated from the moment the family sit down in the room; and in a time of crisis, to follow the problem closely and expand from there, may be of most value to the family. Here is an example.

A problem-focused beginning (Tracey severely bruised following a family fight)

Sequence 1

S.W.:   *(non-specific) (to parents):* I've heard a bit about the problem from the police and I thought it would be useful to meet as a family; when something like this has been going on in a family for some time everyone has usually got something to say about it. (*to boys*) – I don't know your names. (*to youngest*) You're. . .
Bob: Bob.
S.W.:   Bob, and you're how old? Let's see now.
Bob: Thirteen.

S.W.: Thirteen, and which school do you go to?

Bob: Grange Hill.

S.W.: Is that the same school as Tracey?

Bob: No, she's still in Nursery.

S.W.: Will you introduce me to your little sister?

Bob: This is Tracey.

S.W.: Hello Tracey, how old are you?

Tracey: Six in September.

S.W.: Nearly six: so you'll be going to the same school as Julie. Hello Julie (*Julie seated between Bob and Mum*).

Julie: (ten): Hello.

S.W.: You look well placed to tell me what's going on.

Julie: Well, there's been a lot of fighting.

S.W.: Tracey do you know about this? (*Tracey nods*)

S.W.: I see; was it at home, did anyone get hurt? (*Tracey points at Dad*)

S.W.: Dad got hurt?

Tracey: No, Dad hit him. (*nodding at Bob*)

S.W.: Dad hit him; did he hit anyone else?

Tracey: He hit me.

S.W.: He hit *you*. Who did he hit hardest, you or Bob?

Tracey: Bob was naughty.

S.W.: Bob was naughty, so he hit him. Were you naughty!

Tracey: No, I tried to stop him.

Mum: She got in the way like: they were fighting.

S.W.: Is Tracey the one that gets in the way most when people are fighting or does anyone else? How about you, Julie?

Julie: I keep out. I keep in my room.

S.W.: So you keep out, and Tracey keeps the peace; where are you, Mum?

Mum: I was out doing my little job.

Father: Tracey's the one; she keeps peace.

S.W.: Uh huh, I see, you're a good peacekeeper – well that must be quite a difficult job at five years old.

Middle stages

To illustrate the issues of the middle stages of the initial interview, I will continue with the same family. Later in the session, the social worker is trying to make the children sort out and agree on their reality in such a way that they can do some work on it in an age-appropriate manner. She is using the children as experts on the details of their own problems.

Sequence 2.

S.W.:   Well, make sure that's what she's trying to say.

Julie: I think that's what she's trying to say.

S.W.:   Well make sure, ask her.

Julie: Is that what you're trying to say?

Tracey: No.

S.W.:   Are you sure that you two understand each other – let's just get straight what really happens between you two. (*Focuses*) Now, Tracey what happens when Julie won't come and rescue you?

Tracey: Well, I shout at her to come in and stop them but she won't, she just watches.

S.W.:   How would you like her to rescue you?

Tracey: If she would just go to the shop for Dad it wouldn't happen.

S.W.:   So you'd like her to do more for Dad?

Tracey: Yes because of his leg, it hurts him.

S.W.:   So then the problem is you two, is that right, you have a quarrel, a fight and you run in Tracey, to sort it out.

Tracey: Yes.

S.W.:   Is there anything else?

Tracey: No, that's most of it.

S.W.:   How does that lead you to be hit by Dad?

Tracey: Because he says I shouldn't stick my nose in, but I think we should look after him when Mum is out ...

S.W.:   So you would like your Mum and Dad to sort out who is to look after Dad when she's out; it looks as though the responsibility ... who's in charge ... needs sorting out here. Who would you like to discuss this with, Tracey, your Mum or your Dad ... which one would you like to talk to first?

The sick father was the central person in the way the family organised itself, and rather than challenging the organisation, the family were helped to rethink the pecking order, so that Tracey was kept out of fights between mum and dad, and dad and Bob.

In this last example we are moving towards the middle stage of a first interview. The social worker should now have in mind the question of what will be achieved by the end of the session and the links to be made to future work.

It is important to accept and to confirm the protective aspects of the system the family bring, however dysfunctional it may appear in the social worker's eyes, and not to let the family go away without this sense of confirmation well established. Only if they have received a confirming message somewhere during the interview are they likely to accept any initiated change, and to continue working in between sessions, and want to come back. Where a family have felt that their reality has been understood, accepted and confirmed as the best they can do in terms of the options they saw as open to them, it becomes possible to challenge what is going wrong in the system in a variety of ways.

It is also important to note that for each social worker there will be some families that they will personally be unable to work with or to confirm in any way. In such cases it may be essential to bring in a colleague who has a different perspective or to pass the case to someone else. Aspects of family life that are unmanageable by one worker, may be seen by another quite differently. A consultation leading to reframing of the family dilemma for the social worker may classify those aspects of pattern the social worker cannot get a professional stance on alone; either because of its complexity or because of a particular mix of pattern that reflects something from the social worker's own background. The use of a colleague as 'consultant' or 'team' is discussed further in Chapter 11.

5
Divorce and the Single-parent Family System

Family pattern has so far been considered as an entity developed through the repeated impact of daily mutual influence. Parents who separate and divorce are different from parents who stay together. In deciding to separate they take a deliberate decision to push the marital system beyond the usual limits of its pattern. In order to create new ways of living, old ways have to be disbanded. The difficulty of achieving this kind of change should not be underestimated, since in spite of the changing outlook towards divorce, the process itself is rarely emotionally easy. Sensitivity to the violence, rage and acute personal turmoil that accompanies divorce should always be part of professional awareness when involved with families going through the process.

In this chapter the focus will be on aspects of the adjustments that families have to make while going through a systemic change from two-parent to one-parent family systems and from one-parent into other kinds of family balance, such as cohabitations, step families and the maintenance of relationships with absent but still intermittently present parental figures.

The divorce process

Most people get divorced without coming for any kind of therapeutic help. The focus here will be on some aspects of the divorce process as these present in members of families going through the radical changes that divorce requires. Sometimes these processes produce dysfunctional patterns in the temporary adaptations made by the family system, which results in disturbance that is sufficiently distressing to lead to referral by self or others. Richards (Richards and Dyson, 1982) has pointed out that 'divorce is not an event, it is a process'. Aspects of the process attended to here relate:

1.   to families currently going through the divorce process at the time
     of presentation;
2.   to families who have recently completed a divorce and are living
     as a single-parent unit with the other partner in a visiting role;
3.   families who have lived apart for a number of years but do not
     appear to have negotiated aspects of the divorce process in a
     way that leaves them sufficiently free of the original marriage
     to have independent emotional existence.

The problem may come in any shape or form; for example Alice (8)
cutting electric leads, filling the Hoover with a potential explosive and
destroying furniture. Annie (7) soliciting strange men and inviting
them to come with her for walks. Coreen (7) nervous ticks and grunts,
Danny (14) attacking his mother violently following the father's
leaving the marital home. Jim (13) being attacked violently by his
mother, provoked by his teasing. The social worker may also meet
whole families who are depressed or disorganised following a divorce,
where there are symptoms in one or more family members.

From a family systems' perspective, divorce is not seen as family
dissolution but as an alteration in the family balance (and family
structure) from which an altered family system of relationship will
evolve. In the process of change, pain is being located or experienced
more in one part of the family than another. All of the original family
members may and often do continue to play significant roles in the
new family shapes which evolve, and parents may continue equal
parenting. The structure of the family will however change radically
and change always involves loss, however good what is moved on to
becomes. The professional seeing the family has to keep in mind these
two aspects of the process: first, the continuity of the *idea* of the family
and, second, the loss of the original *shape* or *structure* which will
inevitably need to be housed. As one exhausted mother said to her
children following a row about Christmas access: 'I think it's the idea
of the family together as it was that you're missing, even though it's
better now Dad and I don't fight so much.'

Developing an approach that takes the *structure* of the family as the
centre of the therapeutic work the family need to do, and helping the
family to reorganise successfully, does not preclude emotional issues.
On the contrary it highlights them and cathects the emotion on to the
different aspects of daily living structure that are being attended to.
Mother is less likely to find herself hysterical with rage and futility if
she has done advance planning on getting through the weekend with
three children alone; father less likely to be overcome with blame and
recrimination, if, when he arranges to take over the in-house child

care while mother goes out, he does not find all their school clothes are dirty and that no food has been left for them to eat. For younger children, knowing who is collecting them from school or taking them to a hospital appointment; for all ages, knowing where they can sleep when they visit the out-of-home parent and where they can leave some possessions; for older children, knowing whether they can have a key there, being clear about what the arrangements are for 'dropping in', these are the assurances of continuity of a form of life together that helps the family handle its own adaptations to the new structure successfully.

Families who are going through the process can talk about these daily things without being overcome by guilt, blame and rage, if the professional believes in and insists on their importance. A useful focus for the social worker involved therefore is on the maintenance of developmentally appropriate structures for the kids in spite of whatever chaos the adults are going through.

Divorce is still a psychosocial transition most people feel sorry to have to make, even though it may simultaneously be felt as a great relief. Families who arrive in crisis are not usually finding the process 'a new developmental drama rich with possibilities for growth' at the time they come (Walters, 1981). However this potential for alternative development that new structures offer needs to be held on to by the social worker on behalf of the family. Meanwhile professional recognition also needs to include the knowledge that the family life space is altered. Multiple drastic changes have taken place which may include loss of home, loss of role and status as formerly defined and perhaps above all loss of routine; the pattern of those daily habits that enable people to cruise through the dullest bits of life and save energy for new ideas and emergencies. Physical and emotional energy are instead required all the time in the process of new family and personal organisation. Such adjustments of the whole psycho-social biological system simultaneously, which is what divorce entails, can be exhausting and parents, especially those with primary responsibility for the children, may need to be reminded to eat, rest, sleep and physically look after themselves.

The interaction between the couple and the way they keep channels of communication and negotiation open are crucial to how separation is managed. Clearly this is the area that most often breaks down completely. However any conciliation work at this time can help improve the quality of future relationships and the way decisions are taken on access, finance, shared parenting, and so on. Wallerstein and Kelly (1980) and Richards (1981) have suggested that this is a crucial variable in the children's subsequent adaptation to the di-

vorce of their parents. The emphasis of conciliation work, developed
through the probation service, the Bristol Conciliation Service and
other independent groups (Robinson, 1982b) is on the continued
tasks of shared parenting as a vital job which continues following
separation and focusses on the boundaries necessary for this to be
carried out successfully within a clear, structural framework agreed
by both parents.

Separating the parental quarrel from the children's lives, and
freeing them from the overt guilt of the separation is another important issue during this period. Mummy and Daddy are separating – a
parent is not leaving the family because of something the children
have done. It is often at the point that this is clarified that the child
can move from problem behaviour to getting on with the divorce
process. For example:

Mother: I find the situation at home quite intolerable.
Simon: What does that mean?
Mother: It means I don't like it – it upsets me.
S.W.:   Can you tell the children a bit more about that – I think that
would be very helpful.
Mother: I feel there isn't any place in the house for me really except
my bedroom at the top. Everything is so muddled, the house is in an
absolute mess; it's not how I would keep it if it were mine.
Father: But it is yours you see – that's the point we're making – it's
you that's opting out of the house, not the house that's opting out of
you – not the family that's opting out of you – you could have it any
way you want it.
Mother: But I don't want it – I don't want to be there anyway – it's
horrible – it's very difficult to explain.
Simon: But Mummy it is your home.
Mother: No it's not really my home any more.
Simon: It is, you live there.
Mother: No . . . there's always a lot of noise.
S.W.:   Can you finish that with Simon because I think that's very
important – you're saying it *is* her home, you're saying it isn't – can
you tell him why.
Mother: In a way it's my home because I'm with you but I don't
think my home is with Daddy, that's why I don't think it's my home.
Simon: It *is* your home.
Mother: It is because *you're* there, not otherwise.

The immediate divorce period involves children in many worries
about how their parents are going to manage on their own as well as

manage their parenting. Issues such as who is looking after them on which days, who is responsible for shopping, clothes washing, school appointments and pocket money are preoccupying alone, without adult responsibilities of rent, rates and bills. Adult worries and child-sized worries often need appropriate working out. Supporting parents struggling with the economic reality of not being able to afford two dwellings and the shift-work child care of in-house, out-house arrangements, seem to me of primary importance, rather than a focus on the ways in which parents may be failing their children.

Mother on her own

There are many aspects of the reorganisation into a one-parent family to do with survival. Hetherington *et al.* (1978) have shown the decrease in parental competence that follows the immediate separation and the increase in aggression shown by mothers with custody towards their children, especially their sons. Where one person holds all roles of both authority and nurture within the house they are likely to be tired. At a time when the raw emotion of separation is still a part of daily experience, a sense of being drained, helpless and unable to do even simple things, can complicate daily management and parenting. Children can become very enmeshed with their parents in an attempt to comfort them, and help them in their daily struggle. Often such help is inappropriate for that age and stage of development. Jenny, aged seven, sought men out not just because she was missing her father but because her mother was missing her father. She brought two men home, an electrician and a plumber. When it was pointed out that she seemed to be choosing men who would be helpful to her mother, without her mother having to be emotionally disloyal to the husband from whom she had not yet decided to separate, Jenny and her mother experienced both shock and relief and some further work on the different issues involved took place. Six sessions with this family stopped Jenny seeking out men, got Jenny out of mother's bed; moved her back into her peer group; got her sleeping on her own (with some gerbils which she looked after) got mother enjoying free time in the evening and some agreed times between mother and child when they could be separate and be together. Simultaneously mother sorted out arrangements with father, with decreasing involvement of Jenny in the ongoing rows between them. The professional work emphasised supporting mother as an adult, allowing Jenny not to be an adult and to enjoy being a seven-year-old, got her out of the triangle of rows between mother and father and allowed mother and child to express and grapple with some of their anger towards each other and the situation of which they were both a part.

The temporary inbalance in which a child feels responsibility for the emotional management of a parent is shown in the delicate interplay of a mother and a little girl in this extract.

S.W.:   Does your Mummy tell you lots of things!
Tracey: Do you, Mummy!
Mum: Do you think I do!
Tracey: (*to S.W.*) She doesn't sometimes, she tries to keep it to herself but I know she will tell me in the end.
S.W.:   Do you think you help your Mummy!
Tracey: Do I, Mummy!
Mum: Do you think you do. Sometimes you do!
Tracey: Do I help you more or do I not help you more!

This last question is one that I think many children bring in the disguised form of 'problems', and social workers in the process of their interactions with the family can help make the parent–child boundaries clearer.

Father on his own

In 1979, 7 per cent of divorced fathers had custody of their children. Jones (1983) has considered some of the dilemmas peculiar to work with father-led families where the worker is female, highlighting the belief professionals so often fall into, that of their indispensability to the family. She emphasised instead the value of helping the family map their social and intimacy network so that they can make their own decisions about who to use for support more clearly. Where fathers do not have custody, their contact with their children tends to decrease over time, (Hetherington *et al.*, 1978; Burgoyne and Clarke, 1982) and so does their influence. This finding needs to be noted and turned into a positive strategy by social workers carrying out post-divorce work – children, especially boys, do better over time if a good paternal contact can be maintained (Wallerstein and Kelly, 1981; 1982). Where the quality of contact is negative or abusive however, it is likely to create poor relations between mother and child.

Each family or household creates its own routines and structures within which the universals of separation, loss, anger, despair and hope that divorce entails are housed. In psychotherapy many therapists choose to work with their patients directly on the emotions and the underlying human and developmental factors that make these at times unmanageable. The structures of family life may be bypassed. In family work however, the structures provide an essential route into the particular organisation of the family and allow the social worker access to as much of the emotional chaos as the family can manageably share at any one time. By focusing on the daily reality of how key aspects of family routine are different now from how they used to be; who has taken on new jobs now that father has left and how these are managed; who helps in the preparation and cleaning up of food; who sits down together at mealtimes; who is the one who doesn't let mother have any peace in the evening and why that might be, the pursuit of issues of loss and change within the small details of daily living, attend to the larger issues within a frame that helps the family to avoid immobilisation. Living daily lives in a new way is the focus.

As Parkes (1972) has pointed out crisis provides an opportunity to re-examine familiar assumptions. Old ideas and traditional viewpoints can be examined and new ones planned and rehearsed. Rappoport (1970) writing of short-term crisis-oriented casework with individuals, suggests that the focus of intervention should be on cognitive mastery of the event and help geared towards reality adaptations, with direction, advice, information and ideas offered to enlarge the person's sense of autonomy and mastery; the aim being to develop the client's strengths and repertoire of new solutions. Such ideas underlie a structural approach to intervention with the family in the process of divorce.

One-parent families

The shape of single parenthood is arrived at in many different ways, only one of which is by divorce. The others are by choice, by accident and by death. The structures of single-parent families have some features in common which have implications for the work of the professional, but the manner in which each family arrived at its own structure, its particular storage of patterning, will affect the way the structure is working, and always needs professional attention to its unique qualities.

The first aspect of structure was touched on briefly in discussing the divorce process. There is now only one nominal parent. Marianne Walters, an American family therapist who creates optimism for the single-parent family form, argues for the viability of the one-parent as against the two-parent structure. She argues that since there is only one line for authority and nurture there will be less disagreement about how these issues are handled. She has particularly emphasised the value of the single-parent family form as a context for developing the competence of the children and for initiating family membership into increased sharing and participation (Walters, 1981).

Who becomes the 'other parent'?

Inevitably in a single-parent family, different people inside and outside the family may take on limited aspects of the parenting role to a greater extent than is found in a two-parent family, especially if mother goes out to work. Sometimes an older child takes on such a role and 'becomes' the parent to an extent that impedes their own development.

Jim, aged sixteen, had survived as a healthy male child of a mother who had three cohabitees, two of whom had died by violent means as a result of drink and drugs. Jim's dilemma was that – in representing a man who survived – he had become a family pillar of strength, and the more he was seen in this way the more difficult it became either for him to behave age-appropriately or for his mother to relate to another man more closely than she related to him. When the baby Susan, daughter of Richard who had died of drugs in the parental bed, was ill it was Jim who took her to hospital. Activities with his own age group bored him as 'childish' compared to his wish to show he could be a better father to Susan than her own father had been, and a better husband to his mother than any of her three men had been.

By challenging his mother as a *parent* to Jim as well as to Susan, as well as praising Jim for his understanding of his mother's dilemma and mistrust of her own age group when it came to men who 'died on her', some of the mother's concern to *mother* her eldest son as an alternative to using him as a spouse, became a more open part of the expressed pattern of the family. Jim's younger brother Gary was especially helpful in making clear differences between mothers, fathers and sons and helped Jim see that he was changing the *quality* of his relationship with his mother rather than giving it up altogether 'gaining a son, not losing another cohabitee'. In turn the mother's wish for Jim to have a freer life outside the family where he might be less damaged and have girlfriends of his own was expressed: 'I'm not the one I want him to end up with' (there is ambiguity in the choice of words 'end up'; but still there was a wish for Jim at least to 'end up' separately from her.) Jim was able to separate enough to get a job, which could be seen as another way of supporting his mother by bringing money into the family, and gave him some regular life with a mixed age group outside the home.

Becoming the 'other parent'

Social workers know about the danger of inappropriate overinvolvement with families whom they can undermine by being overhelpful. However the single parent can involve the social worker in a peculiar combination of real helpfulness and make-believe, in which it becomes hard to sort out what is appropriate and what is really fantasy. That is unhelpful since it may prevent the parent from making another more real relationship with someone else more full-time and permanent in their lives. Such people include friends, sisters and grandmothers. Common fantasies in the social worker's head include themselves as replacement partners for the single parent or themselves as parents to the children. They find themselves wondering if they could take the family out for a drive or take the kids for a Christmas treat; and constantly have the feeling 'If only I could do more...'. The chief safeguard for this is to have a supervisor or colleague to share these feelings and wishes with and to get them to help keep to the task of helping the family reorganise in a more adaptive way, that does not include the need for a social worker as an *emotional* component of family life.

Grandmothers

Grandmothers can provide stability, warmth and daily child care without making their daughters feel inferior. They can simply assume that their job is to provide for their grandchildren as part of their culture. However the single mother in Western culture may find that the greater proximity of grandmother makes it more difficult for her to act autonomously and in an adult way that meshes with her perception of herself as an independent woman. Grandmothers may infantilise mothers, reducing them to the same level as the children, both in the manner in which they behave towards them in front of the children and in the way in which they take over aspects of their adult capacity to think for themselves.

In families where grandmother attempts to alter a new balance achieved by mother in a destructive way, it is possible that she may be envying a stability achieved by her daughter with her own children from which she herself is excluded. One way of upsetting this balance is to criticise the children and the mother's child-rearing pattern. Where mother has a partner she may have someone to laugh about it with. Where she has not she may feel extremely persecuted. If the children in turn observe their mother undermined and themselves criticised, they can turn against the weaker and more accessible party; their mother, rather than the stronger party their grand-mother. Such confusion of loyalty will be further complicated where mothers are 'protecting' their own mothers and refuse to tell them to be quiet and mind their own business. At some profound level most women/all mothers wish to be on good terms with their mothers, and where their prior relationship has been poor and they have a history of in-care experience themselves, they may continue to hope for good mothering from their own mothers long after the evidence from adult life shows them it is not available.

Work will involve boundary-making between grandmothers and mothers which may include giving grannies a more appropriate place. 'You are a wonderful woman Mrs Gray, but the more you talk for your daughter the less she will learn to talk for herself', or 'You have so much experience of life that you must spend time making sure your daughter has learnt enough from you to do it her own way so she will be able to manage when you've gone', are ways of opening up the issue of intergenerational difference and the passing of time. Mothers make strange time slips when they see their daughters and need to be helped to remember that these are not the infants in arms they once knew, and daughters need to learn to know and respect and make use of their mothers in a grown-up way.

6

Step-families and Foster Families

Crisis in the family means that the equilibrium of the family has been disturbed in such a way that family members are unable to cope with what is in front of them. Remarriage often proves to be such a crisis. Although remarriage is often seen as an event in which a family, having two parents, is now complete again, the effects are not the same as first family formation and should never be treated as such. If we think of the divorce process as one of changing shape in the family with a resulting rethinking of roles, emotions, tasks and space and the consequent internal readjustment of images of self, then remarriage forms just such another new occasion.

When a new second parent joins a family that has been organised as a single-parent family, a number of aspects of the daily family pattern have to reorganise themselves to include new functions from step-father or cohabitee, and a loss of certain functions for each of the family.

Step-families considered as a group include certain structural differences from first families that are often neglected or deliberately ignored by the families themselves. Maddox (1975) has highlighted this reluctance in step-families to be open about the way the family originally got together and the general social tendency to conceal 'step-familyness'. This tendency makes it particularly important for professionals involved in step-family dilemmas to be aware of differences from first families, so that they can think more clearly about crucial but often very simple aspects of family reorganisation.

Burgoyne and Clarke (1982) in a study of forty step-families living in the Sheffield area, highlight some aspects of step-family structure which are often brought to professionals in the form of difficulties. They point out some of the intrinsic complications that the experience of replacement brings for a step-parent who has to accept the coexistence of an alternative parent (who is absent but living) and whose absence is mourned by children who may not express their feelings openly. They examine the different dilemmas faced by step-mothers and stepfathers. Stepmothers in particular reported the problems of becoming an instant parent and the creation of a satisfying domestic life for the family, in which they took responsibility for the emotional and physical wellbeing of the children. Step-fathers tended to see their role primarily in terms of the material and emotional support they could offer the children's *mother*, and the subsequent increased wellbeing of the family as a whole. They also mentioned the contribution of their practical skills to the household as important male aspects of improving the quality of life. Step-parents of both sexes felt the job was easier the younger the children were when they took them on.

Many of the dilemmas of newly-married step families reflect the coming to terms with reality that takes place when fantasies of a healing marriage that will make up for the wrongs of the past, and in particular a first marriage, have to be given up. Fears of recurrence of what existed and went wrong in prior marriages, surface to be looked at; the child relinquishing former aspects of being a parent to another adult has to be faced, and in addition a set of new relationships and boundaries have to be established. Burgoyne and Clarke (1982) point out in addition how the decision to have children of the re-marriage may highlight anxieties about possible repetitions of the pattern of previous experience.

Structural features of step-families

The emotional work of starting as a step family has been discussed by both English and American authors (Visher & Visher, Maddox, Robinson, 1982). In this chapter I will focus on the structural dilemmas as they are presented by families to professionals.

Children in each step family have two biological parents, only one of whom is living inside the family at any one time. The relationship that the main caretaking couple hold with the out family parent will largely determine the way the children are able to manage movement between two families. Continuing tension between divorced couples may be expressed in small but powerful ways that dominate the shared time between step parents and children. For example a mother may always send her children to stay with father and his new wife with dirty clothes, so that step mother's first job is to wash them; or with inadequate amounts of clothing so that father feels 'bound' to buy new things for them. These new things may then be sent back dirty or torn the following week. Similarly a step father may make continual gifts to his step children in an attempt to win them over in a way which the out of house father perceives as a deliberate attempt to alienate the children from him, and mother feels unable or unwilling to mediate. There are many variations on these competitive patterns between adults.

All children in step-families have to cope with movement between two households, and often to cope with radically different styles of expectation and living in each home. Such expectations can be exacerbated by the tension of unresolved quarrels. It may be valuable for the worker to clarify these differences with the children in a straightforward manner: 'Who makes breakfast; how is the time spent between meals; how is space and territory respected; what are the differences in rules governing who talks to whom and when?'

Burgoyne and Clarke (1982) indicate a variety of studies that show how many non-custodial parents gradually lose contact with children by a first marriage. Fathers who often saw their contribution to the family in terms of daily practical and financial input found the constraints of a visiting relationship hard to bear, especially where a stepfather was seen to have assumed these functions. Children, as they grow older, develop friendships and interests which disrupt earlier patterns of access. The payment of maintenance and the exercise of access tended to be linked, so that if a father was unable or unwilling to pay maintenance, he felt unable to exercise his rights of access, and if access was difficult he felt under less obligation to pay maintenance. Many mothers were also willing to forego maintenance where their spouses had taken this on, for the relief of not seeing their former spouse anymore. The authors point out that the ideal which advocates active and spontaneous contact between non-custodial parents and their children is rarely carried out; a distressing finding, particularly in the light of Wallerstein's findings that continued access was of great importance to the growing children and their mental health in her sample (Wallerstein and Kelly, 1982).

In highlighting differences between a step-family under stress and the families they previously lived in, questions around the small details of daily life are of use in getting discussions going about what feels as though it is going wrong and why. How does stepmother manage Sunday lunch as compared to how mother used to do it; how does father spend time with the kids at weekends now compared with how he used to do it before the remarriage.

While initiating *respect for differences* of view between one system and another, the questioner is also making conscious those aspects of previous patterns that may be inappropriately transferred into the current family and that need to change. He is requiring the family to do conscious work on new patterns and creating boundaries between members of the family, and within different aspects of the child, as he moves with the changing patterns of the family created by the adult's decision to remarry.

Within the family presenting for help, there may be radically different styles of viewing life and organisation between the children themselves in relation to that part of life which is family life. Step-parents rarely have a period of time to get to know each other as a couple without children. Sometimes the marriage itself may take away intimacy and protection from exposure to the demands of kids that it was possible to achieve while they were maintaining separate homes prior to marriage. The expectations and behaviour of children have to form a part of the fabric of parents interrelationship from the beginning.

Mr and Mrs James, for example, arrived with three of their teenage children in acute crisis because of fights between Mr James' daughters by his former marriage and Mrs James' sixteen-year-old son. Mrs James felt that the girls followed her around the house picking on the way she organised the family of six children, and Mick, her son, took part in defending her against the girls' idea of how things 'should' be done. Things came to a head around supper each evening which Mrs James tried to manage as a family event, while the teenage children had their own timetables which undermined her plan. The problem was causing her to begin drinking around four o' clock each afternoon in order to work up to a level of inebriation in which she no longer noticed the 'criticism'. The problem was reframed as the dilemma of parenting teenage children who were beginning to move out of the home in appropriate ways, and Mrs James was reassured that she had worked hard and successfully to keep the family together over the previous four years and that it was now time she took a break. It was suggested that she should stop working so hard to create the close family atmosphere that had been required when the family first came together, and only cook a family meal once a week, whenever she chose. On that night, father was to ensure that all the children were present. The parents were also told that it is very important for teenage children to see that their parents could have a good time together without them and that they should find ways of spending time without the kids, which would surprise them. The fact that they had never had time together without the competition of the children to manage, arose spontaneously. Mr James suddenly observed that not many families had such an available supply of babysitters. Mrs James was so amazed to be told to work less hard rather than harder, that her drinking problem diminished immediately between the first and second session, by which time the family showed that they had begun to reorganise in a different way, as a family handling the normal problems of teenagers. Burgoyne and Clarke (1982) highlight the value it may be to step parents to reframe their family problems within that of normal developmental dilemmas, rather than within the guilt surrounding divorce or remarriage and the effects on the children.

What makes reorganisation difficult

It is often the concealed depth of affect that is still attached to the family that originally existed, or mourning over the loss of the family system as it was formerly constituted, that makes the formation of a different system difficult. It may never have been openly recognised by each family that the previous family is gone and that something went with it. Two different frameworks for thinking about this can make it clearer. If we divide human systems in an arbitrary way along the two dimensions of behaviour and affect, we can see that patterns from the past within one lifetime are hard to change, particularly when many aspects of the life of the family will continue in a similar way. Meals will still have to be cooked, clothes washed, rooms tidied, children got to school. The potential for routine to evoke affect belonging to the same behavioural sequence in a previous situation like a former marriage is large. What can make a difference is the potential for new behaviour in a second spouse, and therefore the potential for different affect related to the routine. Often children will resist the new qualities in a step-parent that their own parent admires and try to provoke other behaviours they can fight against. When a seven-year-old complains of the way his stepmother fries his egg and chips and says that he is being looked after by his father, his sister and friends outside the family, the social worker will know that step-mother has a problem on her hands. Father may think he has married an excellent provider but his son may like his egg runny and his chips greasy like mother made it. Very small discussions of this kind which contain large residues of family tension are very effective in helping step-parents be more conscious of areas where they may need to exercise particular tact in respect of an absent parent rejected by their *spouse*, but not by their step-child.

From one to two

In other families the key reorganisation that has to take place is from a one-parent to a two-parent system in which child and parents have to recognise that there is now another adult whose importance has not been taken into account. In the Whitely family, mother had lived with her son Murray for four years, before her remarriage to Bill. He in turn had separated from his wife Jean, leaving his son Dale with her in the North of England. The family presented in acute tension around the issue of fighting between the boys when Dale came to stay, although it quickly emerged that mother was the one who was extremely anxious about losing control, with two averagely robust boys in the house. Mother was fighting a rearguard action against 'allowing' her boy Murray to grow up, being accused by stepfather of keeping him in cotton wool. Murray was dressed more like a toddler than an eight-year-old. The strength of mother's defence against a change from a one-parent to a two-parent system, in which father's voice was heard effectively only became apparent when Murray suddenly volunteered that he liked Dale coming to visit and didn't mind the fighting.

Sequence 1

S.W.:   So everytime Dale comes to stay that's a testing time for you: is that how you feel, Murray.

Murray: Well I'd like him to come and live with us.

Mother: But then . . .

Murray: I *would* like it.

Mother: But after he's been here about three days there's a big sobbing in your bedroom.

Murray: No, there would not be.

Mother: But there is – you've got to be realistic.

Murray: If he would be here longer than he usually stays, then we would get on – if he learnt what I like.

Mother: But there's no reason really why he should learn what you like and there's no reason why he should play with you at all because he's a lot bigger – occasionally he might play with – I think the horseplay business is irrelevant really because there's a lot of difference in their age.

S.W.:   (*Puts to Mum that there will be times when they play together and times when they don't get on and adds*) Do you know, you have a great expert on boys in this room.

Mother: Boys!

S.W.:   Do you know who it is?

Mother: No.

S.W.:   I think it might be your husband. I think that he told me about fifteen minutes ago that he used to fight a lot when he was a boy. Would you like to ask him about that?

Sequence 2

Later on in the session the topic recurs.
S.W. (*to Mrs Whitely*):   I don't think you like fighting very much.
Mother: Not really.
S.W.:   Do you think it's something Mums ought to be able to teach their children?
Mother: I don't think you should teach them – I really don't believe in it.
S.W.:   You had to look after Murray for quite some time didn't you?
Mother: Four years.
S.W.:   So in a way you had to be both Mum and Dad.
Mother: It was very much just the two of us – we didn't really have anything much to do with anyone else – he's not a one that plays or brings children in to play.
S.W.:   So I guess it's very difficult to hand over some things.

Sequence 3

(*Later in the interview, Dale is also named as a potential asset and resource.*)
S.W.:   I'd like to bring Dale in here because Murray gets something from Dale.
Mother: Well he's proud of his big brother.
S.W.:   That's terrific – I think you can do something here.
Stepfather: 'Cos Dale was very much like Murray as far as fighting is concerned at about the same age ... he learnt to fight to protect himself, but now he's often the one that puts the punch in rather than waiting.
Mother: But he's not co-ordinated, see Murray's not co-ordinated.
S.W.:   He is four years *younger*.
Mother: But we've had six-year-olds playing and he can't keep up and he's getting into trouble at school because he can't play football and it's because *I* haven't taught him.
S.W.:   Well *you* don't have to teach him now. There are *two* other people here (indicating stepfather and Dale). I think you've got some very skilled resources here in the men in your family and it's very difficult to hand over to them and say they can look after one bit while you look after another. I think Mr Whitely has got a real job on his hands convincing you he can look after the fighting and that Dale can help.

The Rose family

The Rose family provide an interesting example of the use of a family intervention at a point where the law and social services were undecided whether to use a 'justice' or a 'welfare' model (Hoggett, 1981) in approaching the offence. The family consisted of mother, her second husband Ted and her son Cliff. Cliff was on a supervision order to the Social Service Department, who involved a local family therapy team at the Child Guidance Clinic in requesting an assessment of Cliff's mental state, and an assurance that it was safe for him to stay at home on a supervision order. The alternative was that a care order would have to be made. The fear had been expressed that a placement away from home, possibly even in a closed unit in a community home might be necessary. The social worker took a risk in asking for a supervision order to be made with family sessions as a condition of the order, and the court agreed to this on a report-back basis.

Cliff's offence involved taking an army knife that was hanging on the wall at home and chopping his stepfather's arm off at the shoulder, severing it sufficiently severely for him to have three months off work.

At the first interview it was clear that the family did not wish to come to explore any differences between them and were only coming because they feared Cliff would be 'put away' if they did not come. The family referred to the violent behaviour as 'the incident' as though it were a minor mishap in an otherwise close and united family. Mother in particular showed that she wished to keep the men in her family close to each other and equally valued. The social worker found her own attempts to promote discussion or enactment were consistently disqualified. At the simplest level of hypothesis it seemed that Cliff had in reality been demoted from the role of the man in mother's life, that he had held for the eight years he lived alone with her prior to her marriage, but that this had not been made clear between them. A message was sent to the family by the co-workers acting as 'team' to the social worker in the room (see Chapter 11 for further discussion) labelling Cliff as very protective of mother and saying that she would need to find ways of letting him know whether she required his protection. Mother's response was one of surprise, denial that she needed a protector, and thoughtfulness. At the end of the session the message was repeated and strengthened with the suggestion that Cliff should stay out of rows between mother and Ted, however much she appeared to need Cliff's protection. In the following session Cliff reported that he had managed this and spent more time out of the house with his mates. A number of occasions on which he might have been involved in rows were discussed in detail. The family reiterated their closeness and Cliff was asked to be in charge of bringing a family map in which all *stepfather's* family were drawn in.

In the third session the new pattern was maintained, and the family again expressed the belief that they were a close, loving and integrated family who did not need any outside interference. A gentle but persistent exporation of 'who was closest to whom' in the family in the context of all of them being close produced the following difference from stepfather:

The Rose family

Session 3

Ted: He's closest to his Mum, he's closest to his Mum ... he's closest to his Mum.

S.W.:   Could you tell him that is what you think?

Ted: Well, he knows it.

S.W.:   Yes, I'm sure you have talked about that before but perhaps you could tell him that is what you think.

Ted: He *is* closest to his Mum, it's obvious; if I was in his position I'd be the same, wouldn't I ... (*Clasping his hands to show closeness*). I ain't sort of meaning this, or nothing like that – don't get me wrong when I say that.

S.W.:   No.

Ted: He's closest to his Mum all the time.

Mother: He hasn't known Ted as long as he's known me, has he?

Ted: It's a natural thing, isn't it.

Mother: He's had me for fourteen years, he's only had Ted for a year.

The team decided to agree with them but sent them the message, 'In such a close and united family such events may come like bolts from the blue. What would the family need to do to arm themselves against fate striking in this way again?' The family returned, apparently united as before and 'without having thought about the message until the night before they came'. Mother and Cliff, however, showed a different perspective on the family pattern than in the previous meeting.

Session 4

Mother: I suppose honestly before I met Ted we were on our own and obviously Cliff would be a bit protective for me because he was the man of the house, wasn't he, and to be fair, ever since he was small I've always spoken to him more as an adult than a child, he's been included in everything and if adults were in the room he'd be included, he wouldn't be sent to bed, and so I suppose he's a little in advance for his years. He really has to drop down a step.

Therapist: I think you're right and I think *that* change is very hard.
Mother: Now if I want something I obviously talk to Ted more ... if I wanted something to discuss ... if Cliff and I were on our own I would say, 'So and so and so and so' and now I would say it to Ted.
Cliff: (*to Ted*) Now *you're* the man of the house, isn't it.
Mother: Yes, look at it this way, before if I had a new dress or something I would show it to Cliff first, now I would go to you first and him second.

In this family therefore, a simple structural shift, to create a parental alliance in which the child was not triangulated into arguments between mother and step father was achieved by:

1.   re-labelling the aggressive behaviour as protective;
2.   agreeing with the family's view of themselves as united; *but*
3.   sending a message with enough curious features about it to make them aware of the nature of the event in a different way.

The Knowles family

Mr and Mrs Knowles and Tim and Jean came in a state of high anxiety presenting a long list of problems because of Jean's destructive behaviour in the home, such as cutting the wires of the television, unscrewing the legs of the table, putting polish into a vacuum cleaner, as well as stealing things, and sometimes throwing them away and sometimes hiding them. Both parents had been the targets of this behaviour. Jean usually said that she could not remember the events and disclaimed any association with it even when it was proved. Mr and Mrs Knowles and the children smiled a great deal – they were a pleasant family who frequently emphasised that they were nigh on perfect. Both kids were very likeable and Jean showed no evidence in sessions of the premature delinquency described at home.

A number of themes were apparent. These were to do with this being a happy and perfect family. Before the arrival of Mr Knowles three years ago, there was however considerable violence and the family had to take refuge at a secret address for several months after separating. Mr Knowles therefore had to be careful not to become 'the monster' that the previous dad was.

Mother: I didn't want Mike to do the correcting because I didn't want Jean to turn Mike into the monster – I didn't want Mike to be the villain of the piece. I didn't want anything to go wrong between Jean and Mike so I thought it was better for me to correct her.
S.W.:   But we do have to talk a bit about the monster.
Step-dad: Yes, and suffer the consequences, whatever they are, when we get home.

S.W.:   What was it like before, who got hurt.
Mother: All three got hurt.
S.W.:   Who's going to tell us a bit about what it was like?
Mother: I'd like the children to talk about it.
Tim: I know he done some good things in his life, not many but one or two.
Mother: He wasn't a *terrible* monster.
Tim: I used to see me mum very hurt and cry – I've never seen me dad, since he's married my mum, hurt her, and she's never cried like that.
S.W.:   Jean, do you remember getting hurt?
Jean: Only once.
S.W.:   Can you tell us about that?
Jean: I was about five and I went in to your room and found you and John fighting . . . (*etc.*).

Jeans destructive behaviour was bringing her a great deal of attention within the family and she was closely watched within the home, mother accompanying her upstairs in case she committed further violence on the house. It was Tim who reframed Jean's behaviour as naughtiness, or ways of getting attention. Stepfather picked this up and differentiated between being naughty and getting attention – 'You can get attention in other ways'. He was asked to elaborate on the other ways and went on to give two or three different ways of getting food and bad attention: 'Tell Jean and we will listen.' Tim volunteered his own set of ideas: 'I slam doors to get attention, and if I have little tears in my clothes I make them a bit bigger so I can take it to Mum and spend some time while its being mended.' He pointed out to Jean that the kinds of things he did, although naughty were not as naughty as the things his sister did and only got him into a little bit of trouble as well as a lot of rewards in terms of interaction with his mother. When asked how she got attention Jean said 'taking things'. Tim offered her a range of ways of being angry, like bashing her pillow, and the children showed that they could make plans and work together.

The family were set a task to carry out in between sessions, which was designed to shift the balance of relationships in the family so that Mike could take more of a nurturant and gently authoritative role with Jean; while Tim helped her plan more appropriate and less drastic ways of being naughty as a 'normal' part of eight-year-old behaviour. Mike and Jean were to find time (three times a week stepfather decided)) to get together and discuss how children can get attention in ways that don't upset their parents, and Tim and Jean were to think up naughty things to surprise them. Mum was not to know which of the 'naughty' things had been planned by the two of them, and which were 'spontaneous', although she could guess and let the family know at the next meeting.

Mother later reported this series of tasks as being very successful because'. 'It brought Jean closer to Mike and I was nicely out of the way for a while so the usual switchboard stopped operating.' Jean and Mike got much closer and Jean's needs for a cuddly father began to be met. The family came back for further work six months later when Tim, who had carried the role of peacemaker up to that time became a stubborn, angry and naughtier twelve-year-old and the family again had to readjust to allow Mike to handle this in ways which would not frighten Mum.

The patterns transferred from the past included, therefore, mother's and children's fear of provoking violence in her new husband, turning the 'gentle giant' into the 'monster', (Mike's flexed muscles in the first session were proudly displayed by Tim, but they had to be kept to guard the family, not to be used within it). In addition, Tim's pattern as the eldest child of watching the parents for signs of trouble and always keeping the peace had to relax. It would be hypothesised that both Jean's actions in provoking her parents and Tim's later 'troublesome' behaviour were both stages in testing out stepfather to see whether his strength could be used 'safely' for them rather than against them. Stepfather needed help and support to negotiate this role, which required mother to stop protecting both Tim and herself. The perfect marriage had to become an ordinary 'good enough' marriage in which arguments took place and were negotiated, and in which the children could see that the new family would survive.

Foster families

Much of the family work described above also takes place in foster families, except that both parents will be 'on trial'. The ways in which each set of foster parents will have to negotiate transferred patterns of expectation from children is usually taken into account in planning a placement, but it seems that foster families are less often referred as *families* for help. It is always essential to look not only at how children transfer expectations and behaviour from previous situations, but at how the parents respond or are inducted into behaviours that may recreate previous patterns in the children. It is useful to help foster parents anticipate and rehearse trouble spots, and think of ways of responding that are not going to recreate previous crisis patterns in the child or young person's life.

Jackie, fifteen, had joined her foster family after a career including drug-taking and thieving. Her former foster family had asked for her to be removed after furious rows between them about her drug-taking. After two months she informed her foster mother that she was hanging out with a drug-taking crowd and had been 'experimenting'. Her foster mother reported: 'I was cooking at the time and I thought why is she telling me in this way'. She knows if I tell Bert that he will be very angry and she wants to see what I will do and whether the same thing is going to happen again.' The social worker and foster parents discussed a strategy in which the foster mother used the 'weight of her experience' to talk about all the girls she had known and some studies she had read of the path from soft drug-taking to hard drug-taking. She gave statistics of deaths through misuse and neglect and talked sadly of wasted young lives. She said that it was difficult for adults bringing up young people, as they knew young people had to have their independence and decide what to do with their own private lives. She added that she knew her husband felt the same about these matters but he got very angry instead of sad about it, and had spent some time airing his views on the subject in general when they had seen the social worker the previous week. Her husband meanwhile managed some extra time with Jackie at the weekend, swimming and running (which Jackie also enjoyed) and managed (with some difficulty) not to mention the drug issue.

Within ten days Jackie chose another supper-time cooking hour to inform her foster mother obliquely that 'she had given all that up now'. A week later she added, as though the conversation was still going on: 'I wanted to see what you'd do, what your reaction would be.' She picked up a much more active life with her friends in the evening, and also gave up smoking.

By not giving Jackie attention in the same way, through reactions of indignation and outrage but by offering her firstly, an oblique comment on the pointlessness of her chosen way of life; secondly, increased time with her foster father doing something pleasurable rather than punitive; last, a model of a couple who handled conflict in a different way; it was possible for Jackie to break a transferred pattern of expectation and behave differently. Further work with a foster family is described in Chapter 8 on work with adolescents.

7

Young Children and Violence in Families

The law has known for a long time that people are capable of treating children badly, although its notions of what is bad have varied alongside the notions of society. The special vulnerability of children is only acknowledged by those who have a sense of development and difference, and one of the paradoxical aspects of babies and young infants is that their primitive power has the capacity to delete an awareness of this difference from those who are looking after them in 'the battle of babycare'. Where an awareness of vulnerability is maintained in the care giver, the child can be seen as having special needs. A collection of research findings from different surveys now suggests how this difference between care giver and infant is wiped out at times of family stress.

Babies and their impact on parents

One of the most obvious things about very small children, which is easily forgotten by those who are not currently looking after them, is that they are noisy, active and bursting to explore the world around them. It is a tiring job looking after them, especially if their sleeping pattern is irregular and interrupting their parents' expected sleep pattern. This in itself makes for additional instability in a developmental stage in the family lifecycle, when the pattern between parents is particularly open to changes, and the initiations of entirely new behaviour, and fluctuations in old patterns, will be well beyond the usual balance of the couple, because of the required adaptations made by the process of becoming a parent. Feelings of incompetence and inadequacy are common. Graham (1980) interviewing 120 women with one-month-old babies found that 61 per cent admitted feeling angry with their babies and 81 per cent said the experience of an infant had made them more sympathetic to baby batterers. Anger and rage typically surfaced in situations where mothers were coping with tiredness, and husbands could play a crucial role in providing a safety valve for a persistently crying child.

Frude and Goss (1980) in a postal survey of 111 mothers with children of between eighteen months and four years, also found a high proportion of reported violence. 96 per cent of mothers said they had days when everything got on top of them, and 57 per cent admitted that at least on one occasion they had lost their temper severely and hit their child really hard. 40 per cent feared this getting out of control. This group tended to use physical punishment more frequently, to be more irritated by the child's crying and to be more bored and lonely in the house.

Parents who are tired and irritable often forget that they have been and possibly may again be a resource to one another at some time. The pattern of attending to the needs of querulous or demanding children may override a prior pattern of communication between adults, however intermittent. In addition many young mothers, now unable to work, find themselves very socially isolated. Richman's (1976) study of young mothers with husbands on a housing estate, showed that many of them did not talk to adults from the time their husbands left for work in the morning to the time they came home at night.

Wolkind (1982) reported that the installation of 'phones in the flats of young mothers reduced their reported depression dramatically. These studies indicate in different ways that it is worth helping all parents to achieve many varieties of support system from other adults; playgroups, mothers' groups, and baby-sitting circles, so parents can go out.

In many families there is only one adult, or one of the parents may through absence, illness or erratic behaviour have effectively abnegated the parental role. We have considered some of the dilemmas arising from single-parent structures in Chapter 5. Here the focus is on the message that the child may receive, in terms of the parent's need for closeness or companionship, which may arise equally in one- or two-parent families, where the child responds to the parental need.

Tracey (7):   Sometimes my mummy tries to keep her worries from me but she tells me in the end.
Brian (6):   Now my dad's away (*in prison*) I have to be the man of the house and my mum has to do what I say. He told me it was my job now.
Paul (9):   I used to see my mum hurt very badly and I would try and stop it but I wasn't strong enough.

Social workers will be familiar with many forms of this dilemma of children trying to do more than they are actually able to do. To help parents develop a clear idea for themselves of what a child is or is not capable of can be not only essential for the psychological development of the child, but sometimes a matter of life and death, since when children are *perceived* or experienced as though they were adults, they are often fought with as though they *were* adults in size and strength.

Minuchin (1982, 1983) in demonstrations of work with children, has shown how persistently diminishing the assumed power of the child in front of the parent effectively makes a generation boundary between child and parent, in which both realise that it is the parent's job to take control of the child's behaviour. 'Your mother will help you not to do what you don't want to do. You don't want people to be frightened of you. Four years old is not so big.' Such techniques as getting the child to stand up beside his mother can make this point simply. In other situations a struggle for control may have to be had between child and mother which the professional keeps out of, but helps the mother to win.

It is also worth remembering some of the simple but important aspects of development that can be promoted by parents talking clearly with their children. A number of independent research studies (Madge, 1983) have indicated that one of the most successful skills a parent can develop is talking with their child, and that this correlates subsequently with successful integration into school, and good developmental profiles on a number of different assessment measures. This is not surprising when we remember that children need words to master the world and its many complex events and the feelings inside them that these provoke. Several studies have identified the sophisticated capacity of three- and four-year-olds to make sense of the world in quite complex sentences, which of course enables them to adapt more successfully in a number of ways to unexpected happenings. Rutter (1982) has indicated that a key factor in helping children with stressful situations is the way in which it is talked about at the time.

Many studies of communication in families show that confusion in message-giving can contribute to specific forms of behaviour disorder and mental confusion, so that it is always worth helping parents be clearer in sorting out their meaning with their *children*, even if they can't manage it *with one another*. The social worker can make themselves the person to whom issues have to be clarified and by slowing the process of explanation down, can bring it to a child-sized explanation: 'I don't know what you mean, can you explain to *me* what you want him to do and we'll see if that's what he thought you meant . . . no, I really don't understand when you say that', etc.

'He's doing it to get at me' – non-accidental injury

From the many reports on non-accidental injury (N.A.I.) which have helped us understand the viewpoint of the parent who batters, bruises or deliberately ill-uses their child in small persistent ways, some features can be highlighted as aspects of parenting to be worked on (CCETSW, 1978; Frude and Goss 1980). Some demonstrate the ways in which parents perceive the child as older and more capable than he or she could possibly be, and in many cases as the parent that the parent never had and always wanted (Skinner and Castle, 1969). The implications for work from these studies therefore are that the parents will need a good deal of 'professional parenting' themselves in being helped to distinguish what kinds of loving behaviour a baby or toddler can legitimately give; and may in addition need a great deal of education in what a child of different months and years of age can normally be expected to do.

Non-accidental injury represents a challenge to society as well as to professionals, by continually demonstrating an area in which civilisation breaks down, in spite of the development of health, welfare, educational and social services. British work in this field had been valuable in highlighting differences between those who do and those who do not hurt their children severely. Although the group of families most likely to be at risk in inner-city areas will be young, immature and predisposed to aggression as a form of dealing with the world (Gorell Barnes, 1978b; Kellmer Pringle, 1980), this reflects social class effects (that is, earlier marriage, and housing and other economic pressures). Hyman (1980) distinguishing family circumstances as predictors of stress found different features. She found a high proportion of one-parent families, a high proportion where a birth had occurred within a year of a couple living together and a high rate of unemployment among fathers.

However the most outstanding feature in her two samples, both inner city and out-of-town areas, was the high reported rate of ill-health in the mothers, psychological ill-health being a particular feature of the *non* inner-city group. There was a failure in sensitive interaction and reciprocity between infants' requirements and their mothers' response, despite maternal anxiety. Hyman emphasises that stress was distributed equally throughout the social class structure and throughout the average range of intelligence.

In considering work with families where non-accidental injury has taken place or is suspected, there are therefore a number of contextual dimensions that can be used to think about how the family can both work on itself, and be worked with.

1. How isolated is mother and what is her adult support system – does she have an intimate relationship with a man and how is that going at the moment – can anything be done to improve the adult interaction in the family.
2. If there is no other adult, who else can be used – as an emergency resource, as part of the development of a support group over time; to help develop mother's self-esteem in a lasting way.

Immaturity

Almost all studies of N.A.I. populations agree that parents are 'immature'. The implications of immaturity can be seen as both that parents are doing the best they know how at the time, and that there is room for growth. Hyman (1980) makes the important point clearly that mothers who abuse physically do not have raised levels of guilt and apprehension, but lowered levels of integration and control. This has important implications for what may need to be learnt of particular skills and attitudes. Mothers' transactions with infants will be affected by multiple factors, and in working to reduce tension it is always worth helping parents develop their own observing eye and self-monitoring capacity, in relation to those trigger events which make them feel violent. When they are more familiar with these and have brought them out to have a look at openly, it becomes possible to begin to plan ways of reacting other than with feelings of anger, powerlessness and violence.

It is one of the powerful paradoxes of the abusing situation that at the moment where parents victimise their child, they are most likely to be feeling a victim themselves; either a victim of the child or of some other person or force. Minuchin (1983) has placed the analysis of violence within the larger context of the coercive aspects of society, and the legal and welfare system that can be seen as persecuting by violent families, and points out how many of the surveillance systems that are created increase the family sense of persecution, and reinforce rather than decrease the pattern of violent interaction within the family.

How can work with abusing families be done?

Many of the roles which social workers are expected to carry conflict with the possibility of work to help the family change. Mumford (1983, in preparation) has outlined the preconditions for successful family work as including managerial responsibility held by a 'boss' with permission to carry out intensive work given to the social worker who can then hold the authority, knowing they have the backing to do therapeutic work as well. However the realities of time are crucial. Is the input that can be offered persistent and sustained enough to make a change in the family's experience that will lead to a less violent series of interactions around the same events? If not, a 'surveillance' job will not help the family – it is only the anxiety of the local authority about whether it is doing what is required by the law and society. In order to change established habits of perceiving and relating that are infused with violent emotion, sustained series of other ideas and modes of relating will be needed. Parents will need to be convinced of their competence in relation to provocation by their children and in the face of their provocation of one another, before anxiety can diminish.

Studies of child abusers (Gorell Barnes, 1978b, c) agree that only a small percentage of abuse stems from a position of deliberate cruelty. The majority of violence towards children is committed from a position of helplessness in which the parent feels like the victim of the child. Some strategies for increasing parental competence are therefore worth considering.

1.   *Observation*
Increasing parents' observation of their children and encouraging them to wonder what it means when he whines: 'does it mean he's hungry, or is he in pain; does he want a cuddle or for you to play with him – what do you think it means?' increases parents' sensitivity to child's behaviour having a meaning, and encourages parents to look at their own part in the development of the behaviour by giving it different meanings. Observation in itself can change a whole family pattern of relating: 'Coming here has taught us to look at one or two bits and pieces, if you like, and now we watch things more.'

2.   *Talking to their children*
1.   Helps the child acquire language, so he can relate more freely to the world.
2.   Gives mother and children some shared things to do and develop into play and learning.
3.   Helps mother to realise she can relate to child with words not just blows.
4.   Helps children develop and later do well at school (very important to mothers).

3.   *Management skills*
Short-term: Help to handle outbursts of rage and impulsive feeling in

mother, by describing actual strategies that other mothers use which involve getting a distance between self and baby; a physical distance, say by putting baby in the cot, with the door shut, or if no door then putting the radio or TV on full blast till the mother has cooled down; bringing in, or going to a friend or neighbour, going for a walk; counting to ten or deep breathing, stamping or violent slamming of doors. Frude and Goss (1980) additionally report 'remembering the child is small and dependent', 'thinking of a happier time'. Where a spouse is involved in the violence it may be most difficult since the rage increases. Triggers that help the parents remember the baby's immaturity and vulnerability are therefore most important. Fathers may also need to be helped to modify their imput from 'Why is your child still crying?' to something that makes the mother feel more competent, rather than more inadequate. Each family will need to work out their own repertoire but with encouragement and reinforcement these minimal boundaries for feeling safer can be built into the pattern of home life.

Long-term: The aim of the above 'safety measures' need to be in the context of improved long-term competence and self-assurance in each parent towards the child and in some degree towards each other. Development can be put to them as a force on their side. Children do increase their self-management as they grow older. Minimal educative input must include:

1. Normal child development – expectable behaviour and naughtiness at different ages and stages.
2. The disadvantages of physical punishment as a method of control, and discussion of viable alternatives; 'what will work for you'.

Okell-Jones (1980) in a follow-up study of abusing families has emphasised the importance of planning treatment strategies for the family as a whole, as treatment aimed only at the child may further *endanger* the child.

Unless the home environment can be modified to accommodate changes in the children, professionals may be exposing the children to further risk by stripping them of a variety of adaptive models of behaviour (albeit psychopathological) which have high value in a dangerous environment. Learning, competence, exploration, initiative and autonomy are not encouraged in many abusive homes and may even be the basis for assault by the parents.

Treatment is likely to require an understanding of the difficulties the parent may have in changing from the basis of their past experience; although the focus of the *work* may be rather on developing skills in current contexts. The Marlborough Family Unit has developed a therapeutic programme based on parents facing management issues with their children that allows rehearsal of different ways of resolving issues other than violence (Asen and Stevens, 1982).

Where the family is not viable: authority issues

Local-authority social workers are often brought into families at the wrong time in the wrong way. The whole form of care proceedings places their agency in opposition to both parents and child, and then expects it to become a substitute parent. The social worker will have played a part in the decision to proceed, will have to give evidence against the parents and may even have to represent the authority as an advocate. He will have to carry out the court's order to supervise or remove the child, and may have to provide an impartial home assessment for the court. The social worker may be caught too many ways to do therapeutic work, and may need to find a neutral colleague or group to help from within his own department, or from a child-guidance or children's hospital team. The separation of the management function from the therapeutic function is seen to be helpful by some social workers who have developed colleague pairs working on selected cases within their own teams. Other workers, such as the NSPCC Special Unit in Rochdale, prefer to use the authority they have as a central feature of the work they do, so that the family has to work with the reality all the time.

Where the child has to be removed the parents will feel angry, blamed and without power. It is a very rare family who will agree that it is for the infant's good, at the time of removal. The social worker is also faced with issues of the restricted role, if any, the parents are likely to play in the future and needs to make some plan with the family that is as comprehensible and realistic as is manageable, including facing them with the restrictions of their future role where necessary. Using the welfare of the child (1980, section 18) as a paramount consideration may help to guide the social worker in making boundaries between what the child actually needs to grow and thrive, and the parents' wishes for their offspring, which may predominantly reflect their own needs.

It is important to remember that it is particularly within situations of violence that the most primitive feelings are stirred up in both family and worker, and that just as the family should not be left feeling less competent than before at the end of a session and should not be left in charge of their children feeling more raw, angry and vulnerable, so social workers will also need some support or consultation about the feelings they are left with. For social workers who have not formed a regular alliance with a colleague or group for this purpose, audio recording of sessions can be a valuable aid in providing the opportunity for a later objective review of the session and an analysis of its strengths and weaknesses. Working with a colleague and other methods of self-monitoring and self-support are discussed in Chapter 11.

8

Adolescence

During the years commonly grouped together as adolescence, the young person has to negotiate a number of different tasks to do with internal and external growth. Rutter (1976) examined the literature on adolescent turmoil, and found on the basis of a number of surveys, that while a percentage of adolescents experience misery as part of growing up, the figure for marked disturbance in children is roughly the same at all ages (about 10 per cent). Two aspects of internal state which intensify are upsets and depression, and there is a marked increase in the development of school refusal. In these families, more alienation from parents correlated with increased parental and marital difficulty so that it could be argued that the impact of such difficulty 'matured' during these early teenage years of the young person's development.

Farrington (1978) and his colleagues, explored the family background of aggressive youths over a period of fourteen years from eight to twenty-two. Violent delinquency was most closely associated with harsh parental attitudes and discipline; criminality in the parents, poor parental supervision, separations and low IQ. Non-violent delinquents were less likely to have experienced these factors in the family. Aggressive boys had also displayed their aggressiveness as early as eight years old, when their class-mates rated them 'daring'. Marital disharmony was a prominent predictor of teenage aggression.

These studies, which represent two large longitudinal research projects, show that the family factors related to adolescent disturbance are very often present for the child *from an early age*. That has important implications for preventive work from health and educational services, as well as social services, on those many occasions when the welfare state is brought up against aspects of developing aggression, as it presents in the different settings of health clinic, general practice and school. Social workers may be reluctant to take on didactic or educational functions in relation to the families they meet, but there is nothing to stop them asking the family pertinent questions about its future development. 'How do you see the future for your children – do you think they will leave home by going into care/running away/going to borstal/to prison?' can begin a discussion that changes the family track at least minimally for younger acting-out children, and there are a number of occasions on which minimal interventions may have a long-term cumulative effect. Confrontative techniques are not a familiar part of social work repertoire, but when couched in terms that make the family confront themselves in the service of the children, they may be found more acceptable.

In this chapter the focus is on three kinds of adolescent crisis that social workers commonly meet – the young adolescent who is frightened of never being able to make it, and becomes the 'victim' of his or her peers (the suicide threat); the adolescent who has got 'too big' for the parent and therefore cannot be controlled; the adolescent who 'recognises' the crisis that growing up and leaving home is going to cause in the family.

Early adolescence: the suicide attempt

Families where the young person is facing this kind of dilemma are more likely to present in hospital settings or child-guidance clinics than social service settings, perhaps with phobic symtoms or as a result of attempted suicide. Brief focal work with the earlier history of the family can bring a different perspective to the current anxiety and relieve the crisis for the young person.

Philip lived with his mother, his stepfather, his younger sister Jane, and the son of the new marriage, Derek. His own father had 'disappeared' into prison some ten years earlier, and mother had subsequently divorced him. He was only spoken of in a denigratory manner by his Nan, and all photos of him had been hidden so that the children would not think about him. At the time of referral Philip's sister was attending school irregularly, had run away from home for three nights having stolen a large sum of money and had been brought back by the police. The family were seen once, but Philip refused to come. He then took an overdose of sufficient severity to keep him in intensive care for some days. Following his return to school he agreed to come with his mother and sister for a session to talk about his real dad. The family was defined for this session as Mother, Philip and Jane, excluding stepfather and the son of the new marriage.

The focus of the session was on what the children knew about their first dad; the social worker pointed out that it looked as though Mum (and Nan) could never think of anything good to say about him. 'You must wonder what kind of man you're going to grow up to be.' Mother was asked to remember the things that had drawn her together with father in the first place, and the positive things that he had contributed towards looking after the children. Many anecdotes, of the courtship and wedding, and of father's tenderness towards the children as babies, emerged to partially displace the images of a criminal, uncaring man. As mother talked, it also became clear how father had become the family 'victim' rather than being seen as a single person who was a criminal.

Philip's suicide attempt was hypothesised as being related to his having to live with the legend of a no-good father as part of the family pattern that sustained the second marriage. However 'bad' Dave – his second father – was in reality, in fantasy he had been the man who rescued his Mum from managing on her own, and married her, taking on the two young kids. Expressions of curiosity about his own father and his good features were taboo, because they undermined the legend of badness which underpinned Dave's goodness. However his sister's behaviour provoked Philip's fears that 'blood would tell' and led to his attempt at self-destruction before he too went 'bad'. Even relatively brief exploration in which good points about his dad were remembered by his mum (and specifically the fact that his father had looked after him single-handed for two weeks when his sister was born, and changed his nappies and fed him) brought powerful relief from the fear of what kind of monster his unmentioned father might turn out to be, and what he might grow up to be in turn. (The importance of knowning something about the reality of parents has been written about in detail by Bruce (1982) in his work at St Charles Treatment Centre. In his experience, it only became possible for some of the very damaged youngsters in care to make good relationships with other grown-ups, once they had met and done some work on coming to terms with the limitations of their own parents.)

Philip only came for two sessions, working on his family map in the first session, and having managed in the second session to get some photos from his Nan, following a plan we had made about how he might put the request to her in a positive way as being part of his birthright now he was growing up to be a man. After this he wrote saying he wanted to concentrate on passing exams. Some nice feedback from his mother took place in the greengrocer's seven years later. He had become an outstanding trainee in the firm he was working for, having received special commendation and prizes. His choice of using his head for survival was apparently serving him well enough.

Young people who have got too big for their parents

The following example shows in some detail the need for persistence, humour and the determination not to be put down which work with young people may require. The Booth family were referred to a small social work team specialising in family work in an independent setting from the probation department. A number of charges were hanging over them, pending their being taken back to court. Mother had a suspended sentence hanging over her, and the youngest son was on a supervision order for failing to attend school and for a number of minor burglaries. The closeness and loyalty of the family members to the family as a whole was the protective mechanism that the social worker observed and used throughout the session to counteract the denigratory comments of the boys, to build up the self-esteem of the mother and to enable her to confront the family with the paths open to them.

The Booth family

The three boys, sixteen, fifteen and thirteen were living with their mother and grandfather. Denny, although the youngest, showed himself as having male supremacy in the pecking order, being the only one who was fully trusted by Mum. He had moved his girlfriend into the house and she was taking up much needed space, having been allocated a bedroom which caused envy and rivalry between the other brothers. Mother revealed that she had taken her in because she sympathised with her unhappy home life and that she herself had not had a family at that age.

Session 1 Sequence 1:   *Emphasising the warmth and closeness of the family*

Mum: Well, when I was her age, thirteen, I never had any family life, when I was thirteen my Mum died, that's why I had more than him (*indicating oldest boy*) because if I peg out; and it's a horrible feeling being on your own, you remember that from when you were thirteen, well, when I was eleven, she went into hospital, so I wasn't with her then, and five days after I was thirteen she died. And it's a terrible feeling being by yourself; I mean when you were at school, everyone was on about it's Ma this, and Ma that, and I got nobody to talk about, you know, you stand out like a plum, and (*pointing at girl*) her family is all mixed up, I mean there's dramas at home. I'm not having that, I pay the rent, and I say to them; I mean we all sit round the kitchen table and they have a moan, but you know it's hard when you ain't been brought up in a family, you don't know what a family is supposed to be. It's supposed to be normal.

S.W.:   So it's difficult for you now, because you don't know what it's supposed to be, normal.

Mum: No, I don't know what it is supposed to be.

S.W.:   So you were happy to take her in.

Mum: Well, there is no way that I would leave a bird out on the street. It ain't in me to think like that.

The social worker began to 'frame' the family as close and protective. 'People in trouble like coming to this family.' This was explored round each of the brothers, and each of them confirmed that their friends when in trouble came to this family. 'It's nice in the summer holidays when they all run away, they run away round to our house, I mean my lot they *never* run away.' In the next sequence some differentiation between the brothers in terms of what each of them contributes to the home is attempted. This is leading towards exploring issues of authority in the home in terms of decision-making about Denny's future ('in care' or 'back to school').

Session 1 Sequence 2

S.W.:   Is their problem really about authority? When it comes to who's going to tell the boys what to do?

Mum: Well, it is and it ain't. I mean take him (*pointing to the eldest*) he is very short-tempered. Of course he is that much bigger than me and tougher than me.

S.W.:   How old are you?

Clarke: Seventeen.

S.W.:   Well, that's a man, isn't it.

Mum: Sometimes he is, sometimes he isn't.

S.W.:   Do you think mother treats you as a man now?

Clarke: Sometimes.

S.W.:   She doesn't try and tell you what to do?

Clarke: Sometimes.

S.W.:   What do you do then?

Bill: (*laughing*) Bollocks.

Mum: That's all you get out of him; that or two fingers. I could never rely on him, nor him (*pointing to Clarke*). Him (*pointing to Denny*) 100 per cent him. (*Pointing to oldest son*) He has his grub, and he brings his laundry once a week, puts down his £15 and that's all he does.

S.W.:   What more do you want him to do?

Mum: Well, if he's going to live like that, he might as well go and live in a bleeding hotel, know what I mean. I ain't a bloody housekeeper.

S.W.:   (*persisting*) Well, what do you expect him to do, after all he's older than the other two (*to Clarke*). Do you know what mother expects of you? (*to mother*) What do you expect of this boy/man of seventeen who is living in your house?

Another brother, protesting: He ain't a man.

The dilemma for the family and for the adolescents in it, was framed as the difficulty of moving from the warmth of the house to the relatively cold and uncaring world outside. 'In a way that's nice, in a way that makes if difficult perhaps to go outside the family, for example, to go to school. Clarke's managed it. Maybe he can help.' The youngest son feeling his position under threat finally puts the challenge to the social worker: 'Look, how can you help us?'

Session 1 Sequence 3

S.W.:   You're a family with a lot of ideas, and I don't think your Mum wants you (*to Denny*) to go into care. Do you (*to Mum*)? Is that right? So if you don't want him to go into care, there are some things you may have to sort out as a family, is that right?

Mum: Well, look I know that I ought to get up in the morning, but I'm no bloody good at getting up in the morning; and I think fuck it, I can't be bothered.

S.W.:   Right, so it's *all* of you, that needs to do some thinking about how he's not going to go into care. You're going to have to sort it as a family. Use your experience and your eldest son's.

Some extracts from the second session a fortnight later follow. The family are woorkking further on whether to do any work as a family. Denny is still due to go to court, but his girlfriend has moved out and there is less friction at home. The question of how to stop him going into care is being discussed.

Session 2

Mum: I was in care at his age, it's not good, what you don't learn out, you soon learn in, and it just ain't no good.

S.W.:   So, you want to keep your family together, and the other boys, they've said they don't want the youngest son to go into care (*family giggle nervously*). The question is *how* you do so. Maybe this is something you lot have to discuss together, just how are you going to keep Denny in the family? Can you do it or are you going to have to let the authorities take over for you?

Mum: (*to family*) I think coming here could help us all.

Clarke: (*points to Denny*) He won't be here.

Mum: Well, he might be.

Denny: What's going to happen?

Mum: Well, you have got to come and talk about it here. It all come out here about Janine, and now *she's* gone.

Denny: Huh, that didn't help, it was me, it's because she didn't get on with me.

Mum: Yes, I give you that but it comes out here, it's got to be helping, coming here brings things out in the open (*challenging*). What do you think about coming here?

Denny: It's no good, keeps your bollocks small. (*boys laugh*)

Mum: (*persists and turns to oldest son, Clarke*) What do you think?

Clarke to Denny: Yeah, Mum is right, you don't give nothing a chance.

Mum: So what do you think?

Denny: I ain't coming to no child mental health.

Mum: It ain't child mental, it's family. It's family therapy. It's for the whole family.

Denny: Look, Mum, it's shit, it's bollocks.

Mum to Denny: That's the only words you know, it's about time you got back to school to learn a few more.

All roar with laughter (Mum has definitely scored, within the family circle of permitted hits). The family agree to give 'talking' a chance.

The social worker consulted with her colleagues and decided to continue to reinforce the closeness of the family, and their capacity to find solutions by talking things through, while backing Mum and Clarke as having the authority in the family. She observed to the family that Clarke as the older brother was holding the balance with the world of 'men' outside the family, by going in and out. Mother was still in charge of her two younger boys who were not yet men and she would not let this mean they were forced out of the family before the right time (by a care order being taken).

In the third session three weeks later, Denny had returned to school (where he remained for the rest of the school year) and the focus shifted to anxiety about mother's suspended sentence and how the family would manage if she had to do her year in prison. At this point the family worked in a far more open and direct way on their rivalry, their anxieties about managing without Mum, and their wish to keep Grandpa from going into a home and revealed more developmental differences in what they would and couldn't do for themselves than they had expressed before. They also engaged the social worker and her colleagues as allies and resource providers as 'members of the gang', with a particular kind of experience and authority.

The use of supervision and care orders

'When they were younger I could hold them to me but I can't now because they've got different ways of thinking and different ways of going on.'

Many of the parents who contact social workers have had depriving experiences in childhood and adolescence. This sometimes makes them more determined to hang on to their children and give them a different experience, as in the previous example where mother maintained some respect and authority in her family and could manage with the help of a supervision order to keep the family together. Parents are often faced with continuing to parent their children beyond the age when they themselves were parented. At the same time, in providing something 'better' for their children, they envy the experience they themselves have not had, so that 'ordinary' rebellion or violence from the adolescent may be magnified and construed as monstrous ingratitude. The parent may also not have the physical or emotional know-how to deal with violence as an adult, since it may provoke violent 'unmanageable' responses in them. If in addition they do not have a spouse who has some experience inside *them* of what a 'family' should be like, it may be extremely difficult for them to provide a shape and structure of any kind. As Mrs Booth said, it is difficult to know what a family is supposed to be like when you haven't had one. Where children are acting up physically and where violence has become a common exchange in the family, the issue of how to contain strong emotions and actions has to be faced by the social worker, as the parent is likely to seek help when *they* feel they can no longer manage. As one mother who was fighting with her teenage children put it:

Mother: When we were teenagers, we couldn't get our own way – we had to work because we had to live, and we couldn't live if we didn't go out to work.

S.W.:   (*confirming*) There was nobody to cry on.

Mother: No, that's what I mean, I'm telling them. It's all very well, I want this, I want that. What if they had nobody? What would they do? Where would they go . . . what did I have to do? I used to be able to manage them when they were little but now they've got too big for my apron strings.

Where the violence is intergenerational as part of an inbuilt family pattern, and the spiral cannot be broken by the introduction of new sequences of behaviour, it may be more useful for the social worker to accept the burden of control for a period of time. In the Harber family for example, Rick's continual provocation of his mother, whose depression and attempted suicide had taken her in and out of hospital following his father's abandonment of the family four years earlier, had caused her to fight with him in such a way that she feared killing him. She had beaten his head against the wall on one occasion and her weight was great enough to overcome him. The function the fighting played in keeping the mother alert and involved in her maternal preoccupations with Rick and with the younger children, rather than preoccupied with her internal misery and her deprived past (in and out of care and fighting with her own mother), was grasped by both Mum, Rick and Rick's two younger brothers and a therapeutic system of behaviour was set up, in which at the peak of the crisis, a different set of behaviours were to be brought into play. Rick was to close his door on his mother and mother was to go downstairs to cool off (time out) while treating herself to something she enjoyed. This system worked for a month but a powerful unrecognised element rendered it unworkable over time – the grandmother who returned from a visit to the mother's brother and who provoked her by saying she was not controlling her sons properly and ought to beat Rick more – sending up the therapeutic plan as evidence of mother's softness. Rick then felt constrained to fight his grandmother on his mother's behalf, saying he didn't like to see her put down. Mother in turn, always hoping that the grandmother who had never loved her properly as a child would one day back her up, beat Rick more fiercely, and broke the therapeutic plan by following him into his room instead of going downstairs. The beating she gave him then frightened both of them. Grandmother proceeded to condemn her daughter for her violence, saying it showed that she was not a good mother. Mother cut her wrists and went back into hospital and Rick was placed on a care order, while grandmother competently took over the other boys in the home, appearing the heroine of the piece.

It was clear in retrospect that the cycle of violence was intergenerational and that no plan could have worked without including grandmother. In spite of careful liaison with all of the mother's care team in the hospital, and the care team for Rick, Rick subsequently chose to live separately from his mother and grandmother, and he only went home for visits.

In many families a period of separation is necessary between a parent and an adolescent. Persistence in family interviews, structured at regular intervals (varying from once a fortnight to once a month), maintains contact and as development takes place family members may be able to meet again with a better understanding or greater control of themselves or others.

In one family for example, a care order was used to effect a separation over some months where a father had become out of control in relation to his daughter's sexual behaviour. The degree of his violence, its associated 'protectiveness' to his child and his own experiences as a parentless teenager during the London Blitz in the Second World War were discussed in six sessions involving the special residential worker, the head of house, the social worker and the family. The family (father, mother and two sisters) themselves got a lot of relief from hearing the views of younger people, whom they could not entirely dismiss, on 'sex and violence' today, and were able to modify some of their own views in a vigorous running battle with the 'younger professional generation; who provided a more neutral forum to explore ideas than their own daughter did.

In all families who bring violence to therapy as a part of their problem, the behavioural changes that are initiated early on, if successful, decrease the tension that is preventing the family from working effectively on the underlying causes. This is a positive way for the social worker to provide a 'holding' situation, in which members learn to 'hold' their own violence before they begin to understand its causes. The more precarious the situation, the more vital is this early creation of a safety net around the family.

The crisis of leaving home: a foster family

A technique which may mobilise the positive feelings in families where violence is occurring is to link violence with concern. Tony came with his foster parents because he was systematically breaking up their home. He had joined the foster parents when he was ten and they were in their early forties and childless, and now he was sixteen, 6 ft 2 in and theoretically on the way out; he provided a continual focus for their concern. The crisis of his imminent removal to a reception centre for further placement was explored in the context of his arrival, what his parents had gained from him joining the family, and how things would be different when he had gone. The wife denied that the husband had gained anything, but the husband thought the wife had gained more interest.

Session 1   Sequence 1

S.W.:   So what will she miss when he goes?

Father: It's a difficult question – he will be missed by both of us but hard to say what.

S.W. to Tony: What do you think they will miss?

Tony: (*laughing*) Me.

S.W.:   Yes, what about you?

Tony: Not having me there I think.

S.W.:   Who will miss you most, Joan or Fred?

Tony: Joan – it's something to look after you see; not just having herself to look after – something to do in the day.

Mother: (*retorting*) I had plenty to do before *you* came along.

Tony: Well, you didn't go to work only – I mean you didn't have to worry about what time I was going to come in did you.

The social worker observed that Tony might be trying to make the foster parents angry so that they would miss him less.

S.W.:   I think he's worried about what's going to happen to the two of you when he's gone and I think he's trying to make sure you won't miss him when he goes. He's stepping it up now so that you'll be grateful when he goes – maybe he's wrong.

Mother: I wouldn't have thought of that: as far as I'm concerned if you don't like a thing you say so.

Tony: I didn't say I don't like it; it's so you won't miss me when I'm gone.

Mother: But if you carry on like this there won't be any choice, you will be taken away. (*to social worker*) You see I think maybe there's something in that. Then I wouldn't have to decide for you when to go. But if we've suddenly had enough he'll have to go – Fred's had enough already.

The social worker told the foster parents that they hadn't yet heard the message from Tony about how hard it was to separate and added to Tony that it was not necessary for him to go on breaking things any more – as she understood what he was trying to do for his foster parents. She then asked the parents what signs they would want, to know that he was ready to leave home, 'because we don't think you'd be happy to let him go till then'.

Session 1 Sequence 2

Father: We hear from everyone else he goes to that he behaves very well. He never has a bad report from school – he seems to behave quite differently outside from how he does at home.

S.W.:   What does he need to learn?

Mother: Language, manners and treating other people's property with respect.

Father: Putting others first and not self.
S.W.:   How long do the two of you think he will take to learn those things?

  The foster parents went away and discussed this and came back with the opinion that it would take another two years for Tony to learn these things. Tony's violent behaviour decreased to an insignificant 'banging of doors'. They were told that he could move away into a number of different settings, depending on what they felt was right for him. They decided to keep him at home in order to make sure the things they believed were important were learnt first, before he moved away. The social worker subsequently pointed out 'when both of you took the same line and stood firm, something changed for Tony. It was a very important part of what makes it possible for a young person to leave home and to come back again'.

  Haley (1980) has defined the dilemma of leaving home as involving confusions of responsibility and hierarchy within the family, and advocates an approach in which the parental handling of the young person's behaviour becomes the focus. The professional sides with the adults in the family in the task of getting the young person appropriately organised to leave. All other conflicts in the family are regarded as secondary to this task. Developing this authority in parents, while also linking mad or bad behaviour by the young person with its protective function, can be very valuable in helping families relate less explosively and more flexibly with one another.

9

Adults as Patients

Relatives and the patient

Relatives have always had an ambiguous part to play in admitting their nearest but not necessarily dearest ones to hospital, as legislation since the eighteenth century has recognised. Restrictions on the power of the family to 'put away' relatives are demonstrated by the required professional balance on admission to hospital which specifically requires no kin relationship between professionals and family (for details see Hoggett, 1976, pp. 59–70).

Nonetheless the translation of temper, misery or contextual suffering into 'madness' within an individual continues. A study in the North of England found recently that many doctors called to diagnose mental disorder with a view to admission, were dealing with the product of a marital row where the 'patient' had behaved more forcibly than usual. For reasons of this kind one of the doctors involved in admission is required, where practicable, to have known the patient previously so that present behaviour can be placed in a wider perspective. Within the constraints of health and social service practice, the determination to hold the family as the unit of collective responsibility has been limited. Scott and Starr (1981) write from detailed experience of a large mental hospital about the ease with which patients are admitted by telephone consultation at the request of the GP, and without the family being seen. As a result of the development of a twenty-four–hour crisis team, the proportion of admissions to referral dropped to one in four, and the number of long-term hospitalisation halved (over a year). In addition the incidence of attempted suicides was reduced following the recognised stabilisation of the service, in a period where the rate elsewhere steadily increased.

Scott (1973) has conceptually developed and refined the circumstances attendant on the admission of a patient without the clear acknowledgement and responsibility of the family. A barrier is set up in which the family puts the responsibility for 'treatment' and 'cure' on to the hospital authorities and disowns their own involvement. At the same time mental 'illness' is defined as something over which neither patient nor family has any control. Working with teenagers,

Bruggen (1983) and his colleagues have maintained a similar stance of refusal to disconnect the patient from the family. The refusal is based on their considerable experience that 'breakdown' – if accepted as an individual phenomenon – leads to the severance of relationship ties between the patient and his or her intimate network. This condition of isolation and individual responsibility can become defined as a psychiatric space only amenable to the treatment of doctors. Mental illness is established as chronic when these symptoms of severance are no longer seen as having a source in the individual's relatedness to others and become labelled as a 'syndrome' of some kind. Bruce (1982) has written in detail of the work involved in reconstituting the families of disturbed young people in one of Britain's closed treatment centres, and the value this had in helping them come to terms with the reality of the limited but nonetheless real relationships their parents could offer. Only when this had been struggled through, could some of the fantasy relationships resulting in very dangerous acts be dropped, and the young people be freer to make other relationships with adults in the unit.

Considerable thinking is currently being done about the training of social workers in developing special skills required to deal with the delicate, painful and often dramatic work surrounding patients, their families, and hospitalisation. Following the implementation of the Mental Health Amendment Act (1982), a number of opportunities for work with the family can be seen to be possible in the process of a person becoming defined as a patient. Admission or release from hospital, under section 29 (Compulsory Admissions); Section 25 (Application for Admission for Assessment) or upon presentation to a Mental Health Review Tribunal under Section 25 or Section 26 could be seen as opportunities for focused family work. While 'approved social workers' may develop a range of special skills in these focal areas, a wider range of social workers will continue to see people with histories as patients and currently receiving out-patient treatment, or suffering from severe depression or the manifestation of other symptoms such as phobias, bizarre affect (feelings that do not seem appropriate to the occasion) flattened affect (withdrawal of feeling) or paranoia (feelings of persecution). These people will be acting in the range of ways that daily life demands, as spouses, patients, plaintiffs, employees and colleagues. Emotional frailty and some more defined form of mental disturbance are close to one another, and it is important to remember that adult patients are not a group apart from us; but are a group that include us. The context and life circumstances of being unwell are considered here in relation to some of the different aspects of being an adult in the family life cycle.

A career as a patient or a career as a parent?

Many young mothers will present in distress at a stage in their life's career when they could become either more competent parents or become overwhelmed and become patients who are hospitalised and have their children received into care. Harrison (1982) gives an exhilerating account of the use of a volunteer scheme to foster adequate parenthood and rule out patienthood. In the family account below some of the complexities of this struggle with a family are explored.

Mr and Mrs Smith were referred because of the anxiety of the professional network involved in the health care of their young children Deena (three) and Sean (eighteen months). Both children were in a day nursery because of the mother's repeated desertion of the family when feeling unable to manage. She always returned after a few days and the father had coped adequately. The children were often dressed unsuitably and arrived at the nursery unfed. Deena had received several unexplained bruises and on two occasions had to go to hospital with suspected fractures (once falling off the table and once falling down the stairs). The family ostensibly wanted to be helped to keep things running, but pinned the 'blame' on mother's illness.

Session 1 Sequence 1

Husband: My wife got sick after the birth of the second child. She became manic.
S.W.:   I don't know what that means; can we get that worked out between us? Let's have our own definitions.
Husband: Well, what it meant to me was she spent a lot of time in bed doing nothing; she couldn't cope with life or take the children out. After a few weeks she was admitted to the psychiatric wing of X hospital.
Wife: No, you're telling it wrong. I *asked* to be put in, they didn't put me in.
Husband: Well, you were given the option.
Wife: I decided after four months I just couldn't cope.
S.W.:   What were you doing before you had your second child?
Wife: Well, after the first kid I carried on working as a manageress in the store where I had been before I had married. After the second kid, I had to give it up.
S.W.:   What would you like to be called? Do you want to be Mr and Mrs Smith, or shall we use first names?
(*Husband and wife agreed they want to be addressed as Ann and David.*)

Ann: At first I did try to carry on working with two of them, it was a full-time job.

S.W.: How realistic was that, with two kids under four?

Ann: Totally unrealistic.

David: Another of our problems was that we had taken on a mortgage that was much too big for us.

Ann is sitting on the floor with the kids, and they are playing in quite a contained way, while the father is drawing at the table, both for the kids but also for himself. Later on in the session the social worker comments on how well the mother is handling the children in spite of the two of them being very active and busy.

S.W.: 'I think you're handling the kids very well.

Ann: I am sorry I can't talk very well, I can't explain it properly.

S.W.: It is difficult to talk when you have got two kids under three running around the room and making so much noise. What is it between you and the kids that worries you?

Ann: Well, David and I don't see eye to eye.

S.W.: Okay, that is an issue between you and David and not an issue between you and the kids. Is there anything in the way you get on with the kids that worries you?

Ann: Well, things are getting too much for me; ever since the baby-buggy was stolen, I haven't had a pram and I can't walk around with two of them, then it's hard to do the shopping.

S.W.: These are the problems of a mother with two children under three. How many other people do you know with two children under three? Two children under three is a very difficult experience.

Ann: Two children under three and manic depression is a very difficult experience.

S.W.: I think the two may be pretty closely intertwined (*to both parents*) – it's very easy to frame Ann as a problem without taking into account the context of being a mother of two children under three.

Session 1 Sequence 2

Ann: I've been completely catatonic.

S.W.: I don't think words like catatonic are useful.

David: They're Ann's words.

S.W.: I don't think labels are useful unless you're able to describe exactly what you mean; you could be putting yourself in the wrong category. You see, I could put in the category of a mother, a woman who had been a working woman and had been exposed to the panic of managing two children under three. Many women get into a panic when they have only *one* child.

The frame that the social worker fixed on was a normalising frame that placed the mother's dilemmas among those of all young mothers. She felt this would give more room for exploring dilemmas and solutions than the label 'catatonic' or 'manic depressive'. Reframing is often extremely valuable in helping parents refocus what they need to handle (Gorell Barnes, 1981). The alternative frame is maintained when later in the session, Ann describes her murderous impulses towards her youngest child.

Session 1   Sequence 3

Ann: He was standing just at the top of the stairs and I had this impulse to see if I pushed him, would he keep his balance? He was so nearly on the edge, that's what frightened me.
David: I began to get worried about the kids when Ann is looking after them. I didn't know if they would be safe.
Ann: So I just gave him a little push and he toppled down the stairs, then my mother rang up so I told her what had happened.
S.W.:   Didn't you know that many mothers have murderous feelings towards their children?
Ann: (*shakes her head–cries*)
S.W.:   (*in an incredulous voice*) You mean no other woman has ever said to you that she feels like murdering her kids?
Ann: (*shakes her head*)
S.W.:   So you thought you were the only one who was mad, bad or dangerous.

The dilemma for Ann, as for many patients was that she felt most crazy where she would like to have felt most safe, in the context of the family. The family can feel like a cage which imprisons the patient, constantly watching them and judging their dangerousness to others; keeping them locked up in a cycle of misperception into which they 'contribute' a ready part. Ann's 'giving in to' the impulse to push Sean down the stairs shows a willingness to act 'crazy' which creates further suspicions from David, the health visitor and the whole safety net of the 'child abuse machinery'.

Work continued with this family along confrontative but normalising lines, in which boundary making and limit setting played an important part. Ann was encouraged to devise ways of separating her impulses to hurt from her actions; in her case by thinking of the vulnerability of the children and of her pleasure in seeing them learn new skills. Physical separation at times of stress was encouraged. David and Ann planned the evenings in a different way, so that the children were out of the way early enough for them to have some time together in the evening. For this family a relatively brief involvement of ten sessions, in addition to the ongoing support given by the nursery, and Ann's re-involvement in a part-time job, was enough to reorganise them into a family group managing the difficulties of two young children.

The discharge from hospital

John, twenty-six, as the youngest of four brothers, three of whom have left home demonstrates the dilemmas of leaving home and facing life as an adult, and the alternative pulls of hospital and family. His oldest brother was successfully married, his second brother had joined the army, and his third brother was in the process of getting married. All came home at regular intervals to see their parents. Following his second discharge from hospital, John was referred for family work to a small social work team working independently of the hospital. In this extract the family are being encouraged to explore what they have done to contribute to John's improvement which they tended to see as being all the hospital's doing.

Session 1 Sequence 1

S.W.:   So it wasn't just John that had to change things?
Mother: No it was the family, we all had to.
S.W.:   And how have you done that, because I think it is necessary we understand how *you* have made the changes.
Father: Well, we said to John, why don't you have more meals with us and you didn't used to go out much; we live about twelve miles from Eastbourne, but he never used to get there.
S.W.:   (*persisting*) But to go back to the meal, he never used to eat with you.
Mother: No, I used to say 'your meal is ready John, come downstairs', and he wouldn't come, so I gave it to him in his room. Then I changed that and made him come down and eat with us.'

The social worker moved on to focus on the other boys leaving home and the implications for those left behind. The complexities of decision making; who has power over whose thinking becomes more apparent.

Session 1 Sequence 2

S.W.:   Your other boys have grown up and left home, haven't they?
Mother: Yes but I suppose it was difficult, our eldest boy wanted to

go back to our roots in the North. To be quite honest, I had to encourage Bob to leave home, he was very much a mummy's boy.

S.W.:   He was very close to you.

Mother: Yes, and I felt that he had to decide; he had to have me to decide for him all the time what he was to do. He had a very good training and all kinds of opportunities and I thought that he would do better in the North. He was offered two jobs and he wanted me to make the decision for him.

S.W.:   But do you think that it was really your decision that he had to leave home?

Mother: (*blushes*) Yes; I think he thinks that it was really his decision.

S.W.:   It does seem quite important to see how families manage the crisis of children leaving home. It is a crisis in every family to help children become less dependent and manage to leave home and it is going to be a crisis for John.

Mother: (*nods*) Yes, yes.

S.W.:to mother   And who made the decision about Brian going into the Army?

Mother: He made it (*laughs*). To be quite honest, I've never tried to influence my family because of my husband never doing what he wanted to do.

S.W.:   You feel your husband missed out doing what he wanted?

Wife: Yes, I do – he did really.

S.W. to mother: So you are very sensitive to your children's needs.

Session 1 Sequence 3

(*Team phone-in*)

S.W. to mother: The team are commenting that there has been a boy in this family for nearly thirty years, and they were wondering how you feel you are going to manage when John leaves home?

Mother: Well, I just don't know, I suppose as a matter of fact I don't really want him to leave home, and at the same time no matter what I want, I want what is best for John.

S.W.:   You want what is best for him. What does he want?

Mother: Yes, I'd love to keep him here; I'd love to keep him all the time but no matter what we want, we can't always do this sort of thing can we?

In working with adult patients and their families, the very delicate and complex meshes of confusion in which the family live together and maintain their previous balance need a carefully attuned ear. 'We want him to go but we want him to stay', a message explored in the previous chapter, can be seen spelt out again in the example above. As mother said about disagreement in the family:'Of course we disagree but non-verbally.' The unravelling process is likely to take time and even when begun will require persistence on the part of the young person, the social worker and the family. As Nadia (Chapter 2, pp. 8–9) said: 'Getting out is only one step, you know; keeping out is what's difficult.'

Once the social worker knows the family, the protective and confusing veils evident in the extracts above can be lifted more openly and some detailed discussion initiated about different expectations and hopes within the family. Nadia and her family for example, were greatly helped by a persistent initiation of an unresolved discussion between herself and her father about whether he might smoke in the living room, which she would not allow because the smell of his tobacco contaminated her knickers, which she dried in the same room. Re-establishing a boundary in which father's right to smoke in his own living room also took account of her meticulous cleanliness, led to him finally insisting she dried her clothes elsewhere. The imaginative reader can play with the meaning of this event in a number of ways. The essential part of this negotiation – the establishment of difference of needs and rights within the household and the possibility of these being met in other ways – was one in a series of small steps that led Nadia to feel sufficiently different to separate and to begin a life outside the family home.

The work of the schizophrenia group based at the Institute of Psychiatry (Vaughan and Leff, 1980), is organised around the finding that relapse of schizophrenia is more likely if patients live with relatives who are excessively critical and/or overinvolved. Such relatives are designated high EE (expressed emotion).

High EE families appear as ones who cope least well with the crises surrounding illness, and are most worried and upset. They may have an over-intense relationship with the patient or may be resentful of his or her behaviour. A characteristic of these families is that they emphasise the personal impact of the illness on *them* rather than its impact on the patient. For example one wife described her husband as 'hanging round my neck like this microphone . . . There's no way I can lose him – he's like a sore or a mole.' A mother described her relationship with her son as perpetually watchful: 'I watch him upstairs, I follow him, I can't help it. I'm just watching him all the time: it's nearly broke me.' A husband described the anxiety of trying to behave correctly: 'I was tensed up all the time, wondering what I was going to do that was going to be wrong next.' Parents are particularly likely to become emotionally overinvolved and to start treating the patient as a child again, as the case example given earlier showed. One mother, talking about her thirty-year-old son, said: 'He and I, we're very close . . . he usually gives me a ring during the day [from work] . . . if anything I feel even more protective' (Kuipers, 1979).

In contrast, low EE families are more tolerant and cope with distressing incidents calmly. The team distinguished *critical* remarks, as those which showed that relatives disliked, resented or disapproved of the patient or his or her behaviour; from *hostile* remarks, in which *content* might be enough to reveal the same negative affect. The disturbing aspect of *critical* remarks is that the *content* is often neutral. For example, 'everyday he has the same routine' can be a neutral statement or a highly affective one, depending on the tone. The experience of a continual series of apparently neutral comments uttered in a negatively affective way can be extremely confusing for the patient, especially when the relative, if accused of being unfriendly, asks: 'What did I say?' Over a nine-month period of social intervention using family and group work the schizophrenia group found there was a highly significant reduction in criticism, with a marked difference in the relapse rate between the social intervention group and the control group (9 per cent compared to 50 per cent). The team consider that part of the formula for success is the setting out of clear aims from the beginning, and recommend that anyone entering this area of clinical work should have as a target the reduction of face to face contact and of critical and overinvolved attitudes in the relatives.

Some general principles can be drawn from this work which can guide work in families, where one of the members is currently mentally ill. The team do not think that their work is relevant only to schizophrenic families (Berkowitz, 1983, personal communication) but also to families of depressed patients.

1. Clarify what is being said when confusing statements are made towards the patient.
2. Reduce the negative emotion expressed toward the patient.
3. Reduce where possible the amount of hours in which patient and family are mutually exposed to negative interaction. (This may mean spending time helping the patient and his or her family find different contexts for being together in which it may be possible for them to behave towards one another in different ways.)

Different contexts: different behaviour

The work of the Marlborough Family Services Day Unit offers some interesting examples of how patients can be helped to remain parents through the use of different social contexts offered within the course of each treatment day (Asen and Stevens, 1982). Three main groups of families come to the clinic.

1. Chaotic or under-organised families.
2. 'Intractable symptom' families. The most striking feature is the presence of a symptomatic member, sometimes labelled 'psychotic' or 'schizophrenic', around whom the whole family structure has become organised.
3. Reunion families. These are families where one or more of the children or parents have been separated from the rest of the family because of hospitalisation for instance, or because one or more children have been taken into care.

The work of the Family Day Unit aims at changing dysfunctional behaviour. The following general goals are set. Firstly, the presenting symptom(s) in the identified patient(s) are attended to. Secondly, an attempt is made to provide an alternative experience of family life – to show families that things can in fact be better; for example, to help parents and children to develop successes with each other. This is done by getting all family members to identify their individual strengths and resources, and by encouraging them to make use of these in different settings. Similarly all family members are helped to overcome the usual obstacles they encounter and to increase their behaviour repertoires in the face of their difficulties. These include the encouragement of the development of appropriate parental authority, by counteracting the family's customary measures to undermine it. Thirdly, children are helped to cope with a normal school setting and to overcome the difficulties they normally experience. Another goal is to increase the family's ability to use outside agencies appropriately, and to enable the families to operate more effectively within a wider social context.

Parents' fears of 'contaminating' their children

A final example leads us into another delicate area, which parents who have had the experience of dangerous disturbance in themselves may need to discuss, and that is the fear of 'contaminating' their children. Many parents have to continue parenting while in states of acute mental distress. Some parents, who may be impervious to the effects of their disturbed behaviour on their children, may have to be helped to formulate plans with their partner, or with another adult, about how to protect the children from the more serious aspects of their behaviour. Children can survive many things resiliently as long as they are clear that they are not to *blame* for what is happening. However in some forms of illness, particularly when the children and parents are interacting intensely, they *are* contributing substantially to the tension that triggers off violence in the patient. To pretend they are not contributing can be unhelpful and dangerous. When a mother describes a knife actually 'slipping' from her hand and cutting the leg of a four-year-old, necessitating fourteen stitches, a need for temporary protection of one from the other may be indicated if no other adult is around to provide a safety net. This is different from having the impulse, but knowing it can be restrained. The social worker will want to know in some detail *how* mother knows about her own restraining mechanism. Many families can help the children deal with illness in one parent by discussing it openly: 'This is what daddy is like when he has to go into hospital, but he will not stay like that', and can be honest that they do not know the causes. Much of mental illness remains a mystery to professionals and family alike and children can manage depressed, irrelevant or frightening parents better if they know that it is not their fault and it is not a permanent feature.

Some parents are extremely anxious about the effect their illness may have or is still having on their children. This brief extract shows one ill and anxious father in the process of getting better and beginning to take charge of his children, following major explosions with the social workers involved in the Clinic Family Team, whom he continually disqualified as incompetent. Personal survival over time and the maintenance of challenging good humour in diminishing the ferocity of his attacks spread into the way the family handled angry feelings and their behaviour between themselves. Father and son had each been referred individually for 'mad' behaviour, the boy attacking his teacher or his class-mates unexpectedly, apparently without provocation.

Session 4　Sequence 1

Father, mother, male social worker (2) female social worker (1)

Father:　I just don't believe that in 1982 people with problems of mental illness like I have got shouldn't be able to get proper treatment.

S.W.1:   Yes, I'm wondering now you've been seen both as an individual and as a family with Jonathan, how you see the difference.

Father: Well, Jonathan is a lot better, I wish we'd tackled this earlier. Oh yes, he is. He has grown up a lot, he is much better altogether. But I could have just have left his basic problem untackled, that's what worried me.

S.W.1:   You're still worried that there might be permanent implications are you?

Father: Yes, that's what worries me.

Session 4 Sequence 2

Father: That's the National Health Service for you, put one foot out of line and they chuck you out. You only have to put one foot wrong and they put you out the door. That's the NHS for you.

Mother: But you're much better dear, aren't you?

Father: Yes, that's because I'm in a situation where I feel that I can get angry and I'll still be seen next time. I don't usually get the treatment I need, unless it's a drug. How come with patients as ill as me, the two of you haven't put me on drugs? I don't think you're doing your job properly; either give me some drugs or injections, better stop me. (*laughs*) I know it is not fair getting back at you, you're only doing your job, it is a way of making contact back with the people who treated me badly in the past.

S.W.1:   Well, we seemed to have survived you so far.

Father: Well, I don't know, I'm worse than I was last time. I think it helps me to get angry if you want to know, I'm usually shown the door if I get angry so I might as well get as angry as possible before I'm shown the door, that's what I think *door* therapy does for the patient. Technical incompetence.

S.W.1:   So what do you think our function would be Mum, other than being punch-bags for the National Health.

Father: (*laughs*) Well, that sounds silly, you're making a good point there and absolutely valid. There's no reason to blame you for other people's behaviour, though whether you behave any better yourselves is doubtful.

S.W.1:   You have been setting us quite a lot of teasers here, in this meeting because you say on the one hand we're really nothing better than punch-bags. (*Father, laughing* 'That's a use.') And you say on the other hand that people who walk out on you or say that perhaps that's not a very useful way of passing the time, are just deserting you like rats desert a sinking ship.

Father: I'm really enjoying this, this is terribly rational. I'm usually just kicked without any discussion in fact, I'm actually communicating this time, we're actually communicating!

S.W.1: Look let's try and sort this out, do you want to see us as punch-bags on a regular basis for workout time; or do you want to use us as punch-bags on demand when you feel that something is boiling up and needs working out. (*Turns to S.W.2*) How strong are you feeling today Jack, are you strong enough to stand going on being a punch-bag?
S.W.2: Oh yes, I think so.
S.W.1: That's great, how long do you think you could go on?
S.W.2: I don't know, I should think quite a time.
Father: (*amazed*) Well I don't know. I know one thing, it is these people's jobs to treat patients, whether they are good, bad or indifferent.

The open invitation to fight further in a safe context was transferred to the family; Mother and Father should team to fight safely so that their children could see that they now knew how to handle it (rather than fearing that each fight might lead to Dad being ill again). The playful aspect of the fighting (that fighting can be intimacy as well as violence and can link to good sex) was also discussed. Violence, over four months, was 'normalised' into a more viable family form and the fear of contamination diminished.

10

Styles of Family Work

Family work requires flexibility on the part of the professional. Whatever one's context one needs to think out certain things for oneself at regular intervals. Each person needs to define a baseline way of working for themselves, a safe theoretical frame to fall back on and a series of related moves for when they get stuck. When they are clearer about these they will feel able to take risks safely. In this chapter a structural approach to work with families (developed through a group of professionals working with delinquent boys in the American equivalent of approved school or borstal in the 1960s and later refined through the work of the Philadelphia Child Guidance Clinic) is presented first. A brief discussion of ways in which elements of a strategic approach – incorporating some of the thinking of the Mental Research Institute in Palo Alto – can be added to a structural base, follows. Thirdly the approach brought to this country via the work of the Institute of Family Therapy in Milan, and the difference between this and a structural approach are discussed briefly. The relevance of different approaches to the families seen in the different contexts social work encompasses is too large a topic to discuss in depth here, but some comments are included along the way, and references to the more detailed work of other people in this country are given.

I have not written about a psychoanalytic approach to work with families which has recently been described (Box *et al.*, 1982) because therapies dependent on a lot of time and space and a relationship with the therapist have less chance of being properly sustained in a social service setting. The transformation of many crucial aspects of successful psychotherapeutic work into a *family* form, particularly the containment of violent and persecuting emotion, has been discussed by different British writers in Walrond-Skinner (1981) and in Bentovim, Gorell Barnes and Cooklin (1982), demonstrating the integration of psychodynamic understanding with a different way of interacting between therapist and family.

A structural approach: changing daily patterns

The structural approach created a developmental focus for systemic work with families, and related the thinking that a professional had to do on looking at the pattern of a family to the tasks that the family were confronted by at any particular stage. In structural family therapy the therapist works from the premise that the energy of the family, and therefore the energy for change, goes into the multiple interactions between family members, that repeated day-in day-out over time form the family system. Changes in the transactions will lead to the possibility of change in the experience of the individual. 'In family therapy transformation or the restructuring of the family system, leads to change or the individual's new experience . . . the change occurs in the synapses – the way in which the same people relate to each other' (Minuchin, 1978, p. 111).

Change is therefore approached in small ways, the units of interaction in sub-systems being the main focus of attention. If transactions can be transformed, the changes will affect other aspects of family life. In systems containing many interconnected homeostatic loops (like families) the changes brought about by an external impact may slowly spread through the system (Bateson, 1973, p. 416). Just as Blake could see 'life in a grain of sand', so the therapist can see the essence of the family system in the minutiae of one repeated behavioural sequence which may involve two or more people. 'Can I have some money for sweets, Mum?' 'Shut up, I told you I haven't any.' 'Don't always shout at the boy.' '*You* tell him then.' The philosophical premise is of seeing the larger significant pattern in the small circular sequences of family life, from which developed a technical emphasis on highlighting, interrupting and re-enacting these in different ways that lead to different outcomes.

A structural approach to problem solving suggests that professionals should be able to offer families workable solutions (Walters, 1978, p. 190) states:

> I think change requires that families be presented with concrete alternatives to the impasse or dilemma which brings them into therapy, and that they try them on in the interview. I try to give the family a new perspective of the situation they are in. This business of giving the picture a new frame is as important for the therapist as for the family . . . I need to create a workable reality; to select and reframe a piece of the action where some change can be initiated.

Aponte (1978) has additionally emphasised the need for professional help to be firmly linked to the peculiarity of the family's own style of structural organisation. The work may be slow, may not generalise, and may particularly require the involvement of family allies other than those immediately involved in the nuclear family group.

Ground rules for the therapist

Intensity and persistence
In many aspects the piece-by-piece changing of dysfunctional family interactions, on which structural work is based although incorporating symbol and metaphor in the issues worked on, has characteristics similar to the best behaviourally-based work; teaching skills to mentally handicapped clients, or work aimed at changing aspects of patient interaction with their environment. Intensity; creating a very focussed experience of emotionally charged interaction; *persistence*; concentrating on these long enough to make a difference to the problem patterns brought, and creating *take home tasks* which transfer what has been learnt to the home context, are all essential in creating and maintaining small changes. One of the most important lessons such work can teach a family who do not talk things through is that if they themselves persist with mutual discussion they can arrive at a number of different solutions. It needs the professional as boundary keeper for a family to arrive at the experience of a different pattern of 'changed transaction'. For some families it can happen in one session; for more families it will take a number of sessions, and for others it will take longer. If social workers are allowed the flexibility by their agencies, they can also experiment with how often their input is needed. Three sessions over two weeks may be followed by a month's gap allowing a crisis to resolve, on the basis that a follow-up to see whether a more functional organisation has been achieved is also built into the plan.

Working with detail
Structural work is based on close observation and analysis of the process in the room. Small repeated transactions between any two members are taken as material for examination, once the therapist is aware of the overall patterning. The frequency with which a parent selects one child out for negative comment as opposed to another, and with which a parent smacks a child as a form of communication are aspects of the pattern of interaction that a social worker can see as showing something about the larger whole. To comment negatively upon observed behaviour at the point of joining a family is both

discourteous and unlikely to link to further work. However to link the intervention to the complementarity in the system, the *good* and the bad feelings, may move things on.

S.W.:   So then you took a knife, how big was the knife?
Teenager: *(reluctant)* So big. *(with his hands, not really telling)*
S.W.:   Show me properly, I don't understand. Could your little brother lift it?
Teenager: He could, but not without hurting himself.
S.W.:   You look after him well – but *you* are fourteen, you wanted to protect your mother.
Teenager: Yeah, it was lying there and they were fighting.
S.W.:   Was the door shut – do they fight behind locked doors?
Teenager: Well usually they do, but this time Mum ran down the passage to the kitchen.
S.W.:   Did she ask you into the fight?
Teenager: Not exactly, but ...
S.W.:   OK, go on ... where was your little brother?
Little Brother: He told me to fuck off, he did.
S.W.:   He didn't want you to get hurt; he's your big brother – he was looking after you.

Confirmation and increasing competence
The therapist will always aim to confirm the existing competence within the family. Seeing the positive connotations of behaviour that may also maintain aspects of pathology in a family system is a very important feature of structural work. Labelling positively (for example, an over-disciplinary father as very caring) leads to the next step – a suggested change in the participant's perception of the interaction in a frame to which they can respond: 'You're a caring father. You want your son to grow up to be a proper man. You know the more you beat him, the less quickly he will grow up to think for himself.' Discussing areas of the son's competence might then be brought in through other activities in which he is known to succeed, for example looking after his younger brother, excelling at pool, stealing without getting caught, and the question put: 'How can you help him to be competent in *this* area?' That aspect of the parent that is motivated to increase the competence of the child is heavily relied on in this approach. Most parents do find something they like to tell about their child, but persistence in the social worker may be required. Mr Miles for example, who berated his son for hours about his stupidity and incompetence, admired the quality of his son's statement to the police following a charge of theft – he thought it clear and well organised and

it showed his son wasn't stupid, even if he was out of control. This provided some baseline evidence for building up a different picture of his son, and a possible relationship between them.

Restructuring operations

It is only possible to comment briefly on some of the more important structural techniques.

Enactment

Enactment involves a request to the family to move from description to showing the problems between them in the room, thus supplying direct information on the ways in which they normally fight, support one another or undermine each other's positions. Specific comments like, 'Will you talk with your wife about that', or 'If you want to talk to your father you must look at him, not at me and convince *him* you want his help', move the family in the direction of taking responsibility for working with *each other* on their problem in an atmosphere of heightened consciousness. It is essential for the social worker to have a number of ways of *removing him* as a channel of communication in order to throw the family back on talking to each other, unblocking blocked channels at the point where they habitually get stuck. Looking at your shoes, moving the chair back, and moving out of the chair on to a desk or window sill away from the family, are all useful methods. Once families are engaged and have accepted that talking to *each other* directly is a rule of the session, a brief indication without words that they talk with each other may be enough; for example, pointing to the relevant person or drawing two chairs in a few inches. Some families may need the specific instructions: 'Talk with your son (father, wife) and I will help you if you get stuck.'

Changing space

Moving bodies to intensify an interaction or create boundaries remains a regular practice in structural work, because of its power to shift a system that is stuck. If a daughter complains in a general way about her mother's behaviour, direct the two to move close to discuss this face to face: 'It's no good talking into thin air Doreen, your mother needs to hear your voice directly', and move Doreen's chair, while the rest of the family temporarily sit back and bear witness. This carries considerable power and, by intensifying the mother/daughter interaction, attention is clearly focused on issues within that sub-system that need to be resolved in order to achieve a different balance.

If a mother and father never confront one another directly, but always involve the children or a particular child as a channel of communication, *blocking* that triangulation by removing the child from between the parents makes what is happening clear to both parents and the child and clears the way for the parents to face each other directly. 'Let's get Cliff out of the middle here so the two of you can sort it out together/fight it out straight/don't have to use him as a punchbag.'

Creating boundaries

The clarification of boundaries and the way family members 'hold' each other's voice is a feature of structural work in action. 'Do you let him have your voice for you?' 'Do you want your son to let you be his memory, or do you want him to have his own?' As a way of proceeding it can be linked usefully to age appropriateness – 'How old do you think your mother treats you – four or fourteen?' 'How old do you think your daughter is behaving, seven or seventeen?' – and then – 'If you were four it would be OK for her to have your memory for you – how can you convince her you are fourteen and need your own?' These issues of individuation appropriate to age are a constant feature of structural work, and are valuable from babies through to young adults who have not managed to leave home.

While the ideas discussed here related to family fusion and helping people be separate enough to see more clearly are familiar to social workers, this way of going about it is not necessarily familiar. As a way of bringing violent sequences into smaller and more manageable 'bits' which parents and children understand and respond to, it is very useful. It can be of great value when working both with parents of very young children, who are experiencing them as tyrannical and feeling out of control; with potentially battering mothers where it helps restore a workable reality which can have some built-in safety measures, and with adolescents who are still living at home.

Strategic work

In structural work, the intensity and persistence the therapist brings to the issues of dysfunction in the family may be enough to bring about change, if the family's persistence does not override the therapist's, in between sessions.

It seems that many families are additionally helped by a message which reframes the meaning of the dilemma they bring to the social worker in a different way. Such messages may be given in the form of words, or tasks which direct the pattern towards change without express declaration.

Watzlawick who formed part of the group from the Mental Research Institute in Palo Alto (Watzlawick, Beavin, Weakland and Fisch, 1967) that originally defined how to help people by *not trying to change them*, defines reframing as 'an alteration in the conceptual or emotional setting or viewpoint in relation to which a situation is experienced' and the placing of the experience in 'another frame which fits the facts of the same concrete situation equally well or even better thereby changing its entire meaning'. This reframing is often accompanied by a task or set in the form of a task. The capacity for seeing a thing in more than one way is highly developed in Britain, a nation reared on seaside postcards with double meanings, and has an honourable tradition in six hundred years of British puns, music-hall humour and BBC comedy radio which preceded TV. Humour cuts across class barriers although it does not always transfer across cultural barriers, and often succeeds where a straightforward or serious interpretation or intervention would not (Cade, 1983).

An example of a relatively simple strategic task in work with an adult patient follows.

The Sewell family
In the Sewell family the presenting patient was the father, who was referred at his own request by his GP to an adult mental health setting. The referral stated that he believed he was schizophrenic and was requesting hospitalisation. The psychiatrist who received the referral noticed that there was little prior evidence of schizophrenia other than by the father's own report, and made a chance referral onwards for family work with the question, 'Is there anything you can do?' The family were approached by 'phone and agreed to a family interview, with two professionals working as a team in the room, one as therapist and the other as observer and commentator. In the first session a protracted and tedious pattern of arguing was noted in which the father always ended up in a corner with the mother and the two sons unwillingly but somehow inevitably aligned against him. At the same time the family denied that they believed in arguments or rows. The team of two colleagues in the room decided to move from content to pattern.

Session 1 Sequence 1

Mother: Yes, well you see . . .
Father: *I'd like* to change it.

Therapist: *How* would you like to change it?
Father: Well, two against two.
Derek: I wouldn't like it to have any sides at all – I would like it to be one or four.
Father: Yes, well I was only joking really, because I suppose if there are to be divisions . . .
Colleague: Louise, you are not to let Father get away with that as a joke.
Therapist: Yes I think it's a *very* serious statement. Who would you like on your side – you've got three to choose from here.
Father: I don't want any *one* of them on my side. If we get to a state of two against two it's still going to be an argument and there shouldn't be any arguments I don't think. When it's one against three at least I know where *I* stand.

The theme of one against three was pursued throughout the session and the systemic pull in which the pattern was maintained by father backtracking rather than pursuing his point of view was observed many times . . .

Sequence 2

Derek: Mum does go on a bit; she goes over and over the same points!
John: I can tell that you don't understand . . . I can tell without looking at you that you don't understand.
Derek: It's not that you don't understand . . . it's that you don't seem to be taking any notice.
Father: It's just that it's easier for me to say I agree, so that it gets over the lecture quicker . . .
(Father attempts new resolution and this time therapist interrupts)
Colleague: Hey, Father was just about to say something important here, let him finish.
Father: I think I do get the message but if I don't necessarily agree, rather than argue with it I say I understand so that . . . well . . . maybe I can get on with what I'm supposed to be doing.
Colleague: This is a way I think, Louise, of Mr Sewell remaining one against three.
Therapist: *(to Father)* Yes, you've just explained very clearly I think how it happens; would you like him to argue with you?
Mother: Yes – if he can.
Father: But if I argue with you it only gets more and more heated.
Derek: An argument's *not* a row.

John: If you can understand it then it might not happen again – if you understand, if you can compromise.

Because the family clearly needed to change the way in which father and the 'problem of arguing' were framed, the team worked out a task for the family which addressed the system as a whole. The task names the problem behaviour as healthy and prescribes the symptom producing pattern in an open manner.

Sequence 3: Task

Arguing in a family is a very important and healthy function: It's something that families ought to do. We think there's a lot of talent for arguing in this family but that you're not doing it enough and you're not doing it properly. One of the things that's not happening properly is that arguments are not coming to an end point.

So we are going to give you some homework *(everyone smiles)* to do before we meet again. And that is, that we want you once a week to spend an hour arguing. We would like you to sit down around the table and each of you take it in turns for fifteen minutes to argue with the person of your choice and the other two are not to get involved or comment. So each person has a time to select someone to argue with for fifteen minutes and the others keep silent – and whichever of the males is not involved is to keep the time . . . because we think you need practice in arguing . . . and in arguing healthily and enjoyably and well.

In the following session a fortnight later the family reported that they had not been able to stop arguing, so they had not 'done' the task as given to them. They had enjoyed themselves tremendously. There was an obvious change in the relationship between mother and father who displayed tenderness and some sexuality towards each other (an area of their relationship they had asked us by letter prior to the first session not to discuss with the boys). The family asked to do some work on why they had got stuck the way they had, and a brief genogram (see Ch. 11, page 122) was done in which the different patterns and expectations they had brought in from their families of origin were revealed, which included a strong taboo on men being allowed to argue in father's family of origin.

Session 2

Father: Yes I think a lot of the problem in the past is I don't enjoy arguing. I go for the quiet life you see. But I've found out the last few

weeks that I've been able to enjoy an argument and join in.
Therapist: (*indicating Mother and two boys*) So it's not only these three who have a talent for it?
Father: That's right.
Mother: Yes ... I think a lot of that was just depression. That it was that ... you are not allowed to argue. Even now, in his own family, if there is a difference of opinion, you don't open your mouth.

Father was congratulated on his adventurousness in choosing a wife who could teach him to argue and bring to their own family the liveliness that had been prohibited in his family of origin.

One further session confirmed that the boys were now staying out of parental arguments and that these had been 'arguments, not rows'. 'We've kept out because we know they can match each other, I suppose.' On follow-up six months later, the family described themselves as remaining 'adventurous'.

The Milan approach

From Italy a more solemn version of strategic work developed from the ideas of the MRI group and Bateson's writing, linked with a psychoanalytic team reintroduced a focus on an additional dimension of human and family systems, that of loyalty. The Milan group (Palazolli, Boscolo, Cecchin and Prata, 1978) advocated that professionals work from a stance of not being seen to try to change things, but from one of neutrality, observation and description. By gathering information about the ways the family view the problem in a meticulous and structured method, the professional is then able to describe back to the family the systemic meaning of the behaviours that are taking place as he or she is currently able to understand them. Although in its theoretical stance this is similar to 'reframing' it is very different in method and style.

Those aspects of the Milan approach which are of greatest relevance to social workers include:

1.   the idea of a team or partner in thinking, whose objectivity will be greater than the person who is interviewing the family;
2.   the formation of a hypothesis, which has led to a wider attempt to understand the protective function of symptoms in systems;
3.   the need to retain neutrality or objectivity when making an overall map of the family and its functioning;

4. the interlinked nature of events and behaviours and the meanings ascribed to these by different members within families;
5. an understanding of the importance of rule systems within family organisation, and over more than one generation.

The Milan group offered what appeared in many ways to be the first coherent application of systems thinking to families, in that they linked their clinical work to Bateson's ideas about the levels of learning and change of which biological systems are capable (Bateson, 1973). They offered a way of viewing the interrelationship between meaning and behaviour within systems that were families, in terms of the family's own perception and definition of itself; illuminating how this must necessarily be different from the point of view of the observer (or social agency). Their thinking did not overtly include any broader developmental or social idea of how a family 'should' be which was contained in the structural model. The structural model explicitly takes a position of changing the family towards a better realisation of social and emotional development – the Milan approach believes that if you offer the family a description of itself based on correctly elicited information, but with the different perception of the professional built into the overall formulation of what these behaviours might mean, the family should then be left to reorganise themselves.

The lack of an explicit change orientation in the Milan model can make it difficult to use in situations where change is urgently required by the family. The lack of developmental focus can also make it difficult to use theoretically, in work with babies and young children, particularly that aspect which assigns equal 'responsibility' to all members of the family system, irrespective of their age or developmental capacity.

The power of the method, developed in its original form with extremely rigid families of adolescents or young adults, is likely to be of less relevance to family systems that are *already* unbalanced. Such families may require advice or help with reorganisation on a smaller scale. The approach also needs to be adapted to different settings appropriately, particularly taking into account the abstract conceptual capacity of the family and the language that makes sense to them.

As a method however it is very appealing to social workers who want to work systemically but do not want to use themselves actively in creating change in the process of the session. For those who want to adapt a psychodynamic technique of engagement through a controlled process of gathering information and understanding, it may be a more useful way of working than the active proximity required by a structural approach. An account of the different uses made of the Milan approach in different settings in this country can be found in Campbell and Draper (1984, in press).

Within family therapy and within this book, the issue of how to address the rules relating the problem behaviour with the family system is a key one. What is the difference the professional can offer that will lead to an effective difference in the family organisation and functioning? The attempt to answer this question has resulted in many innovations in therapeutic technique, devised to invite or organise the family into reframing their dilemma in such a way that therapeutic work can take place on a number of levels. The size of the system that is seen by the professional as relevant, and the time scale required for the change in the system to be worked through, are among elements contributing to diversity of approach and technique used. The flexibility or rigidity of the family system according to their degree of dysfunction is likely to be another element. The context of the professional, his or her own time, energy and the support system available in the agency add a fourth dimension which may be equally crucial in determining the way of working. In the final chapter, a number of ways of using colleagues as consultants, teams, teachers and supervisors will be considered, so that potential flexibility in the social worker's own agency, which is often put forward as the most rigid system to be struggled with in professional life, can be considered in designing strategies to create space for learning and maintaining standards of work.

11

Supervision and the Use of Colleagues

Supervision of family work should be directed towards making aspects of family pattern visible as it perpetually replays itself, as well as to making the professional's own process as they get trapped by this visible to them. A further aim would be to increase the skill and effectiveness of any professional, enabling them in addition to develop their personal creativity.

The traditional method of reporting on individual interviewing by remembering and reporting as much of it as possible to a supervisor, appeared increasingly inpractical to family workers as it became apparent that the report on two-, three- or four-person interactions was bound to be extremely partial and told the supervisor more about the therapist's confusion as a result of memory overload than the pattern of the family interaction.

Four aspects of pattern that may need supervising can be highlighted:

1. the overview of the family pattern itself, with resulting objective ideas about desirable change;
2. the overview of the professional's pattern itself, independent of the family, that is, their behaviour in a *number* of families which therefore gives the supervisor some chance to isolate this as a constant variable;
3. the professional's pattern as interdependent with a particular family;
4. the professional's behaviour according to a method of procedure, that is, a frame of therapy such as psychodynamic, structural or strategic therapy.

Depending on whether the supervisor is trying to get a clearer view of the family pattern, the professional pattern or the systemic interrelationship between the two; or relate the therapist and the work to a third thing, a body of theory about a method of change, the choice of supervisory method should differ.

Making pattern visible

All supervision of family therapy attempts to help the worker become clearer about the pattern of the family, the process that maintains it and the part played by the professional intervening. The emphasis is on making pattern and process more visible for the worker, so that he or she in turn can be clearer about what is being done for the family. Many supervision techniques are therefore about *making patterns more visible* – roleplay, genograms and sculpting each do this in different ways.

Where the supervision group is trying to get a clearer idea of *family patterns*, visual aids such as a genogram, which looks at a family over time, or a map of the current family drawn in terms of closeness and distance between members are useful.

Where it seems important to isolate the *professional pattern* because a therapist is constantly getting stuck in the same kind of position in work with different families, sculpting can help isolate the position and can be used to explore the professional's own family of origin, in the form of various tableaux that relate to his or her feelings of powerlessness. However, this is very time-consuming and often tedious for the rest of the group, and genograms which can be done in one's own home, and brought back to the group or supervisor for clarification and further exploration are both more economical of time and more far-reaching in the pertinent self exploration they lead to (see p. 122). In exploring the interrelationship of professional and family, the family map and the professional's own family map can be placed side by side to explore similarities, and possible reasons for 'stuckness'. However where the interrelationship of family pattern and therapist pattern is being explored on a particular case in terms of a *method of procedure*, some form of live material in addition, like audio tape, is in my view essential. The precise way in which families 'fix' workers or render them less competent can really only be learned in detail by hearing or seeing them in action, and ways or freeing them within a framework of developing particular skills requires precision in return.

Supervision in family work was found to be more effective when brought to a group than an individual; since different members of the group picked up different aspects of the process of interaction between family members, and between members and professionals. This soon led to a wish to re-enact aspects of the process to get the worker's experience in the interview into the room in a more direct way. Several methods evolved from this including the roleplays, sculpting and audio tape replay mentioned above.

Roleplay

In roleplay, different people take different family parts and are given as much of the real family description and script as the professional chooses. A number of factors operate against this being an effective method of supervision for the *family*:

1. the process of the interview has been subjectively filtered through the worker in the recounting, *and*
2. it is subjectively filtered again through the imaginations of the participants who bring their own idiosyncrasies to bear on the parts;
3. the group will therefore inevitably form its own process which may or may not be similar to the family process.
4. However, the worker overwhelmed by the force of the roleplay family, may experience feelings of impotence, frustration, and so on, and tell the roleplay family how exactly like the real family they are. This is of course not true. What is similar may be a *conjunction of pattern* that leaves the worker in a fix.

Roleplay may therefore be an essential aid in isolating aspects of family patterns that leave the worker in a fix, and in helping him or her develop recognition, understanding and skills to get out of feeling 'fixed' in relation to particular patterns.

Roleplay is not a technique in my view for supervising the nuances of the unique pattern of interaction of real families, although it can isolate aspects of 'families in general'. It is an essential aspect of helping those who work with families develop survival strategies and skills in getting through different aspects of the process.

The professional who always feels anxiety when confronted by an angry father can make up a family in the room so as to try out a variety of new responses with the encouragement of colleagues. The professional who deals with personal anxiety by 'taking control', can be rehearsed into new ways with affectionate teasing and honest feedback about the resistance he or she provokes. It is usually better to rehearse one small sequence several times, than try to cover large chunks of a session.

Sculpting

Sculpting has a quality of stillness, pattern fixed in a particular way, which allows the therapist to work *at* it rather than being fixed *in* it – and to be in charge of the process of arranging how he or she wants it to be looked at – a process perhaps not to be had with the family itself. Since the sculpted creation of a still 'frieze' of the family as the social worker sees it is based on a personal perception of interrelationship in the family, it is again a subjective perception of pattern rather than offering raw data for others to analyse. It is valuable for the professional to place him or herself in relation to the pattern of the family, and to ask themselves why they feel 'fixed' the way they do. For this reason the sculpt is often arranged with the professional placing him or herself in it, in the place which feels right after the family has been 'shaped'. Thus if the worker finds they are having a great desire to fight the father in the family a way has to be found 'into' the fixed family pattern of the sculpt to do this – or if it is recognised that the experience of wishing to fight the father might be held on someone else's behalf or the worker would be asked to rearrange the family pattern in such a way that the fight could take place. The moving of bodies is a very powerful experience and the sculptor often finds that a great deal of personal insight is being gained in relation to 'families' in general. For this reason the worker may be invited to sculpt his or her own family of origin, using the same 'bodies' as were used for the client family and to work at the way he or she has matched perceptions of the family being seen against perceptions of his or her family of origin. This is likely to illuminate who is equated with whom. (Illustrated accounts of sculpting can be found in Walrond-Skinner, 1976; Gorell Barnes, 1978a.)

Audio tape

The use of video in social work is impractical for many reasons; its expense, its manoeuvrability and the amount of time required to convince the agency of its value being the main ones. Audio recording as a regular aid to learning about family pattern and the effectiveness and coherence of one's own input is invaluable. All departments can afford audio recorders and many social workers would find that the value of their recorder in improving the confidence in their work makes the time spent a very good personal investment. Tape can be played back at any time and analysed more dispassionately, either on one's own or with a colleague.

Over the years certain rules for bringing audio tape to peer-group sessions have evolved, which make the use of the group time far more effective.

1. The social worker responsible for the session listens to the session in advance and notes one or two passages of two or three minutes which *demonstrate* how they get stuck in the work or how the family get stuck in a particular series of sequences which do not lead them on to fresh thinking.

2.   If there is time the social worker transcribes 'nodal points', those key aspects of mixed sequences of communication which are confusing. This has the advantage of making the worker analyse very minutely what is going on, allowing the group to look at it in detail, and developing each person's overall powers of listening and noting detail of pattern, in other words those minute aspects of interaction which demonstrate the power of the whole to keep things the same.

Working with a peer group

There are many advantages to setting up a group of colleagues with the focus of learning to work with families. This can be done either within a team, across teams within a borough or an area large enough to drive within the hour, or in a neutral outside setting. As the task of the group is to focus on a common area of interest independent of the structure of the department, complaints about the department should be dealt with in relation to achieving the task.

In principle, groups of this kind act as support systems to people located in their work setting and offer the following advantages:

1.   the development of knowledge about a method of work;
2.   the focussing of energy to take back to the agency to apply the method of work;
3.   development of clarity and focus around specific areas of skill (the group requires greater precision of ideas to feed back to agency);
4.   the development of very practical advice and crucial management skills, that is, how to talk an anxious colleague round to a new method of work, how to find a hidden video tape resource, how to handle statutory responsibility on a particular case in *family* terms.

The group as a long-distance team
In practice the resources of such a group can be expanded in a number of ways. Roleplay, sculpting and the use of genograms have been discussed. In addition the group can be used as a *team*, which has an impact on the work with the family. From my experience of consulting to groups containing probation officers, field workers, FSU workers and others engaged in work with 'hard to engage' families, the use of the group can be an effective medium for boosting the impact of the lone worker.

Group members are asked to tell their families that they are working with a team who meet regularly to discuss how their work with families is getting on. Sometimes the emphasis is put on the worker – 'I am trying to learn more about families and the way they find solutions to problems' – and sometimes on the family – 'As a group we are meeting regularly to learn more about the ways families find to deal with the stresses life throws up.' The family are told the team will be very interested to hear about their solutions, or the areas in which they feel stuck, and may send them messages or letters from time to time. The team are essentially benevolent and on the family's side, but have the freedom to put their own ideas into the work the family and social worker are doing. Similarly the family are told that the group know their own ideas will often not be right. Families, even very paranoid families, have responded positively to the idea of this unseen team taking an interest in them. Usually the group spend about an hour getting to know each family initially through the account given by the social worker concerned, but then may only need fifteen to twenty minutes for exploring subsequent sessions and sending further messages.

The use of tape recorders   Where a tape recorder is being used regularly as part of the social worker's ongoing work, the flavour of the family's response to the team's message can be heard directly by the team and taken into account in sending any further message.

The value of a team working in this way with a colleague is that it brings some of the advantages of having colleagues behind a screen, or sitting in the room, to workers who are out working on a home visit basis most of the time. It frees them to think not so much 'Am I doing right?' but 'What does this family system need in the way of new ideas or a new way of "seeing things" that will help them develop a fresh approach?' and allows the social worker to concentrate on gathering information as clearly as possible, knowing that the team will help with some of the thinking.

Bringing families in for consultation

In addition, the knowledge that the family have of the team means that if the worker is feeling anxious, stuck or as though the situation is getting out of hand he or she can say to the family: 'I would like to bring you in for a consultation with my team to see if there are any other ideas we can all work out together.' This model has been in use for the last four years now at the Institute of Family Therapy in London, and is adaptable to any setting where there are two adjoining rooms and approximately £400 to spend on a camera and monitor, or to any setting where the worker is prepared to work with a colleague or colleagues in the room.

Setting up video supervision This requires a fixed angle camera attached to one corner of the room and two leads running through to an adjoining room, where the interview can be watched on a TV monitor. The cost of setting up is within the reach of most agencies. If video *recording* is required as well, the cost is increased to buy a video recording deck and video tapes. However effectiveness is greatly increased, since tapes can be used to analyse work retrospectively and to help others in the agency learn about family work. Confidentiality of material has to be handled carefully, and most agencies who use videotape have devised forms which the family are asked to read and sign after the session, giving their permission as to how the tape may be used.

Working with a colleague in the room

Detailed accounts of working with a colleague in the room have been given by Kingston and Smith (1980). The method, which provides the advantage of immediate support and clear thinking to the primary family worker, relies on co-operation and trust between the team members involved. In working this way it is important that turns are taken in being the primary worker and the supervisor in the session, so that learning in the different skills involved takes place co-equally.

In using this method, the emphasis is on one worker engaging with the family and the process of the interview, while the other worker remains a little apart as observer of the family–professional process (an example of this is given in Chapter 10, p. 109). However, a number of inventive ways of using the team in the room have developed in different social work contexts. In work with families where the social worker has a statutory role as 'parent' for example, a colleague has been brought in to act as worker for the whole family group, in which the regular social worker includes herself on a level with the family, and allows herself to be interviewed as a part of the family system. Using a colleague as 'consultant' to the family in this way can clarify issues of power and competitiveness between family and professionals. Use can be made of local child guidance or hospital settings to achieve greater neutrality from the usual interaction of family and social worker, and will give such consultations greater weight; but where the purpose is primarily for clarifying the process of work, a colleague coming to the home will do very well.

Colleagues as friends

The use of a colleague who takes a more distant position from the family can be developed in a number of ways working in the home, and has been discussed in this book in terms of offering new ideas to family and worker. It is perhaps appropriate however to end with the simple, but crucial function of support that discussion with a colleague can bring in clarifying the complex processes, both internal and external, that working with families can generate. The experience of kindliness and interest, after a day of distress and antagonism, can in itself create a difference which frees the social worker to think afresh about their work with families. Their work and intentions within the social-work, welfare state system, need to be connoted positively by their colleagues in the same way as those of family members do, in understanding the ways they behave within the family system.

I would end by suggesting that the rules of any colleague group set up to support and monitor one another's work should always include that idea. Within the frame of a positive intention to help one another develop, rather than a destructive competitiveness about who can do the 'best' work, social workers can develop simple and practical formulas that will help them consider their own professional work with families, and personal development, side by side.

Exercises

Making a family map: the therapist's own family of origin
The following exercise (to do on your own or with a colleague or group) is both fun and very thought provoking. Much family therapy involves making the invisible more visible. This map making is designed to make the balances and alliances in families more visible so that forces that are not understood can be better worked on.

Each therapist has his or her own map affecting the way he or she is able to see and 'frame' relationships in a family. It is suggested that each member should spend some time working on a personal family map, as a way of getting to know some of the patterns in their own family of origin. If they are married it is suggested that they make such a map with their partner and also make a map of the partner's family to look at similarities and differences in the partner's family of origin.

How to do it

Symbols:	women	men	death	divorce
	○	□	✕	⚌

Exercise 1: Begin with whoever you think of as the most influential person in your childhood. If it is your mother, place the symbol on one side of the sheet of paper and add brothers and sisters. Then add the generation above that. When you have mapped out one side of the family proceed to the other side.

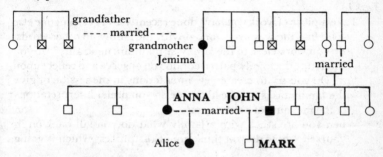

For example if *Mark* is drawing the map (genogram) he starts with his mother. He notices that mother Anna is a younger sister to two brothers. *Her* mother Jemima was the oldest sister to two brothers. Mark has an elder sister, Alice. He notices that his father John is the oldest of a family of five, with a youngest sister.

John often treats Anna like a younger sister, but Anna is encouraged by her own mother Jemima (who was an older sister to two brothers) to stand up for herself and not be put down by her husband. Alice, Mark's sister, despises her mother for being treated like this by John her father. Alice, and Jemima her grandmother have a secret alliance against 'men and brothers' which Mark, as a younger brother, finds uncomfortable.

Exercise 2: Look at the alliances in *your* family of origin, both open and 'secret'.
1. Which ones were comfortable?
2. Which ones were uncomfortable?

Exercise 3: How do you think aspects of the pattern in your family:
1. Affect what you look for in a family?
2. Give you strengths as a therapist?
3. Leave you exposed to certain areas of emotional tension which you find hard to deal with 'professionally'?

Exercise 4: If there has been a time when your family could have used a family therapist:
1. How old would you have been?
2. How would this map have helped then?

Skill tasks (to do with a colleague)
Both these tasks are to do with defining your style when you work with families and getting someone else to develop and increase your skills as defined.

Task 1
1. Take a piece of work you have done recently and get someone else to define the way you worked with the family, in other words, do you work close to the family or maintain neutrality? Do you interrupt the family pattern or do you observe and reflect upon it? Do you try to create new interactions in the session or give the family tasks to take home, or do you prefer interpretations of the meaning of behaviours?
2. When you are stuck with a family what do you fall back on in yourself – how do you think about the process which is going on?
3. In the opinion of your colleague and yourself what additional skills do you need to build on in order to become unstuck?

Task 2
Next time you see a family write down two aspects of self that most handicap you in the session.

Then talk to a colleague about how these handicaps can be turned into an asset or seen as strengths – for example passivity can be seen as the capacity to wait, tolerate uncertainty and allow interactions to develop, or intrusiveness as the capacity to interfere with established pattern of family transactions and allow the finding of new solutions.

These handicaps could be defined as general, or related to particular family members – for example dominating mothers, provocative adolescents, passive (cold) fathers.

In the group, formulate a way this handicap could be turned into a strength in the next family session and try it out. Then check back with the group for further clarification of what did and didn't work. Develop your own variations.

References

Adams, R. and Hill, G. (1983) 'The Labours of Hercules: Some good reasons why social workers should not try to be different and practise family therapy', *Journal of Family Therapy*, 5, pp. 71–80.

Adcock, M. and White, R. (eds) (1980) 'Terminating parental contact', *ABAFA Discussion Paper No. 2*.

Adcock, M. and White, R. (eds) (1982) 'The role of the local authority as parent', BAAF/DHSS research project, *Adoption and Fostering*, 6 (2) and 6 (4).

Aponte, H. (1978) 'The anatomy of a therapist', in P.Papp (ed.), *Full Length Case Studies*, London and New York, Gardner Press.

Asen, E. and Stevens, A. (1982) 'A day unit for families', *Journal of Family Therapy*, 4, pp. 202–15.

Ballard, R. (1983) 'South Asian families' in R. N. Rapoport, M. P. Fogarty and R. Rapoport (eds) *Families in Britain* pp. 179–204.

Bannister, K. and Pincus, L. (1965) *Shared Fantasy in Marital Problems*, London, Tavistock Institute of Marital Studies.

Barclay Report (1982) *Social Workers: Their Role and Tasks*, London, N.I.S.W. and Bedford Square Press.

Barrow J. (1982) 'West Indian Families: an insider's perspective' in R. N. Rapoport, M. P. Fogarty and R. Rapoport (eds) *Families in Britain* pp. 220–32.

Bateson, G., Jackson, D., Haley, J. and Weakland, J. (1956) Towards a theory of schizophrenia', reprinted in 1973 *Steps to an Ecology of Mind*, St Albans, Paladin, pp. 173–98.

Bateson, G. (1967) 'Style, grace and information in primitive art', in (1973) *Steps to an Ecology of Mind*, St Albans, Paladin, pp. 101–25.

Bentovim, A., Gorell Barnes, G. and Cooklin, A. (eds) (1982) *Family Therapy: Complementary Frameworks of Theory and Practice*, London, Academic Press.

Bentovim, A. and Gilmour, L. (1981) 'A family therapy interactional approach to decision making in child care, access and custody cases', *Journal of Family Therapy*, 3, pp. 65–78.

Berkowitz, R. (1983) Schizophrenia Research Project, Institute of Psychiatry De Crespigny Park, London S.E.5 (personal communication) (see Vaughan and Leff reference).

Bloch, D. (1973) 'The clinical home visit', in D. Bloch (ed.), *Techniques of Family Psychotherapy*, New York, Grune & Stratton, pp. 39–46.

Bowlby, J. (1982) *Attachment and Loss: Vol. 1 Attachment*, 2nd edn, London, Hogarth Press.

Box, S., Copley, B., Magagna, J., and Moustaki, J. (1981) *Psychotherapy with Families*, London, Routledge & Kegan Paul.

Brennan, M. E. and Stoten, B. (1976) 'Children, poverty and illness', *New Society*, 36, pp. 681–2.

Brown, G. W. and Harris, T. (1978) *Social Origins of Depression: A Study of Psychiatric Disorder in Women*, London, Tavistock Publications.

Bruce, T. (1982) 'Family work in a secure unit', in A. Bentovim, G. Gorell Barnes and A. Cooklin (eds), *Family Therapy: Complementary Frameworks of Theory and Practice*, pp. 497–515.

Bruggen, P. and O'Brian, C. (1983) 'An adolescent unit's focus on family admission decisions', in H. Harbin (ed.), *The Psychiatric Hospital and the Family*, MTP Press Ltd., pp. 27–48.

Burgoyne, J. and Clarke, D. (1982) 'Reconstituted families', in R. N. Rapoport, M. P. Fogarty and R. Rapoport (eds) *Families in Britain*, pp. 286–302.

Byng-Hall, J. and Bruggen, P. (1974) 'Family admission decisions as a therapeutic tool', *Family Process*, 13 (4).

Byng-Hall, J. and Campbell, D. (1981) 'Resolving conflicts in family distance regulation: An integrative approach', *Journal of Marital and Family Therapy*, 3, pp. 320–1.

Byng-Hall, J. (1982) 'Family legends: Their significance for the therapist', in A. Bentovim, G. Gorell Barnes and A. Cooklin (eds) *Family Therapy, Complementary Frameworks*, pp. 213–28.

Byng-Hall, J. (1982) 'Family legends: Their significance for the therapist', in A. Bentovim, G. Gorell Barnes and A. Cooklin (eds) *Family Therapy, Complementary Framework*, pp. 213–28.

Cade, B. and Southgate, P. (1979) 'Honesty is the best policy', *Journal of Family Therapy*, 1 (1) pp. 23-33.

Campbell, D. and Draper R. (1985) *Applications of Systemic Family Therapy: the Milan Method*, London, Academic Press (in preparation).

Cade, B. (1983) 'Humour and creativity, *Journal of Family Therapy*, 41, pp. 35–43.

Carter, E. A. and McGoldrick, M. (1981) *The Family Life Cycle*, London and New York, Gardner Press.

Central Council for Education and Training in Social Work (1978) *Study No. 1: Good Enough Parenting*.

Child Health Services Committee (1976) *Fit for the Future*, DHSS/DES, HMSO.

Clarke, A. (1980) 'Therapy: that's a different story', *Journal of Family Therapy*, 3 (3) pp. 211–27.

Coffield, F. (1983) 'Like father, like son: the family as a potential transmitter of deprivation', in N. Madge (ed.), *Families at Work*, pp. 11–36.

Cooklin, A. (1982) 'Change in here and now systems versus systems over time', in A. Bentovim, G. Gorell Barnes and A. Cooklin (eds), *Family Therapy: Complementary Frameworks*, pp. 79–110.

Cox, S., O'Hara, G. and Brain, M. (1981) 'Families for families', *Adoption and*

Fostering, 104 (2) pp. 12–16.

Dare, C. (1979) 'Psychoanalysis and systems in family therapy', *Journal of Family Therapy*, 1 (2) pp. 137–53.

Davies, M. (1981) *The Essential Social Worker*, London, Heinemann Educational Books.

De'Ath, Erica (1983) 'Support and intervention: help or hindrance', in E. De'Ath and D. Haldane (eds), *The Family in a Political Context*, Association for Family Therapy, Aberdeen University Press, pp. 25–35.

DHSS (1978) *Social Service Teams: The Practitioners' View*, HMSO.

Dimmock, B. and Dungworth, D. (1983) 'Creating manoeuvrability for family systems and in social services departments', *Journal of Family Therapy*, 5, pp. 53–69.

Fagin, L. H. (1981) *Unemployment and Health in Families*, London, DHSS.

Farrington, D. P. (1978) 'The family background of aggressive youths', in L. A. Hersov and M. Berger (eds), *Aggression and Antisocial Behaviour in Childhood and Adolescence*, Journal of Psychology and Psychiatry Supplement No. 1, Oxford, Pergamon Press Ltd, pp. 73–94.

Frude, N. and Goss, A. (1980) 'Maternal anger and the young child', in N. Frude (ed.), *Psychological Approaches to Child Abuse*, London, Batsford Academic and Educational Ltd, pp. 52–63.

Goldstein, H. (1977) 'Theory development and the unitary approach to social work practice', in H. Specht and A. Vickery (eds) *Integrating Social Work Method*, pp. 60–72.

Gorell Barnes, G. (1975) 'Seen but not heard: Work with West Indian families in distress', *Social Work Today*, 5 (20) (21) and (22).

Gorell Barnes, G. (1978a) 'Group methods in clinical and non-clinical settings', *Social Sciences, Social Work, Community Work and Society*, DE20611, 12, 13.

Gorell Barnes, G. (1978b) 'Family violence and child abuse', in *Good Enough Parenting*, CCETSW Study No. 1, pp. 131–40. Obtainable from CCETSW, Derbyshire House, St Chad's Street, WC1H 8AD.

Gorell Barnes, G. (1978c) 'Infant needs and angry responses: A look at violence in the family', in S. Walrond Skinner (ed.) *Family and Marital Psychotherapy*, London, Routledge & Kegan Paul, pp. 68–90.

Gorrell Barnes, G. (1980) 'Family therapy in social work settings: A survey by questionnaire, 1976–78', *Journal of Family Therapy*, 2, 357–78.

Gorell Barnes, G. (1981) 'Family bits and pieces: framing a workable reality', in S. Walrond Skinner (ed.) *Developments in Family Therapy*, London, Routledge & Kegan Paul, pp. 298–323.

Gorell Barnes, G. (1982) 'Pattern and intervention', in A. Bentovim, G. Gorell Barnes and A. Cooklin, pp. 131–58.

Gorell Barnes, G. (1983) 'A difference that makes a difference 1', *Journal of Family Therapy*, 5, pp. 37–52.

Gorell Barnes, G. (1984) 'Systems Theories and Family Theories', in M. Rutter and L. Hersov (eds) *Child Psychiatry: Modern Approaches*, Oxford, Blackwell Scientific Publications Ltd.

Graham, H. (1980) 'Mothers' accounts of anger and aggression towards their babies', in N. Frude and A. Goss (eds) *Psychological Approaches to Child Abuse*

Haley, J. (1975) 'Why a mental health clinic should avoid family therapy', *Journal of Marriage and Family Counselling*, 1, pp. 3–13.

Haley, J. (1976) *Problem Solving Therapy*, New York, London, Harper Colophon.

Haley, J. (1980) *Leaving Home*, New York, McGraw-Hill.

Harrison, M. (1982) 'Working with young families in their homes', *Adoption and Fostering*, 6 (3) pp. 15–18.

Hetherington, E. M., Cox, M. and Cox, R. (1978) 'The aftermath of divorce', in J. H. Stevens, J. R. and M. Matthew (eds), *Mother–Child, Father–Child Relations*, Washington DC, National Association for the Education of Young Children, pp. 163–70.

Hinde, R. (1978) *Towards Understanding Relationships*, London and New York, Academic Press.

Hoggett, Brenda (1976) 'Mental Health', in *Social Work and Law*, London, Sweet & Maxwell.

Hoggett, B. (1981) 'Parents and children', in *Social Work and Law*, 2nd edn, London, Sweet & Maxwell.

Hyman, C. (1980) 'Families who injure their children', in N. Frude (ed.), *Psychological Approaches to Child Abuse*, London, Batsford Academic & Educational Ltd, pp. 100–19.

Jehu, D. (1961) *Learning Theory and Social Work*, London, Routledge & Kegan Paul.

Jones, E. (1983) 'Leaving whom: motherless families: problems of termination for the female therapist', *Journal of Family Therapy*, 5(1), pp. 11–22.

Jordan, W. (1972) *The Social Worker in Family Situations*, London and Boston, Routledge & Kegan Paul.

Kellmer Pringle, M. (1980) 'Towards the prediction of child abuse', and 'Towards the prevention of child abuse', in N. Frude (ed.) *Psychological Approaches to Child Abuse*, London, Batsford Academic and Educational Ltd.

Komarovsky, M. (1940) (reprinted 1971) *The Unemployed Man and his Family*, New York, Octagon Books.

Kuipers, Liz (1979) 'Expressed emotion: A review', *British Journal of Social and Clinical Psychology*, 18, pp. 237–43.

Leff, J. P. (1979) 'Developments in family treatment of schizophrenia', *Psychiatric Quarterly*, 51, pp. 216–32.

Lewis, J. M., Beaver, R., Gossett, J. T. and Phillips, V. A. (1976) *No Single Thread: Psychological Health in Family Systems*, New York, Brunner/Mazel.

Lindsey, C. (1979) 'Working with rage and anger – the establishment of a therapeutic setting in the homes of multi-problem families', *Journal of Family Therapy*, 1 (2), pp. 117–25.

Loader, P., Burck, C., Kingston, W. and Bentovim, A. (1982) 'A method for organising the clinical description of family interaction: the "Family Interaction Summary Format"', *Australian Journal of Family Therapy*, 2 (3) pp. 131–41.

Madge, N. (1982) 'Unemployment and its effects on children', *Journal of Child Psychology and Psychiatry*, 24 (2) pp. 311–20.

Madge, N. (1983) *Families at Risk*, SSRC/DHSS Studies in Deprivation and Disadvantage No. 8, London, Heinemann Educational Books, Ltd.

Maddox, B. (1975) *Step-parenting: Living with Other People's Children*, London, Unwin Paperbacks.

Mayer, J. E. and Timms, N. (1970) *The Client Speaks: Working Class Impressions of Casework*, London, Routledge & Kegan Paul.

McLaughlin, A. and Empson, J. E. (1983) 'Sisters and their children: Implications for a cycle of deprivation', in N. Madge (ed.) *Families at Risk*.

Minuchin, S., Montalvo, B., Guerney, B. G., Rosman, B. L. and Schumer, H. (1967) *Families of the Slums: An Exploration of Their Structure and Treatment*, New York, Basic Books.

Minuchin, S. (1974) *Families and Family Therapy*, London, Tavistock Publications.

Minuchin, S. and Fishman, C. (1981) *Family Therapy Techniques*, Cambridge, Mass., Harvard University Press.

Minuchin, S. (1982) *Consultation to Hill End Adolescent Unit*, teaching tape available from the Institute of Family Therapy (London), 43 New Cavendish Street, London W1.

Minuchin, S. (1983) 'Child Abuse in a Family Context', London Conference Institute of Family Therapy, April 1983.

Mumford, D. (1983) Personal communication: Child Abuse in a Family Context, London Conference, Institute of Family Therapy, April 1983.

Oakley, R. (1982) 'Cypriot families', in R. N. Rapoport, M. P. Fogarty and R. Rapoport (eds), *Families in Britain*, pp. 220–32.

Okell-Jones, C. (1980) 'Children after abuse', in N. Frude (ed.) *Psychological Approaches to Child Abuse*, London, Batsford Academic and Educational Ltd, pp. 151–62.

Palazzoli, M. S., Boscolo, L., Cecchin, G. and Prata, G. (1978) *Paradox and Counterparadox: A New Model in the Therapy of the Family in Schizophrenic Transaction*, London and New York, Jason Aronson.

Parke, R. D. (1981) 'Fathering', in J. Bruner, M. Cole and B. Lloyd (eds) *The Developing Child*, London, Fontana.

Parkes, C. M. (1972) *Bereavement: Studies of Grief in Adult Life*, London, Tavistock Publications.

Pincus, A. and Minahan, A. (1977) 'A model for social work practice', in H. Specht and A. Vickery (eds) *Integrating Social Methods*, National Institute Social Services Library No. 31, London, George Allen and Unwin, pp. 73–108.

Pollitzer, A. (1980) 'The medium is the message? How agency setting influences our effectiveness as family therapists', *Journal of Family Therapy*, 2 (2) pp. 225–33.

Rapoport, L. (1970) 'Crisis intervention as a mode of treatment', in N. W. Roberts and R. H. Rice (eds) *Theories of Social Casework*, University of Chicago Press.

Rapoport, R. N., Fogarty, M. P. and Rapoport, R. (1982) *Families in Britain*, London, Routledge & Kegan Paul.

Reiss, D. (1981) *The Family's Construction of Reality*, Cambridge, Mass. and London, Harvard University Press.

Richards, M. and Dyson, M. (1982) *Separation, Divorce and the Development of Children: A Review*, Cambridge, Child Care and Development Group.

Richman, N. (1976) 'Depression in mothers of pre-school children', *Journal of Child Psychology and Psychiatry*, 17, pp. 75–8.

Roberts, W. (1982) 'Preparation of the referral network, the professional and the family', in A. Bentovim, G. Gorell Barnes and A. Cooklin (eds), *Family Therapy: Complementary Frameworks*.

Robinson, M. (1982a) 'Reconstituted families: Some implications for the family therapist', in A. Bentovim, G. Gorell Barnes and A. Cooklin (eds), *Family Therapy: Complementary Frameworks*.

Robinson, M. (1982b) A Working Party Formulating Proposals of a Training Course for Workers Involved in Conciliation in Divorce, obtainable from the author, Institute of Family Therapy, 43 New Cavendish Street, London, W 1.

Rowe, J. (1982) 'Long-term fostering project', *Adoption and Fostering* 4 (4) 5 (1) 5 (4) and 6 (2).

Rutter, M. (1975) *Helping Troubled Children*, Harmondsworth, Penguin.

Rutter, M. (1979) 'Protective factors in children's responses to stress and disadvantage', in M. W. Kent and J. E. Rolf (eds) *Primary Prevention of Psychopathology*, vol. 13, *Social Competence in Children*, Hanover, New Haven, University of New England.

Rutter, M. (1981) 'Stress, coping and development', Emmanuel Miller Lecture, *Journal of Child Psychology and Psychiatry*, 22 (4) 323–57.

Rutter, M. and Madge, N. (1976) *Cycles of Disadvantage: A Review of Research*, London, Heinemann.

Rutter, M., Quinton, S. and Liddell, C. (1983) 'Parenting in two generations: Looking backwards and looking forwards', in N. Madge (ed.) *Families At Risk*, SSRC/DHSS Studies in Deprivation and Disadvantage, No. 8, London, Heinemann Educational Books.

Sainsbury, E. (1975) *Social Work with Families*, London, Routledge & Kegan Paul.

Scott, R. D. and Starr, I., 'A 24-hour family-oriented psychiatric and crisis service', *Journal of Family Therapy*, 3, pp. 177–86.

Skinner, A. E. and Castle, R. C. (1969) *78 Battered Children, a Retrospective Study*, London, NSPCC.

Smith, D. and Kingston, P. (1980) 'Live supervision without a one-way Screen', *Journal of Family Therapy*, 2, pp. 379–87.

Specht, H. and Vickery, A. (eds) (1977) *Integrating Social Work Methods*, National Institute Social Services Library, No. 31, London, George Allen and Unwin.

Tonge, W. L., Lunn, J. E., Greathead, M., McLaren, S. and Bosanko, C. (1983) 'Generations of problem families in Sheffield', in N. Madge (ed.), *Families at Risk*.

Treacher, A. and Carpenter, J. (eds) (1984) *Using Family Therapy*, Oxford, Blackwell.

Vaughan, C. E. and Leff, J. P. (1980) 'The interaction of life events and relatives' Expressed Emotion in schizophrenia and depressive neurosis', *British Journal of Psychiatry*, 136, pp. 146–53.

Vickery, A. (1977) 'Social work practice', in H. Specht and A. Vickery (eds) *Integrating Social Work Methods*, London, Allen and Unwin.

Visher, E. B. and Visher, J. S. (1979) 'Step families: a guide to working with step parents and step children', New York, Brunner Mazel.

Wallerstein, J. S. and Kelly, J. B. (1980) *Surviving the Breakup: How Children and Parents Cope with Divorce*, London, Grant McIntyre.

Wallerstein, J. S. and Kelly, J. B. (1982) Preliminary report of a ten-year follow-up, International Association of Child Psychology and Psychiatry Congress.

Walrond-Skinner, S. (1976) *Family Therapy: The Treatment of Natural Systems*, London and Boston, Routledge & Kegan Paul.

Walrond-Skinner, S. (1979) *Family and Marital Psychotherapy: A Critical Approach*, London, Routledge & Kegan Paul.

Walrond-Skinner, S. (ed.) (1981) *Developments in Family Therapy*, London, Routledge & Kegan Paul.

Walters, M. (1978) Verbal communications; also see 'On becoming a mystery', in P. Papp (ed.), *Family Therapy, Full-Length Case Studies*, London and New York, Gardner Press.

Walters, M. (1981) 'One-Parent Families', paper given at Women's Conference, London.

Watzlawick, P., Beavin, J. and Jackson, D. (1967) *Pragmatics of Human Communication: A study of Interactional Patterns, Pathologies and Paradoxes*, New York, W. W. Norton and Co.

Whiffen, R. and Byng-Hall, J. (eds) (1982) *Family Therapy Supervision: Recent Developments in Practice*, London, Academic Press.

Whiffen, R., Iveson, C. and Sharpes, P. (1979) 'A family therapy workshop: a review of a two-year experiment in a social services department', *Journal of Family Therapy*, 1 (4) pp. 397–408.

Wolkind, S. (1982) *Parents and Children in an Inner City: Longitudinal Study*, Family Research Unit, London Hospital Medical School, Turner St., London E1 2AD.

Younghusband, E. (1967) *Social Work with Families*, National Institute for Social Work Training Series, No. 4, London, Allen & Unwin.

Index